*To the man who will always be the King of Barataria to me,
from his Queen Casilda.
(gold stars to the Gilbert & Sullivan fans who get this
reference!)*

THE Princess PROBLEM

Happy Reading!

THE
Princess
PROBLEM

CHRISTI
BARTH

Christi Barth

Preview of *Ruling the Princess* © 2019 by Christi Barth

Entangled Publishing, LLC
2614 South Timberline Road
Suite 105, PMB 159
Fort Collins, CO 80525
rights@entangledpublishing.com

Amara is an imprint of Entangled Publishing, LLC.

Edited by Alethea Spiridon and Heather Howland
Cover design by Elizabeth Turner Stokes
Cover photography by olgankort and Kad Anti/Shutterstock

Manufactured in the United States of America

First Edition November 2019

Chapter One

In the glorious days of the Renaissance, ink on your fingers marked you as a thinker, a dreamer, an artist. But in modern day Manhattan? It just made Kelsey Wishner feel like a criminal.

"Shouldn't this stuff be gone by now? I got fingerprinted almost two days ago," she said, scrubbing her hand against her black yoga pants. *A.k.a.* her lounge-work-everything pants. Because one of the best perks of working from home was never having to dress up.

Unlike her more practical sister Mallory, who'd gotten her stilettos stuck in grates and broken them off three times in the three days they'd lived here. At this rate, she'd be shoeless before Memorial Day.

Mallory rolled her eyes. "It's your own fault, hashtag overachiever."

True. Safety-first NYC fingerprinted its teachers, and Kelsey had insisted on applying for that second job teaching part-time.

"Manhattan's *expensive*," she shot back. Moving to the

Empire State wasn't scary. Affording it was. As Mallory well knew, since she ran their budget. "Our meal plan is currently ramen noodles, oatmeal, and bananas until we nail down how much taxis and the subway will cost per month. I refuse to let us be those sad-sack transplants that New York chews up and spits out in a matter of months."

"Yeah our budget is tight, but you need to wear the fact that we're here like a badge of honor." Mallory grabbed her hand and raised it triumphantly. "We *finally* made it. We're official residents of the most exciting city in the world. Just think—we can now get anything and everything delivered to our door, twenty-four-seven."

That was definitely a perk. Kelsey tapped the stack of flyers already accumulating on the kitchen counter. "Let's order a pizza at three a.m."

Mallory laughed, her auburn ponytail bobbing. "I said wear this like a badge of honor, not go crazy. I'm not going to be awake then, let alone hungry."

Practicality was so *not* the order of the day. "Call it an early breakfast. You love cold pizza. We'll set our alarms. It'll be fun. A pinching-ourselves, made-it-to-Manhattan moment."

"Didn't we take the ferry out to the Statue of Liberty today for that?"

Kelsey sniffed. "It's a big city. We deserve more than one moment."

"Didn't we have another moment yesterday when you got me up pre-dawn to be at Rockefeller Center for the *Today* show?"

Her hands tightened on the next plate, popping a whole bunch of rows on the bubble wrap. Okay. They'd been cleaning and unpacking for hours. It was clear her sister needed a break. Kelsey ought to give Mallory a pass.

She didn't want to wait, though. She didn't want to miss a moment of watching the excitement unfold around her. Half the fun of a 3 a.m. pizza would be looking out the window to see who else was up, what sort of activity was out on the street.

Luckily, a knock on the door prevented—or at least postponed—Kelsey's argument. "I'll get it."

"Leave the chain on," Mallory said.

Fair enough. They'd lived in a tiny Michigan college town their whole lives. Their street sense hadn't kicked in yet, let alone been honed. Caution was good.

Boring…but good.

Standing behind the door, Kelsey angled her neck to peer through the two-inch crack afforded by the chain, and promptly threw caution to the wind. In fact, she couldn't slam the door fast enough, undo the chain, and wildly beckon to Mallory as she swung it back open.

Because in the hallway was a cluster of *hot* men. Two of NYPD's uniformed finest, biceps bulging against the short sleeves. Behind them were three taller, even *hotter* men in suits.

Dating wasn't on their New York adventure to-do list for at least a month. Mostly because Kelsey didn't want to be labeled as a naïve rube. Or worse, a tourist. She wanted to meet Manhattan men on a level playing field, once she knew the subway lines backward and forward and didn't jump every time a taxi honked.

She was, however, willing to re-prioritize the to-do list.

"Hello."

"Ma'am." The adorable shorter cop tapped the brim of his hat. "Are you Kelsey Wishner?"

"I feel like I should ask *why* before answering."

The tallest suited man, one with piercing blue eyes, elbowed the cops aside. He opened an ID holder to flash… something at her. Something with his picture and a fancy golden crest. "I'm Elias Trebanti. I'm here on a mission for the royal family of Moncriano. These police officers can vouch that they've verified my diplomatic credentials. May I speak with you? Inside?"

Kelsey looked at Mallory. They raised opposite, questioning eyebrows at each other. Then she went on tiptoe to peer down the hall. Nope. No cameras. That ruled out a reality TV prank show. This was weird, but also kind of exciting. In a semi-scary way.

After a brief nod from the cops, she stepped back and waved them inside. Only Elias entered. Elias of the close-cropped dark hair, knife-edged cheekbones, and muscles that the tailored suit somehow did not hide at *all*. He shut the door, glancing around the small living room packed with too much furniture their parents had insisted on sending along. Two steps had him at the kitchen, and another five sent him down the hallway to their bedrooms.

Mallory rushed after him. "Hey. You need a separate invite to go that far. Get back out here."

"My apologies." His heels all but clicked together as he executed a military-sharp turn. "I had to make sure that nobody else is present."

"You could've asked," Mallory snapped with a miffed puff of air that fluffed her bangs. *Now* the stranger was in trouble. Snitty Mallory was no fun whatsoever. Even diplomatic credentials wouldn't protect him from her wrath.

"That wouldn't have proved anything." Softening infinitesimally, Elias put his hand over his heart and gave a micro-bow. Maybe that translated to an apology in his country? "In my business, you can never be too careful."

Now they were getting somewhere. "What business is that?" Kelsey asked. She noticed he was still casing the apartment. His eyes practically drew a connect-the-dots line from each window, to each door, along the top of each framed photo, to the cluster of phones and laptops on the oval coffee table.

"I'm in the Royal Protection Service."

Kelsey couldn't help but laugh. "Then I'm quite sure you've got the wrong apartment. There's nothing for you to protect here."

Those blue eyes snapped right to her, and her laughter died in her throat. Was it possible to feel a zing just from an eye lock? "On the contrary. I'm here for you." Unexpectedly, because he'd been all business and stiff thus far, Elias roughly scrubbed a big hand across his face. "This is going to sound crazy, but hear me out."

"Okay." His accent was faint. Mostly British, but with rolled *R*s that made her think of the rolling hills and sun-kissed grapevines of the Italian countryside. She could listen to it all day.

Drawing himself up into a precise line, Elias slowly said, "You, Kelsey Margaret Wishner, are a princess of the House of Villani."

Mallory gasped. Kelsey shushed her. "We're hearing him out." But she did grab her big sister's hand and squeeze it tightly.

"You were kidnapped when you were three months old. The royal family, the country, the *world* has been looking for you ever since."

Kelsey gaped at him.

No way. She'd been willing to listen about the princess thing. Maybe the Wishners were connected through a great-great-great-*great* grandparent to some distant cousin in a royal family. Sure. She'd buy that.

But a kidnapping?

That was beyond ridiculous. Insulting, actually. Hurtful to her parents, who were wonderful and loving and, oh, had been there her whole life. Right along with Mallory.

Instead of getting angry, Kelsey flipped back to her original hypothesis. It was a reality show. It had to be. She squinted at the lapel of his pale-charcoal suit. No obvious pin-type camera. Not on his shirt buttons, either. She really hoped they'd win money for playing along. Broadway tickets to *Hamilton* just might be in the budget this year, after all.

Crossing her arms reminded her of the faded—no, downright ratty—concert tee she wore. With yoga pants. Not a good look at all if they were being filmed. Kelsey rolled her lips together tight to try and make up for not having on even a leftover stain of lipstick. "And you happened to find me after twenty-five years? Now? Here?"

"You applied for a New York state driver's license two days ago. As soon as your fingerprints hit the database, it set off an alarm back at the palace. I verified the match, ran a background check, and got on a plane to retrieve you."

It was too much to take in. Too much to focus on the absurdity of his claim. Kelsey honed in on the less than respectful wording he'd used. "*Retrieve* me? I'm not a piece of missing luggage."

One side of his mouth tugged up into the start of a smile. It transformed his face, made him look warm. Approachable. Yummy. "Christian warned me I should use the flight to work up a speech. I hate it when he's right."

"Christian? Who's that?"

"Your older brother. His Royal Highness Prince Christian is heir to the throne of Moncriano."

Every new specific the man tossed at her chipped away at what used to be solid ground beneath her bare feet. "You're telling me I have a *brother*?"

"And a sister. Princess Genevieve."

"I already have a sister," Kelsey said fiercely, the words coming out low and hard and fast. Once more, she clasped Mallory's hand. "She's standing right next to me. And at this moment, that's the only thing I know and believe with total certainty, so watch yourself."

"I'm sorry." He gave another micro-bow. "I've a one-track mind on carrying out the most important duty of my life. If you would indulge me a little longer?" Opening the door, he murmured to his fellow suits, then turned back to her with a tablet.

Elias held out his hand, palm up. It took her a second to catch up and do the same, but then he encircled her wrist and traced the ink stain on her fingertip. Something shot through her. Awareness? Interest?

Oh, who was she kidding—it was full-blown lust. From a featherlight brush on a finger. A touch that kicked every single erogenous zone on her body into overdrive.

What. Was. That?

He placed her finger over the top border of the tablet. A blue light flashed.

Two seconds later, what she assumed was her fingerprint flashed on half the screen. The other half filled with another box containing a fingerprint. It moved left. As soon as the two images merged, the word CONFIRMED flashed in bright green caps.

Whoa. That was more...*official*...than she'd expected from a reality show prank.

Her stomach clenched. This suddenly felt all too real, and Kelsey had no idea what to do about that. But Elias apparently did.

He swiftly dropped to one knee. Brought her hand to his mouth, and brushed his lips across the back of it. "Your Royal Highness, I pledge my life and my loyalty to you."

Well, that was certainly a heady thing to hear.

For a moment, the part of Kelsey that had loved the Camelot myth as a child wallowed in the fairy-tale romance of those words.

Then two, no, five sirens interminably crawled past their building. Their four-story walk-up on the edge of Midtown, the one that she and Mallory had planned and scraped and saved to afford. The one that was a culmination of their lifelong dreams. It might be gritty and not at all glamorous, but it was every bit as rewarding to Kelsey as getting the gold in a medal ceremony.

Her new life, here with Mallory—that was all that mattered. Not some fantastical story, with no logical explanation concerning the small fact of how her real parents had birthed her and raised her, about people far away that she'd never heard of before.

She yanked her hand out of his grasp and gave a sharp tug on the hem of her ancient tee. Back in high school when she'd bought the thing, her breasts had been a cup-size smaller, so Mr. Bodyguard was probably getting an eyeful. "Thanks for the heads-up. If you have additional information, you can email it to me."

"Additional information?" His lips, super full and downright bitable if she hadn't been trying so hard to give him the bum's rush, twitched. "What I'm giving you is your life back."

That slick, snarky tone put her hackles up. It was *so* patronizing. As if whatever Kelsey had going on in New York simply didn't measure up to what he offered. "I have a life already. One I'm pretty darned ecstatic about. One's all I need."

"Your Highness, I don't think you understand. I flew here to bring you home. To bring you back to your family and restore you to royalty." Elias stalked to the door and threw it open. "These men outside? They're here to supervise packing your things. We're headed to the airport immediately."

Well, he'd just made this far easier. "I don't believe you, and I'm not going anywhere." Then Kelsey planted a hand on his chest—a brick wall of a chest—and shoved him back one more step so that she could slam the door in his face.

Mallory let out a hollow laugh. "This counts as enough excitement to get me out of three a.m. pizza, right?"

Spinning around, Kelsey was about to let her off the hook. But then the door rammed back open. Hard. Hard enough to jolt it sideways from its top set of hinges.

Elias stood there, canted sideways a little, easing his shoulder back. Aside from that readjustment, he was still slickly suited. Not a hair out of place. Not an inch of his starched shirt untucked. Even though he'd just—sort of—broken down the freaking door.

Damn it, that easy show of strength was sexy but also infuriating. His Royal Protection pay had damned well better cover their security deposit, not to mention the upcharge of getting someone out here right away to fix the door.

He sighed, rubbing the back of his neck. "I get the distinct impression this will not be the only time I give you this lecture. Let me be clear: I am now, officially, your shadow. Not to be an annoyance, not for protocol, but for your safety."

"I can take care of myself. You wouldn't be able to guess how many places we've stashed pepper spray around this apartment." Plus, Kelsey wasn't afraid to use the old reliable knee to the groin maneuver.

"Whether you remember or not, whether you believe me or not, the fact is that you *are* a princess of the House of Villani. That necessitates round-the-clock protection. Protection that will be easier all around if you cooperate."

Mallory stepped up, toe to toe with him. Even in yellow-and-white striped cotton pajama pants and a white tee, she managed to look haughty. She gave Elias a measured once-over from head to toe. Chin jutted out, she asked, "How qualified are you to protect my sister?"

"Right now? I'm wearing two guns and two throwing

knives. I'm an expert in three forms of martial arts. I'm a trained sniper. And, most importantly, I'm willing to give my life to save hers."

Seriously? Elias had known her for maybe seven minutes, and he'd not just throw down for her, but *sacrifice* himself? Kelsey wasn't sure if that fell more on the side of sexy or scary. All she knew was that his somber but factual ticking off of his abilities had given her goose bumps on every inch of exposed skin.

Knees more than a little wobbly, she sank onto the nubby brown sofa they had big plans to recover. "We haven't even finished unpacking. I can start emailing these...people"— because how could she call them family?—"and maybe come for a visit in a year. After we've saved up enough money for the flight. Moving to New York has us on a tight budget."

Elias threw back his head and laughed.

Mallory frowned as she sat next to Kelsey. "There's nothing funny about how expensive it is to live in Manhattan." She was the one in charge of their bank accounts. The one who'd run the numbers eight different ways to make sure that they'd waited to move until their emergency cushion was exactly the right size. The one who'd nixed a stop at Junior's because she'd called spending twenty-seven dollars on a Reuben and a slice of cheesecake "a laughable splurge."

"You're exceedingly wealthy, Your Highness." The laughter dissipated, and Elias became quite matter-of-fact. "The private plane waiting for us at LaGuardia belongs to your family. As does a yacht, several boats, countless cars, three palaces, five manor houses—"

Kelsey held up a hand to cut him off. She'd seen movies, for crying out loud. Flicked through glossy magazines when stuck in line at the grocery store. Royalty equaling immense wealth wasn't something that had to be explained to her. Wrapping her head around the fact—that she'd known for all of, oh, ten whole minutes—that *she* was royalty? That was the sticking point.

"I get it, but you're going to have to give me a minute to freaking catch up."

"I appreciate that. We don't have a minute, however. You don't have the luxury of time to take this all in. Your family needs you. Your country needs you. I'm doing my duty by bringing you back, and I'm going to do my damndest to make sure you do yours."

Duty.

That word struck her, hard. Like a physical jolt to her belly that stole her breath away. Kelsey sagged against the back of the couch. Her parents—the ones she knew, anyway— had drummed responsibility into her.

Elias might not realize it, but he'd just given her a reason that she couldn't fight. If everything he told her was true, then Kelsey *did* have a duty...to an entire country. Her own whims and wishes and dreams paled next to the word "duty." Not that she knew yet entirely what that entailed.

"Can you give us a minute?" Mallory asked.

One dark eyebrow raised, practically to his close-cropped hair. "Her Royal Highness slammed the door in my face. I'm not leaving this apartment again until she comes with me."

Shooing him, she said, "Then go stand in the kitchen. Just give us the illusion of privacy and maybe ten feet of space, okay?"

With a nod, he eased back across the apartment until he stood at the sink and politely turned his back.

Mallory clasped her hands, then pointed with both index fingers at her little sis. "You should go."

The effort it took to refrain from rolling her eyes surely earned Kelsey one of those expensive slices of cheesecake. Because, yes, that was one option, sure. An option that completely decimated the New York dream she and Mallory had worked toward their entire lives. A dream Kelsey craved more than an endless buffet of ice cream and pizza put together.

She buried her face in her hands. "I should crawl under the covers and wait to wake up from this super bizarre dream."

Mallory poked her in the side. "Bizarre, yes, but an opportunity you can't ignore."

Kelsey looked at her sister's wide, excited eyes, and tucked a leg underneath herself, curling farther away from the sight of the ramrod spine of her bodyguard. Because the man had a presence that was impossible to ignore. It was distracting. The last thing she needed was to be distracted from this decision about doing a one-eighty with her life.

"There's so much we don't know right now. So much that doesn't make sense."

"You won't find answers here. You'll find them in Moncriano. If your family has really been missing you, searching for you, for twenty-five years? How can you possibly deny them a visit? Not going, now that they know about you, would be heartless."

Ouch. That angle hadn't yet occurred to her. All she could focus on was the fact that strangers were trying to rip her away from her life. But Mallory made a point that was yet another sucker punch, this time to her heart.

Family was everything.

The love Kelsey had for her sister and her parents was so deep, so much a part of her as to be almost indescribable. The pain the Villani family must've gone through missing their child—*her*—for an entire lifetime had to be horrible. It was her, yes, *duty*, to put that to rest. To put a bandage over that raw wound.

"You're right. I know you are. It's just hard to face." Kelsey lowered her voice to a whisper. "That talk of duty really got to me, too."

"Are you kidding? Anything that hot hunk of a man says in that luscious accent packs an extra punch. If he told me it was my duty to go clean Times Square with a toothbrush, I'd do it."

What was she implying? With a frown, Kelsey said, "Agreeing to pick up and leave America to go meet a brand new family in a country I *swear* I've never heard of has nothing at all to do with the hotness of my bodyguard."

"Of course not. It doesn't hurt, though." Mallory patted her on the thigh. "It'll also help that I'm coming with you."

Relief coursed through her, as soothing as chugging milk after accidentally eating the tiny, fiery chilies in Drunken Noodles. "What? No. I can't ask you to do that. I mean, I want you to. Desperately. But you just got a new job."

"It doesn't start for three weeks. I'm not leaving you to face all of this alone. We're a package deal. Always have been."

That was the truth. They were best friends as much as sisters. Kelsey couldn't imagine being an hour away from her sister, let alone an entire ocean apart. With Mallory by her side, maybe this whole, crazy adventure that Elias had dropped on her was doable.

Kelsey leaned over and gave her big sis a long, tight hug. "Thank you so much. I love you."

"I love you, too. We'll always be sisters, no matter what."

Aaaaand there was the last, hardest punch to the gut.

Did this news mean that Mallory wasn't actually her biological sister? Elias hadn't mentioned that there were *two* kidnapped babies from the royal family. So...was she adopted? Or was Mallory?

Holy crap. "Of course we will be," she said fiercely. "Nothing could ever change our bond. Nobody knows me as well as you do. Nobody else knows that I hate Girl Scout cookies."

"Nobody else knows I gave up the dream of being a doctor because blood makes me woozy." Mallory shuddered. "It's humiliating to have an entire career field out of your grasp with one puke."

Standing up, Kelsey said, "Elias? You can stop worrying about dragging me out of here in a fireman's carry. I'll go to Moncriano with you. On one condition."

"If it's that you want a tiara to wear on the plane, I'll admit I didn't bring any of the Crown Jewels with me."

Was he cracking a joke? "What? A tiara? Why would I want that?" She plucked at her yoga pants. "I'm not coming with you because of glittery princess perks. I'm coming because it's the right thing to do."

Mr. Inscrutable's eyes warmed. And his chin tilted to the side the tiniest bit. "I'm both surprised and pleased to hear that."

"My condition is simple, and not up for discussion: Mallory's coming, too." Flashing her sister a smile, Kelsey added, "We're a package deal."

"That's it?"

"Yes."

Giving another one of those military-sharp corner turns, Elias nodded at Mallory. "You are more than welcome to accompany the princess. I'm sure your presence will be a comfort to her."

"Consider me her emotional fleece blanket." Mallory snatched her beloved green and lavender fuzzy blanket off the back of the couch. "Speaking of which, this will be the first thing in the suitcase."

"No suitcases. No time to pack. We have to be out of this country before word leaks about who and where she is." He cast a sidelong glance around the room. "There's especially no time for you to finish unpacking, and then repack half of it. I'm leaving Lathan and Marko to supervise. A moving company should arrive in twenty minutes."

That—even more so than Elias bringing along the NYPD as an escort—hit home to Kelsey what sort of power he wielded. It was eleven thirty at night. There should be no way he could've arranged to have a moving company come now, with less than a day's notice.

Just what was she getting herself into? She stuffed her laptop, iPad, and phone into a tote. Then it hit her. "We can't leave the country. We don't have passports."

"Arrangements have been made. Nothing will stand in the way of me getting you back to Moncriano." Grim determination coated his voice more thickly than road dust in the summer.

Kelsey had no doubt he would've carried her out of here over his shoulder if that's what it took. She wondered what that would've felt like, but she had far bigger things to occupy her mind. What would her new family be like? What would it be like to be a princess?

What on earth had actually happened to her twenty-four years and nine months ago? And why hadn't her parents told her about it?

Chapter Two

Even though they were twenty-five-thousand feet in the air, Elias couldn't relax.

He couldn't shake the feeling the princess might decide to grab a parachute and bolt at any second. That, in fact, the presence of her sister was the only thing guaranteeing that she'd stay put for the entire eight-hour flight.

Skittish didn't begin to describe the wide-eyed woman across from him. Beautiful didn't begin to describe her, either. Not that he should be surprised. The entire royal family was striking, but he'd known them his whole life. Kelsey was a new, unknown quantity in so many ways.

Not just her pale-blond hair and elfin features. Not just the way he'd fought against noticing how her small breasts rounded tightly against her tank top. Or how that same top clung to a waist Elias was positive could be spanned by his two hands. Or how those thin pants didn't hide the perfect swish of her hips as she'd climbed the stairs into the royal jet.

What *had* surprised him was how hard she'd fought the news of her royal birth. What woman didn't want to be a princess? With Prince Christian as his best friend, Elias had literally spent years watching females throw themselves at the heir to the throne.

Not just because Christian was a decent guy with a good heart and quick smile. No, they clamored to share the bottles of Cristal he ordered at clubs. Wanted to ride in the prince's Ferrari, and sit next to him in the royal box. When he suggested low-key, undercover activities, you could all but feel the *whoosh* of air as they quickly made up excuses to bail on his friend.

Kelsey, on the other hand, had seemed unimpressed as he'd reeled off examples of her newfound wealth. She'd cared not at all for the title he'd bestowed upon her. What had she called them? *Princess Perks.* And she'd said it with a sneer in her tone and on her pretty pink lips.

Lips that he needed to stop staring at immediately. Because this woman was off-limits to him in every way but as a job. A sacred charge. A responsibility. The only way to reclaim his family's tarnished honor.

She was his duty. She was his princess.

So Elias did what he always did. What he did best. He focused on the job.

He propped his elbows on his knees and leaned forward. "You never had any hint that you were kidnapped?"

Kelsey lazily stroked the buttery cream leather of the seat. "You mean besides the ransom note in my baby book?"

If this wasn't his job, wasn't literally the most important thing he'd done in his entire life, Elias would've snickered. But he'd been interrogating her almost since they took off an hour ago and gotten nowhere. Despite her and Mallory making friends with the attendants and trying one of every snack on the plane, he'd insisted that she sit and work with him.

So far? They'd gone in more circles than a carousel. Long

enough that he could see Mallory had fallen asleep in the row just ahead.

"I'm not joking, Your Highness."

Her eyes flicked to his, and Elias swore he could hear the sizzle behind the violet eyes that—although she didn't realize it yet—matched everyone's in her family. "See, to me, imagining my parents as knowingly participating in an international kidnapping is nothing more than a joke. A tasteless, horrible joke."

They weren't getting anywhere. Aside from his respect growing by leaps and bounds for Kelsey's steadfast loyalty to the people who'd raised her. *Despite* the fact she'd clearly accepted she was, indeed, the missing princess of Moncriano. The princess just as clearly hadn't accepted the second part of the equation—that her American parents simply could not be guilt-free in this scenario.

With tremendous effort, he softened his tone. Swallowed back the urgency that pricked at his brain. "I'm not officially making any accusations against your parents."

Although unofficially? It was obvious they knew something. At the very least, they knew they hadn't birthed their second daughter. Where was the explanation for that? And why had they hidden it from her and Mallory for so long?

"Good." Kelsey sipped at her lemon seltzer, then tucked the bottle back into the holder for it beneath the window.

"Were there"—Elias paused, searching for the least accusatory word—"acquaintances of your parents? That perhaps only visited every few years? Or when they did visit, insisted on you girls being sent out of the room so they could speak privately?"

"No." She popped a brie and sundried tomato pinwheel into her mouth. Then she poked at the last triangular ham tea sandwich.

It was difficult to tell if she was genuinely hungry, using

food as a way to mask her nerves, or trying to ignore him. Especially since she'd made him stop in Times Square— pleaded with him to stop, with melting eyes that stirred an urge in him to do whatever she wanted—for the largest cheesecake he'd ever seen. It'd been half gone by the time they parked in front of the red carpet leading to the airplane.

Already frustrated again, Elias rubbed at his temple. "That's it? You're not going to think about it for more than one-point-five seconds?"

"No need. We come from a small town. There's a college in it, so I won't say that strangers never came through. But they never came to our house. We would've noticed. Mom and Dad both work in the hospital. They fix broken legs, give vaccinations, and do emergency appendectomies. They're *not* criminals."

Funny how she thought those things were mutually exclusive. Or not funny...optimistic. Naïve. The harshness of New York would very likely have beaten her down, or at least scarred her, in a matter of months.

No matter how you looked at it, he was doing her a favor by taking her back to Moncriano. So it bothered Elias that Kelsey looked as downcast as if her pet had died. It was his job to protect her, to keep her from being hurt. He'd been sawing at her nerves and heartstrings since they met.

God, he regretted it. There'd been no warning that this would be so hard. Elias had been sure that picking up the princess would be nothing short of triumphant. He'd grant some average American her dream about becoming royal, and be greeted in Moncriano as a hero. More importantly, he'd erase a hell of a lot of ghosts and pain that clung in every corner of Alcarsa Palace.

Instead, Kelsey made him feel like a villain. Like *he* was the kidnapper ripping her away from everything she knew and loved. She'd never tell him anything if she didn't trust him.

Damn. He'd handled this all wrong.

A glance up the aisle showed that Mallory was glued to the window on the opposite side, staring at the Northern Lights. So Elias moved into her seat next to Kelsey after dumping the empty plate on the floor. Loosened his tie at the neck and undid the top button. Hopefully it made him look less official, less unapproachable.

"Look, I'm sorry if I've been hammering at you, but I have to ask these questions. It's my job. I'd like to get them over with now so they aren't hanging over you once we land."

Coolly, as if reciting facts no more exasperating than the alphabet, Kelsey said, "Then let me cut to the chase. There were no clues, no hints. Never any reason to think I was anything but the daughter of Ed and Cybill Wishner. No red flags. No guilty glances across the living room when your country's team marched in the opening ceremony of the Olympics." Her eyes shifted to the side. "I mean, I think not, on that last one. Do you send a team to the Olympics?"

"Yes. Every four years, winter and summer. Not the massive turnout of the Americans, but we do well enough. Especially at skiing and rowing."

Her eyes widened. And the knuckles on the fist in her lap whitened. "I can't do either of those things. Make that reason number eight hundred and four that I'm not cut out to be your princess. There's no point introducing me to everyone if I'll just let them down."

That was…adorable. Which caught him off guard. Kelsey didn't want the job, but she was already worrying about doing it the right way. "Being a princess isn't like being the CEO of a company. You don't have to know how to do everything that your subjects can do."

"I should know *something*, though." Squinting her eyes shut, she covered her mouth with long, tapered fingers still smudged with ink. Kelsey dragged in a deep breath. Then she *whooshed* it out and moved her hands away. "I don't mean to be insulting when I say I've never heard of Moncriano."

Her curiosity gave him hope that the princess was coming around quickly to the idea of belonging to another country. "You're not the first to say that. It is small, tucked in along the side of Italy and Austria and a few other equally small nations. I'll make sure you get a tourist guide to start you off with the basics. There's a good chance your grandmother, the Grand Duchess Agathe, will put all twenty volumes of our history on your nightstand, but you can take your time with those."

"Elias"—she touched the sleeve of his suit coat—"oh, do I call you Elias? Or do you have a title I should use?"

Yet another surprise. She didn't want to disrespect him. Despite how he'd treated her so far. Despite turning her world upside down, without her permission. Despite the fact she outranked him by *miles*. This woman was special. Thoughtful.

And dangerous with how easily she slid under his skin.

He patted her hand. It was a gesture he'd definitely never attempt with Princess Genevieve. Elias lived and breathed protocol, spending his days a hairbreadth away from the entire royal family. But Kelsey seemed to need comfort, familiarity. A…connection.

Elias would give her whatever she needed.

"Your Highness, you are third in line to the throne. You can call everyone except the current king anything you want."

"I don't want to be rude, though. Are you a Lord or a Duke or whatever noble titles exist in Moncriano?"

"I'm not titled, aside from what was earned during my military service. I was a captain in the Royal Navy."

"Of a whole ship?" Kelsey arrowed a searching, skeptical look at him. "Aren't you too young for that?"

"Most assuredly." God, Christian would laugh until he ran out of breath when he heard that one. "Captain is a rank equivalent to the same in your army. A Commander's in charge of a ship."

"That's more plausible."

"Don't make me out to be a youngster." Having memorized her file on the plane ride to New York, Elias knew he was older than her twenty-five years. Then again, he'd known that his whole life. Everyone in his country knew the age of the missing princess. "My thirtieth birthday's right around the corner. There's talk of plans already being made, plans that will no doubt give me the worst headache of my life."

"You'll love every minute of it." A teasing grin lifted the corners of her mouth. "If you end up remembering any of those minutes."

She'd both smiled and baited him. The distraction—albeit at his expense—had been successful. It was a relief to him as the official person in charge of the princess's welfare. But it was an enormous relief to him as a man who appreciated this lighthearted side that he'd thus far only seen aimed at her sister.

Hell. He liked it when Kelsey smiled. It was that simple.

Except that simple fact? It made everything Elias did extremely fucking complicated.

"Would you like me to call you Captain?"

"It isn't necessary." It was easier to fade back into his official role than to think about how much it touched him that she'd offered to show him that respect. "I serve *you* now, Your Highness."

"Oh, for God's sake. Stop that." Kelsey thrust her hands in the air, as if physically pushing aside his words. "Stop tossing that title down my throat."

Elias bit back a laugh.

They'd all been searching—at least in their minds—for a *child*. They'd never contemplated what it would be like to find a grown woman, with her own viewpoint. One absolutely shaped by the free-wheeling, free-thinking democracy in which she'd been raised.

A big part of Elias wanted to make a bowl of popcorn, kick his feet up, and get ready to watch what happened next. He also had no doubt, after just a few hours, that the princess had the spine to stand up to anyone who crossed her. But she'd have a lot of battles to fight in the coming days. She'd have to pick and choose the ones that mattered most, and let the rest go.

Elias would need to help her. Everyone else she was about to meet *expected* something of Kelsey. The royal family expected her to be the daughter they'd pined for. The government would expect her to be the balm to all the country's troubles. The people would expect her to be the perfect princess. He couldn't think of a single person who would be looking out for Kelsey's best interests.

Only him, her bodyguard.

Chances were that she'd fight him every step of the way.

He shifted sideways, turning to face her more. Mostly to pull away from where Kelsey's thigh had rested against his. Her warm, soft thigh. "I'm afraid this is one of those things you can't struggle against. Your title is linked to your name from this point forward. You need to get used to hearing it."

Her lips pursed. Her nose crinkled. Her eyes scrunched shut. It was…adorable. Damn it, why did he keep thinking that? And why did it matter? Elias didn't respond to adorable. Sexy—obviously sexy—women were the ones he aimed for in bars. When you weren't planning on spending more than a night together, going the obvious route just made sense, made everything simple.

So why did her adorable pout as she grudgingly nodded

acceptance of his words strike him as appealing? As an almost-invitation to bend mere inches and lock onto those pink lips with his own?

It'd been twenty-nine hours since he'd slept. That had to be the reason for his complete lack of sense. The moment the computer *ping*ed him with her fingerprint match, Elias had jumped into overdrive and hadn't stopped for a second.

Kelsey half stood, looked left and right, and then sank back into her seat. "We're a minimum of four rows apart from everyone else on this plane. You won't get in trouble. But you will get thanked if you just call me Kelsey. That title's not who I am. Not yet. Maybe not ever."

He'd been right all along—the princess *was* already figuring out how to escape. Elias gripped her arm. It was the second breach of protocol in less than ten minutes. If he didn't get himself under control, he'd be demoted to guarding the stable cats within a week. "You agreed to return to Moncriano, to resume your rightful place in the royal family."

"I agreed to *visit*. Nothing more."

"Your Highness—"

She cut him off with a finger against his lips. "Since you believe I'm your princess, aren't you required to do what I say?"

Wily *and* adorable. And if he didn't move away from her touch, Elias would suck that finger into his mouth in less than a second.

He whipped his head to the side. "Kelsey, your family needs time to get to know you. To get used to the idea that you're really back with them and won't disappear again."

"I wouldn't be that cruel. But there are a lot of unknowns right now. I'd be lying if I said that in the space of less than four hours, I've embraced the idea of becoming a princess. I assume I won't get tossed in the dungeon if I end up deciding to return home."

At least she was being honest with him. "How about you start thinking you've got *two* homes now?"

The empty silence that lasted far too long told him that the princess saw right through his attempt to "handle" her. That she knew her own mind, and wouldn't allow anyone to try and influence her.

Finally, in a low voice, she asked, "Will you get in trouble if I don't stay?"

Undoubtedly.

Definitely.

"I'll protect you wherever you go." Elias reached into his coat pocket. "Speaking of that, here's your panic button. Keep it with you at all times." He gave her a fob smaller than an automatic car key. "If you get into trouble, if you get scared, just press it."

After looking at it for several seconds, she toed her bag out from beneath the seat and zipped it into a pocket. "Mallory will need one, too."

"They're only for members of the royal family."

She gave a slight head tilt, with an imperiousness that mirrored what he'd seen in Christian and Genevieve hundreds of times. "I repeat, Mallory will need one, too."

Message received. "I'll make sure there's another waiting in the car for her when we land."

"Thank you." Kelsey curled her legs beneath her, listing toward him with a sigh. Or a yawn. Probably both, given the late hour. "That'll be the one and only thing I know about what happens next."

"Well, I can tell you your brother will meet you on the tarmac."

"That sounds…bizarre. Almost impossible to fathom. My brother, the heir to the throne?" She made air quotes with her fingers, and he could hear the capitalization in her awestruck tone.

"Yes. But don't get hung up on that. He's mostly a regular guy." Elias tried to come up with something that would put her at ease about his best friend. "Unless you order the same thing he does in a restaurant. Prince Christian likes to have the option to swap plates. Annoying as hell, but not world-ending as bad habits go."

"Uh-oh." She grimaced dramatically in mock horror. And it was…hell, it was *adorable* again. Elias had to get some sleep pronto. It wouldn't count as sleeping on the job. No, he'd justify it as a way to shore up his armor against this woman who incessantly slid past his defenses.

"What's wrong?"

"That just might be a deal breaker for me. I've been known to stab Mallory with a fork if she tries to so much as steal a fry off my plate."

He raised his hands, palms facing outward. "I'm out. You two will have to work through that on your own."

"Does he speak English as well as you do?"

"Better. According to him, anyway." To say the prince was competitive was like saying that water was wet.

"Does everyone in my, ah, family?" This time she only bobbled for a moment before using the word. Elias called that progress.

"Yes. Don't worry. About eighty percent of the country speaks English fluently. Tourism is our major profit center. We neighbor so many countries, English is the one unifying language. You shouldn't have any trouble communicating."

"That's a relief." She closed her eyes. "Tell me something else, please. Something to make this all less terrifying."

That was a tall order. Did Kelsey want to know if there was a McDonalds? Reassurance that she'd like the music on the radio? She hadn't asked about her sister Genevieve, and he was unwilling to open that Pandora's Box.

Elias fell back on a tourist spiel. "Moncriano has

mountains and coastline and lakes and farmland. It's idyllic. Postcard perfect."

"Not so much. Perfect for me is a dizzying array of skyscrapers in a tight jumble on a tiny island." Her words were coming slower now, a little bit slurred with exhaustion. She leaned her head back on the seat and closed her eyes. "Adventure and excitement and possibilities around every corner."

"We do have cities, you know. There are tall buildings and taxis. Even some street vendors, although our sausages are far superior to those waterlogged hot dogs in Manhattan."

"Mmm. What about adventure?"

"Let's start with possibilities. Those I can promise you."

A heavy weight pushed onto his shoulder. Kelsey's head pillowed right under his jaw. Her silky hair snagged in his late-night stubble. Then her whole body leaned into his side.

It was heaven and torture all at the same time.

Damn straight it'd be an adventure with her. Not to mention an exercise in self-control. But not yet. For now? He'd follow her lead and get that much-needed rest.

It would be the first time Elias had ever slept with a princess.

And it would have to be the *last*.

Chapter Three

Kelsey flipped over at the waist and mussed her hair from underneath.

Despite the array of beauty products stashed in the jet's bathroom as big as the one in their apartment, her hair was flat. Static-filled. Plane air wasn't doing her any favors. So she was about to meet her brother—an honest-to-God *prince*—in the crappy outfit she'd worn to unpack their kitchen and with sleep-squished hair.

Mallory's equally crappy gray Skechers came into view. "Are you going to stay upside down like that? Because I'm not sure what statement you're making with your ass in the air."

Very funny. Clearly, a reprieve from her sister sassing her was *not* on the list of promised princess perks. "It says I'm not feeling confident. I feel like I'm doing the walk of shame home right before eight a.m. classes." She stood and didn't bother to look in the mirror. Whatever fluff she'd achieved would undoubtedly dissipate before she stepped onto the tarmac.

"Oh yeah. That mistake of a night you spent with Brad Kim. I warned you never to fall asleep at a boy's dorm."

"You *should've* warned me never to drink tequila shooters before hooking up. What do you think put me to sleep?"

"From the description you gave me? Brad's kisses were way more to blame for conking out. No zip. No zing. No tingle."

"No fun," Kelsey said. She remembered the tingle that had raced up her arm when Elias touched her inked-up fingers. That slight touch that had packed more of a punch than an hour of Brad's slobbery kisses.

She could've sworn she'd fallen asleep on Elias. Warm. Comfortable. Safe. But when she woke up, there was just a lavender blanket tucked around her.

Had she dreamed being that close to him? The man was certainly dream-worthy. And once he'd stopped interrogating her, he'd been...nice. Their conversation had been easy.

Aside from how difficult it had been not to just stare into his bright blue eyes. Eyes bluer than Lake Michigan on a summer day. Bluer than the bird in the Twitter logo. Bluer than Matisse's famous Blue Nudes series.

Not that she'd been thinking about Elias *nude*. Not when her entire life had twisted itself into a corkscrew of confusion. That would be *wrong*. Not serious and princess-like at all. It would be a shallow, frivolous distraction.

Except now Kelsey couldn't stop thinking about what he looked like out of that suit...

The man himself caught her eye as he walked down the aisle. Elias didn't look at all rumpled. He looked slick, a little dangerous with his muscles barely disguised by the cut of his suit, and all business. The softer, open side of him she'd seen last night was gone. One hand on a seatback, he gave a short nod. "Your Highness, are you ready?"

No. No way. No how. Nervously re-fluffing her hair, Kelsey said, "Do I look ready?"

He opened his mouth, closed it. "I'm positive there is no correct answer to that question."

"Smart man." Mallory squeezed his arm. "Look—you only get out of your yoga pants on holidays, girls' nights, dates, and interviews. Today is none of those things. So be comfortable as *you*."

"The cheerleading's appreciated." Kelsey could always count on her. She just wanted a little shared reality check at the massive embarrassment of the situation. "But, come *on*. You're the fashionista in the family. I'll bet you're breaking out in flop sweat at the thought of either of us meeting anyone besides the pizza delivery guy in our unpacking clothes."

Perching on the long coffee table that fronted a banquette of seats on one side, Mallory said, "You got me. I'd give a hundred dollars for pumps and a pencil skirt right now."

Elias looked at the wide-open door of the plane. Then back at Kelsey. Definitely noticed the way she wasn't making any forward motion toward the door. "Your Highness, the prince is aware of the speed with which I whisked you away. He won't judge you on your appearance, I guarantee."

"Easy for you to say. You look all buttoned up and appropriate."

After a beat of staring at her, Elias pulled his tie out of its knot with a soft swish. He stuffed it in his pocket. Unbuttoned the top two buttons of his shirt, which revealed a boundary line of dark chest hair. Last, he spiked his fingers through his hair, leaving it standing on end. "Feel better now?"

Omigod.

He'd mussed himself up just to make her less uncomfortable? That was a swoon-worthy romantic gesture, right there. Kelsey couldn't even risk a glance at Mallory. The chances were too high that her sister's jaw was already on the ground. "I do, but I don't want to get you in trouble with your boss."

"I work for you now, Your Highness. Remember?" With an actual twinkle in those blue eyes, he asked, "Am I in trouble?"

Holy crap.

No, but Kelsey was. *Deep* trouble.

It seemed to go without saying she shouldn't fall for her bodyguard. There was probably a rule about that, and yet she was responding to him as though he was...flirting? Her pulse raced, her nipples tightened, and all sorts of things tingled.

"Definitely not. Thank you, Elias." Sure, the gesture was a little ridiculous, but it helped. A lot. "Mallory, are you coming?"

"I'll be within gawking distance. I figure this moment of meeting your brother should be private."

"Right. Of course." That was classic Mallory. Saying and doing the right thing at the right time. "How did you end up with all of the tact between the two of us?"

Tightening her ponytail, Mallory said, "Putting up with you required that I turbo boost those skills from an early age."

Kelsey took a deep breath and reminded herself she excelled at graphic design. That her clients called her intuitive. That her boss called her easy to work with. That she'd been voted *most likely to make friends in a dystopian society* in her high school yearbook. Prince Christian should be the one nervous about meeting *her*.

Except...he probably was because of that whole sticky layer of he and his family actively searching for her. For more than two decades he'd wanted his sister back.

Kelsey didn't want anything. Aside from not humiliating herself. So she bent down to cinch tight the laces on her sneakers. It was time to dip a toe into her new future by connecting with the past. "Let's do this."

Elias led the way out of the plane and down the stairs. Kelsey kept her eyes glued to each step, refusing to give the universe any shot at mocking her by sending her tumbling into a heap at her brother's feet. But when she hit the purple carpet runner on the ground, she looked up.

"Private" wasn't exactly the best descriptor of how she'd meet her brother. There were three black SUVs, two police cars, four bodyguard-types, and one man under a small canopy by himself at the base of the stairs with his hands tucked behind his back, feet braced wide.

Christian was...well, gorgeous. Tall and broad-shouldered in a bright blue suit. Thick, blond hair topped off high cheekbones and a wide mouth. This man looked like a stand-in for at least four Disney princes.

Most noticeably, the unusual shade of his violet eyes was an *exact* match for her own.

Kelsey wasn't sure what to feel about that, except to catalogue it as more proof that Elias had, indeed, not made the whole thing up.

He gave an identical sharp nod to the ones Elias kept popping off. "Your Highness."

Having been schooled in the proper etiquette by her bodyguard prior to landing, she replied, "Your Highness," and paired it with a curtsey that had to look just plain silly in her yoga pants.

An amused chuckle rolled out, as smooth as the Casamigos sipping tequila Mallory had splurged on to celebrate when Kelsey landed her job with Omni Creative. "That feels all wrong. Shall we start again?"

Oh, thank goodness. "Definitely."

They both leaned in. Kelsey *assumed* it was for a hug. Christian, however, only leaned in from his shoulders to kiss her on both cheeks, European style. To do so, he grasped both of her elbows. So when she tried to go for a normal hug, she didn't make it all the way and sort of rebounded off his chest with her boobs.

Terrific.

Christian let go with another chuckle. "There's no way to make this less awkward, is there?"

Kelsey fought back the instinct to cross her arms over her chest. "Only in that it can't get any worse."

"That's the spirit. Nowhere to go but up." He brought his hands together and held them up to his face for several long, silent moments. But the staring he did was so loud and pointed Kelsey almost took a step back. "Apparently, I've a crap way of showing it, but I've been looking forward to this day for…well, for a long time."

How on earth was she supposed to respond to that? Kelsey went with naked honesty. Begin as you mean to go on, right? "That's more than a little disconcerting."

"I imagine so."

She stared over his shoulder for a second, distracted by a glorious vista of a jagged mountain range still tipped with snow on its highest peaks. "Whatever your expectations are, there's a very good chance I won't meet them. The idea of this life, of being royal, is completely foreign to me. The idea of having a whole second identity is beyond confusing." Drawing herself up a little straighter, jutting her chin out just a bit, Kelsey finished with, "But I'm going to try."

Another long silence. Uh…Elias had assured her that Christian spoke fluent English. Was he working so hard at coming up with the words in her language? Or coming up with something—*anything* to say to her?

He surged forward, throwing his arms around her and squeezing hard. It was a great hug. Kelsey swore she could feel the pent-up longing for his missing sister being released as they stood there, embracing in the light June breeze.

It was a much, much better start.

"Don't worry about anyone's expectations," he said into her ear. "Because I never expected to see you again. So this is already more than enough."

Footsteps made the metal stairs behind them shudder. Christian let go and delivered another knife-sharp nod. "Miss Wishner."

Mallory curtsied. Perfectly. Geez, she'd done ballet for four years pre-puberty. Of *course* her curtsey would put Kelsey's to shame. "Your Highness."

Since he'd known her name, Kelsey assumed Elias had given the palace a mid-flight heads-up that Mallory was her plus-one on this royal adventure. But she wanted to make it crystal clear *herself.* Before they—literally—took another step.

"Christian, I want to thank you for letting me stay at the palace."

"It is your home."

Well, that'd be a discussion for another day. Right now, it was just a glorified hotel for the two-week vacation she hadn't planned. "I'd like to ask that Mallory be given a room there, too. Or shove another bed into my room. I can't have her staying at a Hilton down the street, running a gauntlet of security whenever I need her. Because wherever I go, she goes."

"Understood. We've already prepared a room for her down the hall from your own." He turned to face Mallory. "We'll make you a lady-in-waiting."

Her sister's lips pursed. "Ah, I already have a job."

Did she have to be so literal? And/or so dense? Why, *why* would Mallory argue with a freaking prince thirty seconds after being introduced? Kelsey threw her arm around her sister's shoulders and whispered sharply, "Just say yes." She gave a sharp pinch to drive home the command.

Christian resumed that parade-rest stance, but his eyes crinkled at the corners. Was he amused by Mallory's resistance? Charm sort of oozed off him, like steam curling from a cup of tea. "If you accept the designation, Miss Wishner, you'll receive an unqualified security clearance. You'll be able to go everywhere with Her Highness, only excluding some private family meetings."

"Thank you." Mallory sounded...sullen. Like she was thanking him for giving her detention. Just as Kelsey was about to step on her foot, Mallory sucked in a breath. "I'm sorry, Your Highness. There are a lot of changes happening, and it puts me off balance. I'm a planner. I like to see the next twenty steps carefully mapped out. Discovering my sister's a princess...it caught me off guard. And sleeping in a plane didn't help, no matter how luxurious."

"I'll personally make sure there's a nightcap delivered to your room tonight. A liqueur local to Moncriano. Blueberries left to sit in sugar. Sweet and powerful." Christian gestured at Mallory with one hand, palm up. "Rather like you, I imagine."

Seriously? Her new brother was *flirting* with her sister? That was...well, it was weird. Or maybe she'd imagined the flirtatious subtext? Kelsey rubbed at the corner of her eye, because her sleep hadn't been restful, either.

Elias did that sudden, silent appearing trick of his. "Your Highness, I recommend not staying outside. Too much opportunity for the princess to be seen and photographed and rumors to start swirling before you're ready, even with the canopy."

"Agreed." Then he did a double take at Elias's casually rumpled appearance before leading them down the strip of purple carpet to the waiting SUVs. Elias opened the door. "I'll see you at the palace." As soon as Kelsey and Mallory were inside, he shut the door.

"That's it?" Mallory plastered her face against the dark

tinted window to stare at the prince as he hustled into his vehicle. "That was the big introduction—over in less than five minutes? How dare he brush you off so fast?"

Kelsey scooted to the opposite window, drinking in the mountains again. They were magnificent. And to someone who'd spent her life in the flat Upper Midwest, they were also *breathtaking*. "We had a good moment. Okay, we had two really awkward moments first, but then a good one. I'm not sure there's any protocol for what we're doing. No set time limits for small talk with a stranger you happen to be related to."

"You have twenty-five years to catch up on. Don't you want to ask him a million questions?"

"Honestly?" Kelsey twisted around to look at her sister. She lifted her hands, then let them drop heavily back onto her lap. "I don't know where to start. With Christian, or the king. Let alone with Mom and Dad. But I'm sure he'll get in the car with us in a minute. We'll have the whole ride to play Twenty Questions."

She wished desperately her parents would answer their phones. She'd left messages when they stopped at Junior's, and just before taking off. They must've been swamped with an emergency at the hospital to not return her calls yet. She and Mallory had been trained from a young age to accept that patients came first, unless they *themselves* were bleeding.

Did emotionally bleeding count?

Because she really, really needed to get the down-low from them on what the heck had happened to her twenty-five years ago. They had to know. Didn't they?

The engine started. They pulled away smoothly. *Without* her brother in the car. And without her hot bodyguard.

Huh. Was this her new life? A family that didn't hug on first sight and considered five minutes to be sufficient quality time together?

Kelsey felt even more unsettled than she had when Elias had locked their apartment door behind her.

. . .

Despite his exhaustion, Elias sat ramrod straight across from his prince. There must be something of urgency Christian wanted to discuss. What else would make him ride in a different car than the one carrying his newly rediscovered sister?

"What is it? Has word leaked about the princess? I personally chose everyone on this mission, but it's also true that almost everyone can be bought."

Christian stretched out his legs. "*Almost* everyone?"

"Some of us value honor over money, Your Highness." Elias hoped it was true of everyone in the royal household. But then again, he didn't protect the heir to the throne with something as weak as hope. And there had been leaks over the years, albeit not from the RPS.

"If you're trying to use reverse psychology to get a raise, it won't work. The Captain of the Guard makes those decisions, not me."

Elias winced exaggeratedly. "Guess I'd better hope he has a long-lost sister I can find and bring home to him."

Chuckling, Christian asked, "How'd it go?"

Should he start with how crazy-attracted he was to Christian's little sister? Or save that grenade for later? Along with how damned much Kelsey simply did not want to leave Manhattan? "It wasn't, ah, trouble free."

Christian's head turned to him so quickly there was an audible neck snap. "Really? Who doesn't want to be a princess?"

"Your sister, as it turns out. She was less than thrilled by the news. Not at all easy to convince, either."

"That's surprising. Isn't it every little girl's fantasy to be a princess?"

Aha. There was the problem, just as he'd feared.

The royal family still thought of their princess as the baby they'd lost and sought for so long. Elias suspected this wouldn't be the last time they overlooked the fact that Kelsey was actually a grown woman. A grown, beautiful woman with an interesting mind all her own.

"She's not a girl, Christian. She's a woman who had just started living *her* dream and I ripped her away from it. For you."

"For the good of the country."

"Of course." Country before self. The Villani royal family all believed it, lived it, as did Elias. But would an independent American fall in line to that way of thinking? For a country that didn't yet feel like her own?

The prince pulled a bottle of water out of the pocket in the door. "Did you mention the clothes, the jewelry, the servants?"

"Yes. I got the distinct impression she was pissed at what she interpreted as attempted bribery." Which had shocked Elias. It had also impressed him. Intrigued him. "Besides, you're doing her a disservice. A whole new family's a lot to digest by themselves, let alone giving up your entire life to go live with them. Would you expect Genevieve to throw away her life for designer clothes and a handful of tiaras?"

"She'd step over a black cat and walk under a ladder for a tiara," Christian said dryly. "But I get your point. Genevieve would never abandon what really mattered to her for mere *things*."

"Precisely. You should give your new sister the same credit."

Scrubbing a hand through his hair, Christian said, "You're right. It's hard, you know? To not have any idea what to expect from her. To not make assumptions."

"Here's something else you'd never assume. The princess suggested waiting a year to come to Moncriano. She wanted to put if off until she was all settled in Manhattan and had saved enough money to make the trip."

Laughter ricocheted off every gleaming silver handle and fitting in the car. "That's priceless."

Funny in theory, maybe. Not in reality. Not to Elias. "You laugh, but it may be a serious problem if she chooses not to embrace her inheritance, her birthright. She could turn her back on all of this."

"Nonsense." Only Christian's sudden white-knuckle grip on the handle above the door gave away his unspoken worry. "Haven't you heard? I'm charming as hell. Moncriano's the best country in the world. And once she gets used to having breakfast delivered in bed, she'll realize being a princess isn't a hardship. We'll get her to come around, no problem."

Christian wasn't listening. And he was very likely underestimating Kelsey. That was the last thing she needed.

Elias rapped his knuckles against the window. "I'm telling you, Moncriano's the last place she wants to be. She's a huge flight risk. The least little thing could send her running back to Manhattan. Eight-hundred thread count sheets and having someone do her laundry won't make a difference."

"Fuck. I know." The prince dropped his chin to the perfect Windsor knot in his sky-blue tie. "I'm making light of it because I'm scared."

"You? Scared?" His friend was famously fearless. Even when a healthy shot of terror might lead to clearer thinking. Like, say, preventing him from getting in a fight with seven angry, drunk Swiss Guard with only Elias by his side. Or in Tokyo, when he'd eaten thirds of that sushi that could kill you. *Nothing* phased Christian. "Of what?"

"Of saying the wrong thing, doing the wrong thing."

Now his head dropped lower, to cradle in his hands. The words came out slightly muffled. "My own sister terrifies me, because I don't have a clue how to handle her. Of how not to piss her off. How to sell her on our country, our family, without disparaging her own. How to get my baby sister to love me. Or even like me, after all this time."

It usually required half a whisky bottle to achieve this level of sharing. Even stranger that it was happening before two a.m.

Elias wanted to help, but this wasn't a situation with a rule book. Or even examples of how anyone else handled it, because princesses didn't just go missing for twenty-five years and then pop back up.

All he could offer Christian was normalcy. And their normal was poking at each other. "Did you start seeing a therapist while I was in New York?"

"Very funny." He whacked Elias on the knee with his water bottle. "Help me, damn it. Who else am I going to talk this through with? Papa and Genny have their own issues. I can't lay anything else on them."

Clearly, this wasn't the time to confess how...*attracted* he was to Christian's little sister. That just might be the straw that broke the prince's back. Then again, Elias would probably be wise to *never* mention just how much he'd enjoyed having Kelsey curled up on his chest as they winged across the Atlantic.

"Look, it's an impossible thing to go through, but I promise, she's nice. You're awesome with strangers. You two will figure out how to do this brother/sister thing."

With a hollow laugh, Christian sat back up. "Did you see us five minutes ago? On the tarmac? We were like the Three Stooges bumping into each other. Thank God there weren't paparazzi around to capture it."

Yeah, he'd seen it, which was why he'd sent Mallory down

as an interruption. "I didn't say you'd figure it out right away. Give it more than five minutes. Why the hell aren't you in the car with her now, asking questions?"

"Because I didn't know where to fucking start." As Christian's voice rose, he punched a fist against the leather seat. "I can't ask about her parents. The ones who've hidden her from us all this time. Can't ask about her home that we just evicted her from. What's left—asking if she dips her French fries in mayo or ketchup?"

"You've been seated next to some boring-ass people at state dinners. Spouses of world leaders. Remember that K-pop band who kept trying to sing to you between courses? Just follow the same prep. We'll make a list of questions. Small talk. Safe topics."

"That won't get us anywhere."

"Yes, it will. It'll get you comfortable with each other. Once the walls come down, you can move beyond the great French fry debate. You know, on to important things like porters or IPAs. Red or white."

"At some point I'm going to have to talk to her about more than just what goes on a dinner table."

"Sure, but everyone eats dinner, right? It's a great equalizer. A great place to start."

"I'm not sure if this idea's totally brilliant or totally bollocks."

Elias wasn't sure, either. "Talk to her, Christian. Don't hide behind protocol and titles. Just fucking talk to the woman." He looked out the window as they drew closer to the white and gold spires of the castle. "Did you tell your father about the princess?"

"Not yet. I didn't want to get his hopes up until she was on Moncriano's soil and I'd seen her with my own eyes."

Now he got it. Why the prince had waited, since the king had endured years upon years of false hopes and false leads.

The few photos Elias had scoured from the internet didn't do Kelsey's striking violet eyes justice. "Eyes that are an exact match to yours. And Genny's, and your father's."

"I'm sure Papa will notice that right off. Her eye color marks her as a Villani every bit as much as those fingerprints you sent over." Christian leaned forward again, his jaw set and those violet eyes as serious as they ever got. "You know, I owe you for this, Eli. Hell, the entire country owes you a debt of gratitude. There'll be a knighthood in it for you, at the very least."

"For fuck's sake, that's the last thing I want and you know it."

"What do you want, then?"

Her. Kelsey. The one thing he knew Christian wouldn't—and couldn't—give him.

Elias fisted his hand until his knuckles ached as they turned through the gilt-tipped wrought iron gates. "I just want to keep her safe."

Chapter Four

Kelsey's navy wedges didn't make a sound on the thick carpet. *Nothing* made a sound. For a place with over six hundred rooms and what had to be a staggering number of staff, it was eerily quiet.

"Your Highness?" Somehow Elias, with his crack bodyguard instincts, had picked up that she'd slowed to trail half a dozen steps behind him.

"Just…I need a second."

Kelsey paused for a final mirror check. Didn't take much, considering the lengthy hallway alternated sets of French doors to an elaborate garden with ten-foot-tall mirrors. Mirrors with frames that were thick gold swags of some kind of flower. They were spectacular, over-the-top museum pieces, at the very least. Just like everything else she'd seen so far in Alcarsa Palace. Or castle. She wasn't clear on the distinction, and that was about ten thousand and one down on the growing list of questions she had.

Not to mention the single, overarching question Kelsey had for her parents. Specifically, the Wishners. *What had they done?*

How was she supposed to face her new family without an explanation from her old family? Her loyalty to the Wishners was rock solid, on a foundation of so much love it could never waver. But didn't she also owe loyalty to the people— strangers—blood relations who'd searched for her for twenty- four years?

It'd twisted her up so much that even jet lag hadn't given her more than a few hours of uneasy sleep. At least the fancy clothes should distract from the bags under eyes.

She wore a pale-blue skirt and sweater set that had been left on her bed while she showered this morning. Mallory had received a visit from the magic clothes fairy, too. Everything had been in exactly the right sizes. That had struck them as uber-creepy until Kelsey remembered that Elias's guards had stayed behind to oversee packing up their apartment.

Did she love that two muscled strangers now knew her bra size? No. Not at all. But Kelsey was thrilled to not be meeting the rest of her...family in those damn yoga pants. They'd gotten the lipstick shades wrong, though, so a pale, subdued ghost of herself reflected back in the mirror.

"Come in with me," she said to Mallory.

"Nope." Her stubborn, annoying sister crossed her arms over a matching sweater set in a pale apricot that set off her long, auburn hair. The hair Kelsey had always envied. Had always wondered why *she* hadn't inherited from the Wishner family gene pool, too. "This is a private moment. Like when you met the prince yesterday."

Kelsey rolled her eyes. "Look how well that went. I don't want to replicate that sub-par level of non-success."

"Christian will be in there, right? So you can consider this your do-over with him."

That was intriguing. She did that all the time with her graphic designs for clients. Started one, realized it was a boring mess, and started again. They always got better the second time around. Although sometimes it took four or five false starts...

Kelsey poked at the drooping corners of her eyes. Pushed them up and grimaced. "I'm not a morning person, and I'm jet-lagged."

"Not an excuse." Mallory turned her away from the mirror. "You *are* a night owl. And it's ten hours difference, which makes it eleven p.m. in Manhattan, as well as in your body clock."

They'd had dinner on trays in Kelsey's amazing suite of rooms, slept in stunning canopy beds, and had cocoa and croissants for breakfast. All that pampering had done wonders for Mallory's mood, apparently.

Kelsey, on the other hand, had spiraled into sheer terror as the hours ticked by toward the "family audience in the throne room." And terror made her bitchy.

Scowling, she said, "You're determined to be cheerful, aren't you?"

"Mostly because *I'm* not the one who has to meet a freaking king today. I'd be shaking in my shoes if I did. But since it's just you going under the royal microscope, it's easy to be perky."

"Did you fly thousands of miles to help me or to annoy me to death?"

"The jury's still out on that. Last I checked, the two weren't mutually exclusive." Mallory's giggles echoed, bouncing off the marble down the hallway.

Elias was suddenly at her shoulder. He tucked his head down so his mouth was at her ear. Warm breath popped goose bumps up all over her as he said softly, "You look beautiful. You look like a princess. Please take my word for it and keep walking?"

"God, I'm sorry." It was so easy to forget that her quirks

and moods could affect someone else's job performance. She didn't have anyone who reported to her at Omni Creative. This responsibility for someone else was brand new. Drivers and maids and bodyguards weren't anything she'd asked for, but it appeared they weren't going away. If anything, they were replicating faster than the aliens in *Star Trek*.

"You need never apologize to me, Your Highness."

Oh no. Never, *never* would she turn into the kind of person who didn't apologize, who didn't thank everyone who did things on her behalf. Kelsey gave herself a mental slap on the knuckles. She didn't intend to shirk that responsibility again. "You'll get in trouble if I'm late?"

Elias straightened, tilting his hand back and forth. "It's bad form to keep the king waiting."

Interesting how Elias balanced that tightrope of not actually accusing her of screwing up, while still making her aware that she *had*. Kelsey didn't want to let him down. And as reluctant as she was to meet the royal family, she certainly didn't want their meeting to start out on the wrong foot.

Time to get this show on the road, especially since she'd now run out of clichés.

"As it so happens, I don't condone lateness. Too many of my colleagues pull that artistic temperament crap. Punctuality is common courtesy. So let's hustle."

It only took five more sets of the door-and-mirror combos before they stopped in front of a set of doors topped with an elaborate crest. A man in a morning coat—which Kelsey proudly identified thanks to a recent re-binge of *Downton Abbey*—opened the doors and sort of semi-bellowed, "Miss Kelsey Wishner."

Mallory beamed, giving her two thumbs-up for luck. With his own version of a go-get-'em nod, Elias widened his stance, assumed the fig leaf pose famed throughout centuries of art...which, of course, led Kelsey's mind right back to wondering what he'd look like in that pose *naked*. For purely artistic reasons, of course.

Low-grade lust also served to melt away the worst of her nerves. As a person who always said her thank-yous, should Kelsey later inform Elias of how the prospect of seeing his hairy, muscled thighs helped propel her into the throne room?

Upon entering, it was easier for her art-loving eyes to drink in the massive room than the loose semicircle of people at the opposite end. Deep purple carpet was stamped along the border with golden pinecones. Tall windows overlooked the mountains on one side, and the ocean from the other. In between the windows were colorful flags that she guessed belonged to cities or provinces. Four enormous crystal chandeliers ran the length of the room, bringing her gaze to two—thankfully empty—thrones on a dais. Just above and behind one hung a portrait of a lovely woman with a blond updo supporting a crown.

A woman who looked enough like Kelsey to be, well, her mom.

That jolted her to a stop in her march across the carpet. Who was she kidding? That had to be the queen. Her mother. Her long *dead* mother, according to Elias. But yet here she was, being somewhat included in the family meet and greet. It was almost enough to jostle out a wholly inappropriate giggle.

Kelsey kept walking, encouraged by a smile from Christian. She'd been hoping for a cozy discussion on a couch over coffee. This was…pretty much as far away from that as you could get. Especially when her original plan for today had consisted of painting over some questionable stains on their bathroom walls.

Stepping forward, Christian cleared his throat. "King Julian, I present Kelsey Wishner, whom I solemnly vow and attest is your daughter."

About five paces away, she stopped in front of the older man and curtsied.

The king didn't say anything. He did keep staring at her, though.

What the hell? Mallory had practiced with her last night. Kelsey was positive that her curtsey was, if not on par with a prima ballerina, more than acceptable. What had she done wrong? Was it the borrowed clothes? And why was the woman who had to be her sister looking at her with such disdain?

This whole thing hadn't been her damn idea. She'd forgive the lack of coffee and bagels, but she did *not* deserve to be stared at like a zoo animal shedding its skin. Kelsey's temper burned off the rest of her nerves faster than a marshmallow went from toasty to scorched over a campfire.

Finally, in a soft, reedy voice vibrating with emotion, her father said, "You're really her. You're really here. I can hardly believe it."

Kelsey nodded. "I am right there with you on that."

He reached out an arm, as if to touch her, and then dropped it back to his side. Clearly, touchy-feely was off the agenda for the Villani family. But if not a group hug, then what next?

The silence stretching out was excruciating. In movies, scenes like this had soundtracks. Maybe an elegant string quartet in the background to match the regal room. Or swelling strings, overlaid by brass that portrayed the surge of emotion hypothetically swamping her relatives.

Couldn't they at least open one of those enormous windows to let in a little bird song?

Thankfully, Christian came to her side to fill the gap. He led her down the line, one by one.

"Princess Genevieve, your sister."

The woman was flat-out stunning. Kelsey could think

of two occasions she'd come close to looking that flawless—prom night and college graduation. Both had required the help of professionals at the mall with both hair and makeup. And since graduation had been three years ago, Kelsey's lack of attention/inadequacy in that area was a much more familiar feeling.

Genevieve looked so much like her, only polished and more refined. The same blond hair and violet eyes. A pearl necklace circled her throat, matching the fat pearl studs in her ears. Her pale-green suit had a peplum flare at the waist. Beige pumps had heels skinny enough to use in needlepoint. The only thing that marred the look was the thin, downward twist to her mouth.

Having been briefed on the all-important birth order and protocol, Kelsey curtsied to her older sister. "I look forward to spending time with you."

After all, Mallory was her best friend. Another sister would just be loading on the goodness, right? Two cupcakes were always better than one.

Lips barely moving, Genevieve said, "My schedule is run through my private secretary."

Ouch. Elsa from *Frozen* had nothing on the bitch ice princess of Moncriano. If that was the way it was going to be, one cupcake was fine. Two would just make her fat. Or make her face break out.

Christian nudged Kelsey's elbow to move her on to a woman with salt-and-pepper hair and a plumper build. "Duchess Mathilde, your aunt."

A series of brisk nods was accompanied with a wide smile. "Oh, my dear, this is such a joyous day." Two lines of fat tears tracked down her cheeks.

Well, Kelsey certainly didn't want to make the woman *cry*. But it was gratifying to get some sort of emotional feedback. No hug yet. Although Mathilde did keep clasping and unclasping her hands at her waist. That had to count for something. "Trust me when I say I'm not worth crying over. I'm fairly ordinary."

"There is nothing ordinary about the Villani royal family," snapped the next woman in line, her snow-white hair feathered back from her stern face. "Not after holding this country together for almost seven hundred years."

She wore black, and a blinding diamond pin on her lapel. Or was something that big and flashy called a brooch? And shouldn't there be a rule about saving the more than four-carat jewelry for after lunch? Like the one about saving white tie and tails for after six p.m.?

"Gran, you're not making a speech to Parliament. Dial back the rhetoric a little." With a faint smile of apology, Christian said, "The Grand Duchess Agathe, your maternal grandmother."

Kelsey curtsied again. If she stayed in Moncriano, she'd need to add squats to her exercise regimen to get her in shape for all this knee bending. "Nice to meet you."

"Jumping to conclusions, aren't you? As for my part, I shall withhold judgement until the *end* of this meeting." She thrust a shiny white folder embossed with a golden seal at Kelsey. "It took a great deal of effort on my part to get things organized on such short notice. Do not be late to any of these appointments. Punctuality is the rule here, not the exception."

Too bad she couldn't say the same about warmth and courtesy.

Kelsey gripped the folder with both hands. "*Better three hours too soon, than one minute too late.* William Shakespeare agreed with you. As do I."

That earned her a sniff. No way of knowing if it was good or bad, though. Her grandmother gestured to the folder. "That's only for the next two days. Obviously more will be added, culminating in the public announcement of your return. Then we'll set you up with a real itinerary."

It was odd. They acted as if this was a done deal. As though this life was automatically better than the one Kelsey had worked and planned for in New York. When, in fact, all the croissants and new clothes in the world couldn't just take the place of her lifelong dream. A dream she was in no way ready to give up.

Pride in family was a universal concept. She understood where they were coming from. Kelsey just wished that someone would put in a tiny bit of effort to understand where *she* was coming from.

The king broke off from the line. Kelsey was a little surprised an alarm didn't sound as he left formation. "I'm sorry your old room was unavailable, but we didn't think you'd want to sleep in what used to be a nursery. It'd be far too small for your current needs."

Current needs? Mallory had discovered after their first supply run to an authentic NYC bodega that the twenty-four pack of ramen was too wide to fit on the kitchen shelves. They'd stashed it at the bottom of the coat closet. That was where her head was with "current housing needs."

She swallowed back a laugh before answering. "The rooms are beautiful, Your Majesty. Far more than I need. I think the bathroom is the size of my entire apartment back in Manhattan. If you want to save it for a real VIP guest and move me somewhere else, that'd be fine."

"Valentina, nobody is more important than you."

Kelsey tried not to do an obvious crossing-the-street-left-right-left with her head, if not with her eyes. But who was the king talking to? Had someone else join—

Ohhhhh. That must be *her* name.

Her original name. Her princess name. It certainly sounded royal. Lilting, even.

Shocking beyond words, however, to hear her name for the first time in twenty-five years. How had Elias never so much as mentioned it to her? Or for that matter, how had she not asked? "Kelsey" was cute and spunky and not royal at all. She should've realized that immediately.

It wasn't Elias's fault. It was all hers. Okay, maybe she'd throw Mallory under the bus for at least 20 percent of the blame, too.

She needed to be on her toes. Stop letting change and information steamroll right over her. Stop letting everyone else take charge and herd her along. It was still *her* life. And she was the only one in charge of that.

Kelsey would be respectful and courteous and try her damndest. But she needed to stick up for herself way more. Get out in front of this avalanche of everybody else knowing more than her about, well, herself.

Crap. Being two people at once made it super hard to even think in normal sentences.

"Thank you, Your Majesty. That's a very sweet sentiment. But may I ask a favor?"

"Of course. Anything you want is yours. Everything here is yours." When the king said that, Kelsey caught her big sister's discernible twitch from the corner of her eye. Not big on sharing, huh? Or just not a fan of all things Kelsey-centric? "Name it, and you shall have it."

He really did talk like a king. Kelsey wondered if he kept up all that formality during, oh, game night or playing tennis. Was that stiffness and distance a part of King Julian? Or something she could ascribe to the horrible awkwardness of him loving a stranger and not knowing what to do with that?

"I'd like you to call me Kelsey."

"Absolutely not," snapped her grandmother.

Genevieve tilted her head the slightest bit so she could condescendingly glare down her nose. "That's not a *royal* name at all. It certainly doesn't fit here in Moncriano. It sounds like it belongs to a slutty girl on a reality television show."

What. A. *Bitch*. Kelsey didn't even have time to react to the slur before her aunt jumped in to protest.

"Valentina, my dear, you don't realize how special your name is," said Mathilde. "It was our great-great-grandmother's. And she was an Italian *principessa* twice over."

Their accents, while faint, made everything being thrown at her seem even more, well, foreign. Kelsey had a sudden flash of longing for Elias.

Not a rip-off-my-clothes-and-take-me-now type of longing. Well, that kind, too, now that she thought about it. But to have him next to her as somebody to be on her team. To guide her through this room that felt conversationally booby-trapped. Like invisible lasers crisscrossing a museum after lights-out.

"Valentina—" the king began, but Kelsey cut him off by taking three steps forward, going almost nose to nose with him. Was that even allowed? Was there a personal-space rule that she hadn't yet been told regarding all persons above her own rank?

Well, tough.

Taking a stand required a little drama. Just a little. She wasn't going to make a king talk to the hand or anything.

"Pardon me, Your Majesty, but I'm not the baby you lost twenty-five years ago. I'm a grown woman. With my own history, career, and most of all, my own *name*."

It got quiet again. Eerily quiet. The lineup of her relatives all wore matching, slightly open mouths and wide eyes. Worst family portrait pose ever, but Kelsey wasn't worried. She didn't regret one bit drawing that line in the sand. The only thing she did regret was the flicker of utter sadness that sort of melted across the king's face.

It was gone in a matter of seconds, though.

Christian finally saved the day. "Why don't we all agree to call you Kelsey while we get to know each other? The staff were already commanded to use that name in order to help keep your return under wraps. We can discuss how to address you formally when it's closer to the announcement."

Her father nodded. "That's acceptable. I may slip up a time or two, but it will be purely by accident, I promise. I've had a picture of you in my head, a certain way, for a very long time."

Kelsey would take the compromise. For now. "And I've been this version of myself my whole life. Changing on a dime will be a challenge for all of us, I imagine."

"I didn't mean to upset you." Lo and behold, the king reached out one hand and gave her a gentle pat on the arm. If he could bend, so could she.

"I didn't mean to snap at you." Crap. How long did you have to know your dad before it was okay to lie to him? The answer was probably well north of the ten minutes that totaled her relationship with the king. "Well, I did, but only to make sure you heard me, loud and clear."

"There's a good chance the gardeners in the fountain court heard you," Genevieve sniped.

Kelsey had earned her win for the morning. She'd let that one slide. Turning to Christian, she asked, "Uh, what announcement?"

"The official announcement to the world of the return of the missing Villani princess. It will be in two weeks."

Her grandmother sighed. "It would be nice to have more time to prepare, but there's little chance of keeping the secret any longer."

"Official? You mean a press release?"

"An official edict," the king corrected. "As well as an

introduction to Parliament, and a formal reassumption of your place in the royal family."

Every time Kelsey thought she'd caught her breath, another big wallop of information left her panting in surprise.

What happened to easing into the whole family thing first? Icebreakers, maybe. Whatever the royal version of that was—croquet and tea? Why didn't she have the chance to get to know these utter strangers who claimed her as theirs before worrying about the rest of the freaking *country*?

So she only had two weeks to decide whether or not to do this? To take on this whole other life and leave the one she knew—and loved—behind? Tackling the problem of being— *becoming*—a princess in less time than it took for cottage cheese to spoil?

That was it. Kelsey couldn't stand here and listen to any more without hard-core help. "Is there any possible way we could finish this over coffee? The stronger, the better?"

Chapter Five

Elias didn't pace.

He'd learned to march in his Navy training, and learned to be preternaturally still as part of his bodyguard training. Pacing, however, was frowned on by both sectors. So he stood, hands behind his back, a full three, "I'm not at all trying to eavesdrop" paces away from the doors to the throne room.

But in his head? He was making more circles than a pup trying to chase its own tail.

Meeting a member of the royal family intimidated most people. They intimidated most citizens of Moncriano, who'd lived their whole lives seeing the Villanis on the balcony of their palace, in their box at the theatre, and waving and shaking hands at hundreds of events a year. They were a known commodity here, and still people stuttered and blushed and went all wide-eyed when a royal gave them attention.

Kelsey was *not* used to seeing them. She wasn't used to even thinking about royalty. In the short time Elias had known her, it had been quite clear that she had a spine and a mouth, and the two in tandem could be formidable. Enough to stand up and be herself in front of the king?

Elias wasn't sure. He was, in fact, worried. And full of guilt for sending her in there by herself—not that he'd had a choice. It wasn't as if he could claim that he needed to protect her during a private audience with her own relatives.

Although he did, because Genny could be an intolerable bitch when rubbed the wrong way. And the grand duchess could be downright frightening when crossed. Elias was certain that some part of Kelsey's very American-ness would end up making her grandmother very cross.

The doors opened. Instead of waiting for the footman to open them all the way, Kelsey twisted her body to slide through the narrow crack. Elias sprang to attention and gave a brief nod, prepared to bow if the rest of the family came out.

But the doors closed behind her.

Great. They'd all stayed behind to discuss her. Probably to judge her, given the circumstances. Hopefully, Christian would be a voice of reason.

"Your Highness." Elias stepped in front of her.

"Hi." The tight purse of her lips lifted into a full-blown smile. And the force of it was like a warm rain shower. "You waited for me?"

"Of course."

"Of course?" Just as quickly, the smile fell away. Kelsey moved around him and slowly started walking down the hallway. "Oh. Because it's your job to be my shadow."

"To a certain extent. I'm not the only member of your protection detail." Elias pitched his voice lower as they passed another set of footmen at the doors to the king's private audience chamber. "But I would've stayed here regardless. In case you required...anything...upon finishing your audience."

"Anything, huh? In that case, is it too early for a cocktail? Not even a fancy one. Just line up the shot glasses and keep 'em coming. There must be a bar somewhere in this town that's open."

"It's not even ten a.m. yet. I'm afraid we're not Las Vegas."

"Ooh, way to go with dropping a geographically perfect cultural reference." The teasing lilt in Kelsey's voice proved that whatever had happened to her in the throne room, she was bouncing back already.

Elias gestured for her to turn into an adjacent hallway. One *slightly* less grand and gilded, but not by much. It led to the private wings of the palace. "Just because you've never heard of Moncriano doesn't mean we aren't well aware of all things American."

As he'd hoped, Kelsey rose to his implied challenge. "Really? Prove it. What's weird about the parade we have on Thanksgiving morning?"

"Giant balloons of cartoon figures. Which aren't that odd, all things considered. Did you know that Belgium holds a Bathtub Regatta on the Meuse River every year?"

"With real bathtubs?" Kelsey's disbelief sharpened her tone.

"Indeed."

She paused in front of a French door. The morning sun put a halo around her golden hair. Elias had a sudden vision of it spread across his pillow.

So he looked away. Looked for anything at all to distract him from the pull of Kelsey's beauty. The first thing that caught his eye? A painting of The Sirens—three women lying on Moncriano's beach. Nude.

Even though it was centuries old, it was still naked women.

Elias could *not* catch a break.

Kelsey had turned to walk backward as she tossed him another challenge with a cocky lift of her eyebrow. "Where's the Liberty Bell?"

"Philadelphia. I accompanied the crown prince on a

tour of your Independence Hall and we marveled that your country is so young. There's probably twelve bells older than that one within a mile of our palace."

"Show off. Old isn't always better."

"Cheese and wine disprove your point."

"Stale bread and rancid meat prove it." Kelsey drew an oversize check mark in the air with a flair. "Check and mate."

A laugh spun out of her, not like the tinkle of a harp, but a loud, raucous, triumphant belly laugh. Laughs like that did not erupt in the public wing of the royal palace very often. An honest laugh like that one would never be used by a woman to flirt.

See? This was just fun. This couldn't possibly be him breaking every protocol and *flirting* with the princess. No flirtation in history included the words "rancid meat." Elias was cheering up Her Royal Highness, giving her a laugh. Kelsey only saw him as a friendly shadow. A necessary evil. Perhaps even as unwanted as an ankle monitoring bracelet they put on criminals. She wasn't flirting with him.

And even if she was? It was absolutely forbidden for a member of the RPS to date a member of the royal family.

Also very, *very* frowned upon for a commoner to date a member of the royal family.

And his father's reaction—well, that'd be another problem entirely.

She was in the friend zone, nothing more. It was normal to enjoy a friend's laughter. That was his story and he was sticking to it.

That laughter certainly was an improvement over the pale and tightly drawn cast to her face when she'd left the throne room. And he wanted to do whatever it took to keep that light in her eyes, that smile on her lips. On an impulse, Elias veered to the right and opened the French door.

Kelsey didn't walk through. Eyes narrowed, she shot him

a look of confusion. "Why are we going outside?"

"I thought I'd take you on a walk in the gardens."

The upper half of her body canted forward, but her feet stayed planted on the carpet. "I can't."

"Are you allergic to grass? Roses?" Damn it. Talk about an oversight. What if the bouquets in her room were making her sneeze? Or worse? "That should've been in your file."

"No." Kelsey let out a long sigh. Not one of satisfaction. No, this had a distinct tinge of *dissatisfaction* to it when coupled with the slump in her shoulders. "No, your crack dissection of every inch of my life before ever actually meeting me didn't miss anything."

Elias most certainly did not miss the thick sarcasm frosting her words. "What, then?"

Biting her lip, Kelsey thrust a folder at him and shook it back and forth. "It isn't on the schedule. I've been ordered to adhere to the contents of this folder. Admonished, even."

Oh, for fuck's sake.

He should've known the old lady would immediately start throwing her power around. From what Christian had told him, King Julian was in no shape to control the situation. He was in shock. The official, barely responsive kind of actual shock that had sent his valet sprinting to get the palace physician.

Christian said his father hadn't been much better this morning than when he'd broken the news to him last night. As though the king refused to let himself give in to hope. So however horrid his mother-in-law might have been to Kelsey, the king probably hadn't done anything to rein her in.

Elias grabbed the folder. He beckoned to the nearest footman. "Please take this to Miss Wishner's suite. Give it to her sister."

"Right away, sir."

Foot still propping open the door, Elias swept an arm

out toward the vast expanse of manicured lawns, ruthlessly trimmed hedges, and more flowers than he could name. "I believe your schedule has cleared, Your Highness. Would you care to stroll in the gardens?"

"Why yes, I would."

The key to this brief escape for Kelsey was to keep her out of sight of, well, everyone. So he quickly led her past the dual strips of reflecting ponds edged with rows of white flowers. The fast click of her heels dulled as they switched from pavement to the crushed shell path that took them past the fountain. Elias only slowed once they were—mostly—out of sight and under the trellis sagging under drooping purple jacaranda.

Kelsey raised her arm to trail her fingers amidst the blooms. "When I agreed to a walk, I didn't know it would be a speed walk." From beneath heavy-lidded eyes, she pinned him with a glare. "Were you hazing me? Initiate the newest royal by giving her a blister?"

Was that a glare? Or a *flirtatious* glare?

When the hell had he lost all ability to read women?

And why the hell did it matter when Elias could not, should not, would not date a princess? "I'm sorry. I didn't want to give anyone the chance to stop us. Being truly alone is more difficult than you'd think in a palace with more than six hundred rooms."

"Thank you." She pulled down a branch and sniffed deeply. "I...I did need a break."

"If it makes you feel better, everyone walks out of their first formal audience a bit worse for wear. Honestly? Your grandmother scares me, to this day. And I met her years ago, when I was just a boy."

"How did you—" Kelsey broke off and started taking the pins out of her hair. "She *is* scary, the grand duchess. Can you tell me something? Does she hug anyone? Because I didn't get the vibe she was particularly thrilled to see me."

Elias had to tread carefully. Not insult her American expectations, and also not insult the Villanis. All while holding back a good-sized rage that the grand duchess had stayed so true to form. This woman had been missing for twenty-five years; a lifetime. For God's sake, that didn't earn her a hug?

"Each generation of royals has a different approach to public displays of affection."

"We weren't in public," she quickly countered.

"You were. As far as the grand duchess was concerned." God, he hated that he had to explain this to her. Explain the strictures of royal life to a woman who just wanted to give and receive what would be—to the rest of the world—a standard amount of affection. "Any grouping of more than two people is public. There are expectations to be lived up to. I don't even think she accepted hugs from her family the day her daughter was buried. So no, it isn't you, Your Highness."

Kelsey propped her elbow on a wooden column as she pulled out the rest of the pins. "That's sad. Truly. I wonder—"

"Stop right there. If you're wondering if you could change her once you get close, don't bother. She's not only content in her ways, but she'll fight to her dying breath to preserve them."

"The king?" she asked in a quiet voice.

Her questions weren't getting any easier. Elias thrust his hands into his pockets. "King Julian's struggling right now. But he's a good man who has been known to hug his children. I've seen it with my own eyes."

"Oh good." Kelsey's voice was down to a mere whisper. As though she wasn't holding her breath for that to ever happen to her.

He gathered her handful of pins and put them into his breast pocket. "So, to sum up, I gather this morning was rough?"

"Yes." She dragged her palms down her cheeks. "Very rough. They were...relieved, I guess? Not thrilled. Not doing cartwheels of joy. Relieved to have Valentina back. Oh!" Kelsey thwacked him on his upper arm with her palm.

Elias almost laughed. Good to see her energy rebound, even if it was to attack him. "While technically there must be some ancient law that allows you to hit me, do I at least get to know why?"

"You didn't tell me." Kelsey accentuated each word by drilling her index finger into his biceps.

"I'm quite sure there are a million and five things I didn't have the time to brief you on. Which one is worth bruising me?"

"You didn't tell me my name. My other name. My real name. Valentina." She arced her wide-spread hand through the air as though turning it into a banner.

Shit.

That was...horrible. Unforgivable. So, so, *so* damned stupid of him.

He'd been so caught up in using her title, in insisting that she get used to hearing her title, that Elias had forgotten the most basic fact of all.

"I'm sorry. Your Highness—Kelsey—I'm truly sorry."

"I know it was just a slipup. But I felt...stupid. At first, when the king said it, I didn't realize it was *my* name. How could it be? I already have a name. And Valentina is so fancy. So foreign. Like something out of a Renaissance poem."

"It suits you."

"Omigosh, Elias, it so doesn't." She sank onto a wooden bench and gripped the edges as if to keep from falling over. "That isn't even funny. I spend my life in yoga pants, with no makeup, hunched over a computer working for my clients. There isn't a single fancy thing about me."

Elias had to fix this. He knew the speech to give. He and Christian had debated it over the years as the prince figured out what his contribution to the country could be. Christian, absolutely, should be the one to explain it all to her.

But he couldn't let Kelsey wallow in her self-doubt for another second, especially when his thoughtlessness was partly to blame. He sat down next to her, peeled back her tight fingers, and cradled her hand in his.

As a friend would, of course.

"True royalty has nothing to do with jewels and coaches. It isn't about thinking you're better than everyone else. Or even wanting them to look up to you. Being royal means helping all your citizens to be proud of their nation. They do look up to the Villanis as an example of the best of Moncriano. Aspirational. Inspirational. To be a force for good for the country."

After giving a weak laugh, Kelsey said, "That's a million times harder than dressing up in pantyhose every day."

"Indeed. You have to *care*." Which she obviously already did, or she wouldn't be so concerned about doing a poor job of it. "And I have a feeling you will be excellent at that, Your Highness."

She looked at him sideways from beneath slanted, long-lashed eyes. "If that's the first qualification—having a big heart—then yes, I'll admit I could rock that part of being a princess. Is all that written down in a job description somewhere?"

"On the back of your birth certificate, I believe." Trying his best to keep a straight face, Elias continued. "There's a naming ceremony held over your bassinet where it's all explained to you within twenty-four hours of your birth."

Kelsey snorted out a laugh. Then her hand flew to cover her mouth. "Oh God, you *were* kidding, weren't you?"

"Yes."

Her laughter continued, muffled, from behind her fingers. "Thank goodness. I mean, I *thought* you were kidding. Ninety-five percent sure. But things are so different here. So formal. I don't want to accidentally laugh at a centuries-old tradition."

Elias patted the hand he still held. "You will."

Kelsey gaped at him. Indignation even colored her cheeks a little. "Oh, thanks for all that faith in me."

He looked through the drooping vines at the high hedges of the maze, wracking his brain to come up with just the right examples. "When we were nine, Prince Christian filled balloons with holy water out of the baptismal font in the Palace Chapel."

"That's sacrilegious, in any religion."

"When Princess Genevieve was twelve, she pulled off the *keffiah*, the headscarf, worn by the Emir of Bahrain." Elias leaned in close enough to feel her soft puffs of breath on his cheek. "On a dare," he whispered.

Turning so that her lips grazed his jaw, Kelsey whispered conspiratorially, "Who dared her?"

"If you manage to pry that secret out of the princess, I'd love to know."

Leaning back and putting space in between them again, the playfulness slipped from her eyes. "They were just children."

"Technically, yes. But more to the point, the prince and princess were still unschooled, unpracticed in affairs of state. That's where you are now. You'll undoubtedly make a mistake. Or ten. It won't matter, Your Highness." Elias tightened his grasp on her soft, slender fingers. "As long as you keep learning, keep trying, and remember to lead with your heart, you'll be fine."

Kelsey bit her bottom lip. Gifted him with another one of those half-hearted, wry smiles. "Is giving a gold-medal pep talk a usual qualification for a royal bodyguard?"

"My job is to keep you in one piece. You looked like you were falling apart when you left the throne room."

"You'd be right about that. My life—the brand new life I just started—is gone. Nobody seems to care about *me*"— Kelsey thumped her chest as her voice cracked—"the actual person in here behind the princess title. Except for you."

Her aching vulnerability sliced into Elias like a sword straight through his gut. It tore through the rules and protocol and every layer of common sense.

All that was left was a man watching a lost, lonely woman. It was blindingly obvious what she needed. So he wrapped his arms around Kelsey and hugged her.

She didn't cry, or even tremble. But she did heave in a deep sigh, and when she let it out, her whole body relaxed into his. Except for her arms, which slid into a tight embrace around his waist.

They sat like that for long moments. Long enough for Elias to notice the determined buzz of a bee overhead. Long enough for a peacock to strut past them, its vibrant green and blue tailfeathers dragging on the ground like a train. Long enough for Elias to also notice how his arms wrapped so far around her small frame that the tips of his fingers grazed the sides of her breasts.

He knew he should move. Readjust.

He didn't care about *should*. Elias only cared about making Kelsey feel better. Feel like herself.

Feel that he did, indeed, care for her.

Finally, Kelsey lifted her head from where it rested on his collarbone. "Thank you."

"You're—" But before he could finish the phrase, Kelsey kissed him.

It was just a soft, faint brush of lips over lips. Probably meant to be nothing more than a continuation of her thanks.

Except that something sparked between them. The one, faint touch instantly morphed into *more*. Elias honestly couldn't say which one of them consciously deepened the kiss. It felt organic.

It felt necessary.

It felt right.

They clung to each other, and that soft brush grew into a *real* kiss. The kind he gave after a date where everything clicked, where he and the woman connected deeply. The kind he hadn't given anyone in many, many months.

Kelsey's beauty had struck Elias from the moment that flimsy, splotched apartment door opened. But then, as she stood her ground with such determination, as she sassed him on the plane, as she approached every step of this journey with such bravery, the involuntary, primal acknowledgement of wanting her *body* had flipped over into wanting *her*.

The pressure between their lips, between their bodies intensified. Elias moved his lips harder against hers. Kelsey pushed right back. They kissed and kissed and suddenly their tongues were tangled, tasting and teasing.

Elias groaned. God, she was delicious. Sweet. Tantalizing. And so soft every single damn place they were touching.

His hands slid up through the silk of her hair to tilt Kelsey's head back, to deepen his angle. But then he immediately slid one palm down her back to keep her pressed close. To keep those firm breasts rubbing against his chest as she swayed her upper body.

It didn't make up for the fact they were seated side by side, that their hips and legs and bellies weren't rubbing together. But it was damned sexy, especially sexy, paired with the breathy little moans she kept exhaling.

"Elias," she murmured, as his lips moved down the tantalizing column of her neck. God, he just wanted to keep going. Push that prim and proper sweater out of the way and keep lapping at the pale skin that he couldn't get enough of.

"Princess," he replied.

And then froze.

His subconscious had just saved him. Tossing out that automatic title had been the necessary reminder that he wasn't only kissing Kelsey. Elias was making out with a Princess of the Realm.

Elias almost recoiled but caught himself in time, not wanting to hurt her. This lapse in judgment fell squarely on his shoulders, and his alone. Kelsey didn't know the rules, didn't know they couldn't be together. And there was no time to explain, because he had to get her back inside before the grand duchess set loose the hunting dogs to find them.

Or was it that he didn't have the courage to ruin the moment with such a stamp of finality? Cowardice that kept him from stating just how many ways they could never possibly be together?

So he tucked only a strand of hair behind her ear, slowly tracing down below her lobe to follow the dark pink of desire staining her cheek. "I'm sorry."

Those kiss-reddened lips parted. "For what?"

"For letting things go too far."

Confusion blurred her eyes as she blinked, fast. "Too far?" Laughing, Kelsey waved a hand at the latticework above. "I don't see a used condom hanging from the trellis. We kissed."

"And that was my mistake. Wonderful, but a mistake. Stay here. You're perfectly safe. I'll send out Marko, your other main bodyguard, to escort you back inside." Elias shoved to his feet and executed a sharp bow. "Your Highness."

Disappointment mixed with hurt in those stunning violet eyes. It pouted those puffy, delectable lips. Before Kelsey could say a word, before he could weaken again and give in to temptation, Elias left.

Chapter Six

Be careful what you wish for.

Some fuzzy old Chinese proverb that she'd always mocked for being too negative was messing with her. Big time.

Kelsey stared at the door that had *snick*ed shut only a moment before. The white door with beautiful gold, curlicued molding that, for all she knew, was probably covered in actual gold leaf. Staring at the door was far preferable than turning around to face the unexplained giant racks of clothes.

She'd wished for a life with excitement, a nonstop reckless pace, a constant hubbub of activity. She'd *meant* for that wish to come true in Manhattan. Instead, some laughing, sarcastic genie had farted out a vastly different version of her wish.

The first meeting with the highest-ranking members of the House of Villani—because it had been made clear to her that there were plenty of lesser-ranked members yet to come—definitely felt like it happened too fast, too soon.

Then the kiss with Elias...well, that wasn't too soon, exactly, since the possibility of it had been tickling around the edges of her brain since Kelsey first clapped eyes on those firm, chewable lips.

It had definitely *ended* too fast, though. Then her replacement bodyguard had rushed her inside to meet with a frowning man in what looked like a graduation robe who'd lectured her about Moncriano's history. This happened while Kelsey was given twenty precious minutes to shovel down a scallop salad (delicious), one flaky biscuit (she would've given Mallory's left arm for three more—why didn't being a princess entitle her to freaking seconds?) and a single glass of fruity iced tea.

From the little Kelsey gleaned, Moncriano sounded a lot like Switzerland. Permanently neutral and friendly. Okay. At least they didn't have a blood-drenched history like ancient Rome. Although she kind of wished they'd pick a side when it truly mattered. Maybe she'd missed something important when the buttery biscuit blacked out everything but her taste buds for a few seconds.

Then a frowning woman in a pale-lavender suit escorted her to a study to quiz her. What languages did Kelsey speak? What degrees did she hold? Could she ride? Shoot? What was her level of archery proficiency? Any certifications such as scuba or rock climbing?

Shockingly, Lady Tamara did not even crack a teensy grin when Kelsey proudly mentioned her fireworks launching certifications she'd gotten to personally ensure that the Fourth of July celebrations went off without a hitch. It was one of her favorite holidays.

Geez.

Did she have to give that up? Would Kelsey get in trouble now for celebrating her American heritage? So far she'd enjoyed exactly none of becoming a princess—aside from the kiss with Elias. And she was pretty sure that her being a princess had *not* been a driving force behind his lust.

So yes, her day had been fast-paced with constant activity.

The problem was that Kelsey had chosen none of it. Plus? Her big dream had been to be a *bystander* in New York. To sit back and watch the excitement unfold around her like a twenty-four-seven play.

All of this excitement was happening *to* her. Technically, the basics of her wish had come true. But with an ironic, twisty execution that flat-out sucked, which meant that right now, staring at the door was preferable to turning around and dealing with whichever unwanted surprise was next.

"Dear, you don't have to wait to be announced." The gentle voice lilted with a stronger accent than Elias and Christian had. "Come in, come in."

Kelsey tried to rub out the frown line between her eyebrows that felt like it went all the way through her skull as she turned. The room itself looked like a wide, enclosed hallway. A receiving room? Lots of oversize portraits and more of those kick-ass chandeliers, but not much furniture at all. Just a few lavender velvet chairs along the walls.

And oh, good. No scary grandmother. Just the nice Duchess Mathilde. "Hello. This is…not what I expected to find in here." The unfamiliar and already painful heels clicked against the elaborate parquet floor as Kelsey edged away from the door.

"The clothes?" The older woman bustled forward to grab her hand and pull her along faster. "Normally we'd do this in your own suite of rooms, but with the quantity needed, well, sufficient space took priority over comfort."

"Do what? I'll admit I don't remember the schedule." That sounded plausible. And far more forgivable than the truth, which was that she hadn't even looked at the thing before Elias sent it off to Mallory's safe keeping.

"We have to completely outfit you with a new wardrobe. Well, that's not possible in an afternoon, of course, but you'll have at least the basics while we get the rest custom-fitted."

Was that her first in-person royal "we"? Just then, the fifth rack of clothes rolled forward to reveal a tiny desk and three women clustered around it. They looked impossibly chic. There was what movies had always portrayed as a European flair about them. An artfully draped scarf on one. A patterned tunic that flowed over hot pink cigarette pants on another. The third boasted a statement necklace that Kelsey wouldn't be brave enough to wear even at Halloween.

Had they been briefed on her? Was there a photo in that folder on the desk that showed her in the yoga pants she'd slept/deplaned in? Were they judging her?

On the other hand, wouldn't the whole freaking country be doing that if King Julian actually rolled her out as the lost princess?

And would they find her sorely lacking as princess material?

Before drowning in a panic spiral, Kelsey remembered her tried and true approach to projects. One step at a time. One task at a time. She reached out to stroke the sleeve— holy crap, was that cashmere?—of a jacket. The clothes were absolutely beautiful. About a hundred miles out of her league, but beautiful.

Not wanting to hurt her aunt's feelings, she asked cautiously, "Why is this necessary? Aren't my own clothes here from New York by now?"

"Only an American commoner would presume to call that box of fabric *clothing*." The sneer in Genevieve's voice preceded her sister coming from around the farthest rack. It was quickly followed, however, by a matching sneer of disdain that pulled all of her features downward, sort of like that Dali painting of melting clocks. Only bitchier.

Kelsey could let it pass. She could take the high road and not respond to the obviously intentional poke.

On the other hand, she'd stood up to the freaking king

this morning. She'd decided to start as she meant to go on. If that was a good enough way to treat the king, it was the right way to go with her sister. While true that she'd been raised a commoner, and an American, the one thing Kelsey was *not* was a pushover.

"Only a discourteous snob would insult someone's personal belongings. Or are basic manners just an American thing?"

Red washed across Genevieve's face. Not in a single, rosy perfect blush, but in hot-looking blotches. Even better, she didn't say another word. Kelsey notched that as a win.

Duchess Mathilde crooked a finger to beckon over the three…courtiers? Dressmakers? Style servants? Kelsey had no clue. Which was pretty much par for the course for how her day was unfolding. "Your clothes are being pressed. The Royal Protection team who packed didn't have, shall we say, a delicate touch. But you are about to have a full to bursting schedule. We don't expect you to know the requirements of every function. It is the Villani family's duty, and my utter pleasure, to supply you with a wardrobe for the social calendar we've thrust upon you."

Smoothly done. Kelsey knew darn well she'd just been handled. So expertly, though, that she didn't mind it at all. "You're the family peacemaker, aren't you?"

"I like everyone to be comfortable. In their heads"—she tapped Kelsey's temple—"and in their clothes, as well." She held up a lacy dress the color of sunshine, then switched it out for an identical one in a paler daffodil hue.

Scarf lady started to pull off Kelsey's sweater. It was disconcerting, to say the least. "I can do that for you." Awkwardly, she twisted away and tugged off the cardigan. She'd watched every *Downton Abbey* episode at least a dozen times. It had always baffled her that the lords and ladies would stand there while other people dressed and undressed them like dolls. It wasn't as though slipping out of a sleeve required a ton of effort.

"Dear, let Marie help you. She has to take all your measurements. European sizing is a different scale than what you're used to. We must start from the ground up."

That sounded long and involved, and like something Kelsey had no intention of suffering solo. "Why isn't Mallory here? Doesn't she need new clothes, too?"

"Mallory doesn't need anything from us. She isn't a princess," Genevieve said, her tone dripping spite. She popped up in between the racks when she had venom to spew. Like a snake, hiding in the grass until it was ready to strike. "She's no one."

That was probably the cruelest thing Kelsey had ever heard. Also, the absolute most incorrect. Her family—the one she'd grown up with and loved every day that she could remember—was her Achilles' heel. Her softest, most vulnerable spot. Any attack on them was the same as dropping a match into a cylinder of rocket fuel.

She'd defend them with her whole heart, for her whole life. It was that simple.

It was also a fact far more pertinent to share with the room than her neck circumference.

Kelsey stepped away from the semicircle of outstretched measuring tapes to confront Genevieve head-on. "I realize I'm a guest in your house, which is the only thing keeping me from plowing you to the floor. But let me be perfectly clear about Mallory. You don't ever, *ever* say a single nasty thing about her or to her. She matters more to me than literally every person in this country."

Looking down her nose—only possible because her needle-sharp stilettos were at least two inches taller than Kelsey's heels—Genevieve said, "Oh, it's always been clear that *you* are the important one. Even though you weren't here." Without bothering to leave space, she brushed shoulders with Kelsey as she hurried from the room.

What. Just. Happened?

The duchess sighed as she patted her roundly shellacked helmet of gray hair. "Ladies, I see that we're missing refreshments. Would you please go ask the footmen to get us some lemon water?" The stylish gaggle immediately withdrew, so she had to raise her voice to catch them at the door. "And a bottle of Riesling?"

That was...an unexpected choice. While Kelsey was more than ready for an alcoholic panacea to the day, her *aunt* requesting it made her wary. "We're going to need wine for this talk?"

"I might. I'm not sure you will. I already see the strength of your spirit." The older woman patted her hand, then used it to pull her over to one of the gilded chairs along the wall.

That was a lovely thing to hear. Mathilde seemed nice, approachable, even. So she volleyed back a little honesty. "I'm not always strong," Kelsey said as she sat. "I wouldn't have been strong enough to come to Moncriano without Mallory by my side."

"You're lucky to have had that relationship, to have someone who bolsters you. Princess Genevieve was not so lucky."

Boo-freaking-hoo. Okay, that was immature. Insensitive. Thank goodness she hadn't slipped and said it out loud. But her older sister's snitty attitude made Kelsey want to revert to the childhood they hadn't shared and just spat with her. "She's a princess. Isn't there a whole castle full of people for her to lean on?"

"Full of people, yes, but not the one person who mattered the most. She has always felt the hole in her life left by her missing little sister."

This time a snort did slip out. "She's got a funny way of

showing it."

"Genevieve has had to live her entire life shadowed by your disappearance. Every choice, every move she made was colored by the overhanging threat of another kidnapping. Many choices were taken from her, which was always explained away as a result of what happened to you, ah, *Kelsey*." Mathilde leaned hard on the name, as if wanting to prove that she could say the right one.

The effort was appreciated. As much as her words themselves were not. "You're saying it's my fault that Genevieve's a bitch to me?"

"Of course not, dear." Another pat of the hand. "But she believes it is your fault. You're just going to have to prove her wrong, show her why it is best to bury the past and move forward shoulder to shoulder, as true sisters."

"Great. I'll just add *overcome decades of deep-seated bitterness* to that schedule the grand duchess gave me."

"That would've made your mother very proud."

Um, number one? Did sarcasm not translate well in Moncriano? Because Kelsey had absolutely not been serious. And B? Pretty crafty of her aunt to administer a dose of dead mother guilt. She had to give Mathilde props for that.

• • •

A pillow to the face was *not* an acceptable replacement for an alarm.

Even when the throw pillow was a cloud of tufted silk. Being hit was jarring, period. Kelsey sat bolt upright, arms up to ward off another attack. Because this was not her first rodeo with her sister.

"I'm pretty sure these pillows cost more than our apartment's rent. I'm also sure there's got to be a 'no hitting the royalty' clause in whatever etiquette manual they live by here."

Looked like somebody had paid attention to Kelsey's wardrobe rant about equality among the Wishner sisters, because the same pajama fairy had visited Mallory. Her navy satin set matched the lavender set that had been laid out in waiting for Kelsey once she was finally allowed to escape back to her rooms.

Mallory dropped the pillow and climbed up—yes, using the actual tiny step at the foot of the bed—to sprawl next to her. "Hey, desperate times call for desperate measures. I haven't talked to you in an entire day. It was like they scheduled us to purposefully keep us apart."

Leaning back against the upholstered headboard, Kelsey scrunched up her nose, because something definitely smelled off about that situation. "You noticed that, too, huh?"

"Oh yeah. For the record? That was the House of Villani's one gimme. Due to the surprise and suddenness of having you back maybe having caught them off guard. But one day is all they get to hoard you all to themselves. I can't help you adjust to this if I'm not by your side."

And just that fast, something *settled* deep within Kelsey. She and Mallory were a team. They'd always been a team.

Going it alone yesterday had been rougher than rough. Moncriano really was a whole new world. One where Kelsey didn't have the faintest idea of who to trust, who to believe, and most of all, how to avoid accidentally causing an international incident.

But side by side with Mallory, she'd be more confident. More discerning. More able to not just tread water, but swim amidst these unfamiliar and no doubt treacherous waters.

Basically, she needed a buddy. And if that made her sound like kindergartners crossing the street in pairs? Well, she dared anyone else to discover a whole new family and fly across the ocean to a whole new country and discover that her brand-new sister hated her...and handle it even a teensy bit better than she was.

Oh. *Oh.* Kelsey wriggled up even straighter. Because, even separated from Mallory, she'd had someone in her corner to lean on, at least for a little while. "I've got something to tell you."

"One thing? Are you kidding? I want to be filled in on every moment. On every meal, every glance, every gilded wall sconce you saw." Mallory reached out to touch the carved post that held up the fringed canopy. And there was considerable awe in her wide eyes. "We're in a freaking palace, Kelsey. We're basically living out a Hallmark channel movie. The only thing missing is the tall, dark, titled sexpot ready to kiss you senseless."

"That's what I have to tell you." It was weird to admit. Confusing. Talking it through with Mallory was the only way to get clarity, especially since Kelsey had zero idea of how to reach out to the man himself.

Did she have to wait to talk to him until he showed up for his next protection shift? Was there a code on the bedside phone? *Dial 184 for bodyguards, dial 186 for tea and scones?*

"You can't kiss anyone with a title." Mallory underscored her point with a severe finger wag. "You're probably related to them. Or at least, for safety, you should assume that until we do the research."

Ewww. "Pretty sure I'm safe with my bodyguard. Double entendre totally intended, BTW."

Mallory's hands flew to her mouth as something close to the squeal of a boiling teapot escaped her lips. "You kissed Elias?"

"Yes."

"Was he amazing?"

"Yes." Kelsey traced the outline of a golden peacock in the bedspread. "It started out sweet, and then things got real. Real hot. Scorchingly hot. Then he stopped, said it was wonderful, but a mistake, and practically sprinted away." She locked eyes with her sister, hoping to read an answer in the flurry of fast blinks. "What the heck is the takeaway supposed to be from that?"

Mallory's eyebrows had shot up to meet the edges of her mussed bangs as Kelsey's story progressed. They plummeted back down into a pinched frown. "Let's unpack this one step at a time. Where did this knee-melting kiss happen?"

It was easy to pull out the memory. Kelsey was certain she'd remember every moment of it for the rest of her life. Not just for the kiss. But for his listening and understanding as well. "Under a flowering trellis in the formal gardens. The air was scented, the birds were trilling. Basically, the most beautiful place possible."

Fanning her cheeks, Mallory said, "Okay, so hot *and* romantic. I approve. But as much as I approve...I think it's dangerous," she added, slowly drawing out the words.

Her sister's nervousness—no, *skittishness*—about the potential to be mugged or burglarized in Manhattan had been annoying, but at least understandable. For Mallory to be pulling the same shtick behind gated walls literally guarded by an infantry was ridiculous.

"You actually think some crazed person who doesn't even know who I am could get past all the palace security to get the jump on us while I'm kissing my bodyguard?"

"Uh, no. Not at all. But I think it's dangerous in that he more or less works for you. Or at least your family. So you two getting together puts Elias in a difficult situation, job-wise. Long-term? That could put you in a difficult and dangerous situation, heart-wise."

Geez. Talk about taking the protective older sister thing to extremes. Yes, in the sixth grade, when Kelsey crushed on Nate Bierson and then he touched her hand when they were on the sidelines during flag football, she'd written *Mrs. Kelsey Bierson* over and over in her journal. With a heart over the "i," thank you very much.

But the next day he'd sat with Barbie McCloud at lunch, and she'd used a fat black Sharpie to scratch out the entire journal page.

"We kissed. Once." She stuck her index finger in Mallory's face for emphasis. Just the one finger, with the rest folded away. "For three solid minutes of sheer nirvana, but only once. It's way too early to be worrying about the state of my heart."

"It is never too early for me to worry about that. Do you remember David Czimenski in the tenth grade? He kissed you, invited you to the backward dance, and then dumped you two hours later when Heidi Marshall asked him out. You were crushed."

"I was fifteen." Why were they both suddenly thinking back to their childhood? Was this quick, familiar dip into the past a way of dealing with the fish-out-of-water feeling that being the Alcarsa Palace gave them? And if so, could they maybe dip into memories where Kelsey didn't come off quite as pathetic? "I think I've got a more stable emotional footing now. Dumb things like that are supposed to happen at fifteen."

"He hurt you. That's why I TP'd his house."

Nice to have that mystery solved. Dissolving into giggles, Kelsey fell sideways across Mallory's lap. "That was you? I thought you told Mom you had nothing to do with that. I mean, his parents called the cops."

"Which is why I said I didn't do it. I'm not stupid." Mallory gave a gentle tug to the ends of Kelsey's hair. "But your broken heart needed to be avenged."

Her sister was a badass. Kelsey rolled back onto her semicircle of down pillows. "Thank you. For future reference,

I'm good with the two of us just going for mani-pedis, or having a Kahlua-and-cookies night."

"Duly noted. Now to finish up with your bodyguard. Him walking away was probably one hundred percent about him and his duty. Men like Elias always have hang-ups about duty. And he may not even be allowed to *be* anything other than your bodyguard."

"Since *I'm* his duty, I think that's at least a little about me."

With a wry smile, Mallory poked her in the shoulder. "You should talk to him."

"That's the same advice you always give."

"Because it's always true. Work, family, friends, sex... being open and talking about a problem has a cure rate of about one hundred gajillion percent."

A knock on the door had Mallory dragging the covers up to Kelsey's neck. "Come in."

"You don't know who it is," she said in a furious whisper. Because she was far, far from ready for this sister-time to come to an end. "Why did you tell them to come in?"

"Because it's coffee and croissant-o'clock. Who else would it be but breakfast?"

A short man in a lavender-and-white striped vest with a ruthlessly sculpted goatee hurried across the thick carpet. "Good morning, Miss Wishner. Miss Wishner."

Kelsey didn't dare look at her sister. How were they not supposed to giggle at that identical greeting? "Hi. Now that you've seen me in my jammies, could I maybe get your name?"

"My apologies, Miss Wishner. I'm Sir Evan McCandless, your private secretary. I've been briefed on your, ah, background, but most of the palace staff are still in the dark. Might I add that it is a relief and a thrill to have you home."

At least he hadn't bowed to her. "Thank you."

"I've brought your schedule." He put a white folder—identical to the one her grandmother had handed over yesterday—on the bed.

"That is very much not the croissant I was hoping for. Also, I already have a schedule." Somewhere. Or Mallory had it. Honestly, Kelsey didn't even know which drawer to look in to find her underwear.

"You had a draft." His blue eyes rolled, as though the very idea of it was absurd. The dry humor in Evan's tone made Kelsey wriggle up straighter to fully engage with him. "The best we could whip together on short notice. We've now had a full day and night to refine it." He walked around to the other side of the bed and set a considerably thicker binder next to Mallory's legs. "This is an introduction to royal protocol. It should be a good primer for the two of you."

That looked—and sounded like—it'd require actual studying. And even when done in a four-poster bed with what Kelsey hoped would be a magically appearing chocolate croissant, studying still sucked. Her brain rocked at the creative. Rote memorization? Not so much.

"On a scale of one to ten, how important is it that we read it?"

Thank goodness, Mallory was a step ahead of her. Hopefully Evan would be like a really good waiter who had the balls to tell you the truth when asked to choose between two items on the menu.

Evan's personality came blazing out at them as he busted out a snort/eye roll combo. "My advice is to think of it as your full-time job to get up to speed on royal protocol."

Oh. *Oh.* Time difference aside, it was Monday now. Which meant her job back in the States had to be told that she wouldn't make it in today...or any day for the next two weeks. It proved just how upside down her life was that Omni Creative and her stack of clients hadn't even crossed her mind.

"I need to call in sick."

Giggling, Mallory corrected her. "You need to call in royal."

"That's not a thing, and you know it."

"It is now."

"Please, nobody believed Chad had anything other than a wicked hangover when he called in with purported Dengue fever the day after his bachelor party weekend. So I promise you nobody would believe I somehow became a princess since I signed off on Friday." Kelsey scooted across acres of bed to retrieve her phone from the nightstand. The one that still didn't have a return text from her parents.

"I should check my emails, too. There's a day of orientation, a.k.a filling out paperwork this week for my new job so I can hit the ground running. We'll come up with a more solid excuse than Dengue fever as soon as I come back with my phone." Mallory slid off the bed and sprinted out the door.

"Evan? Sir Evan? What should I call you?"

"Anything you'd like, Your Highness." He tugged at the bottom points of his vest. And then winked. "Although a good teacher might point out that if you read the protocol manual, you'd find the answer."

Kelsey liked his style. "That behemoth's not getting cracked until I spend a good hour on the internet catching up with my real life. But a good student could be bribed into looking at it this afternoon if you'd tell her how to get coffee. Is there a Keurig in a kitchenette at the end of this wing or something?"

"The 'or something' would be a fully staffed kitchen capable of handling a banquet for one hundred fifty, and a reception for six hundred. I'll have breakfast for you and Miss Wishner sent up."

"Thanks." Her mind was already scrambling through what possible explanation she could give to stall half a dozen projects simultaneously. Projects that she'd been excited about. The deadline on one was this week. She'd have to play the family emergency card. Kelsey had the strong suspicion that the contents of the folder didn't leave her with free afternoons to stay up-to-date on her project list. But she hated lying to her clients and her boss. Hated leaving things undone. Thrusting her responsibilities onto someone else.

Being a princess was complicating everything. Immensely.

Just like kissing Elias had complicated things. Immensely.

Chapter Seven

Elias cupped his hands around the steaming mug of coffee and wished he had some whiskey to doctor it with.

Because it turned out that finally living out the dream he'd had for so many years—that of telling his father that he'd found the missing princess—in no way matched his fantasy.

In his head, Albert Trebanti would've fist-pumped the air, given him a rib-cracking hug, and layered on the praise like whipped cream on top of apple strudel.

It wasn't the accolade so much that Elias had dreamed of. It was finally taking that haunted look out of his father's eyes. Lifting the shroud of the past the man walked around with every damn day and making him happy. That by finding the princess, his father would turn back into the laughing, lighthearted man Elias couldn't remember, but had seen in photos.

Yeah, *no*.

"Look, I'm sorry I didn't tell you sooner, Papa. But duty required the royal family be notified first. You know how that goes."

"Of course. Our duty to the Villani family is more important than anything." It was a sentence he'd repeated to his son growing up as often as telling him to comb his hair or do his homework. Albert put a plate of eggs and bacon in front of Elias, then immediately turned back to the stove. Or, more to the point, turned his back *on* Elias.

As an attempt to stop this conversation, it was laughable. Elias never gave up. On anything.

Least of all, getting to the bottom of why, when his father should be relieved and ecstatic that his twenty-five year ordeal was over, the man was as stoic and closed off as any other Monday morning.

He looked around the small kitchen of the stone house he'd grown up in. White curtains still hung at the window overlooking the mountains. Copper pots still hung from a rack above the wooden table. But the explanation for his father's relentlessly dour mood was nowhere to be seen. "So you're not mad I've known for four days and only told you now?"

"I'm not mad."

"You're not happy, though, either. Not truly." Eli pushed his coffee away to clasp his hands on the blue-checked placemat. "Papa, you getting this news should be like fifty birthdays and a hundred Christmases all rolled together into one magic burst of happiness. Your honor has been vindicated."

"I'm proud of you for bringing Princess Valentina back where she belongs. But it doesn't change or in any way diminish the *dishonor* of how badly I failed her all those years ago." His father brought his own filled plate to the table and sat.

Neither of them picked up forks to so much as touch the food.

Searching for something to break the silence, Eli said,

"It's Kelsey, not Valentina. She wants us to use the name she's known her whole life."

A ghost of a smile almost flickered at the edges of his father's mouth. "I cannot imagine Grand Duchess Agathe being happy about her granddaughter abandoning her royal name. Especially in favor of one so...very American."

"Yeah, well, luckily my job is not to keep the grand duchess happy." In an attempt to keep that smile flickering, Eli fell back on relating gossip about the guards. Because aside from his son, the bodyguards were the only thing in his father's life. "Did you hear that she fired August Terrani last week? The man had twenty years in the Protection Service. Worked like a dog to be assigned to the inner circle of the Villani family. He didn't last three days guarding her."

The grand duchess's temper was legendary. As was her biting wit that could sheer a person's skin off with a handful of icy cold words. Elias worried about Kelsey holding her own against the formidable old woman.

On the other hand, maybe he should worry about *Agathe* holding up against Kelsey's infectious spirit.

With a stiff nod, Albert picked up his fork. "I appreciate you bringing me this news. I'll be sure to come to your medal ceremony."

"What ceremony?"

"For finding the lost princess, of course. At the very least, the king will give you a medal of honor. At the most, a knighthood. Possibly a manor house to go with it."

Fuck. Elias had assumed Christian had just been poking at him with the threat of a reward knighthood. Keeping the Villanis safe was all the reward he needed. He wasn't one of the privileged elite. He *worked* for a living, and was damn proud of it. Sitting on his ass raking in money other people earned on his behalf was not how he planned to spend his life.

Now he'd have to find a way to head that off at the pass. On top of working out elaborate security plans for a princess who had to go incognito for two weeks.

And *that* was on top of working hard not to think about how good Kelsey had felt in his arms... Like a dream come true. Except more real, more fantastic than any dream.

But just as fleeting as a dream.

Maybe that was the problem. Maybe his father needed to *see* her to believe she was truly real, and not just a figment of his imagination. "Come meet Kelsey. I'll look at her schedule and find a time. You'll like her. She's a breath of fresh air."

"No."

Right. The decades of embarrassment and guilt were holding Albert in place like quicksand. But Eli was throwing him a rope. All he had to do was let Eli pull him up. "It'll give you closure. Once you see the princess, in the palace, you can finally put the whole thing behind you." Having a plan kickstarted his appetite. He smeared a thick layer of loganberry jam on the toast.

"Why would she want to meet me?"

"She's meeting an entire country's worth of new people. It's...disconcerting. Difficult. The princess trusts me, feels at ease in my presence in a way she doesn't yet with most others in the palace. When I say I want to introduce her to my father, she'll do it, no questions asked."

"Your father, yes, I'm sure. But why would she want to meet *me*?" Thumping his fist against his sternum hard enough to make a knocking sound, he continued in a much louder tone. "Me, Albert Trebanti, the guard who let her be kidnapped?"

Elias shoveled in a forkful of eggs to have an excuse not to respond.

Because, *hell no,* he hadn't told the princess about his own, very personal connection to her disappearance. He'd barely talked her into leaving Manhattan as it was. Knowing that his own flesh and blood was—technically—to blame for her abduction wouldn't have given her any reason to walk out the apartment door with him.

His dad had raised him, knew his tells. And even after years of training to keep Elias stoic and poker-faced through any and everything, a parent always had intuition about his child.

Albert's eyes narrowed. Then, with the most emotion he'd shown all day, he pounded on the table.

"Aha! The princess doesn't know, does she?"

He dodged the accusation with as much finesse and speed as when he'd dodged Christian's rapier-thrust when they'd fenced last month. "We've thrown a lot at her in a very short span of time. There's only so much she can take in at once. I think it's up to King Julian or Prince Christian to relate the official version of what happened when she was abducted. Right now, they're too busy plotting her future to bother wallowing in the past."

There. That sounded reasonable. Believable.

Not at all like it was already knotting up his gut to keep this from Kelsey. She'd poured out her heart to him. How was Elias repaying her? By half truthing it on one of the biggest pieces of his life.

The entire reason he'd joined the Royal Protection Service was to try and give his father the assurance that the Trebanti name would reclaim its honor with his devotion to the royal family. His best friend was the prince because he'd had free rein of the palace due to his mother being lady-in-waiting to the queen. And the disappearance of Princess Valentina had shadowed his life every bit as much as it had the Villanis.

"Son, this is a mistake. You need to tell her Highness before she finds out from someone else."

"There are about a million and ten things she needs to know right now. Everything's a top priority. A pair of Siamese octopuses couldn't juggle everything being thrown at the princess." His phone shimmied on the table as it vibrated with a notification.

Odd that it was from Sir Evan. They weren't exactly drinking buddies. Why would Duchess Mathilde's secretary need him? She had her own protection team.

One swipe gave him the answer. Or rather, a whole truckload of trouble. Short on detail but big on impact, it read,

THE PRINCESS IS ON TWITTER!!!!!!

Normally, Eli would roll his eyes at the string of exclamation marks. But today? With this news? They were barely enough to convey the enormity of the situation.

He pushed back from the table, took a fast swig of coffee. "There's been a complication at the palace. I'm sorry, but I have to go. Please think about meeting the princess."

"That would be a mistake."

Well, it wouldn't be the first of the day. This situation with Kelsey could flip from a huge mistake to huge danger in a matter of minutes. Three bites of breakfast were not enough fuel to get him through this next battle. So Eli called in reinforcements, texting Christian to meet him ASAP in the palace's south wing.

Because there was no way Kelsey could be allowed on the internet.

· · ·

Elias made sure to stay at the prince's elbow.

Striding through the halls of Alcarsa Palace together meant he had to add on a couple of layers of formality. At least, to any observers they passed.

They were walking too fast, however, to be overheard. So Elias let it rip.

"Did you get whacked in the head with a mallet when you fell off your polo pony last weekend?"

"Destiny isn't a pony. He's a full-blood Arabian that stands at seventeen hands. And I didn't fall off. I got unseated."

"Either way, your brains have to be semi-scrambled. I heard you put fifty *litva* into the Harbor Protection's pool for tonight's soccer game."

"Betting's not illegal. I'm going to go down there and watch the game with them. A few wagers will make it more interesting."

True. Plus, he appreciated this gift-wrapped chance to hassle the prince. As a friend. As a citizen and an employee of the royal family, however, Elias knew better. "But you bet *against* Moncriano's team. What if word gets out?"

Christian gave an evil grin, full of teeth and threat. "I hope it does. Then the coach will finally realize he used his balls for brains when he traded our three best defenders. The team is a disgrace this season."

They stopped in front of the double doors to Kelsey's suite. Elias nodded at Lathan, who was bowing to the prince. "It'll probably get loud in there for the next few minutes. How about you take your break now?"

Lathan shook his head. "I couldn't possibly desert my post." But Elias caught the way the corners of his eyes crinkled in amusement.

Damn it. Sir Evan must've blabbed. Lathan wanted to stay and listen to the show. "You eavesdrop like an old woman."

"I collect information."

Annoyed, Elias used the side of his fist rather than his knuckles to deploy a volley of knocks. "Your Highness? Are you decent? May we come in?"

"I'm still jet-lagged, so the chances of my behaving with total decency are down to about fifty-fifty."

He and Christian exchanged faint smiles. Apparently, the grand duchess hadn't scared the stuffing out of her. Yet. Elias opened the door for the prince and followed him in.

It was after nine, so he'd expected the princess to be up and about to launch into Sir Evan's formidable schedule. But he hadn't thought about jet lag making her sleep later.

He also hadn't prepared himself for the sight of Kelsey *in bed*.

Her hair was mussed, mussed in the way it'd be if he spent the night in bed with her. Sunlight flooded the room, so her violet eyes practically sparkled. And oh, sweet Lord, the *ideas* it gave him to see her centered in the four-poster bed amidst tumbled covers and a stack of pillows.

His mouth went dry. His pulse jack-rabbited up. Elias could all too easily imagine how soft and warm and pliable she'd be underneath the duvet. Hell, he could all too easily imagine swiping his tongue across her lips to taste the marmalade he saw glistening on the corner of her croissant. Undoing those lavender buttons with his teeth to slide a hand under her top and knead her breast while they kept kissing...

Mallory's squeal pulled him out of his lust daze. Holy hell, how had he not noticed that her sister was over by the window? Then there was a thud as her knee hit the table as she tried to jump up and curtsey at the same time. It knocked over the chair, and almost knocked her sister on her ass.

Good physical comedy more than made up for the coffee he hadn't gotten to finish.

"Your Highness." On the second try, Mallory sank into a deep, flawless curtsey that looked utterly respectful even in pajamas and bare feet.

"Good morning, Miss Wishner. Kelsey." Christian gave

both sisters his half-assed, official smile, along with a nod of his head.

Guess he was nervous about laying down the law to Kelsey after their less than stellar meeting two days ago. Hard to be strict with someone while you also wanted them to instantly connect with you. Clearly, Elias needed to get a move on that conversation-topics list for the prince.

Kelsey didn't budge or smile. "Two of us are dressed wrong for this meeting," she said dryly. "How about you give us an hour to shower and get dressed, and then we'll regroup for whatever this is?"

"I'm afraid this can't wait."

"I'm not fully caffeinated."

"Join the club," Elias muttered. Shit. That was probably too familiar, too relaxed of a comment to make in front of Christian. Luckily, the prince's attention seemed to be focused on the *other* Miss Wishner, who had moved behind the heavy draperies swagged at the French doors. Her head angled sideways around them as she unhooked the tasseled rope pulling them back.

"Mallory, what are you doing?"

"I don't have a robe in here. I can't stand in front of the *prince* in my *pajamas*."

Kelsey rolled her eyes. "Last Halloween you wore a bikini with hay sticking out of it to prove scarecrows could be sexy. Since when did you turn into a prude? I'll bet you five dollars—wait, what is it you use for money here? Euros?"

Rubbing his forehead, Christian winced. "Not yet. Ask me again in six months to see if the answer's changed."

Elias couldn't believe she'd managed to step right onto that conversational land mine. Maybe he should make a list of topics for Kelsey of questions that shouldn't be asked…yet.

She poked at a thick white binder with her foot from under the covers. "I'll bet you five *whatevers* that there's nothing in this protocol manual that says it's against the law to wear PJs in front of the prince. Right?"

Christian put his hand on his lapel and inclined his head. "In fact, when in my bedroom, I quite stringently uphold the opposite of that rule."

Mallory's eyes widened. Kelsey waited a beat before crawling to the foot of the bed where Christian stood. "Did you just make a dirty joke?"

"Yes." This crown prince who regularly handled conversations with world leaders, Nobel prize winners, and working-class people equally smoothly cast Eli a panicked, "oh crap, what have I done" glance. Then he extended his arm, palm upraised, toward Kelsey. "Unless it offends you, in which case I'd write it off as something going wrong in translation."

A wide smile broke across her face. She planted a palm in the middle of his chest and pushed. Caught off guard, Christian staggered back a step.

"Are you kidding? That proves you're getting comfortable. Breaking down the formal walls. You made a thoroughly inappropriate joke. That's the best thing that's happened to me since we landed." Her gaze slid up, over his shoulder to where Elias stood near the fireplace. "Or at least the *second* best."

Eli's pulse soared again, but this time out of apprehension. Was she going to just blurt out to her brother that they'd kissed?

Was their kiss really the best thing that had happened to her?

He couldn't risk giving her the chance to bring it up. "Your Highness, we're here on a matter of some urgency. I apologize for not stipulating this previously, but you need to be on social media lockdown. No emails, no Instagrams of the palace, and definitely no Twitter."

"What? You can't cut me off like that. This isn't a police state. Is it? I'm still an American citizen. I have rights, and one of the main ones we hold dear is freedom of speech. If I have to march out of here straight to the American embassy, I'll do it." She'd climbed out of bed and gone toe to toe with Elias. Her eyes flashed and her chest heaved and holy hell, she was beautiful all worked up like that.

After clearing his throat, Christian added, "You also need to quit your job."

Whew. Glad Christian took the lead on that pronouncement. It should at least shift her ire to the prince for a few minutes.

Instead of more fiery anger, Kelsey deflated. The corners of her pale-pink lips drooped. Disappointment muted her like fog rolling off the ocean and blocking the sun. "And here I thought we were making progress." She crossed over to Mallory and whipped away the curtain. "Stop being ridiculous. We have bigger problems than your sudden, weird shyness. Christian's family now. Get used to it."

"He's not *my* family," Mallory muttered. But she did sit down in a chair. Drew her knees up to her chest and hugged them in tight with her arms, though.

Kelsey stayed by the French doors, one hand tight on the gilt handle. Eli hoped she wasn't about to make a break for it. She'd be safe on the palace grounds, but it'd be harder to keep her true position a secret if she streaked across the formal gardens in her nightclothes.

She put her other hand on the side of her throat as if her head was too heavy to hold up by itself. "Christian, you can't tell me what to do. Perhaps technically you can, since you outrank me. As my brother, though? Nope. Ask Mallory. She's tried to boss me around our entire lives. Does it ever work?"

"Almost never," her sister affirmed in a disgusted tone.

"And, Elias, unless you're giving me an order that'll get me out of the way of a bullet, you can't tell me what to do, either. I'm fairly logical, reasonable. If you talk to me like a person, with, oh, explanations for a request, I'll listen with open ears and a mostly open mind. Ordering me around? That'll just make me dig in my heels."

Eli didn't dare risking a look at Christian. No doubt his friend regretted the way they'd handled this as much as he did. Why had they charged in, issuing commands? Was it a knee-jerk reflex to Kelsey being an American, rather than thinking of her as a Villani? Or was it an instinct to overprotect because they *knew* she was the princess?

One thing was undeniable—they'd screwed up. And he wouldn't wait for Christian to kick off the apologies. Elias needed to do this for himself. For her. To keep the tenuous trust they'd built so far.

"Your Highness, I'm sorry if I came off as high-handed. We were concerned, convinced that every lost second could result in another tweet you fired off."

Her hands fell to her sides. "What on earth is so concerning? Do you think I'm leaving bad reviews for your country on Yelp?"

Elias bit back a grin. It would draw Christian's attention if he reacted. "Right now, very few people know we've found you. Revealing your return will require considerable strategy. For every one thing we control, there will be a hundred world-wide actions and reactions that are out of our control."

Batting away his words with her hand, Kelsey said, "A surprise, yes. A headline blip for a few days, but after the big reveal, there isn't any more news. Then it's just a private matter as we work out how to be a family."

Christian, in his own half-assed apology, squeezed her upper arm. "It is considerably more complex than that. You've come back to Moncriano at a...tricky time. Our country is caught up in a divide the likes of which hasn't been seen for centuries. Tensions are high. Everything the royal family does has a ripple effect on those tensions."

She gathered her hair into her fists and held it on top of her head. The motion pulled her top taut against her breasts, and Elias honestly wondered if he'd get an erection in front of the prince for the first time in his life.

Unprofessional.

Unacceptable.

Almost unstoppable.

He looked away, over to the antique clock on the mantel. It was fanciful; pale-green porcelain with pink roses and gilt curlicues around the edge. Staring at it dropped his lust surge immediately.

Then Kelsey laughed. And Elias realized there was nothing that could tamp down his attraction to her. "Considering I didn't know anything about Moncriano a week ago, I can easily promise not to weigh in on whatever this is. I'm not qualified to go spouting off opinions."

Shaking his head, Christian said, "Your mere presence will be an influencer. You see, there's a vote coming up about our joining the European Union. I presume you know what that is?"

Mallory's legs fell to the floor, and she straightened. "The grouping of twenty-five nations that came together politically and economically approximately twenty years ago."

Evidently spouting facts cured her shyness.

It earned her a tight smile of approval from the prince. "One faction sees it as a leap toward the future. The other faction would prefer to cling to the nationalism of the past. Support of the monarchy is a big piece of that."

Something that looked an awful lot like hope brightened Mallory's eyes. "If you join the EU, will it dissolve the monarchy?"

It was almost laughable how much these Wishner sisters considered being a princess a *problem*. In fact, Christian's mouth twitched and came damned close to breaking into a grin at the ridiculous prospect.

"No, but how we reveal the princess, every statement made about the royal family being made whole again, those will trigger a strong—to put it mildly—response by the monarchial party. It could be seen as us trying to tip the vote. When, in fact, we bend over backwards to *not* do that. That would, of course, enrage the other side. Nationalism versus opportunism."

Kelsey hoisted herself up onto the foot of the bed. "I only emailed my boss to explain that I'd be unavailable for two weeks on a family emergency. Then I emailed a profuse apology to the man who's going to be stuck covering for me. Oh, and I tweeted a happy birthday gif of a cat drinking beer for my friend Priscilla."

Thank goodness. Of course, Eli would still comb through every post she'd made to check. "At first blush, that seems harmless, yes? But what if someone sees it as a Marie Antoinette moment? That now that you're a princess, you've embraced a life of drunken debauchery and urge your friends to do the same."

"It's a burping cat, with its little paw covering the hole in the can to shotgun the beer. PETA might give me side-eye, but it certainly isn't debauched."

"Things on Twitter can escalate fast," he said grimly.

Christian had wound up sitting across from her sister. He pointed at her now. "What if you and Mallory post a selfie from the garden? Pretty roses behind you, nothing outrageous. Except that there's an accidental photobomb of the prime minister in the courtyard. There wasn't a meeting on his public schedule with the king. Is this proof of collusion? Are we secretly insinuating ourselves into the voting process?

Buying favor with members of Parliament?"

"That's ridiculous," Mallory shot back.

Elias didn't disagree. But that didn't change the facts. "That's the internet. That's why, Your Highness, you have to stop. As royalty, everything you do or say will be picked apart through a very different lens."

She crossed her arms under her breasts, forcing him to look away again. "I didn't agree to stay past two weeks. If I don't stay, I still need a job. The rent won't pay itself."

This time Christian did laugh out loud. "You have an immensely large trust. Since you were never declared dead, it's been held for you. You won't ever need a job again."

"Needing isn't the same as wanting. I like my job. I like what I do. I like having a *purpose*."

Elias adored her dogged refusal to back down, even though it made his job twice as hard. This woman knew what she wanted.

Christian was holding onto his patience well. Even though Elias knew he didn't have the ten minutes to spare today that they'd already spent in here. The prince said calmly, "Do you like it enough to not leave them in the lurch? Even if you don't stay in Moncriano, your world will be turned upside down. You won't be able to continue the life you had before. That isn't a command. It is simply a fact of what comes with your new status."

A status that hadn't quite kicked in yet, which gave Elias an idea. Normally, he wouldn't contradict the prince in front of others, but he couldn't take the sadness that drew her mouth into a kissable pout.

"What if we give the princess a week to wrap up a few projects? To post all the memes she wants on Twitter. Instead of going cold turkey—which never works—we ease her off gently?"

Christian's eyebrow shot up at Eli's public challenge.

Then, after a brisk nod, he strode to the tall double doors leading to the hallway. Decision made and discussion over. "You can have one week. That's as long as we'll be able to keep your return a complete secret. Maids talk. Members of parliament talk. We can hold off the official announcement, but I guarantee rumors will be swirling by Saturday."

He left without waiting for any acknowledgment from the Wishners. Elias had no choice but to follow him. Christian may have thought the matter settled.

Elias knew better. And he knew, *hoped*, Kelsey would need him.

Chapter Eight

Kelsey got her first C on a test in tenth grade.

She'd studied, knew the material, and thus felt comfortable staying up late binging rom-coms. Except it'd made her so sleepy the next day that she'd forgotten to turn *over* her test. Missed the whole back page. Entirely preventable, and entirely her fault. Frustration had her choking back dry sobs, until her mother handed her a pair of leggings, a sports bra, and told her to go run it off.

The first life lesson she learned from that was that it was impossible to cry and run. The need to suck in air superseded any petulant tears. The second lesson? It was possible to run off just about any bad mood. Or at least the worst of it. She really hoped that translated in a foreign country.

Because that ridiculous argument with her brother and her bodyguard wasn't out of her system. Sure, Christian delivered his edict and left as though everything was resolved.

Nothing was resolved.

Except for a much stronger feeling that she did *not* belong here.

Kelsey paused at the end of the raked gravel path to get her bearings. Right in front of her was an oversize pond shooting off a fifteen-foot fountain. About a hundred steps led up to a towering brick arch topped by four golden horses pulling what she assumed to be her (give or take a few greats) great-great-grandfather. With at least another hundred steps down the other side, it seemed like a big enough challenge to sweat out her mood.

Righteous indignation got her up the first fifty steps. Righteous fury the next fifty. And the surprise fifty after that? Kelsey let the oldie but goodie "life's not fair" propel her to the top.

Thank goodness there was a stone balustrade to hang on to as she bent over and panted. To her mom's point, concentrating on breathing *did* clear out all the other stuff. For a few minutes, anyway, until she straightened to take in the view. A fairy-tale palace, colorful flowers in meticulous patterns around reflecting pools…and a bodyguard running hell-for-leather toward her.

Elias had ditched his suit jacket, revealing the shoulder holster strapped around the white shirt that barely contained his muscles. It was like watching an action movie hero coming to rescue her. Until Kelsey remembered that Elias represented the problems and the palace she was running *from*.

So she took off down the steps on the other side without a sufficient rest. Pain stabbed rhythmically under her ribs. Her calves burned, too. In a palace with so many employees, maybe there was an early Zumba class she could join? Or cardio kickboxing? Even if the instructor didn't speak English, she could still follow most of the steps.

At the edge of the pond, Kelsey turned left. Away from the palace. Away from her new/original/infuriating family. Away from Elias. And promptly body slammed right into said bodyguard. Guess he knew a shortcut.

So much for running off her problems.

Elias curled his big, warm hands around her bare shoulders. "Your Highness, what are you doing?"

"Does this outfit not translate?" Kelsey looked down at the black spandex layered over her whole body. "It sure says *running* to me."

His eyes flicked down and then up her body. "It says... something. Where'd you get the clothes? They don't look like an outfit that Duchess Mathilde would pick out."

Funny how Elias had asked exactly the wrong, most awkward question. Still, she didn't want to lie to him. Kelsey also didn't want another argument before she was done sweating out the last one. "Are you going to yell at me if I tell you?"

He let go. Stepped back and crossed his arms with patronizing amusement blaring from the smirk that lifted his lips. "Should I?"

"No. No, you most certainly should not get that stern tone in your voice and aim it in my direction ever again."

Elias loosened the knot of his tie. A little. "You can trust me. In fact, this whole bodyguard thing only works if you trust me."

Kelsey had trusted him from the moment she agreed to leave Manhattan in his care. Aside from Mallory, Elias was literally the only person on this *continent* that she fully trusted. Sure, he'd yanked her away from home. But he'd had a mission, integrity.

At least, as far as she could tell.

So far.

She had to believe there was someone solely on her side, right? With his entire agenda and purpose being to keep her safe, Elias seemed to be the most reasonable choice.

"Anya, my maid"—and how freaking weird did *that*

sound?—"borrowed them for me. From Genevieve's closet." Without asking first. Not that she'd let Anya in on that hiccup of courtesy. "The woman already hates me, so I figured it didn't make any difference."

He speared his fingers through his hair. Which made Kelsey realize that the utterly controlled, soldier facade Eli wore like a uniform...well, it slipped off when it was just the two of them. "I'll see what I can do about getting your own clothes delivered ASAP."

"Good. Is that all?"

"No." He looked from her over to a tall fence, then triangulated back to the palace. "You weren't...were you running away?"

"From my problems, yeah. But here you are anyway," she said dryly.

"I meant, were you running away from the palace?" Elias reached out to grip her shoulders again. His fingers dug in just a little too hard, as if some of his control had slipped away. "Because that would be dangerous."

Ohhh. He'd been worried about her. The sweetness of it blew away some of the sting of being caught. "I told you, I won't dodge my responsibility. I'm here for two weeks no matter what. I promise I'm only out here to blow off steam— not to blow off the House of Villani."

His arms dropped back to his sides. "Kelsey, you can't run like this. You're in hiding, remember? It isn't, ah, usual for anyone to go racing through the formal gardens." He indicated the park-like grass and flowers and water features and trees as if she'd be unclear on the concept of where *not* to run. But at least he wasn't yelling. Explaining was... acceptable. "If you're seen, questions will be asked. Staff wouldn't dream of doing it. The royal family has their own gym. The prince goes down to workout at the Navy barracks. That leaves a grand total of one burning mystery woman that'll make everyone start buzzing."

Message received. Freedom was off-limits.

Kelsey eased into a calf stretch. Mostly for her calves, but also somewhat to have an excuse not to look at Elias while she got these words out. "I hear you, truly. I didn't think through the ramifications. I just needed to get out. Get my emotions out. Without swearing a blue streak at the top of my lungs. I thought running would be more, ah, expedient."

"I'll take you to the family gym. Or for a walk around the gardens. If you need to stretch your legs, we'll make accommodations."

She'd thought being kicked off social media was the ultimate proof that her whole life had done a one-eighty. Or even being told to quit her job.

Turned out those weren't big picture *enough* changes. No, what most made Kelsey realize that nothing would ever be the same again? Being told that her desire to do something as basic and uninvolved as jogging required "accommodations."

It knocked the wind out of her. Along with her notion of the freedom of being an adult. If she wanted a grilled cheese at midnight, could she wander down to the kitchen? Or would she have to take into account selfishly waking up a cook to do it for her?

On the more complex side…not having a job? How'd she lose *that* choice? If freedom of choice was what Kelsey had to trade to keep her tiara, then she honestly didn't know which choice she could live with.

Or would she be able to live with herself if she made the wrong one?

Did staying here mean giving up all autonomy? Obeying commands, turning into a shell of herself?

But was going back home the ultimate in selfishness? Would she—*could* she—let an entire country down, as well as the king and her siblings? Not to mention—would it really be that different? Aside from the easy access to TV shows in English and Times Square hot dog carts, wasn't it naïve to think she could slough off princess-hood? A Moncriano tiara could very well cast its shadow all the way across the Atlantic.

Kelsey looked out across the pond to a pair of winding paths that curlicued around each side of the riotously colored beds. It was beautiful.

A beautiful prison.

"I don't care how expansive the grounds are," she murmured, not caring if Elias heard her rambling thoughts. "I feel like a cloistered nun."

His gaze burned through her spandex. Kelsey expected to see steam coiling upward from where it tightly contained her breasts.

"You're no nun." The words ripped out of him like a spray of gravel from behind a Harley. Rough. Fast.

Elias did a quick three-point check of their surroundings. Then he took her hand. "Come with me. Please." He led her behind the brick edifice to a row of skinny pine trees shaped like the flame of a candle. They slid sideways between them and were suddenly in an entirely different garden.

It was more of a forest—barely claimed by humans. It was wild and overgrown and teetered on the edge of messy. Vines crowded along the edge of the dirt path. Tiny white flowers were sprinkled randomly, like a gigantic dandelion had exploded. A stream ran past them, surprisingly wide for being in the middle of a garden.

Down about a hundred feet, the path rose to the entrance to…well, *not* a gazebo. The structure looked like the latticed and fanciful turret to a dollhouse—just all by itself atop a wide shelf of rocks that had water spilling over the ferns and stone outcropping. The walls were mostly square glass panes, but it was impossible to see inside from the glare and angle of the sun.

As Elias led her inside, he asked, "Are you upset about this morning?"

Even fifteen minutes ago, Kelsey would've flipped out at such an obvious question. But she'd calmed considerably since...well, since Elias put his hands on her. So her words were tinged with humor rather than heat.

"Are you so dense about women that you need to ask?"

"Prince Christian and I apologized for being..." He fumbled with the door latch, probably as much for cover of not knowing what to say next as due to warped wood.

"Jerks?" Kelsey tossed out with a helpful, tight grin. Because it was turning out to be a little bit fun watching her smooth operator of a bodyguard so awkwardly dig himself into a hole.

"Ah, insensitive, I'd say."

"Also true." She followed him into the cool gloom of the octagonal room. There was a large grouping of well-cushioned wicker couches and chairs in the middle. Instead of sitting, Kelsey faced Elias. Better to clear the air now. "I appreciated the apologies, but it takes more than a finger snap or even a well-crafted, sincere apology to fix some things. Many things."

"Understood." He was silent for a moment. "What can I do? Because I pledged to be the person you could trust, could turn to."

Ohhh, that offer was better than an apology, more meaningful. If she wasn't trying to set a precedent, Kelsey would've forgiven him right on the spot. "Time usually helps me cool down. After glancing at the schedule my grandmother put together, I realized I don't have much of that, so I went for a run. To work off my temper before I accidentally unleashed it on anyone else."

"I do the same thing. Run until all my thoughts disappear and all I can feel is the need to breathe."

"My mom taught me to do it. My, ah, American mom."
What was she supposed to call her now? And why on earth
hadn't she returned Kelsey and Mallory's string of phone calls
yet? Blaming it on the time difference didn't cut it anymore.
This radio silence from their parents *worried* her. The Villani
royal family could answer her questions about centuries of
ancestors and proper etiquette, but they couldn't answer the
number one question burning in Kelsey's brain.

How had she ended up with another name, with another
family, in another country?

Elias took her hand again and drew them down onto the
green- and yellow-flowered cushions. "I'm not stopping you
from running. Merely requesting a change of venue. Perhaps
five minutes advance notice so I can change into more
appropriate shoes." He stuck out his leg, with the polished
black loafer at the end of it and wiggled it back and forth.

He looked ridiculous. And that broke the last of the
tension tightening her chest.

"I understand. I'll follow the rules. But it's a bigger
picture problem. The running that I can't do out here"—she
gestured at the trees outside the glass panes—"represents
everything I'm cut off from, every opportunity, every dream
that I'll potentially lose if I stay in Moncriano."

"It's an adjustment, not an end of the road. A shift in
lanes, as it were. One you didn't ask for, but one full of its
own unique joys."

Meh. All in the eye of the beholder. And so far, she
didn't behold anything that compared to her dream life in
Manhattan, working with her clients on fulfilling projects.
Did they even have pizza places in Moncriano that delivered
at three a.m.? Kelsey snarled, "The princess perks."

"Not just the clothes and jewels and palaces and yachts.
Although you might want to give yourself the chance to enjoy
all of those." His eyelids lowered to a level of pure smolder.

"I think you'd look spectacular with pearls and diamonds dripping down your throat."

On the rare occasions Kelsey ditched her uniform of tees/yoga pants, she only upscaled to jeans and a snazzy shirt. Fun, artistic pieces she grabbed at street fairs were as fancy as she got. "I don't have an outfit that goes with pearls and diamonds."

"I didn't say you'd be wearing anything else in this particular fantasy."

Oh. *Oh.* Evidently, now that they were shut away in a hidden garden in the very private summerhouse, Elias could drop his "yes, your royal highness" routine. It was the real Elias with her at this moment— like when he'd dropped the proper bodyguard facade on the plane and held her.

Just like when he'd kissed her in the garden yesterday.

Kelsey had a feeling she'd enjoy playing out his fantasy. But how did you ask your scary as hell new grandmother, *hey, can I borrow the crown jewels for a make-out session?*

Despite her dry mouth, she managed to get out, "Princess perks aren't enough reason to give up the life I planned."

Elias gave her *that look*—the one he'd given her over and over again since their first meeting. The one that declared her to be extraordinary and unfathomable. Characteristics Kelsey had hoped to pick up after living in Manhattan for at least a decade. After watching other people do exciting things, have interesting adventures. After learning how to live it up.

Because Kelsey knew she was ordinary. She lived in yoga pants, wore yellow-tinted glasses occasionally to cut down on the blue-light glare after staring at her computer monitors for ten hours straight, and had lived an utterly boring life.

Manhattan was her chance to—eventually—change all that.

Being stuck inside a gilded prison, even with pearls

around her neck, did *not* hold up well in comparison. And Kelsey hadn't gotten the impression that this could be a part-time gig. This choice wouldn't merely effect or shape her future; it would *become* her life.

A life sentence.

"I've never had to sell someone on royalty before." Elias took her hand. As he held it, he slowly rubbed his thumb across the top. "Let me take another stab at it."

"Go ahead." Heck, she'd let him recite the periodic table as long as he kept up the soft rubbing. *Almost* soft. His fingers had callouses that were just rough enough around the edges to be intriguing. To make the fine hairs on her arm stand at attention.

To make all her nerves stand at attention.

"Kelsey, the perks that come with being royal aren't surface frivolities. It is the honor of knowing that the entire country looks up to you. That they see you as a role model. You can give hope and courage, strength and laughter to all of your subjects."

Talk about a tall order. Elias did a good job of selling the position of princess, just like he had on the plane. He made her a believer for a moment. But it didn't last, because the way Elias described being royal sounded…awe-inspiring.

Number thirteen of all the things Kelsey *wasn't*.

It didn't feel right, or fair, to mislead an entire country. To force them to curtsey to an imposter who hadn't even known they existed a week ago. To ask them to respect someone who didn't know their language, their customs, or even the color of their flag. Someone who would, inevitably, let them all down.

That was her selfless reason.

Selfishly? How could she make Elias understand that life in New York had been her focus and goal for the last decade? That this fiery dream that had blazed in the forefront of her mind was being extinguished?

More than that, she *needed* him to understand, needed to morph him out of the stern shadow of her brother and back into her protector. Back into the man who'd promised to be on her side...even if that meant standing up to his prince.

How could she make him understand anything when her whole being was centered on the circles his thumb made on her now overly sensitive skin?

Kelsey dragged her gaze up off her hand to the blazing blue eyes locked on...her lips? Instinctively, her tongue flicked out to lick them.

"I can't stop being a part of my friends' lives, especially if I'm an ocean away. Keeping up online is the only way. They're important to me."

"You can look, stay up-to-date. You just can't post yourself."

Sighing, she moved on to the next big problem he and Christian had presented. "I can't stop working."

Elias started to laugh. Probably thought better of it once he caught a whiff of the stink-eye she was aiming his way. "Believe me when I say you *will* work, in a...different way. A change of careers."

He wasn't getting her point. "Manhattan was going to be my own personal movie. I wanted to watch a world of adventures unfolding in front of me. Like unlimited cable channels—I'd get to choose what to watch, when, on my own terms. Now? *Nothing's* on my own terms."

He stilled, with an intense glower around his eyes, as if holding an internal battle with himself. After a quick shake of his head, those blue eyes cleared. Putting one arm behind her on the edge of the couch, Elias leaned over. Sort of hovered right in front of her face, while that steel wall of his chest pressed along her arm. "There's one thing that can be on your own terms."

"What?"

"Me." Then he stayed there, only touching the edges of her. Along her upper back, arm, and thigh. He was so close that gravity should've done its thing and nudged him the final few centimeters.

Oh. But that was the gift Elias had given her. No need to wait for gravity. No need to wait for him to soldier past his list of responsibilities and reasons why they shouldn't kiss. It was all on her terms.

So Kelsey accepted the gift. She lifted her chin just a bit. That was all it took to have her lips make contact with his. Just a touch, a brush. It was the green light Elias had evidently been waiting for.

He rounded his shoulders to cage her in with his other arm. But was it really a cage when it was precisely where Kelsey wanted to be at this moment? In fact, this was the most free she'd felt in *days*.

And she was suddenly glad she'd brushed her teeth while waiting for Anya to riffle through Genevieve's workout gear for her.

Elias kissed her. His lips worked across hers, kneading and pressing and sending little flares of heat into the center of her body with every single change in pressure. He was slow, steady, methodical in his approach to varying softness and firmness, speed and finesse. It wasn't just as good as the last time.

It was better.

Better because he—or gravity, finally having shown up to the party—was slowly pushing her over sideways. As soon as her head hit that flowered cushion, Elias covered the rest of her body with his. Heat and weight everywhere, a million times better than the coziness of being under the warmth and heaviness of a down comforter topped by three afghans during a blizzard.

His heat radiated through the thin material of his dress

slacks onto her bare legs, through his shirt to her belly and breasts. Even through the buzz cut of his short hair as she ran her nails through it. And all of that was nothing compared to the heat at her core.

Elias teased her lips apart. She was no dummy. Kelsey parted them and immediately tangled her tongue with his. It was a dance, really. A twining, swirling dance first in her mouth, then in his, to the point where she lost track of whose was whose.

It was fantastic.

He broke off the kiss and raised up on his elbows. "You're so beautiful, Kelsey. And you look so delicate, fragile even. Until you kiss me back with such fierce passion that I can hardly restrain myself."

Something about the way his speech patterns—which were the only clue that English wasn't his first language, aside from the lilting hint of an accent—tended toward the formal struck her as unutterably sexy. Maybe it was a naughty professor fantasy she'd never realized lurked in her subconscious? When he spoke to her in those longer, almost old-fashioned sentences, it just curled her toes.

"Don't."

That popped him from his forearms up to his hands, practically planking above her as he lifted his body. "Don't kiss you?"

"Omigosh, not that at all. Don't *restrain* yourself." More sure of herself now—or more sure that Elias and his strict adherence to rules wouldn't hold her at bay—Kelsey curled her legs around his calves to pull him back down. Then that felt so good that she kept going, wrapping them tight just below his ass.

Then she *undulated*, half to drive Elias crazy, half because she simply couldn't stop her hips from moving against his. Not when it rubbed her against a very long, very hard bulge in his pants.

One that she now craved to see out of his pants.

The movement spurred Elias back into action, his momentary hesitation *gone*. He buried his face against her neck, biting and licking and sucking his way from the hollow below hear ear, across where her racing pulse beat frantically against her skin, down to the hollowed notch in the center of her collarbone.

God, she loved how methodical he was.

Elias surged back up, taking her mouth once more. More...recklessly. A little rougher, a little less polished. More...urgent. Lips more insistent, tongue more persistent. Somehow, he made her shiver and flush with heat at the same time.

A man who could tweak the laws of science with his kisses was a good man, indeed.

It was so quiet in the summerhouse that their increasingly harsh pants were louder even than the tree branches the wind tapped against the glass panes. That made it all more real. That there wasn't a pulsing techno soundtrack to distract, or even the sharp symphony of taxi horns she'd fallen in love with in her two days in Manhattan.

There was only their breath. The proof of their mutual arousal.

It was exactly what Kelsey needed as an antidote to the morning.

His big, facile hands circled the bare skin above the waist of her shorts. But shoving her sports tank up only gave him access to the tight band of the built-in bra. And by tight, she meant locked down tighter than San Quentin during a riot. Kelsey could swear she came close to dislocating a shoulder at least once a month while fighting to remove her sports bra.

Clearly, he knew not to fight a losing battle. Instead, he rasped his thumbnail across her taut nipple, poking hard against the tight spandex. It wasn't his mouth on her, which Kelsey longed for. But omigod, it made every nerve ending squeal in delight, especially when he squeezed and pinched the other one, too. Twin bolts of bliss arrowed from her breasts to the hot, needy ache between her thighs.

"I want you, Kelsey," he said in a gravelly, thick voice. "I want to have you. All of you. Naked beneath me, on top of me, surrounding me."

Oh, she was all in. But, as Elias had so gallantly offered, on *her* terms. So Kelsey asked, "Is that another order, or a request?"

"It is my most fervent desire."

Kelsey had been with other guys. Men. She'd had satisfactory sex, no complaints. But she'd never, ever been someone's fervent desire. It was both romantic and a remarkable turn on. "I'm rather fervent with that desire as well."

He kissed where her breasts swelled over the spandex, then her nose, her forehead, and ended with a slow, sweet kiss on her lips. "But not here, and not now."

"What happened to being on my terms? Which would be right the heck here and now, by the way."

Elias grimaced, wiping his hand across his close shorn hair in embarrassment. "No condom."

She didn't bother to hide her giggle as he sat up and smoothed her tank top back down into decency. "Isn't that number one in a protection necessity right behind a gun?"

With a chuckle, he said, "Not for when I was guarding your brother. It hadn't, ah, come up as a security measure. Besides, you've got a full schedule yet this morning. Sir Evan is probably about to stalk the security cams to find you." Another brush of his lips against hers that didn't match the darkness and desire that had blown out his pupils. "I don't want to rush with you."

It was a good sentiment. Thoughtful, generous, and one that left her with an unspoken promise of undoubtedly more than one orgasm.

The only problem?

They sort of did need to rush, because Kelsey knew her time here in Moncriano was ticking away fast.

Elias might end up as just one more princess perk. Like a sparkly tiara, something she got to try on, but ultimately, would have to leave behind.

Chapter Nine

"Your Highness, we should stop before we accidentally cross over into Austria and piss off their border guards," Elias shouted into the wind. Because he'd been doing nothing but sucking wind in Christian's wake as they'd galloped through the forest for the last half hour.

The heir to the throne yelled back over his shoulder. "Can't keep up?"

Smug jackass. Christian was riding an Arabian gifted from the King of Dubai sired from a line of the fastest horses in the world. His name, Bariq, translated to *lightning*.

Whereas Elias sat on a...serviceable...Irish Hunter kept in the royal stables for guests. Silvester was calm. And unenthusiastic about Eli's need to keep up with his prince. A professional jockey a hundred pounds lighter than Elias couldn't keep up with Christian on this horse.

Which the prince knew damn well.

"Simply a reminder that our horses have to get us *back* to the palace as well. This isn't a one-way ride. Unless you want to pull a dick move and call for a helicopter to come pick you up when Bariq runs out of steam."

Christian slowed his mount. He turned in a half circle and broke into a wide grin at the rest of the security detail trailing by at least three hundred feet. "We smoked them."

"Funny, I don't recall you mentioning we were in a race. Next time maybe a heads-up would make it more fair?"

"More fair. Not more fun." Christian undid the chinstrap of his helmet and took it off, scrubbing his hand through his hair. The helmet was their only nod to traditional riding attire. This was exercise, not on the official calendar, so they got the rare chance to relax in jeans and tees, which almost never happened once they left college. The Royal Navy had required uniforms, and it turned out that life in Alcarsa Palace had its own uniform code, as well. "I needed the run."

Talk about a moment of déjà vu. "Funny, that's precisely what your youngest sister said this morning. Perhaps you two have more in common than you realize."

Christian pulled the reins to a full stop, and then pierced Elias with the violet eyes that were a dead match for Kelsey's. "I still don't see how I can craft an entire conversation around that. Damn it to hell, I hate that the most I've interacted with her was our argument."

"Siblings fight." He'd watched Genevieve and Christian bicker and snipe at each other their whole lives.

"True, but an argument isn't usually the sum total of their history together." He leaned forward to stroke along the side of Bariq's head. "I came at her like a prince, not a brother."

If only Elias could remember to come at Kelsey as a bodyguard, and not a man who desired her. Because he'd sure as hell forgotten his place, his duty to her, and his country in the summerhouse.

"You can't be both all the time. Sometimes a choice has to be made."

"Damn it, I *want* to be her brother. I want to throw duty

and caution to the wind and just get to know her."

If only the prince knew exactly how much Elias echoed those sentiments. He still couldn't pin down what had made him say the hell with duty. To risk so much by kissing Kelsey... *again*.

The first time had been an accident, a mistake. One he knew should not be repeated.

The second time? Definitely not an accident. Definitely a conscious choice to act on the lust churning through him. A choice to act, to make her smile, to give her a distraction.

To give her himself.

Which wasn't really a gift that he *could* give. Because Elias belonged to the Crown. He'd made that vow to his liege lords, to his father, and to himself. The country, the House of Villani—that was where his allegiance lay. He had no right to carve off a portion of himself to give to Kelsey. The royal family deserved 100 percent of him.

As did Kelsey.

And as much fun as their interlude in the summerhouse had been, he was wracked with regret. Not for the actions themselves, but for the lack of a clear path forward for the two of them.

If she returned to America, they had no future. His life was pledged to Moncriano. If she stayed, embraced her role as princess? They still had no future. He could never have a real relationship with a royal, let alone turn his back on his duty to House Villani when they'd trusted him to keep the princess safe.

But facts didn't stop the *want*.

Elias, too, removed his helmet to enjoy the feel of the summer sun warming his head. "I've worked up those talking points for you to use with her. Maybe try them at the next meal you share. That is, if you're not too nervous to sit down with her one-on-one?"

"Is that a challenge? Damn it, Eli, you know I can't turn down a challenge."

Bariq snickered his displeasure at the stillness, so Christian and Elias began a slower trot back toward the stables.

"Indeed I do. I also know the princess is perhaps as eager to get to know her brother Christian, rather than His Highness Prince Christian. So stop being a coward and talk to her."

"You know I could have you arrested for calling the heir to the throne a coward." Christian frowned. It was probably an attempt to channel the death glare that King Julian used when displeased, but that sort of overkill never worked on Elias. He knew the prince too well to be intimidated by him.

Instead, he pushed right back. "Yes, but then you'd have to make public the reason *why* I insulted you. Which would simply highlight your yellow-bellied cowardice all the more."

"You're an ass." Christian gave him the finger to drive the point home.

"I'm your best friend. Pretty sure that's in the job description. Be an ass when nobody else will dare push back at you."

"Can I demote you to a bodyguard for the rest of this ride?"

Elias snorted. He tried that gambit at least once a week. "No. Here's my first idea of what you can ask the princess: *What sort of music do you listen to?*"

"Isn't that a basic club pickup line, one that should be screamed over a techno funk beat while flailing your arms and holding a plastic cup of beer?"

"Holy shit. Is that really one of your lines?" Elias's laughter echoed off the cliff wall beside them. They could follow the stream at its base all the way to the edge of the palace grounds. "Christ, it's a good thing you're the heir to the throne and can get women with your title alone."

"It works." Christian paused to let Bariq drink from the clear water. "But I don't think it'll work with Kelsey. What else have you got?"

"Where do you stand on the ramifications of globalization?"

"Am I trying to get to know my sister, or am I at a global economic conference trying to convince a bunch of foreign ambassadors I know my ass from a hole in the ground?"

"If you don't want to do small talk, I thought you could try and get a feel for her worldview."

"You suck at this. Did you lift that last one from my trade meeting in Croatia last month?" Christian asked.

Actually, yes. He'd forgotten about his promise to come up with talking points for Christian until last night because 1) it was stupid that the man was scared to talk to his own sister, and 2) he'd been all in his head thinking about Kelsey nonstop.

It was the first time he'd ever come close to forgetting to carry through on a request by the prince. Which proved that getting in any deeper with the princess was a dumb, horrible, idiotic risk to take. Equally horrible for both his career and his friendship.

"Of course not." He lifted one shoulder. "Maybe I remembered something like it."

"You suck at this," Christian said flatly.

"Well, I'm not in your communications department. I'm the hired muscle. I can kill a man with my bare hands. Reassemble a weapon in four-point-five seconds. Defuse seven kinds of bombs."

"So a limited skill set, then. Remind me of this during your next performance review."

"Now who's being an ass?"

Christian laughed. "This feels good. The fresh air,

bullshitting with you. Not worrying about which courtiers are hovering about trying to overhear our conversation. We should do this more often. We used to."

"Yes." Elias missed that freedom, too. But neither of them got to put their own wishes and desires first anymore. The good of *Moncriano* came first now. Always. "Back *before* you fully assumed all the duties and responsibilities of the Crown Prince of the Realm."

"Fuck." Christian sounded almost as frustrated as Elias. "I'm not even thirty. I'm too young to have such a regimented life. I want to be able to go for a ride more than once a week. To not feel like I'm playing hooky to hang out with my best friend. To not have to work through two sets of schedulers in order to simply have a conversation with my sister."

The simplicity, the ease of the ride when weighed against Christian's complaints gave Elias an idea. "What about a vacation?"

"You know everything is on lockdown until this vote on joining the European Union is behind us. No unofficial trips for us. No fun."

"I'm well aware." The king's private secretary himself had laid down the law in that regard. And in a belts-and-suspenders move, had made sure to alert the security details for the entire royal family of the fact. As if they were supposed to barricade them in their rooms if a fun getaway was mentioned. "But *after*. After everything shakes out, one way or the other in a few weeks. What if you all got away?"

"The whole family? Aunts and uncles and cousins? It'd be a circus, and probably break the budget."

"No. Not the hangers-on." The string of barely related bootlickers that circled the court were as numerous as the pine trees in the forest around them. "Just you, Genevieve, Kelsey, and the king. A forced bonding experience. Like boot camp."

"We don't go away as a family. Not ever. All of that shut down once Valentina...I mean, *Kelsey* disappeared. No group travel that included the heir and the spare, for safety's sake."

How messed up was this life they led that a family of four couldn't go on vacation together?

"What's the use of being in charge of the country if you can't occasionally screw the rules?" That's what he *said,* anyway. To lighten Christian's pissy mood. What Elias *meant* was that he'd turn the entire Royal Protection Service inside out to pull this off, if he got the okay. "We'd keep you safe. And keep it under the radar. What if you went to the Seychelles, or hell, even hiking in New Zealand?"

"Can you imagine the look on Genevieve's face if we told her we were going hiking for a week?"

She wore heels *everywhere.* Even with all the time he spent in the private royal apartments, he hadn't seen her barefoot in the palace in at least a decade. Casual was not Genevieve's style. "Yeah, that might've been an overshoot. But lounging around in a bikini on a yacht *is* her speed. Lots of opportunity to talk or not, just *be* a family. No courtiers. No photo ops. Totally off the grid."

"The idea has merit. The Villani family road trip." Christian threw him a lightning fast grin. "Papa will probably laugh himself silly when I suggest it."

"Perhaps, but I'm sure he'll see the value in it. And, ah, I'd suggest it sooner rather than later."

"Why?"

"The only way this works—the whole slotting Kelsey into this foreign, weird-to-her situation—is if you give the princess roots in Moncriano. And roots mean family to her." She'd commented at least half a dozen times about not managing to speak to her parents yet. Probably twice as many that he hadn't heard. Her closeness to Mallory was evident from the get-go.

"We welcomed her back into the family in the throne room. We said the words. She is a part of the royal family."

There Christian went, thinking with his title instead of his heart again. "Actions speak louder than words. If you and the king present her with a plan for this trip, it would be proof you don't just see her as the missing princess. As a body to prop up the tiara. Proof you see her as a daughter, a sister, whom you *want* to be with on a very personal level."

"Well said. Food for thought, for sure. I'm promoting you back to best friend status." Christian looked up to the vista of snow-capped mountains that would still be tinged with white through the summer. "How much of a flight risk do you think she is?"

Talk about a loaded question.

He'd barely been able to get Kelsey out of America. The situation hadn't exactly improved since landing in Moncriano. She wasn't getting the warm and fuzzies from the family. She chafed at the restrictions that came with her sudden royal status. Her days were being filled with lessons and lectures and not a single thing to show her how wonderful his country was.

Elias had no doubt that Kelsey would honor her promise to stay for two weeks. But the chance of her embracing her title, her new country, and staying past that? He sure as hell wouldn't put his own money on those odds.

No matter how much he wanted her to stay. For the sake of his country. For the sake of Christian and his family.

And, selfishly, for himself.

None of which he'd say to Christian.

"It's too early to predict. She's being bombarded, immersed in a life and a culture that she didn't choose. If we go to a restaurant and I order you salad, when you've had your heart set on a juicy steak all day...would you be excited to eat the salad?"

"No, of course not. God, that's the saddest metaphor I've ever heard. You're saying that *I'm* salad? Fuck, Eli. I've got to be filet mignon wrapped in bacon and chocolate cake for Kelsey to want to stay. Now I get it. I just don't know how to fix it."

Elias seized the opening he'd been waiting for. Obviously her part-time job teaching computer design at a high school was over, no matter what. But her other job didn't have to be. After checking to be sure the rest of the security detail was still out of hearing distance behind them, he said, "I've got an idea about that. What if you tell her that she *can* keep her job?"

"Impossible."

"No, hear me out. She could do it under a false name. We'd announce she was quitting, but at the same time her company could bring in a 'replacement' for her." He looped the reins around his wrist to lift both hands to make finger quotes. "'Amalia Winterhooven' could take over her roster of clients. We'd set up a series of email server hops so that nothing could be traceable back to Moncriano, let alone the palace. She'd have the freedom to still pursue her passion."

The idea had come to him once they left the summerhouse. Who could blame Kelsey for not wanting to give up what she'd trained for, dreamed of, gave her a reason to get up in the morning? What father, what brother, would deprive her of that if there was an alternative?

Christian's dark blond eyebrows squiggled up and then together. He looked down as they traversed a rocky slope. It took him a full five minutes of mulling before stating, "Being a princess is a full-time job."

"Not necessarily. Everything about Kelsey breaks the rules. Why not bend this one? The country's managed without a second princess for twenty-five years. Other countries let the sixth or seventh in line to the throne have full careers that aren't even secret."

"She's not that far down the line of succession. She's third in line."

Now Christian was just grasping at straws, because he *would* be king. Not for decades, probably, but the crown would go to him. "Not for long. I've heard the king pressuring you to wed. And by wed, I mean pop out a string of heirs."

Bariq startled at something in the bushes. Or he simply reared up because he'd channeled Christian's distaste for discussing his inevitable marriage. "He's made his feelings known on the subject. As have I. You know I'm not going to put up with being pushed into a marriage simply to propagate. I'm not a stallion, extending the bloodline."

"You rather are. It's in the job description, as I recall." Which had been fun to laugh about as teens. That being prince *required* Christian to have sex. But as they matured and sussed out the full impact of being expected to marry and have kids *no matter what*—well, it stopped being even a little bit funny.

"And you're demoted down to just bodyguard again. If I won't marry to get Father off my back, I certainly won't do it so that my sister can live her dream life."

"Even if she did it part-time, it could be that olive branch that gets her to consider staying."

The fact that the idea of Kelsey remaining in Moncriano made him smile was just a side effect. Not selfish at all.

"I do hear you." And then Christian shot him a sideways glance that seemed to have already seen too much. "I hear Kelsey's happiness seems to be your top priority."

Damn it. Of all the times for Christian to suddenly be perceptive. So Elias deflected, fast. "Would you rather have a part-time princess, or one who pops back to America for good?"

"Look, even if I see the merit in what you're saying…" Christian sighed. "Maybe in a few years, once things have settled down, but to do it now? It's impossible. The situation is too volatile. Both that of the country *and* her potential danger."

Shit.

Christian was dead-on with his assessment. Elias had blanked on the biggest reason why they needed to keep everything the princess did streamlined. Because her happiness did not get to be the number one consideration. Not for him. Not when her very life could be at stake.

He'd put what was good for Kelsey ahead of what was good for the country. And in doing so, he'd completely overlooked the most important part of his job.

Protecting her.

"You're right. Guess that's why you get to be our Supreme Leader one day," Elias said, making sure to frost the words with about an inch of sarcasm. That mostly covered up the equally thick layer of guilt now weighing him down.

"Have you told Kelsey yet? That as soon as she's revealed to the world as the missing Princess Valentina that she'll potentially be in danger?"

"You mean tell her the kidnappers might be drawn out and try again? Since they obviously failed the first time?" Elias tilted his head side to side, cracking his neck. It did nothing to relieve the tension. "Uh, that'd be a no. She's gotten enough sucker punches. I thought I'd wait to scare the crap out of her until she came around to trusting at least one other person in this country."

"But you *will* tell her?"

The urgency in Christian's voice had nothing to do with a strategic timeline to roll out the bad news. No, Elias saw right through him to the heart of the issue. "You mean so *you* don't have to?"

"I was hoping you'd, you know, offer."

"You're scared? You're pulling the 'I delegate what I don't want to do' scam?"

"How's this? If you do, I'll have them saddle Bariq for you next time instead of that trail turd you're riding now."

Elias had always planned to break the news to Kelsey about her danger. But if hedging a little got him a ride on that magnificent beast, he'd turn the guilt-screw a little bit more. "You're bribing me to piss off and/or scare your sister?"

"Rather than do it myself? You bet." Christian pulled on the reins, and both their mounts stopped at the edge of a clearing. One that let them see just how far back the rest of the security detail was. The prince glanced over both shoulders. Then he leaned sideways in the saddle toward Elias.

"Have you told her about her, ah, adoptive parents? Christ, I hope they didn't actually file paperwork to adopt her. That'd be a legal mess."

"They didn't. Not that I could find." A fact that made the elder Wishners all the more suspicious to his eyes.

"So you're going to tell her that, too? About how we, ah, detained them?"

That was a load of whitewashing. "You mean how we had the local police throw them in jail as suspected abductors before my plane even landed in New York?"

"Yes. That. I'd bet she'll be more upset about us arresting her parents than the potential danger."

"I'll bet that 'upset' doesn't come close to covering it. Dealing with the blowback for you may just earn me my own Arabian racehorse," he said jokingly.

The fact was that Elias would always do anything and everything the royal family asked of him. After Princess Valentina disappeared, they could've thrown his father in jail. Hell, they could've executed him for dereliction of duty. Instead, they'd kept him close, kept him on the job. They gave his father not only his life, but respect. And he would forever be in their debt.

The intensity...desperation?...in Christian's eyes matched the fervor in his voice as he leaned over to squeeze his friend's arm. "Thank you. No joke, Elias, whatever you want. It's yours."

What he wanted was more make-out sessions like this morning. But Elias had a feeling that once he did Christian's dirty work, kisses would be the last thing on Kelsey's mind.

Chapter Ten

"Is it possible we're in Narnia and not some country we've never heard of?" Mallory asked.

Kelsey wriggled out from under the high bed. She'd been looking for her phone. After Christian's edict on Monday, when she got back to her rooms the phone had been downgraded, with the addition of a safety filter. Like how you kept kids from accidentally one-clicking on porn sites. Except in her case, it was social media sites.

On Tuesday, her email had stopped working. The cause had officially been given as connectivity issues due to her foreign plan, but neither she nor Mallory bought that for a second. Now, on Thursday afternoon, she couldn't even find the thing. Which was a problem, because she'd stayed up all night finishing two projects for Omni Creative. She wanted to send them off before she lost all access to the web.

"I think a country we've never heard of is at least marginally more realistic than a land with a talking lion. Why?"

Her sister twirled—*twirled* like a Disney princess—out

of her closet. "Every time I go in there, your clothes have magically multiplied."

Kelsey got up to look inside her walk-in closet. Well, the very large room with cupboards and shelves and even an island full of drawers that they called a closet. The amount of skirts and dresses had doubled overnight. Again. As had the shoes and purses. It was strange. Magical indeed. She kind of wanted to put a cookie in there tonight and see if they turned into a half dozen by morning.

"Too many dresses. Way too many heels." Still, despite her strong preference for comfy clothes, Kelsey's built-in femininity couldn't deny the absolute gorgeousness of the rainbow of couture apparel. "They are all ridiculously pretty."

"Soft, too." Mallory twirled back in and came out with a cashmere cardigan in pale green, stroking it like a kitten.

"Go pet your own clothes." She started unmaking the bed to look for the phone. One princess perk that did not at all suck was the maid service. Oh, guilt still punched her in the sternum each day when Anya bustled around, folding her favorite fuzzy blanket from home and making the bed. But the guilt didn't prevent her from enjoying it.

Mallory carefully set the sweater on the table by the window to refold it. "My closet doesn't have the magical expansion pack."

"Is that so?"

"Don't get in a huff. I have the clothes I brought, as well as at least a dozen other outfits that they did provide me. Very generously. Remember, I'm not a princess."

Gritting her teeth, Kelsey did, indeed, huff. "I would very much like to be able to say the same thing."

"Still not feeling…regal? Special?"

"I…" She trailed off, remembering how she'd felt with Elias over the past few days.

He listened to her with an intensity that made her feel

treasured and brilliant and, yes, very special. He didn't *just* listen, but asked questions, too. The right questions that drew out the conversation whether it was about her demanding clients or her delight at the array of pastries presented at the daily tea with Duchess Mathilde.

"What?"

She perched on the dainty chair at the table, looked out the window at the acres and acres of manicured grounds and burbling fountains that evidently were her birthright.

Kelsey didn't feel like she had a right to any of it.

And she wasn't at all sure that she wanted to turn into the sort of person who *did*.

"Mallory, you love me to pieces, but you wouldn't call me special. I've never done anything to make myself stand out."

"Stop it."

Mimicking her sister's tone, she said, "What?"

"Stop putting yourself down. You've spent the last six days whining about not being special enough to be a princess. You *are* special, Kelsey. You don't have to have medals or trophies to stand out."

"No, I do not feel worthy of an entire country hanging on my every move. I want to be the one watching *other* people's spectacles unfold." Deliberately, she turned away from the window. Geez, unless the phone was surfing the bed's canopy, Kelsey had to admit it was gone. Not lost. No, she had a very strong idea that a certain sneaky bodyguard had asked Anya to confiscate it for him.

Mallory bent over, sticking her face right in front of Kelsey's. Her long ponytail bobbed as she stayed sideways. "Why? I mean, sure, that was your original plan, but why not think bigger? Why not own this change in status?"

Big sisters were a pain in the butt, something Kelsey had always maintained, but now that she suddenly had two of them, she had twice as much proof. She pushed past Mallory and crossed over to the fireplace to get breathing room from this well-meaning but massively annoying inquisition.

"I sit in front of a computer screen all day. Alone, at home. I'm the poster child for unexciting and uninspiring."

"Will you stop putting yourself down? You use your vivid imagination to create amazing designs all day." Before Kelsey could rebut, Mallory held up her hand. "You have a huge heart. You always volunteer to help someone move, or hang out when they're sick even if it means catching a bug yourself. You design original, marvelous birthday cards online for everyone."

"Yeah, but you're the one who remembers to buy paper cards and send them three days early." So old-fashioned, proper. Too bad Mallory couldn't be the princess. She'd be far better at it.

Her sister didn't take the *I need space* hint. Instead, she joined her at the fireplace, tracing a golden vein in the marble mantel. "Both ways make our friends smile. You're the most loyal and caring person I know. You never had that teenage rebellion period with Mom and Dad because you didn't want to let them down. You led the boycott of that bookstore that wouldn't carry the books by Mr. Mason down the block just because they were male/male romance. You care about what is fair and just and right."

"Ah. I'm Superman?"

"You're definitely super. So stop worrying about being enough." With a stern frown, Mallory thrust out her arms to point both index fingers at her. "Just do it."

"Do what?"

"Care about people. Watch their lives unfold and cheer them on. The same thing you would've done in New York—just on a different scale."

"Different country and continent scale. People over here speak multiple languages. They bop across borders for the weekend. I'm like an architectural miniature of that—1/64th to scale. I've never bopped away for adventures."

"That's because Mom and Dad were paranoid. They never let us go anywhere. You'd think we were living in twelfth century, barbarian-filled Gaul the way they didn't trust any cities bigger than ours. The way they didn't trust any people outside of everyone we already knew."

An idea slapped Kelsey right in her frontal cortex. She gasped. "Do you think that was because of me? They instilled a feeling of smallness to keep me safe?"

"I think we don't know anything about what our parents did or didn't know about you. It's pointless to guess."

A knock on the door preceded the footman announcing Elias's arrival. Kelsey flung it open. She'd put a stop to this sneakiness right now. "Perfect timing. Look, I'm onto you. You had Anya snitch my phone, didn't you?"

"Good afternoon, Your Highness. Miss Wishner." He nodded at each of them.

"Skip the formality. You're in trouble, Elias. I've stayed off social media, per Christian's order. So what's with the disappearing act?"

"This is…unfortunate." He slid his hand into the inner pocket of his jacket and held out her phone. "I'd hoped to return it before you realized it was missing."

Even though Kelsey had leaped to the assumption Elias was behind it, *seeing* that he'd confiscated it was a whole different story.

Was it Christian who didn't trust her? Or Elias, who was the only one in Moncriano that she *did* fully trust? Moncrian-an? Crap. She'd better ask Anya how to say it. Her maid filled her in on useful tidbits about the place, as opposed to the centuries-old history and etiquette lessons *officially* on her schedule. In return, Kelsey was educating her on worthwhile American music.

Kelsey patted both hands to her heart. Right at the very sedately cut neckline to her sedate white sundress topped with a sedate white cardigan. She wasn't sure if they were dressing her as a princess or a virgin sacrifice to stave off a bad winter. "Isn't my word that I wouldn't post on Facebook good enough? You're checking on me now?"

"No." His facial features did an allover twitch of distaste, like he'd sniffed milk past the expiration date. "You're not the one I'm trying to check on, Your Highness."

Two "your highnesses" in a row. She'd thought they were past that now, what with the French kissing and excellent handsy-ness in the summerhouse. Not to mention a few other kisses they'd snuck in deserted corners. Therefore, Elias really must not want to fess up.

Too bad for him that wasn't an option.

"That's nonsensical. Who else would be on my phone?"

Elias placed the phone on the mantel, next to the beautiful clock that enchanted Kelsey every time she looked at it. When he turned back to her, his emotionless bodyguard mask was in place. "Miss Wishner, would you excuse us?" After another nod to Mallory, he gestured to the door. "Allow me to explain—*elsewhere.*"

Mystified, Kelsey left her suite and followed him to a wing she hadn't yet explored. It was even more museum-like than her wing, with plush carpets that muffled their footsteps, tapestries on the walls and suits of armor standing sentinel. At the end of the hall, not one but two liveried footmen bracketed a pair of doors with what she now recognized as the royal family's crest.

"What's in there?"

"King Julian's private apartments."

Kelsey flashed back to her dad's study at home. A corkboard hung on that door, covered with bad doctor jokes and cartoons he'd collected over the years. Things like *your x-ray showed a broken rib, but we fixed it with photoshop* and *insomnia is a common diagnosis—try not to lose any sleep over it.* The cheesier, the better. The door was never closed unless he was on the phone with a patient—and always opened again as soon as he hung up. Ed Wishner prided himself on always being available to his daughters.

Somehow she doubted that after a quick knock, it'd be okay to pop on into the king's apartments. If the footmen would even let her within three feet of the door. The thought made her both miss her dad…and miss whatever relationship could have evolved over the years with the king. Was it even possible to start now and end up with something as close and vital as she was used to?

Elias pressed on the edge of the molding in the corner. And then the wall opened up.

She gasped. "There's a secret door? This palace legit has a secret door? Why didn't you lead with that instead of the tiaras and riches and private planes when you were trying to convince me to come here?"

"My apologies." Elias gave her another formal nod, but this one felt sarcastic. Probably because she heard the laughter in his tone and saw the twinkle in his eyes. "If I tell you about the secret entrance to the dungeons, will that be enough to coerce you into staying?" He gestured for her to precede him up a spiral staircase.

"Dungeons? Aren't those more for a castle rather than a palace?" Because Kelsey knew the difference now. Fortifications versus fancy housing.

"Extensive dungeons—more like a prison—are in castles. But you definitely want somewhere to toss wrongdoers while interrogating them. When the original structure was built in the 1600s, times were more violent. Less civilized."

"Will you show me the dungeons?"

"There's a private access to them from your suite. They

were turned into a gym about eighty years ago. Also a pool and squash courts."

"There's no door to anywhere but the balcony..." Kelsey trailed off. This was the coolest thing ever. She couldn't wait to tell Mallory. "There's a secret passageway from my room?"

"From each of the royal apartments. God forbid anyone see the royal family wandering about in spandex and dripping sweat." Elias pushed past her to fiddle with the latch on a wooden door. When that didn't work, he put his shoulder into it, and the timbers creaked before opening. "I'll be sure to get that fixed. Nobody really comes up here anymore, not since Queen Serena died."

"This was her private spot?" Kelsey knew the answer before she'd taken more than three steps inside.

The round shape gave the room away as the turret. Rather than furniture, the floor was heaped with pillows in faded, green-sprigged chintz. A low shelf by the far window was filled with well-worn paperbacks. On top were an assortment of candles, a crystal bud vase, and photos.

She rushed over and dropped to her knees. These weren't official, posed photos. These were family shots. The queen with her children, all as babies. A very pudgy Christian, another with toddler Christian in a hilarious romper sticking his tongue out at baby Genevieve while the queen laughed.

And a third that had to be her, Valentina. Kelsey had never seen a baby photo of herself before. Her parents claimed they'd all been lost in a basement flood. She'd seen Mallory's, but her own baby books didn't start until she'd been more than a year old.

The queen...looked like her, which she'd already noted in the formal portrait in the throne room, but it was more evident in this photo. No crown or poufy hair. The queen—*her mother*—sat on a blanket at the edge of a lake. Christian and Genevieve were wrist deep in a bowl of grapes, both grinning with their mouths stuffed. And the utter happiness and love suffusing Serena's face as she looked down at the tiny blond baby in her arms took Kelsey's breath away.

Or maybe it was the thickening of unshed tears in her throat.

"Kelsey."

"Yes?" She sniffed, and curled her legs beneath her.

"I need to tell you something. I need you to listen without flying off the handle until I get all the way through."

Elias was wearing his very-serious-bodyguard face again. Even though they were very alone. That did not bode well. "Just a heads up that no woman on the planet likes to be told that a man is worried she'll fly off the handle." She held up a hand. "And don't try and tell me it got mangled in translation."

"Fair enough." He closed the door. Stayed over by it, hands behind his back. "I'm the one who took your phone. Don't blame Anya."

"Okay."

"I took it to put a recording…" It was the first time Elias seemed to be stuck on finding the right word in English. It was sort of adorable. "…a listening device in it."

Not okay. *Not* adorable. Kelsey surged to her knees. Sort of. All the pillows making her wobbly reminded her of being a kid in a ball pit. "You bugged my phone?"

"Yes." If Elias was any closer to the door, he'd be on the other side of it. "But not to listen to you. We want the ability to listen in when you talk to your parents."

"Why?"

"That's what you do with suspects."

Kelsey crossed her arms, shook her head, and gave him the should-be-patented "you disappoint me" look learned at Cybill Wishner's knee. "I told you, there's no way they kidnapped me. They're good people, Elias. They love me and

Mallory. They devoted their lives to healing the sick."

But he stood his ground. Elias crossed *his* arms. Ricocheted a patronizing, "you're not as smart as you think" look right back at her. "They know something. You don't have adoption records. Your birth certificate is forged—we checked. Oh, and, of course, your fingerprints prove you're the child of King Julian and Queen Serena. The Wishners may have been good parents to you, but they are *not* innocent."

"I'm sure if you let me talk to them, they'll explain everything." At least, that's what she and Mallory had been whispering to each other every night, in an effort to stave off their growing fears. Because nothing added up about their loving, supportive parents stealing a baby.

"We're giving them the chance to do that, which is what I needed to tell you. We had them taken into custody before you even left New York."

"Custody?" She'd watched enough iterations of *Law and Order* to immediately flash to bars slamming them into a cell. With that distinctive, hollow, double *bing* that always accompanied it. "You had them arrested?"

"Yes. Arrested, then flown to New York and held for questioning while we were granted extraterritorial jurisdiction. Interpol, our own Intelligence and Security Agency, your FBI, and the Kenyan National Intelligence Service—all these agencies were a part of the search and thus now want to be a part of getting the answers. It has been... complicated to work through all the channels."

Holy fuck. Her parents were sitting in jail right now because of her. Because, for whatever reason, they'd chosen to love her and raise her. Guilt almost outweighed her anger at not being notified. At least it solved the mystery of why they weren't returning her calls. "Wait...Kenya?"

"That's where your family was vacationing when you were abducted."

Oh. She'd been to *Africa*? That fact was as surreal as the rest of this mess. Kelsey stood, letting her arms fall to her sides. "But they're in jail? Why?"

"Because it is obvious the Wishners know *something* about the kidnapping, even if they were not responsible for orchestrating it themselves."

Elias kept using their last name rather than referring to them as her parents.

It was obvious he'd brought her up here to this essentially padded room so that she could yell and flail at him to her heart's content. Well, she didn't want to disappoint. After kicking off her heels, Kelsey crossed to stand toe to toe with him.

Then turned her volume all the way up as if they were an entire floor apart. "Damn it, Elias, how could you not tell me?"

He flinched. Which, from Elias, was the equivalent of a normal person cowering in the fetal position under her targeted rage. "I'm sorry, Your Highness."

"Don't you dare retreat behind titles now. You can't keep things from me." She wasn't an idiot. His *duty* was to keep her safe. Droves of people had the *duty* to figure out who took her in the first place. While Kelsey hated it as their daughter, she...accepted that her parents, at the very least, had to be questioned. And that all of that was out of her control, as well as Elias's.

What was *in* his control was the level of honesty they shared.

Dipping his head into one of those annoying nods, he said in a low voice, "I didn't want to worry you. I thought it might be the rug that broke the camel's back."

"Rug? What rug? It's a straw that's the tipping point for the camel."

That broad forehead crinkled above his thick brows.

"But camels don't carry straw. They carry goods, like rugs."

Kelsey threw up her hands. "Omigosh, I truly don't care. Unless you surprise me with the fact that camels are the national symbol of *whatthehellever* here."

"Our state symbol is the white peacock."

They were so far off track it was laughable. So Kelsey gave in and *did* laugh. She put her palm on his wall of a chest, rested her head on his shoulder, and laughed.

After a moment, Elias curled down around her, one arm pulling her close while he laughed with her. And it was a relief to be back on the same page with him.

"Thank you for trying to protect me, but your job is about bullets and crazies—not about protecting my emotions. I'm a grown woman. I deserve to be fully dialed in, and make my own decisions."

He let out a long, slow exhale. "You're right, but it is hard to stand back and do nothing."

"You won't be." Kelsey lifted her head to lock onto those brilliant blue eyes. "You'll stand *with* me. You're the only one here I fully trust. If you blow that—we're done."

"Then I have more to share to clear the air between us."

Uh-oh.

Maybe he'd been *partially* right? That it was too many giant truths to drop on her head at once? Should she ask for the one-a-day plan?

Clasping her hand, Elias walked her over to a window. They both nestled into the pillows, backs against the wall. "Once you are revealed to the world as the missing princess, you may be in danger."

Was that all? Kelsey huffed out a breath. "That's why I have you. To protect me from the throngs of excited royal-watchers."

Hard to imagine herself in the middle of a crowd, shaking hands and accepting nosegays. Maybe it would take her an extra ten minutes to greet everyone, but that didn't sound dangerous. Especially not after having been drilled about how important it was for the royal family to not give opinions on political issues.

His thumb traced the bracket around her smile. "No, far more serious danger. Whoever took you, whatever group was behind your abduction...they might decide to try again. People deranged enough to commit such a serious crime once generally don't respond well to being shown as failures."

It was clear Elias was trying to not just warn her, but scare her. Which, again, was his duty. Fine. But Kelsey simply didn't see it as a credible threat.

"I'm no longer an infant. I can scream for help. Identify evildoers. Fight back. As a grown woman, I'd be too much trouble to kidnap again."

Elias held up his palm sideways, like he was about to karate chop away her words. "If I ever tell you that you're in danger, that you have to do whatever I say in order to save your life, will you?"

Whoa. "Obey? Without question?"

"In that unfortunate circumstance, yes. You may not agree with my assessment of the threat level, but should it come to pass, you must allow me to do what's necessary."

"Yes." It was a simple concession to make, seeing as how it'd never come to pass. "Should we be in a suddenly life-threatening situation, you're in charge. No questions asked. Is that all?"

"Not quite."

"Seriously, Elias? We've known each other a week. How many deep, dark secrets can you possibly be keeping from me?"

"Just the one more."

"Still waters run deep, I guess." At his quizzical look, she held up a hand. Because she couldn't stand a variation on their idiomatic camel debate. "Never mind. Divulge away."

"Prince Christian and I are…ah…*close*."

While karma might have just gifted her with untold wealth, *yada, yada*, there was no *way* that bitch would have Kelsey's new brother and hot hunk of a bodyguard be *into* each other. Was there? No. It couldn't be. Had to be another language barrier thing.

"Use more words, but choose them carefully."

"Christian is my best friend. We grew up together, here in the palace."

"Huh. Kind of a shocker, but I'll take it as more proof that my brother's a good guy, worth getting to know."

"So you can see, this is yet another reason why anything happening between us is an impossibility. Your brother would never allow it."

Christian didn't get a say in who she dated. So what if Elias was her brother's best friend? She barely knew the man. Why should it matter? Aside from the obvious—Elias's unerring commitment to honor. It was sexy as hell.

Albeit not at all convenient.

Kelsey turned sideways to lay down on the mounds of pillows. It was easy to tug him down on top of her. Slyly, she said, "While you shouldn't keep secrets from me, you're more than welcome to keep them from Christian."

And she sealed that invitation with a kiss.

Chapter Eleven

Some men used wealth to get the girl. Lavished them with jewelry or expensive concert tickets. Others used fame, promising the chance to rub shoulders with the high and mighty.

Not Elias. He knew none of that would impress Kelsey. More importantly, he knew what *would* get her.

"Are you ready?" he asked.

"I thought you said we were going on a date." She spun on her heel in a half circle, taking in the long hallway hung with oversize portraits of eighteenth-century Villanis. And, of course, the ubiquitous footmen at each end. "Walking through the palace is not a date."

He snickered. "There is literally an *entire* country of women—not all of them single, even—who would disagree with you. Nevertheless, we are most certainly going on a date."

Francis, the footman with the unenviable job of dressing in eighteenth-century garb every day, raised his spear and winked at Elias. Luckily, he had no idea who Kelsey really was. And dressed down in jeans, sneakers, and a T-shirt, she wasn't even recognizable as the VIP staying down the hall from Princess Genevieve. So his next move felt safe.

Well, still quite risky—but Kelsey was worth a calculated risk or two. Or ten. Which this was. *Nothing* had changed about her status or his. Being together was an impossibility. For sure, in two weeks once she was officially recognized as the princess.

So Elias would steal these moments with her now, as many as he could. Because Kelsey was sunshine and fun and warmth…exactly what he'd need in his memory to get through all the gray days ahead when he wouldn't be allowed to touch her again. That was the bargain he'd made with himself. Knowing there'd be an unmistakable, inescapable end—all too soon—to what they shared made it less wrong to be with her now. Because their time together would be so short, it wouldn't matter.

Except Kelsey was starting to matter quite a bit to him.

Elias pulled on the heavy gold edge of a frame—Queen Anna, circa 1784, powdered wig and all—and it swung open.

"Ohhhhh, the secret tunnel." Kelsey wrinkled her nose. "To the gym? You didn't tell me to dress for a workout. I look all wrong."

The woman couldn't *be* more wrong. And he gave her an exaggerated, playful leer of appreciation to prove it. "You look very, very right."

What she looked was a million times more herself. Like the woman he'd first met in Manhattan who had bowled him over. The jeans clung to her beautifully tight ass in a way that had his fingers itching to squeeze. Just like the border of lace at the top of her white shirt gave him the urge to push it down to reveal more of her creamy breasts.

God, he wanted his hands on her. "Does it feel good to be back in your own clothes?"

"*So* good." She shook her head as he led her inside a low-ceilinged tunnel. "I feel like I'm playing dress up every day in those skirt and sweater sets."

"You dress up beautifully. I like both versions of you. Almost as much as I like the spandex workout version of you." He clasped her hand to hurry her along. Elias had timed their trip down the corridor for right after the day and evening shifts swapped out. Punctuality was imperative at the palace, so everyone would be at their posts and not skulking about back here.

Hopefully.

Kelsey elbowed him in the ribs. "No way. My running clothes can't be your favorite. Access is too difficult. Much like lunging or squatting is too difficult in these skinny jeans."

Elias swallowed. Hard. But it didn't erase the mental image of her naked, on the bed, lunging over him... That's when Kelsey pressed back with the tips of her fingers, and he realized he was white-knuckling her poor, delicate hand. He brought it swiftly to his lips to drop an open-mouthed kiss on her soft skin.

"Don't worry. This isn't the secret passageway to the gym. These are the staff corridors. I'm taking you to my place and cooking you dinner. A one hundred percent normal, non-princess-perk date."

"You live here? In the palace?"

"I do." One side of his mouth pulled down into a grimace. "Just don't expect anything as opulent as your suite."

"Again, for the record, that is so not me. It might as well be a hotel penthouse. I prefer things simple. With access to outlets for my devices without walking more than six steps."

"While I can offer you that, how about we unplug for the night?"

Kelsey tugged free of his grasp. Slamming a hand onto the middle of his dark-gray polo shirt, she made a valiant attempt to both push him against the wall and look fierce doing so. She failed at both, but he played along.

"Hold it right there. Are you trying to take my phone away again for yet more nefarious reasons?"

"If by nefarious you mean kissing you, then yes." In a twist on a karate move, he lunged to one knee and bent her backward over it, kissing the exposed line of her throat until she squealed and laughed. So much for semi-stealth mode. Elias quickly set her back on her feet and hurried them past the final turn. "I'm off schedule for tonight. Blocked out completely. Unless the palace is invaded by alien drones, there won't be any interruptions. Just you and me. A real, normal, Friday-night date," he said.

"It sounds perfect. And I'll turn off my phone"—her smile turned impish, and she pulled her phone out of her back pocket—"as soon as we take a selfie."

"No. Absolutely not. Not out here." They'd tempted fate enough after pausing to kiss.

She stopped and held out both arms, upraised, like a candelabra. "Isn't this whole, vast structure technically my house? Since when can't a woman snap a photo in her own home?"

"You're claiming ownership of Alcarsa Palace?" Elias couldn't help but throw back his head and laugh. Kelsey continually both surprised and delighted him. "Did you just try—feebly, I might add—to pull princess rank on me? That thing you can't abide and haven't even decided yet to accept?"

"I'm trying it on for size. How does being imperious look on me?"

He dug out his key. Then he bent his knees and hoisted her over his shoulder. "Take your damned selfie and find out."

Kelsey laughed and squirmed and, from the *snick* he heard, took the upside down selfie draped over his back as he carried her past three more doors until they arrived at his.

Once safely inside, he slid her—slowly—down the front of his body until she stood. "Welcome."

"Your show of strength is, mmm, immensely sexy." This time she was the one stringing a line of kisses down *his* neck. She had to stand on tiptoe to do it, which canted her whole body forward against his.

Damn it. Elias heaved in a deep breath. "I'm cooking you dinner. Put your appreciation of my muscles on hold until after I've provided you with the aforementioned date."

"Maybe you do things differently in Moncriano. But in America?" Kelsey very deliberately pushed her open hand down his back to cup his ass. "Dates can be all about sex. Start to finish. Soup to nuts."

Maybe things *were* different in America. Because he had no idea he was expected to make soup. Or provide nuts. "I didn't prepare a soup course. Just some sautéed calamari and cheese for an appetizer."

Kelsey immediately let go, falling back several steps. Apparently she needed the extra room to bend over, hugging her stomach, and laugh hysterically.

"If you want soup, I can call down to the kitchens for it…"

"Elias, omigosh, *no*. I'm laughing because it's just a saying. Soup to nuts means…well, the whole enchilada. Which, now that I think of it, probably doesn't translate, either. It means 'everything included'. No actual need on my behalf for soup."

"That's a relief."

"I can't believe you're cooking calamari. That sounds so exotic. I'm extremely impressed."

"We're a nation on the edge of an ocean. Seafood is not exotic here. But I'll take the easy win." He headed toward the kitchen. When he didn't hear footsteps following, he turned back. Kelsey was still in the entryway. Her eyes were wide with shock.

That didn't bode well. Not after he'd bribed his friend

Luisa the chambermaid into doing a…"soup to nuts" cleaning of the apartment. "What's wrong?"

"Nothing. Your place looks perfect. Amazing. Amazingly *normal.*" She did a big sweep of the living room, trailing her fingers along the edge of the green chest beneath his plasma screen television. Crossed the moss and white maze-patterned rug to toy with a branch on his ficus tree. Kelsey ended by leaning back on his grey sofa, looking comfortable and at home.

"What did you expect?"

"Something all gold and delicate and antiqued like the rest of the palace." She pursed her lips, considering. "Or a medieval stone chamber."

"Well, you haven't seen the bedroom yet," he quipped.

"Very funny."

Elias sank onto the matching grey club chair. It was odd, needing to lay out how *not* special he was. Especially when so many people looked right past him, as though he were nothing more than an ambulatory suit of armor next to Prince Christian.

"I work in a fancy place. My best friend is about as fancy as they come. But *I'm* not. I started as a sailor. Now I keep other people's treasures safe. My life's simple, at the core."

"Hardly. You've got focus and honor and a shocking depth of responsibility. There's nothing simple about juggling all of that. Plus, you're keeping a tree alive." She pointed at the robust ficus that almost filled his window.

"Not even close. I only won that from the palace's head gardener a few weeks ago. Odds are that I'll kill it due to shocking neglect before the month is up."

"Won it? Did he not bring enough cash to a poker game?"

It occurred to Elias that perhaps he'd oversold the simplicity of his life. To an American, at any rate. "I, ah, bested him in an archery competition."

"Seriously?"

"Quite. Not only did I hit all my targets, but Ilian accidentally killed an owl."

Kelsey lifted one eyebrow. "Sure, totally normal, because it's all fun and games until a forest creature fatality."

Funny. That was the same joke he'd made as he helped the man dig a tiny grave. Ilian insisted he was completing the circle of life by gifting Elias with a tree to keep alive.

It'd be very easy to keep sitting here, chatting and admiring how right Kelsey looked in his living room. But also very selfish. Elias was determined to give her the trappings of a normal date. Food. Wine. Music.

Rising, he punched on his speaker, and sultry French jazz filled the room. "I should start cooking. The chicken paprika and cheese dumplings have been simmering all afternoon, but the calamari have to be done fresh."

Kelsey scrambled after him, snatching his arm. "Thank you." Her tone was solemn and intense. Oddly so. As though he'd thrown himself in front of her to stop a bullet, instead of throwing chicken into a pot.

Elias cocked his head. "You haven't tasted my cooking yet. I'd hold off on any expressions of gratitude."

"Trust me, I'm plenty grateful for just the attempt." Those big, violet eyes were overflowing with her appreciation and care.

Since she wouldn't allow him to lighten the mood, he'd answer in kind. "You've made it very clear this isn't a life you'd choose. Definitely one you'd never dreamed of. But despite the formalities being stuffed down your throat, I can assure you, it isn't always like that. You can still be you, Kelsey."

"People seem pretty set on the whole title/bowing thing."

"Your inner circle of friends and family won't be that way when you're in private. I see all of this from one step behind

Christian. I can assure you he manages plenty of normal activities. Ordinary nights."

"Christian—but not Genevieve?" One corner of her mouth ticked up, as if already well aware of the answer.

"Normal's not really what she's looking for out of life. She rather enjoys the princess perks." Elias gathered her into his arms. "Let me prove to you that you can be a princess and still have a somewhat normal life. Starting with a home-cooked, traditional Moncriano meal."

"*Starting* by turning this into casual night. Lose the fancy duds." Kelsey slid her arms underneath the sides of his sport coat and up, as if to ease it off his shoulders.

But then she visibly jolted. Her right hand froze, up against the holster to his gun. Because even though it was his night off, he'd never consider walking anywhere on palace grounds unarmed.

"Nothing about *this* is normal," she murmured. And her long lashes fluttered closed over despondent eyes, shutting him out.

• • •

This was yet another in a string of firsts over the last eight days. There weren't supposed to be any firsts left with sex. There was a finite number of positions, only so many parts to go so many places. While lovely, nothing about dating or sex should surprise her anymore.

But trying to hug a man and running into his gun? *Definite* first.

Not to mention a definite mood killer. For as hard as Elias was trying to give her normal, the gun reminded her how different, upside down, everything was in her life.

"Damn it, Kelsey, don't do that. Don't close down on me." He grabbed her chin and tilted it up. She looked into blue eyes sparking with…anger? Frustration?

"We were kidding ourselves, Elias, pretending for one night that nothing's changed doesn't make it real. Just like pretending we can be together doesn't make it real."

His hands slipped down to cup her shoulders. As if he was worried she was about to run out the door. "Maybe I went about this all wrong. I'm sorry for trying to make you feel like you were Kelsey Wishner again, excited Manhattanite. I simply wanted to put a smile on your face."

"I smile every time I think of you. You're outrageously handsome, you know. And when I talk, you make me feel like there's nothing else you'd rather be doing, nowhere else you'd rather be. You make me feel like I matter. Plain old Kelsey Wishner."

"Extraordinary Kelsey Wishner," he corrected softly. He looked over her shoulder and cursed. "Stay here." Then he disappeared through an arched doorway into the…kitchen? She only glimpsed the curve of a small, round wooden table, set with wineglasses and a fat candle in the middle. But there were heady smells coming from the room, a sort of rich tomato sauce with spices she couldn't identify.

When Elias came back, his jacket and holster were gone. "I've turned it all off. Dinner's on hold. Indefinitely."

Oh no. She'd screwed everything up by freaking out about his gun. "You're going to take me back to my suite now?"

"What? Of course not. Kelsey, what your life has spun into is a new normal, for sure. But one with a few perks that I promise are worth it."

Not getting dinner sure didn't come off as a perk. "Such as?"

"Sex with me." His cocky grin and *you want a piece of this* pose with one leg outstretched in front and both arms up was pure, absurd male ego on parade. Apparently, Elias knew it, too, because he only held the pose for a few seconds before laughing. "I'm taking a page from the American dating handbook. We're skipping straight to the sex, because that's the one thing I *know* will get your mind to stop spinning about all the changes in your life."

She could get on board with that. "Consider it my gift to your country."

Elias gripped her upper arms tightly, and his voice was so deep it rumbled. "You're a gift to my country, all right. But the only thing that matters right now is what a gift you are to *me*. Let me show you."

Before Kelsey could pick up her dropped jaw and reply, Elias moved in. He shuffled her backward a few steps until she was pressed between him and the wall. Pressed tight enough to feel the steel wall of his pecs against her already hard nipples, massive thighs caging in her legs, and the gratifyingly hard and long bulge against her belly.

Oh, and while they took those few steps, his mouth *devoured* hers. Heat and speed, yes, but mixed with a thoroughness that left her lips a little bruised and a lot electrified. There was no doubting the depth of his desire.

There was no denying the depth of hers.

Kelsey gave back as good as she got. Her fingers raked across the top of his skull, delighting in the soft brush of his super-short hair. Her tongue danced and tasted and licked.

It wasn't nearly enough.

She wanted her bodyguard to stop guarding her body, and start using it.

Boosting off the floor, she wrapped her legs around his lean hips. It shifted the solid length of his penis to notch right between her legs. Kelsey moaned. Elias swallowed the sound, then broke free.

"Christ, you can't move. Not at all. This can't be over in two minutes against a wall."

"Why? Because I'm a princess? Because it wouldn't be

proper?"

Because Kelsey liked the sound of that. Very much.

"Because you deserve better," he said. And it was the sweetest thing she'd ever heard. The man had a raging hard-on, but wanted to slow down on her behalf. The way he cared for her, cared about her, grounded her in the moment, in *him*, more than even the fiery kisses.

"Save better for later," she ordered. "I don't want to wait. I'm so turned on I could eye-fuck you to orgasm."

His hips bucked once. Hard. "Holy—that's worse than moving, my treasure. No dirty talk, either." Yet his lips kept trailing across the side of her face, her neck, down the vee of her shirt...

Oh, this was *fun*. And her heart almost exploded from his touching endearment. "You know how you can make me stop? By filling me up with your cock until I literally can't form words."

"How do you do it? Make me discard common sense. First, you talk me into putting off dinner. Now this."

"Now what?"

"This," Elias repeated. He unzipped his pants. Kelsey put her feet back on the ground, happy to help. Then he cursed again, fumbling to undo the buttons at her waist. "Jeans. Even harder to get into than spandex. Turn around."

Two quick yanks got her jeans to just below her ass. She heard the metallic rip of a foil packet. Whew. Good to know birth control was as standard an expectation over here as in America. And then the thick head of his penis was right against her.

His warm breath stirred the fine hairs in front of her ear. "Are you sure, Kelsey?"

"Sure that I want you? Yes. Sure enough to almost make it a pseudo-royal command."

"Your wish is my pleasure to fulfill." After that sexily

formal turn of phrase, Elias sank into her in one smooth stroke.

If she could do a Facebook post about this moment? It'd be that exploding fireworks background behind the single line #worththewait.

"Do it again," she...ordered? Urged? Begged?

"Of course, Your Highness."

Okay. This one time, she'd acknowledge that hearing Elias use her title, in a deep voice pushed through gravel, well, it *worked*. Kelsey scrabbled, clawed at the wall. Thrust her ass at him as best she could with her knees locked by her jeans.

"Trust me?" he asked, pumping in and out in a steady rhythm.

"I really, truly do."

"Then relax."

She was wound tighter than a violin string. But in this one, particular case, she'd obey. Consciously, she willed her shoulders down, her arms to her sides, and her knees lax.

Sure enough, Elias had her. One arm clamped across her waist tighter than a restraint bar on a roller coaster. And the other? Oh, he had that hand angled down from her hip, so that the tips of his fingers tapped at her clit. And without her straining for it anymore, her orgasm just washed over her. No warning. No time to do anything but try to scream his name...and get stuck at "*Eliiiiiiiiii—*"

Three more fast snaps of his hips brought him to the same point. Elias groaned into her ear, a guttural, primal sound that positively thrilled her.

As Kelsey still shuddered a little, he brought his arm up to her chest. Shuffled backward six steps, still holding all of her weight, her feet not even touching the floor. He leaned on what she guessed to be the arm of the couch. From this angle, it was simple for Kelsey to slide off and pull her pants back on.

Or so she thought.

Elias's hand shot out to stop the upward tug of her clothing. "I think not."

There wasn't exactly cuddly afterglow after up-against-the-wall sex. And she'd already derailed his big plans for the date enough. "I thought you wanted us to do dinner?"

"Exactly. That was only the appetizer." With a wolfish grin, he spun her sideways into a fairy-tale hold, her knees draped over one arm. Although those fairy-tale princesses were never depicted half undressed with their bare asses hanging out. "I'm going to feast on you for the main course."

He carried her down a short hallway to his bedroom. Her heart triple-time fluttered the entire way. Elias set her gently on the bed. He tugged on a chain that turned on the overhead chandelier. Oh, nothing grandiose like the rest of the palace. It was rustic, wooden, and curved and looked like it came straight from Gaston's tavern scene in *Beauty and the Beast*. Kelsey had time to stare at it while Elias disposed of the condom and stripped off his clothes.

More importantly, she stared at *him* as he bent over to riffle through a nightstand drawer to pull out another three condoms and place them strategically on the pillow. Naked, the man was stunning. All hard planes and bulging muscles. His legs and arms were covered in a light mat of hair a few shades darker than the near-stubble on top of his head. It in no way covered the definition in his calves, the thick thighs, and arms that she already knew possessed remarkable strength. If she saw Elias on a beach, he'd be gasp-worthy.

Alone, full of anticipation of the whole night ahead of them, the sight of his utter manliness made her toes curl.

A dark strip of hair ran down his rippling abs to a penis that appeared to have rebounded in astonishingly record time. Kelsey sat up to trace the line with her nails. But she only made it halfway before she remembered the jeans locking her knees and sort of fell over sideways.

"Crap. I swear I've got sexier moves than this," she said, wriggling them down her legs.

"Stop." Elias lifted her hands and kissed the backs of them. "You're a present, my treasure. Let me unwrap you."

So. Romantic.

So. Swoon-inducingly. Romantic. The man actually treated her as if she *was* a treasure, worth untold value. Elias made her feel so special, so…seen and understood and valued.

"I'm all yours," she said simply, dropping her hands to the forest-green comforter.

He slipped off her shoes and socks…and then kissed along the tender and sensitive arch of her foot.

He slipped off her jeans and panties…and then kissed up her calves, stopping to do something swirly and special behind both knees.

Then Elias straddled her, and that eyegasm almost happened for real. He was just so big up close. Big and brawny and with an overwhelming sensuality in the way he touched and kissed and stroked. Like every part of her and every part of him had been declared an official erogenous zone. Like being naked with her was wholly comfortable and second nature.

Like he thought this night was every bit as sublime as Kelsey did.

"Feeling good?" he asked, pulling her shirt over her head.

"That's an understatement." Kelsey rubbed her palms in circles over his pecs. "I'd like to be feeling more of you."

Lips in the crook of her elbow, he said, "How about we make that the theme of round three?"

Oh, a very acceptable compromise. From beneath half-lowered lashes, she asked coyly, "Will that be tonight?"

"Definitely. Or possibly round four, as I've still to taste you properly." Elias tossed her bra into the corner. He paused to stare with raw longing at her exposed breasts. Her nipples puckered just from the heat of his gaze. "I don't believe your uncomfortable heels will be the reason you can't walk straight tomorrow."

Stroking and circling and caressing, the man made love to her breasts. Up and up and up higher, he whipped her into a frenzy of need. Kelsey's head whipped back and forth on the pillow, and the sounds coming out of her mouth were very much un-princess-like. When he paused to roll on a condom, she stopped him.

"You've got to let me do this. I've got to touch you."

With a nod—one of *those* nods he gave all the time that she'd never see the same way again—Elias presented himself, hands flat on his thighs. Kelsey hitched herself up to a sitting position. At the first, tentative stroke of her index finger down his velvety length, he gulped in a breath. When she did it a second time, he twitched forward, seeking more of her touch.

After that, she couldn't linger, as much as she wanted to learn the path of every vein. Because neither of them were going to last much longer. All Kelsey would allow herself was a soft, sucking kiss on his very tip, savoring the salty tinge to his skin. Then she rolled on the condom.

The moment the rubber snapped against his root, Elias sprang into action. He shifted his knees to the insides of her thighs, and then pulled her legs up and over them, which lifted her ass and positioned her exactly at that long, glorious penis. Blue eyes piercing her with their intensity, he entered her. Slowly. Then pulled almost all the way out, just as excruciatingly slowly. The lack of speed focused Kelsey on all of her already inflamed nerves. It ratcheted up her pleasure to a level she hadn't even expected.

He kept going, oh-so-slowly, eyes never leaving hers. His

arms were columns of steel as she restlessly stroked her hands up and down them.

"Elias?"

"Yes, my treasure?"

"Us…against the wall…that was fantastic."

"Agreed."

"This? What's happening right now? There are literally no words—at least not in my language—that would be enough to describe it."

Laughing, which rippled those amazing belly muscles and brightened his whole face, he said, "Who needs words?"

In another display of strength that shocked her, Elias gathered her into his arms so that she was mostly sitting up, only canted away from his body a bit. Then he took her mouth in a hungry, possessive kiss. It matched the driving way he all of a sudden picked up speed and pistoned into her.

Kelsey clung to him, absorbing his heat, his desire, his urgency. Her approaching orgasm spiraled ever closer. It was entirely in Elias's control. She was merely a passenger on this ride. And wasn't that incredibly freeing? To not worry about performing and just let herself be caught up in the vortex of pleasure? This was *his* gift to her. One that she hadn't even known she'd needed.

She scored her nails down the taut muscles of his back, relishing the growl it drew from him. He tipped forward just a bit, holding her at what felt like an impossible angle. But that angle also shifted him deeper. Ground him harder against her clit. And shattered her into sheer satisfaction.

At exactly the same moment, Elias's kiss turned into a long, deep moan that she swallowed as he shuddered to completion.

Simultaneous orgasms? She really *was* living a fairy tale.

Gently, stroking her everywhere, Elias eased both of them back onto the sheets. "I like your American way of dating."

Uh-oh. That wasn't a precedent she necessarily wanted to set. "Well, we don't *always* skip straight to the sex."

"Duly noted." He propped himself up on one elbow. "Let me try it my way next. I'll cook you dinner, and we won't have sex again until you're properly fueled. One caveat, though."

She'd pretty much agree to anything he suggested at this point. "What's that?"

"There's a strict dress code. You're required to only wear my shirt. Unbuttoned, of course."

"Of course. As long as you only wear an apron."

"I don't own an apron."

Even better. "Then I guess you don't get to wear anything."

"I'll have your eyes on me the whole time. That's more than enough."

Oh, wow. Kelsey *adored* this man.

Chapter Twelve

Kelsey looked in the mirror.

It showed the reflection of all the other mirrors in the palace's hair salon. The reflections of Genevieve, Mathilde, Agathe...and Mallory. All lined up like that, under the bright bubble lights circling each station, it was unarguably obvious that she was a part of the Villani family.

And that she and Mallory looked absolutely *nothing* alike. Sure, Elias's fingerprint test had already told her that she wasn't truly a Wishner. They'd done a blood test, too, since she'd arrived. But accepting the words and seeing the proof of generations of blond, violet-eyed women around her were very different things.

Just like watching Elias move with cat-like grace across the gardens and watching that same feline grace as he crawled naked across the bed to her were very different things.

Yup. That'd been her Saturday so far. No matter what she did, or thought, after a maximum of five minutes, her thoughts circled back to last night's date with her handsome bodyguard.

And oh boy, did he *know* her body now.

"Valentina, are you quite all right? You look flushed." Mathilde clapped a plump hand over her mouth. "I'm sorry, Kelsey. Old habits are hard to break, but I do promise I'm trying."

"That's okay. I appreciate the effort, and I'm fine." Her cheeks, throat, and chest were as pink as cotton candy, but yeah, *fine*. "Just nervous about what's going to happen to my hair for this official portrait deal, I suppose."

Reina, in a lavender smock that looked more suited to a spa, patted her shoulder and gave a reassuring smile. But she didn't *say* anything as she kept making tiny snips to Kelsey's hair. Was she, as staff, not allowed to talk? With all the senior royals in confab? Crap. It probably said somewhere in that damned protocol manual.

"The palace stylists are the best in all the land. They aren't going to do anything drastic. Merely give you some actual shape and fullness." Her grandmother's voice had a snap to it. But at least she hadn't come straight out and said that Kelsey's current cut lacked style.

She'd chalk that up as progress.

Mallory angled in her chair to face Agathe. "Thank you, Your Grace, for allowing me the treat of participating today."

Obsequiousness, thy name was Mallory.

Her sister had memorized that enormous protocol binder backward and forward. Which, admittedly, was helpful for both of them, since Kelsey hadn't put nearly as much effort into it once she discovered that it mostly applied to people with stations...titles or lack thereof...below hers.

On the one hand, she bristled at the idea of anyone being seen as *below* her. Both on the feminist, democratic front and because Kelsey knew she was average, utterly ordinary, on her best days. How was it that nobody in this country had noticed this about her yet? And when they did, what would happen? Would they demand the king send her away? Or should she just escape back to America at the end of this trip no matter what, full of relief to make it home before she was called out as a princess fraud?

On the other hand, it did give her a free pass to behave normally toward everyone except the king.

"You won't be included in the family portrait we're taking this evening, of course."

Another almost-barb from her grandmother. Great.

"But we did so want the chance to have a little hen party and get to know you, Mallory. Because you're so important to our Kelsey." Mathilde was great at smoothing things over. And she'd gotten her name right this time. As long as Kelsey didn't walk out of this room with a Priscilla Presley circa 1968 bouffant, this might turn out to be a good afternoon.

Tapping her flawless French manicure against her crystal goblet of lemon water, Genevieve said, "Yes. Do tell us some quaint childhood story where you ate too many cherries and threw up all over each other."

And there it was. Her royal sis bringing the full bitch. Topping the list of things Kelsey wouldn't miss if she hightailed it out of this country in a week...

"Oh, so you know Michigan is famous for cherries." Mallory toed her chair all the way around to beam at Genevieve in the mirror. "It's so lovely of you to take an interest in our home state."

Kelsey's jaw dropped. Holy crap, Mallory could pile on the bullshit. How had she turned that insult so handily into a compliment? She appreciated the assist, but she couldn't let Mallory do it alone.

"Our best childhood stories revolve around gory, accidental medicine. We both delivered a baby in a blizzard back in high school. Oh, and I used a tourniquet and set a broken leg on a friend when I was only twelve."

"Did the baby *and* mother survive the ordeal?" Genevieve asked snidely.

Mallory's auburn brows creased together into a frown that came and went so fast, Kelsey was sure she was the only one who'd seen it. But it was clear the continual digs were getting to her sister. Nevertheless, her voice was steady and even a tad cocky when she replied, "Of course. We had great training."

Before Mallory could go on to explain that it was because their parents were doctors—since the Wishner parents were a touchy subject, at best, with the Villanis—Kelsey jumped right back in. "We're both certified in advanced first aid. Which is a handy, FYI, in case you ever slip on all the marble steps around here and dislocate something."

Yep, she'd like nothing better than to hold a whimpering Genevieve down on the floor and use all her weight to jam a joint back into place. Petty? Sure. But technically, since it'd end up fixing Her Royal Bitchiness, it was okay for a girl to dream, right?

"Goodness. If someone went into labor in front of me? I'd simply fall to pieces and not have an inkling of what to do—and I've given birth myself twice." Mathilde trilled out a laugh. "You must be good under pressure. Just like Genny here. Isn't it nice to discover things you have in common beyond your looks?"

Yes. *Yes*, it was. After all, Elias made it sound like, while Genevieve might be a tad high maintenance, she didn't go around in a twenty-four-seven snit. At least, not until Kelsey had appeared on the scene. It was easy to snap back at her, in the moment. Every time.

Too easy, for sure.

She wanted to be the bigger person. Or at least try a little harder. Because the fact was that she and Genevieve needed to find some way to communicate beyond sniping at each other. Kelsey genuinely wanted to connect to the non-bitchy side of her new sister.

If at all possible.

Maybe she and Mallory should go online tonight and Google royal watcher fan sites. They'd probably be chock full of useful and interesting info. Like a Cliff's Notes intro to the House of Villani. Even something as dumb as who prefers wine to beer, or heck, their college majors, would give Kelsey a starting point for finding a spark of interest to share.

"So, who has an endearing childhood story to reveal about Genny?" The nickname felt too casual, too...*fun*. Genny looked perfect and poised and, well, princess-y every moment. Even now, with a spinning brush fluffing one side of her hair, the other clipped back starkly and wet? She sat ramrod straight with her makeup flawless (how had she not gotten splashed and smeary during the shampoo?).

For a few long moments there, the only sound was the snip of hair scissors and the crinkle of foil for Mathilde's color treatment.

Mallory shot her a panicked glance, which Kelsey promptly volleyed back. Who knew asking for a "she named her pony Sprinkles" type story would shut everyone down?

The squeak of the leather cushion at the opposite end alerted her to a shift by the grand duchess. "Your sister climbed into your crib the night you were born. We hadn't transitioned her out of her own yet. There'd been no attempt by her to get out of it. But she climbed up and out of her crib, toddled down the hall to your nursery, climbed in, and fell asleep with an arm across your swaddling. Genevieve did it every night. After a week, your mother simply let her go to sleep next to you, and then moved her back to her room so you wouldn't wake her up when you needed to feed."

Wow. That was one heck of a monologue. A real, honest-to-goodness grandmotherly reminiscence.

It was a gift, one so unexpected and lovely that Kelsey had no words. But her hands came to rest, together, over her heart. And she didn't need to peek at the mirror to know that her eyes were brimming with tears.

"You never told me that story," Genevieve said. Accusation and annoyance sharpened her words enough they could probably carve a *how dare you keep secrets* into those diamond studs at her ears.

"You didn't need to hear it. Kelsey did."

The grand duchess poked back at Genevieve. Just like a real grandmother! This was going so well. Kelsey envisioned monthly shared trips to the salon with all the women in the family.

If she stayed.

But she didn't *want* to stay. Kelsey was only here out of duty, out of courtesy and respect to the grief of the family, the country that had lost her. Staying meant...turning into someone else. Adding, *accepting* the title of princess would change her. Kelsey didn't even know how to accomplish that big a change. How to become the princess everyone expected.

Did going back home make her a coward? Someone too lazy to put in the effort? A quitter?

This was why she didn't sleep more than a few hours at a time.

Genevieve pushed out of her chair, fury vibrating off of her as she confronted Agathe. "I didn't need to hear a story about my own mother? When I've flat-out begged you for them over the years? When I've spent my life combing websites and microfiche and every possible outlet to compile pictures and videos and memories that show who she was?"

"We didn't want to risk you remembering it yourself. After. When we couldn't get you to stay out of that empty crib once baby Valentina was gone. You cried all night for months."

Crap. Just that fast, the story teeter-tottered from awesome to angsty. Well, it was her fault for asking and thus opening this Pandora's Box, so she'd just have to fix it.

Kelsey murmured, "Excuse me," to Renate as she rose and joined her sister. Even reached out to pat—tentatively, like you would a piranha—Genevieve's arm. "I'm sorry you didn't know, but maybe it's for the best that we both got to hear that story for the first time, together. I'm not taking anything away from you, after all, by learning about it with you."

In a whip-crack fast motion, Genevieve lifted and twisted her arm to remove Kelsey's hand. And her arm stayed raised, fingers outstretched, as if perhaps she was one second away from actually striking her. "You already did. It's your fault my entire childhood was taken away. Your fault that I lost my *mother*. Or didn't you know that she committed suicide on your birthday?"

No. Oh no. Nooooo.

Why had nobody told her their mother wasn't just long dead, but took her own life? That double wallop of pain must've tainted everything, everyone in the palace.

Ripping off her protective cape, Genevieve slammed out the door. Oddly, the stylists hadn't so much as paused in working on the two older women. But Kelsey was damn sure frozen in place by the news.

Did *everyone* blame her?

Mallory got up and gave her a wordless side hug, leading her back to the chair.

Mathilde fluttered a plump hand at her. "It wasn't actually your fault, my dear. Your mother was suffering from severe post-partum depression. She did with all three of you. Your kidnapping simply pushed her over the edge on which she was barely balanced."

That all made sense. Depression was a disease, and could

be as serious and fatal as heart disease. But Kelsey could also see how Genevieve would've needed somewhere to pile the blame in a way to deal with the pain of losing her mother. It made Kelsey worry that others in the family harbored the same bitterness toward her. How many even knew? Did she stand any chance at getting them to overlook her as the trigger and accept her for herself? Or should she give up now and go back home?

How did you decide the entire course of your life in a matter of days?

Renate hovered, comb and scissors outstretched. So Kelsey sat back down and watched her snip and tease and spray her hair into a near-match to Genevieve's.

Which also made her resemblance to the portrait of Queen Serena in the throne room even more striking.

• • •

Elias bowed deeply as the Grand Duchess Agathe swept by him. He halfway straightened as Mathilde also exited, then came up into simply a nod as Kelsey passed through the doors of the palace salon. "Your Highness."

She cruised by him at a pretty swift clip, too. So fast that he couldn't get a full look at whatever they'd done to her in there. "Let's go."

"What about Miss Wishner?" Mallory was still seated with two stylists bent over her head.

"They wouldn't even start her until the bluebloods left. She, ah, *encouraged* me to go get some air. With you."

Two long strides caught him up. And then he did a double take. Kelsey had definitely been made over into Her Royal Highness Princess Kelsey. Her hair was...fancier. Shinier. Bigger. Almost identical to Genevieve's. As was her makeup.

"You look very regal." And then he took another look.

All the layers of powder and lipstick couldn't disguise the turmoil tightening her features. He didn't dare touch her, what with footmen every twenty steps and maids and under-butlers crossing their path. "Your Highness, what's wrong?"

She paused, right in front of a footman, who scrambled to open the door for her. However, Elias knew it was the door to the security division, so he shook his head to stall the man.

Head swiveling left then right, Kelsey threw up her arms and asked, "Which one of these six hundred doors leads outside?"

"Many, but it's raining. Do you want to walk off whatever's bothering you, or do you want to talk about it?"

"I'd prefer to do six shots of tequila."

"Problem solved." He led her up two flights of the carpeted stairs. As they walked silently along the thickly carpeted hall, Elias had a fleeting thought of how much fun it might be to sit around and get buzzed with this beautiful, witty woman. But this clearly was not the right time or circumstance for any fun to be had. Not from the clench of her jaw and the way her hands stayed fisted as they swung at her sides.

They entered the snooker room. It had the green-felted table, of course. A highly polished wooden bar carved—so legend went—from a single enormous tree at the top of Mount Siljikan under which friars brewed up the very first ale in the land.

Total bullshit, of course, but it was a beautifully ornate piece that deserved a good story. As he slipped behind the bar and collected glasses, Elias said, "We're guaranteed privacy. Nobody comes in here but Christian, and he's at an event overnight in Rome."

"Hanging with the pope?"

"The Italian prime minister, actually. Along with the mayors of Rome, Naples, and Venice."

Kelsey's jaw dropped. "Oh God. I was kidding. For a

second there, I forgot I've got a family now that might hang out with the pope for real."

"Pope Linus II isn't so much about hangouts. Christian and his father did dinner with him at the Vatican about five years ago. King Julian made up an excuse to leave as soon as dessert was served. And the king never, ever cuts short an official duty."

She traced the outline of a peacock on the edge of the bar. "What was wrong?"

"Apparently, His Holiness is both boring and pompous. I guess some people take being a direct conduit to God as license to think they're better than everyone." *There.* A wan smile lifted the corners of Kelsey's mouth. He'd have to say an extra novena at Mass tomorrow, but the blasphemy was worth it to lift her spirits.

Kelsey moved to stand in front of the fireplace. She craned her neck to look up at the painting above it of a castle with regiments of men marching away, battle flags unfurled in the stiff wind. "What's this?"

"Castle Navarro. From the seventeenth century. Depicting the last time our troops rode off to war. The palace curator moved it in here to commemorate the four hundredth anniversary. They'll cycle it out before the fireplace gets lit again in the fall. It's too old to risk any smoke damage."

"Does the castle still exist?"

"Yes. Not the best place to vacation. A few bathrooms have been added, but no air conditioning or heat. It's mostly a tourist attraction that helps fund other restoration efforts throughout the kingdom." Elias joined her, because he'd let her stall long enough. "Do you really want to talk about artwork?"

"No. I mean, yes, I do. It's beautiful and fascinating to discover that almost all the paintings have a history. My family's history." She wrinkled her nose at the dark liquid in the small, fluted crystal glass he held out. "What's that?"

"A measure of port. This will take the edge off. Your requested six shots of tequila would leave you in no state for the formal portrait session in an hour."

"You're always looking out for me, aren't you?"

"It is both my job and my privilege." Elias didn't dare risk touching the photo-ready hair and makeup, so he curved his hand around her shoulder. "Let me help you now. Please, Kelsey. Trust that you can reveal any problem to me, and I'll do everything in my power to fix it."

"Ah." With a cynical smile—something he'd never before seen on her—she shook a finger in his face. "You wisely hedged your bets with that 'in my power' phrase, because it turns out you can't fix this. You can't fix the bone-deep sadness weighing me down at discovering that my mother committed suicide."

Ah, indeed.

Maybe it was a bad cliché, but weren't beauty salons supposed to be full of gossip and fashion chit-chat? How on earth had two hours with her sister, aunt, and grandmother turned into a revelation about the darkest moment in their family's recent history?

God, he hoped it hadn't been the grand duchess filling in the details. Her distinct lack of warmth would've made a bad situation unbearable.

This was definitely far, far out of his scope to fix. But Elias *could* sympathize. He set down his drink on the carved wooden mantel and gripped her other shoulder, too. "It is a horrible knowledge to carry, but Queen Serena was very, very sick. I'm told that many tried to help her. Much like an advanced cancer, her depression was simply too great to be treated."

"I get that." She crossed her arm over her chest to squeeze his hand.

"It truly had nothing to do with you, Kelsey."

"Don't worry. I'm not casting blame—or taking it on myself." Her tone was resolute, but not laced with any guilt, which was a relief. "I understand the basics of mental illness. Raised by medical professionals, remember?"

Elias noted her word choice. Was she being cautious in not calling the Wishners her parents inside Alcarsa Palace? Or simply trying to delineate in her mind between those who nurtured her, and those who wished they'd had that chance?

"I wish there was something more I could tell you. Some way of easing the shock and pain."

Her lashes drifted down to lay on her cheeks. "I'm just so sad that she gave up, that she threw away the chance to experience everyday joys. Not only watching Christian and Genevieve grow up, but walking at sunset with her husband. Eating a perfectly ripe peach. Being there for a friend when they have a bad day."

Perhaps he could help, a little, thanks to the basic education that every citizen of Moncriano now received in school about noting and dealing with mental illness. King Julian had insisted on adding it to all health curriculum the same year his wife died.

"I don't think she was giving up. She sought an escape from pain. If it helps, Queen Serena's death prompted an overhaul in the kingdom's mental-health practices. We now have the lowest incidence of post-partum suicides in all of Europe. Doctors no longer take a wait-and-see approach after birth. They're extremely proactive in treatment."

"Well, that's a good thing." Kelsey threw back the entire contents of her glass. Then she stared down into the dregs of the syrupy liquid for a few long, quiet moments. "I'd like to do something about it, in honor of the queen. My mother. Something to help others, to ease their suffering."

There was that giant heart of hers, pushing past her own

grief to think of others. This woman was truly born to be a princess, taking care of a nation, even if she didn't realize it. Elias was so proud of her. "That's a noble sentiment."

She looked up, her violet eyes wide and beseeching. "I don't know what I could do, though. Maybe volunteer an hour of babysitting once a week so that they can go to therapy?"

Elias bit back a laugh. Her heart might act like a princess's, but her head still needed training. "Perhaps that'd be a bit too hands-on. It could spiral out of control quite quickly. And you wouldn't be able to help very many. You could hold a fund-raiser."

"Tiaras and long-winded toasts?" Her nose wrinkled. "I'd like to be more hands-on than that."

His hands slid down to stroke up and down the thin cotton sweater covering her upper arms. "What about a visit to a mental-health clinic specializing in post-partum?"

"Shaking hands? Smiling? What actual good will that do?"

And they were back to the same argument. Him trying to impress upon Kelsey how very important she was to the country. Although it seemed impossible, it had only been nine days, not enough time to absorb even a tenth of her role and what it meant.

Nine days also shouldn't have been enough time for him to grow to care so damned much about her...

"It will give tremendous hope. Pride. Your visit would be the equivalent of a course of penicillin. I know you don't believe it yet, but I think you will once you do your first walkabout, and see the enormous reaction that ensues."

Her brow smoothed out. Determination squared her shoulders. "Okay, but not on September fourteenth. That'd be too sad. At least this year."

"Why not that date?"

"Because that's my birthday. The day she killed herself."

"Ah no." *Fuck.* "The queen took her life on your— Princess Valentina's—birthday. August seventh."

Kelsey stared at him, then she grabbed his glass off the mantel and tossed it back like a shot. Kicking off her shoes, she took a fast circle of the perimeter of the room. She stopped behind a pair of maroon leather-wing chairs.

"My birthday isn't even right? Are you freaking kidding me, Elias?"

What the hell was she getting schooled in all day, every day? How had nobody gone over the basics of her *original* life with her yet?

He crossed the room in three long strides. Then Elias drew her around the chair, sat, and pulled her onto his lap. "Look, that isn't bad news. There's an obvious silver lining. Now you get two birthdays."

It was the weakest of attempts to comfort her. Kelsey wasn't a child, to be distracted with the promise of twice as much cake and presents. But if there was a guidebook that told the right way to handle this constant barrage of strange upheavals that was her reality now, then nobody had damn well shared it with him.

"But I don't know which one is real. Which *me* is real?"

Elias didn't have the answer, and he wasn't sure what to hope that she'd discover. Because whether she returned to America or stayed at the palace, Kelsey wouldn't be allowed to stay with *him.*

Chapter Thirteen

"If you planned to traipse us across the entire palace grounds, why didn't we start earlier, before it got so darned hot?" Mallory lifted her hair off her neck to pull it through the strap of her stars-and-stripes baseball cap. She always wore it in the run up to the Fourth of July. Kelsey just hoped nobody here in Moncriano got offended by the in-your-face Americaness of it.

"The royal family attends Mass every Sunday," Elias said. "I went with them."

Aha. That explained why her official schedule had been so surprisingly empty. It had been nice to lay in bed doing nothing after so many jam-packed days in a row. Kelsey bumped shoulders with her sister. "No complaining. Even in a palace, God trumps everyone."

"We're not Catholic," Mallory reminded her. The snippy tone was probably due to how poorly she dealt with heat. That auburn hair and pale skin made her particularly susceptible…and bitchy. "We don't have to jump to attention every Sunday."

And, boom! There was another reminder of things that were beyond her scope of knowledge. "Hang on. *Am* I Catholic? Christened in the church and all that?"

Elias nodded without breaking his stride as they tromped over thicker grass far beyond the manicured gardens she knew.

"So if I stay, I'll have to learn my catechism and get confirmed?" Oh geez. What if they did mass in Latin? She'd have to learn *two* more languages? This country was piling up reasons for her to take the easy way out and bolt back to New York. Yes, it was surface stuff and not an actual reason to turn her back on her legacy, her duty. But sometimes that all got too heavy to contemplate, so Kelsey focused on the small differences. It helped her cope. She knew, however, it in no way could help influence her actual decision.

"Unlike England, in Moncriano the monarch is not the head of the church. In terms of battles to fight to keep your sense of self, you have a good chance of not being hassled if you choose to remain...what, exactly?"

Oh, it was delicious to catch Elias out. Kelsey did a skip-hop combo to get in front of him. All the better to wag a finger in his face. "Ha! Something your background snooping didn't turn up. I'm shocked. So disappointed in your slacker-hood."

"The Royal Protection Service doesn't snoop. We investigate." He was as haughty and proper as...her grandmother. Until Elias winked at her.

Warmth poured through her body at that naughty wink and the smile that accompanied it. Watching the real Elias leak past the buttoned-up layers of pomp and formality was so much fun. Kelsey almost reached for his hand, but stopped herself just in time.

The gardens looked deserted—did the entire capital city go to mass?—but the outer grounds of the palace were open to public tours. They had to be careful. Or so Elias kept insisting. *Repeatedly.* That if anyone found out, he'd lose his job. And his honor. Because he was a commoner and she was royalty.

Kelsey didn't believe it. What was the good of having the title of princess if it couldn't be used to protect her... what...*boyfriend*? If she could call him that. Considering she might be moving back to Manhattan in a week, that seemed presumptuous.

She'd never ask Elias to give up his life here in Moncriano. No matter how much she respected him...enjoyed him... adored being with him...craved more time naked with him...

Nothing cranked down the lid on the urge to touch him like thinking about religion. "We're Presbyterian, I guess? We mostly went on Christmas and Easter."

"Any excuse for carols and ham," Mallory said.

"Perhaps you'd be willing to undertake a basic education in the rituals, so that when required to attend church as a family you wouldn't feel confused."

Turning in a slow circle to take in the unfamiliar mountains, the glint of the ocean in the opposite direction, and of course, the palace, Kelsey said, "This shouldn't be breaking news, but I'm existing in a *perpetual* state of confusion."

"Stop that. You're doing great," Mallory said stoutly. "You're not a spy cramming for a black op. These things take time. Citizens spend eighteen years learning history and culture and tradition as they grow up. They're trying to stuff it all into you in a matter of weeks. Don't put yourself down."

Kelsey blew her a kiss. Her sister never failed to boost her confidence levels. Something that burbled way below average in her bloodstream. "Habit, I guess."

"A crappy habit, one you need to break. Royalty should be extremely self-assured."

"Like you know."

"Uh, you know how much I love old movies. Lots of them revolve around royalty."

Wouldn't it be nice if she could just binge watch some black-and-white movies with snappy dialogue and great hats and be all caught up? "I watch all those medical dramas. You don't see me posing as a doctor, do you?"

"Not yet. Who knows what next secret about your new life will be unveiled?" Mallory wriggled her fingers and lifted her arms as though lifting a sheet.

They both giggled. It was such a relief to not be tamping down any of their humor in public. Maybe a totally deserted park wasn't very public, but Kelsey was already sick of minding her Ps and Qs all the time. Not in a rebellious, teenage way. Just in a not wanting to be fake way. Serene and stoic did not come naturally to her.

So far, being royal felt a lot like being on a nonstop job interview.

She was positive it wasn't just her relatives doing the judging. Everyone from the footmen to the other security teams to yes, Renate at the salon, who all saw this near-clone of Genevieve walking around with unfettered access to the royal family. They *had* to have guessed who she was already, and been sworn to secrecy. Either way, the only people she could relax, be herself around, were Mallory, Elias, Sir Evan, and her chambermaid, Anya.

Living a lie didn't sound appealing. Giving up who she was on the outside was one thing. Her job, her country, her preferred daily uniform of yoga pants—Kelsey could live without those, if necessary. But giving up who she was on the inside was an entirely different matter. It was as if she was a doll, having her stuffing replaced.

Was there a way to embrace being a princess while remaining her ordinary self? Because she truly wanted to give Moncriano a fair shot. Being a part of the House of Villani was a centuries-old legacy. It'd be immature to turn her back on it just for not being what she'd planned. Yet it felt very mature to realize that she could not truly become a Villani if it meant giving up *everything* that made her Kelsey Wishner...

"Look, there." Elias pointed past the edge of the lake to a copse of leafed-out trees. In their shade sat what looked similar to a Grecian temple. Four marble columns, holding up a pitched roof. Centered under its peak was the image of a crown over the name *Serena*.

Mallory stopped and grabbed Kelsey's arm. "Is that her tomb?"

"Yes."

Whoa. Talk about a bait and switch. Kelsey took in the enlarged black silhouette in relief on pale-blue marble. Its shape was almost identical to her own face. A pair of silver plaques bracketed it, covered in writing she wasn't close enough to read. Curiosity carried her forward even as she shot Elias a stone-cold glare.

"You said you wanted to show me something meaningful on the palace grounds."

Elias put his hands in his pockets, bunching up his jacket, the one she knew he only wore in this heat to cover his gun. To protect her at all times. "It is meaningful, to me. I've been here many times with Christian over the years."

"But I'm wearing shorts." Kelsey didn't think she should be in all black and a hat with a veil. But something more respectful than frayed denim shorts and a concert tee from Elton John's last tour would be *appropriate* for her first visit to her mother's grave. The closest she'd come to meeting the woman who gave her life.

This morning had taken a hard left to the surreal.

The inner corners of his dark-brown eyebrows pulled

together in obvious concern. "I could tell that you were all in your head about her suicide. You didn't relax at all during the portrait session last night."

Not relaxed? That was like calling a volcano a warm mud bath. "I was posing for a family portrait with people I barely know with a heavy tiara shellacked to the top of my head. The grand duchess stared at me, Genevieve wouldn't look at me, and yeah, I was processing everything. It takes a few hours, for goodness' sake."

"You're saying you're better now? Calmer?"

"I *was*," she said pointedly.

His usual nod bent deeper, into a half bow. "My apologies. I'd hoped bringing you here, unannounced, would be akin to removing a bandage without warning. Less painful. Less worrisome."

"And you made sure Mallory came along in case I got emotional." Kelsey had been caught off guard, sure. But the thoughtfulness behind his decision to blindside her with this field trip was inarguable. Better than a dozen roses, or dinner at an expensive restaurant. Elias got nothing out of this. He'd done it strictly *for* her.

With practiced polish, he side-stepped the actual answer as they approached the base of the pavilion. "I'm aware you two haven't gotten to spend as much time together as you'd like."

Kelsey sat on the wooden bench beneath the silhouette. Wondered how to connect to a dead woman. How to not feel as though she were cheating on the woman who raised her. Ponder how to say hello to someone who wasn't even a memory, and yet had loved her so very much. "This is a beautiful spot."

Elias stood at the front of the farthest column, eyes scanning the grounds they'd just covered. His on-duty intensity showed in the taut set of his jaw. The way his hands hung loose, ready to fist or grab for his gun, while his feet were just wide enough to brace himself. Too bad he couldn't join them on the bench.

"It is open to the public, so that all may mourn and remember their Queen. Many do, to this day. But I've taken the liberty of closing the gates for the next hour, so that you may have privacy."

"Thank you. This would be a hundred times more difficult if there were a crowd of strangers." If the urge to cry did take root? The fewer people to witness her inevitable red nose, the better.

Mallory plopped down next to her. "What do you want to say?"

"I don't know. I don't know anything about the queen. Sitting here makes me wish I did. I wish that we could share stories. I wish I knew what made her so special that people still come visit her grave more than twenty years later. I wish I knew...anything," she repeated lamely.

"Perhaps I can help." Prince Christian appeared from the grove of trees. A very different version of Christian than she'd seen before, in jeans and a white polo shirt. Next to him was Genevieve. She was also dressed way down in a simple, pink eyelet sundress. The down-turned corners of her mouth, however, were something Kelsey was already very used to seeing.

Mallory shot to her feet. Then she bent her knees into a curtsey. Which looked *ridiculous* in her sleeveless khaki dress made of T-shirt fabric. "Your Highness. Your Highness. Good morning."

"Miss Wishner." Christian inclined his head in a completely different way than Elias did.

There was no subservience implied, no "I'm at your disposal." It was more of an acknowledgment that, yes, he accepted her greeting, as was his due.

Kelsey didn't believe that Christian meant any slight by it. Even after a little over a week, she'd come to realize that was simply the way things were here. Probably everywhere that had a monarchy rather than an "all things are created equal" democracy.

Crap.

She should probably scrape together two ounces of courtesy and greet her siblings. Not because protocol demanded it, but because she'd been raised to be friendly. Midwestern nice. Even when one of those siblings was staring at her with a level of disdain generally reserved for six-month-old food covered in mold in the very back of the fridge.

"Good morning, Christian. Genevieve." Kelsey didn't get up, though. She'd learned enough to know it wasn't required...until Christian ascended to the throne, anyway. "Do you come out here every Sunday after Mass?"

"Our schedule's not that fluid, I'm afraid. And we don't want to cause a disruption for tourists and citizens who want to visit." He craned his head back to look at the silhouette of their mother. "I can't remember the last time I was here. Genny?"

"I came on my birthday." Her words snapped out. Then she wrapped an arm around the ridged column and leaned against it. Everything softened. The curve of her shoulders, her pinched lips, and most of all, her tone. "I do every year. That's when I miss her the most. It just...seems like a day everyone deserves to be with their mother."

That was such a normal, human reaction, one that tugged at Kelsey's heartstrings, and made her ache for the little girl Genevieve had been. Growing up motherless, coming out to a peaceful but very sad place instead of getting birthday donuts in bed.

For all the loss Kelsey was still struggling to process when it came to Queen Serena, she'd *had* a mother. One who tucked her in every night with kisses. Who scared away the monsters under the bed with a truly horrible tap dance routine. One who listened when Kelsey complained about Mallory getting to do everything first, and told her it was okay to be sad as long as she didn't take away from any of Mallory's joy at wearing makeup or driving or graduating.

All of that added up to her being far, far luckier than the prince and princess standing in front of her.

"Your Highness, would you like me to leave?" Mallory directed the soft question to Christian.

Crap. She'd forgotten all about poor Mallory still standing there, super awkwardly, while consumed with pity for Genevieve. This having *two* sisters thing would take some practice. Kelsey almost told her to stay. That urge was automatic. The need to have her nearby was strong, too.

But she wanted to hear Christian's response. To see if he'd dismiss her (oh, just let him try!) or ask her to stay. To see if he accepted Mallory as family—like it or not—in a way that Genevieve clearly did not, as of yet.

"Pardon me, Miss Wishner. I didn't mean to leave you standing." He took her by the elbow and led her the half freaking step back to the bench. "Please, do be seated."

Was that—omigod—a *blush* coloring her sister's cheeks? Just because Christian touched her? The skin of a redhead always revealed the naughty thoughts roiling around in her brain. There'd have to be questions about this later.

Mallory shook her head. "Oh, I couldn't. There's only room for two on this bench. You or the princess should sit."

This uber-polite dance between the two of them verged on laughable. In fact, Kelsey caught Elias's eye and saw his lips twitch as she wriggled her eyebrows and tilted her head ever so slightly toward Christian and Mallory. And it felt so… *natural* to share that unspoken communication with him. Like they were in sync.

Kelsey reached out and tugged on Mallory's skirt so hard that she sort of fell back onto the bench. "See those five acres of grass in front of us? There's plenty of room for everyone to sit, for goodness' sake."

Christian sprawled on the ground. Genevieve's security detail, who'd been huddled with Christian's guy and Elias, whipped off her jacket and laid it on the checkerboard tiles next to the bench. Talk about high-level protection for a cotton dress!

At some point, Kelsey would learn the names of all the security guards. They all seemed intent on blending into the woodwork, but that didn't fly for her. If these people were willing to give up their own lives to protect her family, she darned well wanted to know at least a little something about them. The basics—their names, if they preferred cookies or brownies so she could make them treats every so often, their favorite bands...

Oh. *That* would entail diving into the music scene here in Moncriano. Or very probably, the entire European music scene. Make that thing number eight gajillion and two that she'd have to learn from scratch.

If she stayed.

"Thank you, Clara," Genevieve murmured as she knelt. And that earned her about two hundred points back in the *not a total bitch* column. Because three minutes ago, Kelsey would've assumed that there was no way Genny knew the name of her bodyguard.

"So why are you two out here?" If it was to drop some other horrific secret on her, well, Kelsey still hadn't recovered from yesterday's big suicide-on-her-birthday reveal. She'd quite possibly grab Mallory and make a run for it.

"Elias requested I join you." Christian looked vaguely amused. "He never asks for favors. Ever. I couldn't turn him down."

"Elias?" she said, swiveling to face him in shock. This asking a favor of his friend thing—on her behalf—seemed huge. Not an optimal way to keep their relationships under wraps, either.

He took a miniscule step forward. "I thought Your Highness might like to learn a bit about the queen as you saw her grave for the first time. Something personal, not in the official histories. Family stories. A way to feel her presence here."

"That'd be really, really nice." Kelsey hadn't wanted to come out and ask anyone. Yes, the woman had been dead for more than twenty years. But she didn't want to accidentally pick at an emotional scab. It didn't feel like she had the right. Not yet. So this was yet another gift from the man who knew what she wanted and needed before she even realized it herself.

She couldn't wait to get Elias alone to thank him.

"Genny here just tagged along. Uninvited." Christian pulled out a few blades of grass and blew them at her from his palm. "She's a brat that way."

Kelsey bit the inside of her cheek to keep from laughing out loud. Their true brother/sister dynamic was showing, and it delighted her. It was as if they'd left their titles back in their bedrooms with the formal clothes. This was *real* family time. It was the key to her actually connecting to them.

Shrugging one shoulder, Genevieve said, "We almost never talk about her anymore. For a while, Papa made an effort, but once we were grown, he stopped. So yes, I want to hear the stories, too. Don't be an ass about it, Christian."

"Don't give Kelsey the wrong impression of me."

"I get the feeling she's capable of coming to her own wrong impressions, without any help."

Was that a dig? Because she didn't let Genevieve run roughshod over her? Or because she'd perhaps lobbed back semi-bitchiness every time it came her way?

Point taken.

And thus, olive branch extended. "I'll take all the help I can get. In every aspect of learning about this family." Then Kelsey noticed that Mallory was sitting ramrod straight, the tips of her toes pointed. A bow with a cocked arrow had less tension than her sister. That needed to stop right-the-hell now. "I'd like to start, though, with you two learning about *my* family. This amazing woman next to me."

"Kelsey, shush." Mallory's cheeks reddened to near-fire.

"No. If I'm going to get to know them, they need to get to know you. We've had time to get over the shock, the weirdness of being in each other's lives. Now we're a blended, modern royal family. Breaking new ground, charting new territory. None of it matters, though, unless we act like a true family. Unless we learn to care, learn what makes each of us special and awesome and lovable."

Genevieve curled her legs underneath her, then she looked Kelsey directly in the eyes. "I will give you free rein to borrow *anything* in my closet—for a day—if you give that speech to our grandmother. Two days, if you let me watch."

"Heck, no." Relieved laughter gurgled out. "I'm passionate, not self-destructive. I've got a feeling the 'missing Princess Valentina' would never reappear to the country if I did that."

"I have a dozen pairs of Louboutins. In case you change your mind…"

The shoes weren't tempting in the least. Bringing out this playful side of Genny, however, was. Kelsey curled her fingers around the seat of the bench and leaned forward. "I just want to start with you two so my brother and sister learn to respect and like my other sister."

"Here, here," Christian said. "I, for one, would be fascinated to learn about Miss Wishner."

"Huh-uh." Kelsey was on a streak, and she'd push it as far as possible. "Her name's Mallory. I understand protocol, *yada, yada, yada*, but when it's just us? Use her name. Please. All this formality only puts another wall between us."

Shockingly, it wasn't Christian that responded first. Genevieve scooted a little closer. "All right then, *Mallory*, tell us one of your favorite things about Kelsey. And vice versa."

"Oh, she'll hate that. I'd better move so I don't get pinched." With a smirk, Mallory jumped up and hustled over to stand by Christian.

Kelsey allowed herself another swift and significant eyebrow waggle at Elias. Then she took a deep breath and held it, because yes, she absolutely hated having the spotlight turned on her. This reversal of praise was not her plan at all.

"She never puts herself first. It sounds selfish for me to say that, doesn't it?" Mallory rubbed at her chest, biting her bottom lip. "I guess it's more that she doesn't think of herself as better, or more important than anyone else. Kelsey always asks how my day is first, even if something big and horrific happened to her. She always lets people with a handful of items cut in front of her at the grocery store. When I'm talking to her, I'm confident I've got her full attention—and will, for as long as I need it. She makes me—and everyone— feel valued and important and *seen*."

Kelsey jumped up to deliver a tackle-hug. As they landed on the grass, she said, "I hated hearing it. But I love that you feel it."

"Well said, indeed." Christian applauded. "Kelsey, what did you want to tell us about Mallory?"

"I'm not as eloquent. Mine's more bullet points. She can stretch a dollar further than anyone. I can't even explain her magic way with numbers, but she's a whiz. She's such a good baker that she placed five years in a row at the state fair. And she bends over backwards to support me no matter what—

including traipsing halfway across the world on ten minutes' notice just so I wouldn't be all alone here."

"Very laudable," Genevieve said. She even beamed a half smile at Mallory.

Christian, on the other hand, winced comically. "And an ironic segue to what I was going to share. *Our* mother was a horrible baker."

Ooh, a personal freedom alert. Kelsey's eyes widened. "She was allowed to cook? Sir Evan told me I wasn't to go down to the kitchens even to grab a bag of chips."

"That's to protect their feelings. Our kitchen staff takes great pride in providing for us. But our mother decided when she first got pregnant that it was a requirement of the role to bake cookies. She practiced every other Thursday night. For seven months."

Mallory's jaw dropped. "It took her seven months to learn how to make cookies?"

"Not even close. Not even practicing for four years helped. I don't have many memories of her, but I do remember the oatmeal cookies she made were so bad that I spit them out. In the middle of a garden party. I got taken back to my room. But at least I didn't have to eat any more of those cookies."

They all laughed. Yup. Mallory was better than a freaking queen at baking. Kelsey laughed with joy at learning a fact so ordinary. So humbling. So darned funny.

Kelsey leaned across to put a hand on Christian's arm. "Tell me something she did as queen that made the title matter more than the tiara."

"That's easy. She gave away all her baby presents. Every time. Even the designer dresses and top-of-the-line strollers and monogrammed pacifiers. She gathered everything up and gave it to single mothers in the kingdom."

That single memory he'd shared told her *so* much about her mother's generous nature. Kelsey loved it.

Genevieve got up and knelt in the grass without bothering to bring the protection of the jacket. "Tell the one about the costume. At that American superhero thing."

"Papa would tell it better."

She lifted her hands to indicate the empty park. "He's not here."

"Mama snuck into a comic conference in full costume so nobody knew it was her."

"Comic-Con?" Kelsey breathed the words with reverence. After moving to Manhattan, it had been her biggest dream to attend someday.

"In what costume?"

"Black Widow."

Kelsey flopped to her back. It was her favorite movie. She'd worn the costume four Halloweens in a row.

A costume her grandmother had carefully altered every year. So now that she finally had a tangible connection to this life and the queen—it was also a reminder of her old life, and the people she loved back home.

Stalemate.

Again.

It was a weird, one step forward, one step back dance. Did that mean that there truly *weren't* two versions of her that Kelsey had to choose between?

That it was okay to love Mallory and learn to love Christian? Okay, maybe learn to *like* Genevieve? That she could still be herself no matter where she landed?

Kelsey did know one thing for certain.

In the midst of all this dichotomy, being with Elias made her feel the most normal, the most real. In fact, Elias gave her *all* the feels. Arranging this session with her brother and sister had been so thoughtful of him. Kelsey couldn't wait to thank him…"properly."

Chapter Fourteen

Sex with Kelsey was mind-blowing. It turned Elias's world upside down.

It was also exhausting. Staying up until four a.m. to wallow in every moment possible of touching her made it tough to report for the daily security briefing at six.

Worth it, no question about that. But he'd guzzled a double espresso while shaving, had a coffee as soon as he hit the security wing, and now that the briefing was over, was pouring an extra-large coffee.

It'd wake him up, for sure. Damn well better not do target practice today, though, because Elias doubted his hands would be steady if he kept up this rate of caffeine consumption.

Marko, Kelsey's relief bodyguard, crowded in, waving an empty mug. "Leave some for the rest of us, why don't you."

"You know how to work a coffee maker. You can make more." Elias would bet an entire paycheck that not a single guard in this room needed the coffee as badly as he did.

"Late night?" Marko cupped his hand around his mouth

and semi-whispered, "Got a good story to share?"

Not in a million years. Especially not to Marko, who prided himself on being a player. "Just didn't get much sleep. I've a meeting with Prince Christian in an hour. Need to be sharp." Elias dumped in three spoonfuls of sugar. He never used it, but he'd take any advantage today.

"We all know the prince is your best friend. I don't think you'd get the axe if you yawned in front of him."

True. Odd that Marko brought it up, though.

Christian never gave him preferential treatment. They were both scrupulous about maintaining a strictly professional relationship when Elias was guarding him. Since their friendship predated Elias's induction into the Royal Protection Service, the rest of the guards never made a fuss about it.

"He wouldn't axe me." Elias ceded the remaining half inch of coffee to Marko, moving to lean against the doorjamb. "But I'd do it myself. We're not friends when I'm on duty. He's my protectee."

Swearing, Marko dumped it in the sink and grabbed a filter. "Not anymore. Not with Princess Valentina back on the scene."

The security teams were all fully briefed on Kelsey's true identity. Technically, they gave everyone the same level of protection, from members of Parliament to visiting diplomats. But knowing you were responsible for the safety of a member of the royal family stepped up everyone's game. And it just might make a difference should that snap second come when a guard had to decide to give his life to keep a protectee safe.

"Well, that could be a temporary assignment. Nothing's decided, which is why I'm staying in the loop with His Highness by meeting this morning."

Not that Elias wanted to think about Kelsey leaving. Or her staying.

Either way, the inevitable end of their relationship.

Normally, if something bothered him, he'd vent to Christian. The prince was a great sounding board, and when he didn't have anything useful to say, doled out sympathy, swearing, and Scotch. But there was no way he could tell his best friend how torn up he was about the possibility—hell, the definite need—to give Kelsey up.

Explaining that he'd fallen for Christian's little sister would be the end of their friendship. The end of his career. Not to mention pointless, since he couldn't change the facts. In less than a week, he and Kelsey would be through.

And all the time he stole with her didn't make that any easier to swallow. The more he saw her, the more he *wanted* to see her. It was maddening. But he couldn't stop.

Marko looked over one shoulder, then the other. There were a handful of other guards still milling about their break room. Nothing out of the ordinary, though. "How about we take a walk before you have that meeting?"

That was odd. Elias thought they worked well as a team. Marko was his preferred sparring partner. And he enjoyed nursing a beer at a bar while watching his friend, the ultimate player, plow through every pretty female. He couldn't think of any reason why they'd need to "take a walk."

Shrugging into his jacket to cover his weapon, Elias said, "Shouldn't you be heading up to Miss Wishner's suite?"

"Soon." Instead of going out the door leading to the main hallway, Marko jerked his head toward the back of the room. They went past the briefing room, past the bullpen, and past the locker rooms and gym. Marko punched in a code and opened the door to the armory.

"What's this about?"

"It's the most secure place I know, and I respect you too much to have anyone overhear this conversation."

That didn't sound good. Elias fisted his hand around

the support for the nearest set of shelves, lined with boxes of ammo. "What the hell, Marko?"

"I should be asking you that." Feet planted wide, thumbs tucked into the waist of his pants, Marko said, "What the hell do you think you're doing fucking around with a Princess of the Realm?"

On a scale of one to ten of badness, this topped out at three hundred.

Denial was pointless. Marko wouldn't confront him over a mere hunch. He *knew*. But how? They'd been so damned careful.

First things first, though.

In a smooth lunge, Elias seized Marko by the knot of his tie and shook him hard, once. "Don't ever disrespect Her Highness with that kind of language again."

The man had enough sense of self-preservation to go lax and not fight him. "Sorry. The disrespect was aimed at you, not her."

"That's the only reason I'm not beating you black-and-blue." Elias let go and stepped back. Smoothed the lapel of his jacket and wished he could smooth the panic pinging through his brain half as easily. "How'd you find out?"

Marko eyed him warily. "Does it matter?"

"Yes, damage control. Have to figure out who else might know, or even suspect."

"Nobody." Then squinting as he reconsidered, he tilted his hand side to side. "Maybe Lathan, but not likely."

"That's not good enough. How, damn it?"

"I heard her talking to her sister. Miss Wishner, that is, not Princess Genevieve. We were in the grotto. They thought I was far back enough I couldn't hear, but their voices just pinged off all that stone and came right at me." Marko grinned. "Apparently, you're 'knee-meltingly wonderful' in the sack."

Christ. Good to know Kelsey appreciated his moves. But he didn't know how he'd be able to look Mallory in the face the next time he saw her. Roughly, Elias muttered, "I don't need a performance review, thank you very much."

"Just reporting the details as I heard them." He opened a box of bullets and took one out to play it over the backs of his fingers. Without looking up, he asked, "So it is true?"

"Yes. The legend of my bedroom prowess is not overhyped," Elias deadpanned.

"This isn't a joke."

"I'm well aware."

Although—if Elias believed in that nonsense—he'd say it was a huge karmic joke. That he'd spend his entire life working to salvage his family's honor, to never make a single misstep, only to be tempted by the most amazing woman that he absolutely couldn't have…

Marko snatched up another bullet to run over his other hand. Guess he really wanted an excuse not to look Elias in the face. "Look, this is awkward, a conversation I never want to have with anyone ever again, let alone a guy who outranks me and, on occasion, can be a better shot than me. But…what are you doing?"

That was the question, wasn't it? Taking his one shot?

Seizing the moment?

Being a reckless fool?

Elias paced in slow, measured steps to the end of the room. Past all the racks of police batons, ammunition, handguns, rifles, automatic rifles, grenades, gas masks, tear gas, and Kevlar vests. It still didn't give him enough time to come up with a good answer, one that would explain away the immense risk he was taking with his career. His honor. And hell, his heart.

But all he blurted out was, "Kelsey's…special."

Marko glanced up enough to roll his eyes. "She's a

princess."

"Not like that. She's a special woman, with a big heart who doesn't care at all about being royal. She just...cares. She's beautiful. A little off-center. With a core of sweetness like the chocolate in the middle of a croissant."

"Don't attack me again, but"—Markus let the bullets fall and loosely fisted his hands, as though worried enough about Elias charging that he prepared—"she *is* beautiful. So is this just a one-off? Every man in the country's been panting after Princess Genevieve for a decade, and Princess Valentina looks just like her."

"It's Princess *Kelsey*," he snapped.

Yeah, he'd spent his whole life worrying about the missing Princess Valentina, just like everyone else. But Elias saw how hard this transition was for her. She might very well accept being folded into the Villani royal family. He had no doubt, however, that she'd always remain Kelsey Wishner in her mind. That's who she was.

And all of Moncriano needed to accept it.

"You really think they'll let her keep that name?" Marko winced, like he'd sucked on a lemon. "It's so American."

"It's Irish, actually." Because yes, the investigative team had checked. They'd looked into the origins of the name Kelsey Margaret Wishner to see if there was any possible clue in it to her abduction. "It is *her* name. If she stays, I have no doubt she'll keep it. We need to not only respect that, but help enforce it."

Cocking his head to the side, Marko said quietly, "I guess you answered my question after all. You like her, don't you? You're having some kind of an actual relationship with her?"

"Yes."

"You're a fucking idiot."

"I know." Elias leaned back against a rack and let his head bang into the shelf. Hard. It didn't shake loose any of his longing for Kelsey, though.

Marko stalked down to lean against the opposite rack, arms crossed. "There's literally no way this can end well."

"I know."

"As soon as she's announced as the missing princess, the country will go nuts. Her official calendar will fill up. The grand duchess will start a husband search for her, if she hasn't already. You'll have to distance yourself."

"I *know*." Did Marko really think Elias hadn't come up with all these points himself? And repeated them twenty times a day? Nothing about being with Kelsey made sense. Except for the time when he was actually *with* her. Then everything in his head quieted, the world faded away, and the only thing that made sense *was* her.

"If you know all that, why'd you even start down that road?" Marko punched him in the biceps. He packed some heat behind it, too. "It's dangerous, man. I don't want you to lose your job. But if anyone besides me finds out, there's no way you can keep it. You're compromised."

Elias straightened faster than a yanked zipper. "I'm not. I'm Prince Christian's primary bodyguard and his best friend. Nobody accused me of being compromised in that role."

"Falling for a woman is entirely different. Doesn't matter if you end up leading with your dick or your heart. All that matters is you're not leading with your head."

"I know," Elias muttered again. And then he broke into laughter, because what else could he do at that point? Keep repeating himself?

"Never in a million years would I have pegged you for a guy to not just break the rules, but break the biggest one of all. Consciously. Willingly. Did I mention that you're a fucking idiot?"

"Yeah, but it bears repeating."

Marko punched him again, only half as hard. "What are

you going to do?"

Time to face the music. Elias refused to try and force Marko to stay silent. It was his mistake, and his alone. He wouldn't drag his friend down with him. "Will you report me?"

There was an extra long beat of measuring silence. "Depends on your answer."

Fair enough. Elias pressed the heels of his hands above his eyebrows. Squinting his eyes tightly shut, as though that'd keep him from seeing the inevitable future, he said, "I'm not going to do anything. Yet. If the princess leaves Moncriano, we're over. If she stays, we're over. Every way this plays out, within the next week, we're done."

"As long as you know that's how it has to be."

"I know," he echoed himself, hollowly. "There's no other option."

"Then I'll let you have your fun." One hand on the doorknob, Marko huffed out a breath and shook his head. "But for Christ's sake, be more careful."

• • •

The desk and coffee table in Prince Christian's study held half of an enormous breakfast. A platter of sausages, a basket of crumpets, a mound of scrambled eggs, a bowl of fruit, and a plate of cheeses.

"Are you expecting someone besides me?" Elias asked. "There's enough food here to feed at least three more people. Or your friend Sergei when he's trying to eat away a hangover."

Christian dipped his head. "I'm hiding. I asked the kitchen to bring us breakfast in my chambers and they got overly excited."

Elias shoveled a little of everything onto his plate. Food

should energize him, on top of the sugar and caffeine. He hoped, at least. "Why are you hiding?"

"Breakfast with the family for the last three days has comprised of arguments about Kelsey."

Elias cringed. "Sounds like something you should be mediating."

"Not interesting ones I'd like to have a say in, but things like what color palette suits her best."

When he'd been on duty, he'd caught some of those conversations, too. "That sounds...boring. Pounding-your-head-on-the-table boring."

"If her fascinators should have veils or feathers. If her heels can be the same height as Genevieve's, or if they need to be shorter because Grandmother saw her ankles wobble the other day and that pretty much predicted the fall of the House of Villani if seen by anyone outside palace walls." Christian threw the crust of his toast down so hard that it bounced off the plate and onto the floor.

Elias picked it up, and was mildly surprised the prince hadn't put his fist through the wall yet. "It's my job to protect you, Your Highness. Therefore, I'm going to insist you hole up in here for breakfast every day. At least until their dithering calms down."

"Thanks, Eli. You've always got my back."

His back...and his sister's front.

It was hard for Elias to stand there, soaking in the smile of gratitude from his best friend, all the while knowing that he'd had his hands all over Christian's baby sister not five hours ago. He didn't deserve that kind of trust. Not the way he'd been abusing it lately.

Did it make a difference that Christian and Kelsey were practically strangers? That she shouldn't be off-limits, in that case? That technically, the prince should barely have any sense of needing to protect her honor?

Yeah, not likely. The only person more loyal to the bone than Elias himself? That'd be Christian. He'd give Kelsey a kidney tomorrow—without blinking—if she needed it. Merely because the blood of the Villanis ran in her veins.

Which made Elias a snake in the grass. Horse shit on a shoe. The lowest of the low. The guilt weighed on him every hour, like the entire island of Malta pressed down on his shoulders. But Elias wouldn't give up a single moment he'd shared with Kelsey, or the few remaining to him in the next week. Not even for Christian.

He started shoveling eggs into his mouth so he'd have an excuse not to look up.

"I'm not merely hiding. Papa and I had an early conference call with the Privy Council." Christian picked up his plate and came around to join him on the blue brocade sofa behind the table.

He did that all the time when it was just the two of them. The prince said he felt stupid and pretentious talking at Elias from behind the desk. Usually, Elias appreciated that his friend didn't want the layers of rank to come between them.

This morning, though, a little space would've been *welcome*.

Elias layered quince jelly onto his crumpet. "A call? Why didn't you meet?"

"It'd be impossible to keep a meeting secret that has the King and the Crown Prince in attendance with the entire Privy Council. Rumors would fly that Papa was abdicating, or some such nonsense."

"That's stupid. If he didn't abdicate after Queen Serena's death, he's not going to do it now."

Christian waved the butter knife, as though cutting through a web of gossip. "Ah, but you see, you're using logic. Rumors are never logic-driven."

"I'll bite. Why the secret call?"

"To tell them the missing Princess Valentina has been found by none other than the valiant Royal Protection Officer Trebanti."

"Damn it. Really? You had to go and stick my name into the narrative?" The last thing Elias wanted was any spotlight shining on him. He'd found her because it was his job to do so. Period. Just like it was his job to stay in the background. Not be noticed. Not draw any focus away from his royal charges.

And he liked that role.

Christian's mouth turned down into an expression of… pity? Like he knew how miserable this would make Elias? "The number one question after *where has she been all these years* will be *who found her*. We can't pretend that Kelsey— out of the blue—walked up to the palace gates and asked to see her family."

They could say space aliens dropped her from a tractor beam, for all he cared. "You can simply say she was located by the Royal Protection Service. No need to go into details."

"Have you lost your mind? The press, the public, the world are going to scrape for every single last detail of this story. From *what was Princess Valentina's last meal in New York* to *can she speak our language yet?* After only two damn weeks."

Elias moved on to a hunk of cheddar. It gave him something to do with his hands besides punch them into the back of the couch in frustration. Because he knew Christian was right—if not underplaying the whole thing. "Her maid's teaching her the important words pretty fast."

"How to swear?"

"Yeah." They both grinned.

"I know you'll hate being in the news. But…welcome to my world." Christian spread his arms wide along the gold curlicue that formed the top edge of the sofa.

Elias shuddered. Seeing it from the fringes was bad

enough. "I don't want to be in your world unless I also get the salary and the cars. The Lamborghini, to be specific."

"Dream on. You'd also have to marry some vapid, foreign titled woman and make her pop out babies in short order. We both know how much you despise spoiled heiresses."

Elias wasn't a fan of anyone who didn't pull their weight, contribute something to life besides spending money. Or, say, know the capital of their country.

Sex was fun, but you needed to be able to talk to the woman before, during, and after. And about more than fashion and fine wines. Some of the women in Christian's sphere seemed to think being pretty was the only requirement to catch the prince's eye. Were they ever wrong.

With another big shudder, Elias said, "As do you, Your Highness."

Christian nodded emphatically. "Which is why I'm not married yet. Thankfully, this whole Kelsey thing will distract the Privy Council from pushing me on it for at least a year. Maybe I owe *her* a Lamborghini."

"That'd work for me. As her protection officer, I'd of course drive her in it. For safety. She isn't used to navigating on the other side of the road."

Bracing his palms on his thighs, Christian leaned closer. His official mask of seriousness slipped into place. "You know, Eli, if you really want that car, I'd give it to you. Tomorrow. Anything you want—name it—for bringing my baby sister back."

Elias didn't need things. Nor did he even need the gratitude of his eventual monarch. Especially not when he'd already been gifted with the reward of getting to know Kelsey. Of feeling twelve-feet-tall every time she batted those violet eyes at him. Feeling at peace in a way he never had before just from holding her hand.

Unable to say any of that, he snarled, "Shall I remind you

again how I was only doing my job?"

Getting up, Christian walked over to pluck his ceremonial Navy sword off the wall, mounted above the fireplace. He unsheathed it and pointed it at Elias. "The king asked me if he should knight you."

"Did you say hell, no?"

"Not in so many words."

"In *any* words?" Because Elias needed a knighthood about as much as he needed a set of diamond barrettes for his hair. It'd look just as ridiculous on him, too. He was a sailor, a soldier. A man who worked, not one who let others work *for* him.

"I told him you'd been so busy guarding the princess and helping her acclimate to her new life that we hadn't had the chance to discuss a suitable reward."

Elias deliberately stood, scooped another big spoonful of eggs on his plate—turned out last night's sex wasn't just exhausting, but it made him famished—and another sausage. "There. Reward duly given and gratefully accepted."

"Breakfast?"

"You said anything I want. And right now, I'm starving."

Christian sheathed the sword. "One day, I'll figure out what you truly want. The favor you need but are afraid to ask. Then I'll finally get to repay you for all these years of sticking by me."

"Or you could feed me again tomorrow morning. Call it even." Because Elias had *plans* for Kelsey tonight. Plans that would undoubtedly make him even more famished and exhausted by this time tomorrow. But he needed to get Christian off this bullshit idea of rewarding him before then. "How'd the Privy Council take the big news?"

Christian pressed the backs of his knuckles into his forehead, wincing. "I've never heard the prime minister squeal before...and let's be crystal clear on how much I never,

ever want to hear it again."

Prime Minister Skeggit was a supremely serious former judge. She smiled while campaigning and at King Julian. Period. Built like a battleship with short, no-nonsense grey hair, she was only slightly less imposing than Grand Duchess Agathe. Elias would've been hard-pressed to believe she'd squealed at age five, blowing out her birthday candles.

"That's very wrong."

"As wrong as a five-headed frog."

"Not just as wrong as a three-headed frog?"

"Trebanti, if you'd heard this—" Christian broke off. He slammed the sword loudly back into the holder on the wall. "I think I'll hear it in my nightmares from now on."

"More to the point, did you agree on a plan? To present the princess to Parliament, and the country?"

"We'll let the protocol police hammer out those details. It'll be days of jockeying for who gets to see her first, gets greeted first, stand closer. All that rigamarole that drives me crazy."

For someone destined to be king, Christian had little patience with ceremony and obsequiousness. Much like Kelsey. "But the timeline stays the same? Another week?"

"Yes, although they'd prefer to do it in half an hour. They're convinced this will boost morale exponentially among our people. The country's been torn apart over this vote to join the European Union. Kelsey's reappearance will help heal it. Maybe even the fact that she's been living overseas will prove that joining with foreigners isn't a bad thing. She could turn the tide of the vote without ever broaching the topic."

It all sounded positive. It did not sound at all, however, like it had been mentioned Kelsey hadn't yet decided whether or not to embrace Moncriano as her home. "Christian. I understand they were excited by the news. But did you tell them she might not stay? That she might leave and renounce the Villani name entirely?"

"Not a chance. She sees herself every time she looks at us. We're family. That's a bond that can't be broken."

How could he make the prince understand? "Still, she *could* choose to return to America. I'd put it at a better than fifty-percent chance. She feels isolated. Her life is so different here than what she'd planned to be doing. I'm not sure Moncriano has given her enough reasons to stay."

Christian clapped him heavily on the shoulder. "Elias, you're my ace in the hole. Do whatever you can to convince her. Make sure Kelsey feels like this is where she belongs."

Holy hell. Elias fake coughed to keep from laughing out loud. If only Christian knew what he'd just given Elias license to *continue* to do to his baby sister...

Chapter Fifteen

A barrage of knocks sounded on Kelsey's door.

Loud, fast, and constant enough that it could only signal one thing—the historic palace hadn't sprung for a fire alarm. She looked across the breakfast table at Mallory. "That can't be good."

A moment later, without bothering to wait for any response, the door flew open. Sir Evan burst in, literally panting. His vest had popped a button, and his tie was askew. Clearly, her guess had been correct. Something was terribly wrong.

He skidded to a stop and frowned at her. "You're in a bathrobe."

"Be grateful you didn't barge in ten minutes ago when I was in far less than a bathrobe." Or a few hours ago, when he would've gotten an eyeful of her both naked *and* wrapped around a naked Elias. She'd stopped wearing her pajamas entirely. Kelsey didn't want to miss any chance to be skin-to-skin with his amazing muscles. But it wasn't just the *fabulous* sex. Sleeping with Elias wrapped around her quieted all the worries and confusion that had kept her awake every night prior to him being in her bed.

She couldn't get enough of him, which was a huge problem, what with their expiration date being in only a week. But Kelsey couldn't think about it, couldn't rack her brain for an end-around of all the reasons Elias told her "they" were an impossibility.

If she did, she'd just curl up under the covers in misery. So Kelsey ignored the impending doom—just like she did with global warming, and the risk of salmonella from eating raw cookie dough.

"My apologies, Your Highness, Miss Wishner." Sir Evan executed the world's shortest and fastest bow. "But there's been a change in your schedule. The king would like to see you."

"It's about time," Mallory muttered under her breath.

Kelsey kicked her with a bare foot. It wouldn't hurt much, but it would get across the point of *save your snark for when we're alone.* "Just me? Or both of us?" King Julian wasn't quite as intimidating as her grandmother, but he was still…well…*king* of an entire country. Every time she'd seen him so far, it'd been with many other people. Mallory was her security blanket.

Pulling himself together, Sir Evan gave the slightest nod of apology to her sister. "His Majesty specifically requested only you, Princess. You must get dressed immediately. Jeans, boots, a light sweater."

"I don't have boots." Because it was June. Who needed boots until autumn?

"Of course you do. Miss Wishner, would you mind retrieving her outfit? We mustn't keep the king waiting."

Perversely, Kelsey wanted to do exactly that. "If he didn't want to be kept waiting, then he could've given me advance notice." She took a big slug of her coffee. Long nights with

Elias were equally exhausting and invigorating. Invigorating to the heart, but exhausting to the rest of her body.

Sir Evan watched as Mallory freaking scampered off to the big closet. Then he folded his hands at his waist and gave Kelsey *the look*. The same one he gave her when she asked why she couldn't wear pants to be presented to Parliament, and why Anya wouldn't stop curtseying every time she came into the room, even though Kelsey had ordered her not to do so.

"Forgive me, Your Highness, but when Mr. Wishner asked you to accompany him on an outing back in Michigan, would you require advance notice?"

Dad would double over in laughter if she asked him to schedule one of their spontaneous trips to Dairy Queen. But King Julian wasn't "Dad." Not yet.

Kelsey crossed her legs and took another long sip of coffee before answering. "That's not fair. Right now, with this running around at the snap of his fingers, you aren't treating him like my father. You're treating him like my king." Positive that she'd checkmated him, she braced her palms on the table and leaned forward in smug triumph. "Which is it?"

"It is now, and will always be, *both*." He had the grace to look a little regretful. "No doubt that will take some getting used to."

"Add it to the list," she murmured.

"I am sorry for this disruption to your schedule. The king will be waiting for you on the west wing loggia in ten minutes, precisely." With a nod, he backed toward the door.

"Wait. You're not going with me?" Going without Mallory was bad enough. Going without any friendly backup made this even more daunting. "How will I find the loggia?"

"Marko's right outside. He'll escort you." As if taking pity on her, Sir Evan paused with one hand on the knob. "This is a good thing. King Julian wants to be alone with you.

Literally every person in this country would kill for that kind of access."

The door shut behind him just as Mallory reemerged, knee-high boots dangling from her fingers. She thrust the pile of clothes at Kelsey. "Hurry up. Put these on."

Clearly, she had no choice, but it felt a tiny bit traitorous that Mallory had been so eager to side with Sir Evan. Everyone in the palace had an agenda for her—one that didn't take into account Kelsey's own wishes—*except* for Elias and Mallory. Or so she'd thought.

Pissyness at this turn of events was a lot easier to vent on her sister than on the messenger—or the king himself. Stripping off her robe, she snarked, "What's with you? Why'd you jump to obey his command?"

"Because this is a big deal. Huge deal. Mount Rushmore on top of Mount Whitney big." Mallory waited until she'd tugged the heather-gray tee on, then put a hand on her arm. Her sister's wide green eyes were so serious, as was the way the top of her lip rolled in where she bit it. "You know I've been studying royal protocol—"

She cut Mallory off with a one-armed hug. "—so I don't have to. For which I'm grateful." Kelsey just didn't get the whole bowing and scraping thing. Especially when it was just due to her DNA, and not anything special or worthwhile that she'd actually done to garner that kind of respect. Mallory had explained that it was like geometry—understanding wasn't necessary. Merely acceptance.

"The king is not accessible. Not even to his children." Mallory waggled an index finger for emphasis. "Nothing is more valuable than his time. Moncriano's neutrality means so many other countries come here and use it as a mediation and negotiation spot. He doesn't just rule this country. He helps balance the rulers of the entire world. King Julian has his fingers in everything."

"The way you describe it, it's amazing he took the time to create three children in the first place."

"Well, he ramped things up after the queen died. Threw himself into work and bringing Moncriano back to the forefront, both for tourism and politics. So if he's carved out time to be with you? You don't want to waste a single second." She knelt to wedge a boot onto Kelsey's foot.

Okay, then. Looked like a quick attitude recalibration was in store. With a gentle tug on Mallory's auburn pony, she teased, "Here I was hoping you had a hot date and you wanted me out of the way."

"Trust me, I'm sad to report you're the only one getting awesome foreign nooky."

"Nooky? We're all grown up, Mal. You can't call it nooky anymore." Her sister had a prudish streak. Kelsey's secret belief was that she hadn't had the right kind of mind-blowing sex yet to shake out the Midwestern repression.

Mallory would never, for example, have sex on a couch in a summerhouse.

She zipped both boots and stood up with a grimace. "*Hookup* feels disrespectful to your new station in life."

Kelsey hated that reason. No, the term "hookup" felt disrespectful to Elias himself. "It's not a hookup. It's so much more than that."

Mallory's face dropped. "You're serious about him, aren't you?"

"If you're asking if I'm head over heels crazy about him, the answer's *yes*."

"And it isn't just the mysterious allure of a foreign hottie?"

"Definitely not." Kelsey opened the jewelry box that had appeared, day two, on top of her dresser. Every day more earrings and necklaces appeared in it. Fancy, tasteful real gems that were probably more costly than her entire college tuition. She grabbed a pair of black—jet? Onyx?—dangly earrings.

"What happens if you decide to go back home? For good?"

That was the sixgajillion dollar question, wasn't it? "I'm living in the moment. Not making any decisions for the two weeks I promised to give them."

"Riiiiiight."

Mallory always could see right through her. "I'm living in the moment," she repeated, heading to the door. "And completely freaking out about one more possible life-changing decision that I'll have to make. I had no idea Elias would be a factor, that he'd feel so important, so integral to me, in so little time. It's wonderful...and horrible."

Rushing the length of the room, Mallory threw her arms around her. "It'll be okay. These are all good problems. Now go be your awesome self with King Julian."

"Mallory?"

"Yeah?"

After gnawing on her top lip, Kelsey took a deep breath. "Why has it taken the king—my *father*—nine whole days to *want* to be alone with me?"

"Maybe you should ask him."

• • •

The king cleared his throat. "I have a present for you."

"Really? It's not my—" Kelsey stopped in the nick of time before saying "birthday." Did the king still think of that more as the death day of his beloved wife? It was a potential conversational black hole she wasn't brave enough to get near. "There's no need for presents. I'm staying in the most beautiful room I've ever seen, and clothes and jewelry keep showing up for me to wear. I've a feeling that's all your largesse."

Largesse? When had she ever used that word before? She sounded like a freaking Dickens character. Or—holy crap— were they actually managing to turn her into a person who sounded like a *princess*?

The king batted away her words like dandelion fuzz in the air. Which there might also be, as they were striding along a path of crushed shells bordered by tall wildflowers and a vast expanse of lush lawn that sloped downward to an orchard. "You need to be properly outfitted. No thanks are necessary for giving you what you deserve."

"I don't feel like I deserve any of it," Kelsey said. There was no point faking anything. This man, like it or not, was her father. She'd tell him the truth…and see where that got her. "Honestly. You may all have these expectations and dreams about what a grown-up Princess Valentina should be, but I'm nothing special."

Beneath the leather brim of his cap, his forehead creased. "Who told you that?"

"Nobody."

"Kelsey." He stilled her with a touch on her shoulder. Then he took her chin between his thumb and forefinger and tilted her head up. "Who told you such a bald-faced lie? I'll send a team of soldiers to cross America hunting them down to give them a royal ass-kicking the likes of which they've never endured."

Okay. That was sweet and hilarious. A giggle burst from her throat, and the king got some friendly crinkles around his blue eyes that made him look…normal. Approachable. Non-regal. "That's a generous offer, Your Majesty. But there's no high school bully that left me emotionally scarred. I'm just ordinary. Which I'm perfectly okay with, I promise."

He spun on the heel of his boot, looking over both shoulders. Then he looked up, and pointed at a man with a basket balanced on a stepstool against a shortish, bushy tree with fruit that looked like a yellow-ish cross between an apple and a pear. Geez. She even had to learn different *fruit* in this country? "Do you see that man?"

"Yes. Picking…?"

"Quinces. He's a gardener. No family. He plays soccer on a bar team, but by his own admission, isn't good at all. Remy shovels compost in the spring, harvests when needed. Does nothing a newspaper might call remarkable, and probably never will. Remy, however, is *not* ordinary. And neither are you."

That was quite the lowdown, especially from a man who was busy remembering international market conditions and heads of state and…well, whatnot. Kelsey cocked her head. "How do you know all that?"

"I talk to him. When I walk along here to the stables every day, when I walk through the orchards to clear my head."

"You talk to the gardeners?" Because her grandmother had turned all snitty when Kelsey mentioned chatting with Anya. Told her not to ever confuse "functionaries with friends."

"Of course. Not because they are my subjects, my responsibility, but because they are people, just like you and me. And everyone matters. Everyone is unique and has their own contribution to society, to friends, to life. Nobody is ordinary. Least of all you, Kelsey."

It was a very fatherly thing for him to say. A perfect segue, too. Because she'd never have the nerve to ask this question of *Julian IV, by the Grace of God Father of the People and King of Moncriano.*

But she'd damn well ask it of the man trying to be her father. "If you find time to chat to your staff, why has it taken you so long to talk to me?"

They kept walking. Kelsey heard the buzz of the bees in the waist-high pink and purple stalks of flowers, the trill of morning songbirds in the orchard on the left. A string of what she guessed to be curses from Remy who shook his hand and licked at it, clearly scratched in the battle with picking the quinces.

Rounding a curve, a gigantic L-shaped building she hadn't yet seen came into view. It matched the style of the palace with its white walls and rounded turrets at each corner, but it was only two stories. Abutting one side was a circle of hard-packed dirt, enclosed with a low, split-rail fence that brought to mind western ranches.

Finally, the king stopped at the end of the path where it met an asphalt drive for the building. He stared straight ahead at a tall, red-flowered bush that covered a corner of the wall. "When they told me you were alive, I was shocked. It embarrasses me to admit, but I'd given up hope. I left a standing order that the search for you never be discontinued, but in my heart, I assumed you were dead."

It didn't sting to hear him say it. Kelsey understood. Holding out hope for all those years would've been so painful. Giving up allowed him to move forward. "That was a safe, smart assumption."

"I couldn't...I didn't...I heard the words that you were alive. I saw you, talked to you in the throne room that first day. But I couldn't do anything more. I knew, *loved,* Valentina, a three-month-old baby who smiled at everyone and anyone who picked her up. That's where my mind was stuck."

Wait. He'd put off talking to her because...he hadn't known what to say? The exact thing Kelsey had been so worried about? Well, she certainly couldn't be mad at him for *that*.

"But last night, I figured out how to start. With this present." He waved an arm to encompass what she assumed to be stables, now that two horses had been led out into the fenced arena.

"I don't understand. What is it?"

"I'm giving you a horse." He pointed at the smaller of the two horses with a coat the same burnished red as Mallory's hair. Next to it was a giant black beast, snorting and stomping. "That one. Branko. He's light, fast, a strong jumper."

"What am I going to do with a horse?" Holy crap balls. That was rude, unforgivably so.

How, *why* had that been out loud? But, in Kelsey's mind, she still lived in a five-hundred-square-foot Manhattan walk-up. This two weeks in Moncriano was the super-bizarre vacation she'd never dreamed of. "I'm sorry. I mean, thank you, Your Majesty. It's just that I don't know how to ride."

"I presumed as much, which works to my advantage. You see, I'd always dreamed of going riding with my little girl. Teaching her. My parents did it with me, and some of my fondest memories are of continuing the tradition with Christian and Genevieve. You may be all grown up, but I can still have this experience, as a father, of teaching you."

Oh boy. That was a lot to drop on her. Like he'd make up for the missing twenty-five years between them by giving her a *pony*?

The hopeful, upraised eyebrows above those high, aristocratic cheekbones gave her the impression the king thought this would fix the empty gap of those missing years. That she'd fall in line and be the perfect princess daughter.

Except…

Maybe that was a leap to the wrong conclusion. An unfair one.

Maybe she was clinging too tightly to her loyalty for Ed Wishner. Maybe this was a knee-jerk reaction to an honest attempt at reconnecting. *Maybe* she ought to give the king the benefit of the doubt.

Just in case, though? She'd lay another nakedly honest truth on him. Because right now, Kelsey had a lot more to worry about the unfairness of what was happening to the parents who'd raised her, rather than the one who'd missed her.

"Your Majesty—"

He cut her off with a rather imperious swipe of his hand. "That's not right. Christian and Genevieve call me Papa. Would you? Or whatever American version you prefer?"

"Well, that's the thing. This all feels like...like an Indian-arranged marriage. Where the bride and groom have barely met before they speak their vows, and are expected to jump into the whole husband/wife/love forever thing in an instant. I don't think of you as 'Papa' yet. I don't know you."

Had that been too harsh?

Was there any way to sugarcoat *that* statement, though?

Frowning, the king said slowly, "I am your father, Kelsey."

"I realize that, but I don't *feel* it yet. You had a baby you loved, and held, and thought of for years. All I have is a stranger, in a literal strange land, asking me to call him Papa."

"There has to be a first step," he said. And this time, his voice sound much less dad-like and more regal; commanding. Insistent. "I made one, with this gift. It is your turn to make an effort."

Crap. Kelsey didn't want to piss him off. Or seem ungrateful. The king was making more of an effort, for example, than Genevieve. She needed to at least thank him, and not be such a stubborn jerk.

She put a hand on his arm. Squeezed once. "I appreciate the gesture. Truly. There's no such thing, though, as an insta-daughter."

The real problem suddenly geysered to the front of her brain. The worry that had poked at her subconscious nonstop, no matter how much she tried to ignore it for the simple fact of not being able to fix it. The sticking point that kept her from politely agreeing to his simple, rational request.

Love, loyalty, family... These were the foundation of her life. Kelsey might not understand all the royal layers of the House of Villani, but she absolutely believed they felt the same. Especially with their family lineage being unbroken for centuries. So, damn it, she had to make him see that it wasn't either/or. Black or white. There was no integration into the Villanis without also bringing the family she already loved into it as well.

She spread her feet wider, hands on hips. Braced for... well, whatever sort of reaction he might throw at her. Kelsey was certain she was about to cross a line with the king, but it was her own personal line in the sand.

"I can't connect with a new father when the one I know and love is in prison and not allowed to communicate with me."

He didn't immediately beckon the bodyguards trailing them up to drag her back to her room. Didn't even look the least little bit mad. If anything, King Julian looked... intrigued.

"I hadn't thought of that. My own fault, really. I'm used to advisors filling in the gaps. But I didn't ask anyone for advice on how to deal with *you*. It felt wrong. You're my daughter; therefore, I ought to instinctively know what to do."

Well, if he could admit he was wrong, Kelsey could throw him a bone. Why had she assumed everyone else was handling this belly-wallop of a life change better than she was?

"The last time you saw me, you only had to know if I was hungry or needed my diaper changed. We've both got a lot to learn about how to communicate with each other."

"That's quite gracious of you," he said with what *might* be the leading edge of a smile on his lips.

"I'm told that's the hallmark of being a royal," Kelsey sassed back. Hey, if he was going to play the dad card, he'd have to get used to *some* sass.

A deep, baritone rumble of a laugh rolled melodiously out. Huh. The king sounded like he might have one heck of a singing voice. "Sir Evan's been getting through to you, I see."

"He tries. I try. We both get frustrated." She rolled her eyes, grinning. "And then we break for lunch and do it all again."

"I also see that it pains you to think of the Wishners being held in custody. Moncriano is not the only interested party, however. Interpol is running the investigation. They're coordinating with several international agencies. At this point, my request alone would not be enough to get them released."

"Seriously?" Kelsey fought back the temptation to scuff the toe of her boot across the path in frustration. "What's the good of having an in with a *king* if not to get people you love out of jail? I'm not asking you to throw around your power like a Bond villain. I just want to talk to them."

"The good news is that I hear the investigation is almost over."

Hope *gushed* into her heart. "They're free to go?"

The king spread his hands wide, palms up. "I'm sorry, Kelsey. I honestly couldn't say. What I can tell you is that so far, as far-fetched as it is, the official inclination is to believe their version of events."

"What does that mean?" Because it sure didn't sound like an "all-clear, come on over to the palace and visit your daughter any 'ol time" statement from her new dad to her other dad...

"It means that the persons who physically took you from us were not the Wishners. What happened after that, and their choices that led to you being raised as their daughter... well, I leave that story for them to share with you."

"So I can talk to them?"

"I will make the request. That is all I can promise." He

paused, and then continued. "They have been treated better than most suspicious persons. The House of Villani made it clear they were to be accorded additional courtesies and accommodations. Whatever else they did, the Wishners loved you and fed you and treated you like a daughter. They raised you to be a woman whom I am honored to welcome back into our family."

He made it sound as though they would've been subjected to waterboarding had he not stepped in.

For all Kelsey knew, that was indeed the case. Talk about an act of graciousness. *She* knew her parents weren't kidnappers. But King Julian didn't. To put his bitterness and suspicion aside out of sheer gratitude for them keeping her safe all this time?

Well, that got to her more than any of Sir Evan's lectures about the meaning of royalty. That was *grace*. It made her want to be that kind, that understanding, less judgmental. More...noble.

More like her father.

"Thank you." She gave him a hug, the one for which she'd ached at the emptiness at not receiving when they first met. Maybe the king wasn't a hugger, but that'd be another thing they'd have to compromise on, then.

After a moment, he surprised her by not just relaxing into it. King Julian bent down to tuck his head next to hers, and wrapped his arms tight around her in a rib-cracking, breath-stealing hug.

"Would you like to say hello to Branko? You don't have to ride him, but he was told he'd be visited by a pretty woman who'd bring him a treat." The king pulled a baggie of baby carrots from his jacket pocket and shook it in front of her.

"It'd be rude to stand him up," Kelsey said.

As they approached the wooden fence, the king spoke again. "Your mother's grandparents were from Romania.

She called her father Tata, in their language. Would that be an acceptable compromise for you to use, just between us? As you get used to me?"

"I like that." The connection to the mother she'd never known made it special. A way to honor her memory, too.

"I wouldn't suggest calling the grand duchess by anything but her title. Until she says otherwise," Julian warned in a low voice.

"Does she scare you, too?"

"She's my mother-in-law. Of course she does."

It was a start. A good start. Either to staying, or...

To building a bridge that would sustain them once she went home. For good.

Chapter Sixteen

Elias didn't get choked up at sad movies. After all, he was a soldier, a defender of his country. But right now? Standing next to Mallory on a square of grass that made a checkerboard pattern alternating with the paving stones in the sunny courtyard? He might actually lose it.

Because his father was talking to Kelsey.

His father, who'd been *buried* under guilt at losing her for decades. Who'd sloughed off all self-respect and trust.

Even though the royal family never blamed him, Albert saw himself as *wholly* to blame. The man had raised him with a single-minded purpose—that Elias's service to the House of Villani might, eventually, atone in a tiny way for the loss of their daughter. That Elias could atone for Albert's biggest mistake. Neither of them, however, had believed that Elias would not just atone, but *fix* it.

This was a moment neither of them thought they'd ever see.

"You need a tissue?" Mallory pulled her sunglasses down her nose to look over their rims at him. "Or is one only allowed to use crisply ironed handkerchiefs inside the walls of the palace?"

"Is sarcasm a gift for all Americans, or just you and your sister?"

"I'd say it's in our DNA...but that'd lead us back full circle to this moment we're trying to ignore so we don't bawl." Looking at Kelsey and Albert seated on a curved bench backed by tall, spiky purple flowers, she said, "Your dad's a sweetie."

That coughed the emotion stuck in his throat right out like a hairball. "Hardly. You know, he's still an active member of the Royal Protection Service."

"Who does he guard?"

"He's on rotation for Duchess Mathilde and a few countesses, people who have a slower schedule. He stays mostly on indoor duty."

Mallory's neck cracked, it whipped around so fast. "I'm surprised he's still a bodyguard. I'm not trying to throw shade, but you let a princess go missing, seems like your job security should be shaky, at best."

"The king himself insisted he not resign, as did the queen. They said that if they, as parents, weren't to blame for losing her, then neither was he."

"I'm dying of curiosity how he's going to tell her."

Elias had told Mallory why he wanted, *needed* his father to meet Kelsey. That way she could engineer them having "private sister time" so that no courtiers would overhear his father's apology. If she ended up going back to New York, this could be the only chance to give his father closure. "I don't know, actually."

"Can we get closer?" Without waiting, she inched along the brick borders of the flowerbeds until they stood, barely hidden, by an archway.

"So you knew my mother," Kelsey said.

"My wife, Alora, was a lady-in-waiting to the queen, a trusted and beloved confidante. They were pregnant at the same time. That's how Elias and Christian became so close—they were together from the cradle. Nothing kept those two apart." A smile ghosted at the edges of his father's mouth.

Kelsey gave him an encouraging grin. "I imagine they got into quite a bit of trouble."

"Trouble..." Albert's face clouded over. "Your Highness, thank you for allowing me to see you."

Damn it. Apparently, the polite chitchat was over just that fast. His dad was determined to martyr himself at Kelsey's feet. Even though Elias had sworn up one side and down the other that it wasn't necessary.

"Of course. Elias has met my family." She leaned closer, one hand splayed across the neckline of her pale-pink sundress. "He knows them far better than I do, as a matter of fact. It's only fair I should meet his."

"No, this isn't what you think. I'm here to apologize. I'm so sorry." Albert slipped to his knees, head drooping. "So very sorry, Your Highness, for I'm the one who was guarding you when you were kidnapped."

Kelsey's entire body jerked, as though she'd been pushed, but her voice was remarkably steady when she said, "Oh. Elias never mentioned that."

"I'm sure he thought you'd never speak to him again if you knew." Albert sounded broken. Old.

Elias wondered if forcing this meeting had been a mistake, after all. Seeing his father slumped in sadness tore at his heart.

"Nonsense." She grasped his forearms and pulled him back up to the bench. "Mr. Trebanti, it wasn't your fault. I'm guessing if someone paid you to look the other way while they scooped me up, you wouldn't still be in the palace. Do you want to tell me what really happened?"

Elias put a hand on the sun-warmed stone. He hadn't ever heard his father tell the tale. Only the official and media versions. And he felt a measure of comfort when Mallory curled her fingers around his.

"The royal family was on holiday in Kenya. No official engagements, so protection was lighter than on some foreign trips. No crowd control necessary, just standard rotations." Albert told it in a rhythmic cadence, as though he'd said the same words, in the same order, hundreds of times. "But the staff at the resort were all natives. One of them must've drugged my drink, just like they did to the nanny. It was an odd mixture of local juices—the taste was so off, I thought the fruit had turned. I threw it into a planter after a few sips."

Kelsey cupped her hand around the side of her mouth, as if about to divulge a deep secret. "I once spit out a walleye cheek and hid it in a centerpiece. Some things can't be swallowed."

There was her innate kindness shining through. That gigantic heart that astonished him constantly.

"When I didn't pass out fast enough, they hit me with a poisoned dart gun. That did the trick." Absently, he tapped at a spot just below his ear. "I was in a coma for three days. When I woke up, you were gone. Everything was different. I'm so ashamed."

"It doesn't sound as if you did anything wrong. It sounds as if you almost died trying to protect me. There's no apology necessary."

"I don't deserve your forgiveness."

"For what—the wonderful life I led? Because that's what I had with the Wishners. I grew up on the edge of a beautiful lake, surrounded by people who loved me. An average American childhood. Thoroughly wonderful in its ordinariness. I wouldn't give up a day of it." She kissed him on the cheek. "Thank you for telling me. I see where your son gets his bravery."

The doors to the courtyard slammed back against the wall. Sir Evan threw his arms wide open. "*There* you are."

Mallory hurried forward, sandals clacking against the stone path. "Yes, right where I told you we'd be. Imagine that."

After sniffing at her—it was his signature move that no one in the palace escaped aside from the king and the grand duchess—Sir Evan gave a micro-bow to Kelsey. "Your Highness, you're meeting with your grandmother in half an hour."

She tilted her face up to the cloudless June sky. "Which gives me twenty-five more minutes of soaking up the sun."

"You can't meet her in that. Your arms are exposed. Your"—he circled his hand at the top of his chest—"is exposed. One must dress appropriately to meet with the grand duchess."

Kelsey glared at Sir Evan. "I'm sorry, Mr. Trebanti. Apparently, I've been sitting here chatting with you *practically naked*." Elias's father snickered. "But I'm looking forward to hearing more stories about your wife and my mother." She locked arms with Mallory and swept inside the palace.

Naturally, Sir Evan managed to slam the doors behind him. His attitude was louder than that purple and black brocade vest he wore. "He's puffed himself up since being appointed as the princess's secretary," Elias commented dryly as he approached the bench. "Amazing how he speaks English perfectly until it comes to parts of the female anatomy."

Switching back to their native tongue, Albert asked, "Elias, do you have a few more minutes?"

"My shift is over, but we shouldn't hang about in the South Courtyard." He nodded at the steps that led out and up to the path to the rose gardens. "Do you feel better, Papa?"

Albert gave a light swat to the back of Elias's head. "Do you just want to be told that you were right?"

"No." Ha! His father would see right through that. "Perhaps. A *little*."

Elias didn't need to be right. He needed to know that the meeting had, indeed, given Albert peace.

"I'm grateful you introduced me to the princess. Being able to tender my apology to her personally was, indeed, satisfying."

"Good."

At the landing he paused under a hanging pot overflowing with pink and purple fuchsia, and turned to face Elias. "But you must break it off with her. Today. I *beg* you. If you're discovered, it'd be the end. For both of us. Not just the loss of both of our jobs, but also the loss of my pension. We'd be ruined. The Trebantis can't live down a second family disgrace."

Damn it, Elias *knew* all of that.

He knew the cost. The danger of being dismissed from the RPS. Of losing his lifelong friendship with Christian. Of him and his father being left with nothing. His father was close to retirement. And who'd hire a bodyguard that the royal family fired? Not to mention that the humiliation would no doubt break his father. Who would, undoubtedly, never forgive him. So he'd lose all that was left of his own family along with losing the brotherly bond with Christian.

All of this disaster would be his own fault.

But no matter how much he cared for Kelsey, it would be over soon enough. Her position, the revelation to the world of her existence, would make sure of it. As would her return to America, if she chose that instead. So he'd damn well indulge in these last few days possible with her.

She was worth the risk. Worth *everything*. In fact, Kelsey was quickly *becoming* everything to him.

So either way, his entire world was about to crash down around him.

The temptation to yank down that damned pot and hurl it across the courtyard with all his strength was...*immense.* "I'm happy, Papa. Can't you see that?"

"I do. And it does not matter."

"Of course not." Elias didn't bother to hide the bitterness in his voice. The prioritization of loyalty had been drummed into him for a lifetime. "Because you always put the royal family first, even ahead of your own son." He should stop there. But frustration, *no,* anger at his inevitable loss of Kelsey forced out the question he'd never once let slip. "Why must *they* always be more important than us, every second of every day?"

"Because the Villanis are the very heart and soul of this country. What's best for them, what keeps them safe and happy, trickles down to the rest of us. The royal family parents us all—the entire kingdom." He curled one hand around the skinny wrought-iron railing. The other he clawed painfully hard around Elias's wrist. "See that you don't let your parents down—the king...or me."

• • •

Kelsey glanced out the diamond-shaped window of the staircase. The velvety violet of dusk clung to the mountaintops. That made it...almost lunchtime back home? She reached for Mallory's hand as they took the final few steps. "Do you think they're still in New York, or back in Michigan by now?"

"Mom and Dad? I don't know. With all this talk of Interpol, maybe they even flew them to D.C. to be questioned more?"

"At least we'll finally get some answers." She hurried soundlessly down the cream-and-gold curlicued pattern on the carpet. Carpet that was identical to several other hallways, but Kelsey didn't think she'd seen this one before. "Marko, where are you taking us to do this phone call?"

"Your office, Your Highness."

Her *what* now? "Since when do I have an office? Why do I have an office?"

"All the senior royals living in the palace have one."

Oh, FFS! "I don't live in the palace." Not yet. Maybe not ever. "I'm just visiting." Why did nobody but Mallory believe her? Did they think she'd get tired of repeating herself and just stay?

Marko halted. "Your Highness, you are a blood princess, third in line to the throne of Moncriano. No matter where you may be in the world, you will always have a home, a bedroom, and yes, an office here in Alcarsa Palace."

"So there!" Mallory stuck out her tongue. "Guess he put you in your highly elevated place."

"As for why you need one, I'd suggest this call with the Wishners is a perfect example. They are on hold. All you need do is pick up."

"On hold?" No. Oh no. "How long have they been waiting?"

"The rest of the world—aside from your family—waits for you. Never the other way around."

Her clever bodyguard had circled the question without answering it. "But they *are* my fam—" Kelsey broke off, realizing arguing with Marko would be a waste of time she didn't have. "Never mind. But pick up the pace."

She and Mallory began running. Sure, their dad had been late to a lot of activities due to medical emergencies. If anything, it made him that much more hypervigilant about punctuality. Waiting for God knows how long would've ticked him off...*royally.* Ha.

Marko indicated an already open door, and they dashed

in. Lunging at the dainty desk, Kelsey stabbed at the speakerphone button. "I'm so sorry we're late!"

"We're so sorry about…everything," replied her dad in a low, humbled tone.

What was it with people today? First Elias's dad rocked the martyrdom, and now her own. Both of which made no sense whatsoever.

She was shutting that down *now*. Kelsey circled the desk and plopped into the high-backed, white upholstered chair.

"Sorry for what? For loving me? Spoiling me? Paying for braces and the trendy sneakers I had to have? No, Dad, I don't want an apology from either of you, and I won't accept one."

In the deafening silence that ensued, Mallory wiggled onto the corner of the desk. Kelsey promptly shooed her off. The desk—like everything else in her rooms in the palace—looked old and dainty and all kinds of fragile. Its white curved legs and undoubtedly real gold trim along every edge and cutout did not look capable of handling a modern American ass.

Pulling up a fringed footstool, Mallory finally said, "Hi, guys. Is Mom there, too?"

"Oh, sweetheart, yes, I'm here, and it's good to hear your voice. I'm so glad you two are together."

"That's the only way the Wishner sisters roll."

"Are they treating you well?" their mom asked hesitantly.

"Like royalty," Mallory deadpanned. It broke the tension. They all laughed. Probably a little too long and a bit too heartily for the level of the joke, but it felt good.

Kelsey didn't want to waste this precious call on chitchat, though. "The bigger question is, are *you* okay? Are you still being held? How much trouble are you in?"

"Don't worry about us." Ed sounded resolute and reassuring—his standard doctor voice. "We always knew this day might come. I think we'll be released any day now. Everyone finally believes we didn't do it."

"What *did* you do? Exactly?"

"We were medical missionaries. We were going to save the world. But we decided to save you, instead." Cybill said it with pride.

While grateful for her life with them, it set off alarm bells to Kelsey that they'd "saved" her. From what?

Mallory shot her an equally worried look. "Um, that sounds ominous. A baby princess doesn't need saving. The setup here's pretty sweet."

"We were in a makeshift clinic in Ethiopia. Long days, treating so many people who'd never had any medical care. It was exhausting and invigorating and we thought we'd found our calling. We'd left Mallory at home with your grandparents, and were thinking of sending for her so we could stay indefinitely."

This was nuts. Their parents had never mentioned being missionaries. They never went anywhere, never took vacations, and basically worked to convince their girls that the big, bad world was far too dangerous to ever be explored.

Ed took up the telling. "We went into the bush one day, and when we came back to our tent, there you were on our bed. Swaddled up, sleeping. There was a note pinned to your blanket. It said, 'We know who you are. We'll be watching you. Take good care of the baby. Tell no one, or you all die.'"

Mallory circled her hands, as if trying to pull details out. "That's it? No signature? No explanation?"

She'd wanted answers. Instead, her parents only provided more questions. Too frustrated to sit still, Kelsey got up to pace around the Oriental rug in shades of pink and lilac in the middle of the floor. "Someone threatened you into keeping me safe? What kind of weird villain does that? Why kidnap me and not ask for ransom, but just give me away?"

Ed gave a long, deep sigh. "As we've said to multiple police agencies, we don't know. The best guess is that at least two people kidnapped you. One of them had second thoughts. Giving you back would've meant getting caught, so they gave you to us."

They made it sound so black and white. Kelsey did not find it so. Who just keeps a random baby that shows up like a pillow mint? "Why didn't you tell the police?"

"We couldn't. It said they'd be watching. And were they just watching us, or Mallory back home, too? Our only choice was to obey the note, which wasn't a hardship. This mission was going to be our last chance to make a difference, or so we thought. Mal was unplanned—it seemed fitting that our second baby was, too."

Mallory plucked a letter opener topped with the shape of a gold peacock and tapped it against the blotter. "How do you smuggle a baby out of a country? And into America?"

"Well, this was before nine-eleven. Security was more lax. We told the head of the mission that your mom had a medical emergency and had to return to the states ASAP. He agreed to help."

Kelsey wanted to jump through the phone and shake her dad into spilling everything twice as fast. Through gritted teeth, she asked, "Help you do what?"

"Get out. The whole trip was a NGO, and the family who headed it was very wealthy. When they heard your mom needed immediate surgery, they sent their private plane to take us home. At the airport, we claimed you'd been born in the bush, and that's why you weren't on our passports. It was simple, really."

"We stayed with your grandparents in Vermont for a few weeks," Cybill added. "Told them we'd adopted you in Africa when both your parents died on safari."

"Really? They believed something so...movie of the

week-ish?"

"They were delighted with their new grandbaby. Meanwhile, we found the clinic in Michigan where we could start fresh. Where nobody knew us, and they'd believe that you and Mallory were our children."

Mallory snagged the hem of Kelsey's skirt on her fourth circuit of the run, pulling her back to the desk. "But what about the news? A royal baby was kidnapped. That was probably the lead story, every day, for quite some time. You never wondered if that explained the baby that appeared in your tent?"

There was another long silence. Dad liked his word to be accepted, no questions asked.

"From what we've been told, you were kidnapped two weeks before being left with us. We didn't see any news while working at the clinic—the generator was only for use treating patients. Once we were back home, we were a bit frazzled dealing with a new baby and making sure Mallory adjusted to instantly becoming a sister. Since she was only thirteen months older, her capacity to understand being forced to share us, and everything else, was pushed to the limit."

Kelsey shoved at her sister, grinning. They'd heard plenty of stories over the years about Mal throwing tantrums for six months straight before accepting Kelsey as a permanent fixture in her life.

"The only truly illegal thing we did was make a fake birth certificate. Your dad went into his old hospital and fudged the records so we could get one for you. We've been upfront about that."

It explained so much. Why they never traveled. Why they didn't want their daughters to move anywhere, let alone to Manhattan.

"No one ever contacted you again?"

"No, but we never stopped worrying." More voices

blurred in the background. "Oh, we have to go, girls. We love you!"

The line went dead. Mallory shook her head. "That fixed...nothing."

"Nope." Kelsey had never believed for a moment that her parents had engineered the kidnapping. She hadn't needed that reassurance. Some great big "aha" explanation would've been nice, though. "But it felt good to talk to them. Really good."

"It did. Will you thank King Julian for me for making it happen?"

"Absolutely." And how odd was that? Her dad pulling strings so she could talk to her other dad? Odd and complicated and it left her unsettled, feeling vaguely disloyal to *both* sets of parents. Was that how the rest of her life would feel—no matter which country she called home? Would she have to choose between them to find any peace?

Wouldn't that choice be selfish? Horribly hurtful to one branch of family? With everyone purporting to love her, why was she so miserable?

Her temples began to throb. Her jaw clenched. Kelsey wanted to pull at her hair and kick something. The pressure being put on her was too much, the decision too impossible. And yet option three that had come to her four nights ago— running away and starting a *third* life where nobody could find her—was dumb. A lose/lose scenario.

But there wasn't a scenario where she got to return to the life she'd always envisioned. So it felt like she'd already lost...

A short rap at the door barely preceded it opening and Duchess Mathilde entering. "Do you like it?"

Mallory popped upright and then dropped into a curtsey. "Your Grace."

The interruption was timely. "Do I like what?" Kelsey asked.

"Your office? I chose the color scheme, worked with the designers. Feminine but not fussy."

"Oh. I had no idea. Thank you." Kelsey turned in a half circle, really taking in the furnishings. The walls were painted a pale green, with white moldings. There was a sage-green chaise lounge, a matching chair and footstool, and built-in bookcases with a sleek TV screen flanked by ornate music boxes. "It's lovely."

"I want you to feel comfortable at home. Which is why I'm here." She put a hand on Mallory's shoulder as she joined them. "Do sit back down, dear. I'm not one for fuss and formality."

"Thank you, Your Grace." Mallory smiled...but of course remained standing.

Mathilde handed Kelsey a jewelry box. "This was your mother's. She had it commissioned once you were born. Your birthstone, peridot. She adored it, and planned to hand it down to you on your eighteenth birthday, after years of 'wearing the love into it.' I thought it might give you some comfort, make you feel closer to her."

"That's so thoughtful." All she could get out were these inane pleasantries. Kelsey's head was still whirling from finally hearing for herself that her parents were all right. Learning that Mathilde had put in the personal effort to redecorate for her, and now this sentimental gift, set her heart to bursting.

She popped open the white velvet box. Inside lay a large teardrop peridot, dangling beneath a trio of tiny diamonds and then two more round stones. Three sets of small gold leaves, also diamond studded, crawled up each side of the delicate gold chain, before ending at another pair of round peridots.

Realizing it had last touched her mother's skin shook her to the core.

Cued in as always to her emotions, Mallory lifted it out

of the box and fastened it for Kelsey. She led her over to a gilt mirror on the sidewall. "Look at how pretty it is."

"I guess the queen had great taste." She trailed her fingers along the stone, then closed her eyes to just feel her heart beat against it. Aside from her time in the tower room, it was the closest she'd felt to her unknown mother.

Kelsey whirled around and hugged Mathilde. "Thank you so much. For remembering this, for understanding I needed something tangible to connect to her."

"I loved your mother dearly. She wasn't just my sister-in-law, but my best friend. I want to do right by her. To make sure that you feel and know Serena's love for you. How happy she would be to see you reunited with your family. Back where you belong." The older woman pressed a kiss to Kelsey's cheek, waved at Mallory, and hurried out of the room, dabbing at her eyes.

Kelsey dragged through a slow circle in the center of the carpet. She looked down at the intricate pattern—and then back up at her sister. In a voice on the edge of breaking, she asked, "Where *do* I belong...that's the question, isn't it?"

"You're running out of time to come up with the answer. Did talking to Mom and Dad make it harder?"

"Yes." She stroked a hand down the necklace, staring at it in the mirror. Tears filled her eyes, choked her throat. The necklace was her mother's legacy to her, but Kelsey herself was Serena's legacy to the *country*. How could she turn her back on that? How could she risk hurting the people who'd abandoned *their* dreams to raise her by turning her back on them? "Everything that happens every day makes it harder."

From behind, Mallory wrapped her arms around Kelsey's waist, propping her chin on her shoulder. "Even Elias."

"Yes." Even. Especially. He was the wild card that made it harder to think. He clouded her brain, stole her attention, and Kelsey could barely suck in a breath when she thought about leaving him. "Do you know what today is?"

"Something awesome like National Hot Fudge Day?"

"It's Wednesday."

Mallory's reddish-brown eyebrows drew together. "So?"

"It's the day we had matinee tickets to our first Broadway show. We're missing it."

"Are you saying missing the show makes it hard? Because it sounds like you now have the money to *more* than cover the very expensive tickets. And I'll bet there's a big fancy theatre within spitting distance here."

Kelsey turned around, frustrated beyond belief. "It's one more damn thing, Mal. One more concrete example of what I'll miss, what I am missing, if I stay. One more dream that isn't coming true."

Slowly, Mallory moved her arm in a circle to encompass the pretty office. "Not all dreams come true. But some would call this life of yours a dream. Being stubborn about a million little things can't be how you make a choice this big."

"I know. I'm just annoyed and venting."

"I wish I could help you. You know I do love to tell you what to do. But I can't this time. I can't even share my opinion. This decision has to be wholly your own."

Crap. "I wonder if they sell Magic 8 balls in Moncriano…"

Chapter Seventeen

Elias knew his three-person team was unobtrusively providing protection for the princess. On top of that, Kelsey's true identity was still on lockdown. And her strong resemblance to Princess Genevieve was obscured by a long red wig, enormous sunglasses, and an oversized floppy sun hat. That didn't stop him from scanning the evening crowd as they walked along the river. Vigilance was second nature to him.

Until he scanned down to the river, where they were reflected in the glassy water. Then his instincts as a bodyguard took second place to his instincts as a boyfriend. "I don't like the outfit Mallory picked for you to wear tonight."

"Why not?" Kelsey shrugged, which sent the off-the-shoulder ruffled blue top sliding even farther south of her collarbone. "I don't look at all like a princess, right?"

"No, you most certainly do not," he growled. Micro-white shorts exposed miles of leg down to high-wedged sandals with little leather flowers. She looked sexy. Edible. Tempting.

When what she *ought* to radiate was a "don't touch me"

vibe. Unapproachable. *Don't even have a passing thought because my boyfriend who has been trained in sixteen ways to kill a man with just his hands will get jealous…*

"That works, since I still don't feel like a princess." Kelsey stage-whispered the last word, cupping her hand around her mouth and not quite hiding a grin. Which just made her even more adorable.

But maybe he could turn this into a useful conversation. Part of tonight's planned lesson. Casually, he asked, "What's a princess supposed to feel like?"

She gripped the old-fashioned, wrought iron light pole with both hands. It was topped with a glass lantern and a black crown that matched—in miniature—the official state crown used in coronations. "Wise. Caring. Just. Patient. Kind. An extension of your people."

"You're describing a saint." It was hilarious, how far from the truth it was. The public might put them up on a pedestal, but Elias knew all too well that the Villanis were merely people. Ones with problems and heartache and worries like everyone else in the kingdom. "I can't speak for your sister, but I know your brother wishes he had far more of those traits. Especially when he loses to me at darts. The only one he thinks he's nailed is caring."

"Well, he's not king yet," she said.

"I doubt the king feels all those things, either. The royals try. They work at it. Their commitment to caring is the key. And you're a natural at that."

Planting one foot on the base of the pole, she spun around it in a wide circle. "I don't know who I'm supposed to care for. Or about. I only know Americans. Their grit and independence. A streak of 'we can do anything' a mile wide."

He caught her by the waist and lifted her high overhead, continuing to turn as she laughed in joy. Didn't even worry about what the rest of the detail would think. Their convenient cover tonight was to "pretend" to be on a date.

Marko's idea. For which Elias owed him a very nice bottle of vodka.

Elias set her down. Then he pulled the hat a little lower over her face. "That's part of the reason behind tonight's excursion. You've been sheltered in the palace. No wonder you haven't connected to the citizens of this country."

"I never thought I'd want *out* of a palace, but I'm thrilled to be in a noisy crowd, on the street, sucking down scooter fumes." Kelsey tipped her head back, holding her floppy brim with her fingers, and inhaled deeply.

Okay, that was weird, but still adorable, which just showed how completely *gone* over her he was. And ignoring his feelings for the princess was like trying to ignore gravity. It was simply there, whether you acknowledged it or not. Still, he was pissed at his lack of self-control at falling for Kelsey in the first place.

So his response came out terse. "We call them motorbikes."

"Potato, potah*toe*. They're painted in sherbet pastels. Pale green, pink, peach. No self-respecting motorcycle would put down its kickstand next to one of them."

Amused again, he asked, "Would you prefer it black and painted with flames? Or skulls?"

"I mean, *I* wouldn't be brave enough to ride it. But it would be bad-ass. Very fun to watch."

"Well, I brought you here to watch something else." Elias led her up the slope of the double-story stone bridge. The height at its apex gave a perfect view of the town square in front of the towering pink cathedral.

Kelsey did a double take as the wall of sound hit them from the enormous crowd. "Wow, there are a ton of people down there."

"Indeed. Do you see they brought picnics, children?"

"Is it a festival?"

"Ha. Of a sort. See those people on the steps of the cathedral? They're here to talk about what happens if Moncriano joins the European Union."

"A debate?"

Her American-ness was showing. Elias firmly believed they had a better system. "No. A debate turns into an argument, or worse, a shouting match."

Kelsey shrugged. "That's politics."

"Where you used to live, definitely. Tonight?" He pointed. "There are five main speakers. Each gets equal time to speak their piece. Then anyone else can stand up and share their own views. No interruptions."

Her jaw dropped. "Seriously? Hundreds of people are giving up a beautiful summer evening to listen to fervent *monologues* that either pro or con joining the European Union?"

"Not just here. It's happening every night this week in the six biggest cities in Moncriano. The crowds will be just as big at every location."

"If I saw it in a movie, I wouldn't believe it." Kelsey tapped her temples and then exploded out her fingers. "You're blowing my mind a little right now."

"Good. I thought it'd make an impression on you." It was satisfying to hear the awe in her voice, see the spark in her eyes. For his people. For *their* people.

She laid a hand on his crisp white shirt. Worry knitted her brows together. "Will it stay peaceful?"

"If history is any measure, then yes. These people aren't grumpy at doing their duty. They're making a night of it, listening to all sides, all opinions offered, because they want to do what's best for Moncriano."

Was he coming on too strong? Elias didn't have the luxury of taking baby steps. Kelsey's two-week deadline was almost up.

Christian had asked him to show Kelsey *why* she should stay. This gathering wasn't the waterfalls at Mount Llubejc, or a concert in the high meadows. Those things were merely pretty wrapping.

What she watched now was the beating heart of the kingdom.

Elias hoped it was enough.

"Everyone's wearing blue and white. Everyone." With a laugh, Kelsey plucked at her top. "Even me, accidentally."

"They are the colors of our flag."

Her hands flew to cover her mouth. "Oh. I didn't know. That's silly, isn't it? It feels like a basic, like the Pledge of Allegiance...which I don't even know if you have something similar here. I'm failing at Princess one-oh-one."

Elias slapped the wide stone railing with his palm. No wonder she hadn't realized. Everything in Alcarsa Palace was the purple of the royal standard. How could he make her understand a lifetime of devotion to the realm, when she didn't know as much as a child entering primary school?

He picked her up and sat her on the railing. Now only the few pedestrians passing them on the bridge could see her face. Elias couldn't resist the instinct to minimize the admittedly slim risk. "You aren't failing. If anything, we're all failing you. Jamming centuries-old history down your throat. Telling you how to address servants and soldiers. None of that matters until you know the *people*."

"You mean the ones I'm not allowed to interact with at all?" she said drily. Because it had been a battle to even get Kelsey out of the palace tonight. The prime minister herself had tried to stop it once she caught wind of the plan.

Elias wasn't sure if it was out of concern for the princess's safety, or more because Skeggit's self-importance insisted that she be on the dais when Kelsey was revealed to the world. He'd been forced to go to Christian to get permission to spring her.

If anything happened to the princess, it would be on him.

"I'm sorry. You've no idea how much negotiation it took to give you this glimpse."

"I'm sorry for being snippy." Kelsey craned around to look down at the river. "This is beautiful. The old buildings, with such bright shutters and trim in all the colors of the rainbow. The cobblestones underfoot. It's like I stepped into the pages of a fairy tale. Something I never aspired to, trust me, but I love it."

"Good."

She twisted back to stare at the crowd, still growing even as the first speaker had begun. "They care so much," she murmured.

"National pride is strong here. Love of country and love of the royal family go hand in hand; for to us, they're one and the same. I wanted you to see it now, when you aren't being treated as royalty. So that you'd know their passion has nothing to do with protocol."

"Thank you for bringing me." Kelsey flattened her palm over her heart. "I feel it. Truly. For the first time."

Good, because it wasn't safe to linger out here with her. Now they could move on to the part of the evening that wasn't about Moncrinao and monarchs. It was solely for the two of them.

Elias lifted her down. "I think you'll like the next view even more. Someplace where you can watch people like you wanted to in New York."

"People watch," she corrected with a shake of her finger. "You got it backward."

Please. He didn't feel at all bad about one tiny stumble in all the time they'd spent together. "Once you start talking to me in *my* language, then you can pick at my idioms."

"That could take forever. I've never learned a language before." Kelsey pulled her sunglasses down her nose to look up at him sideways from beneath fluttery lashes. "Maybe twenty-five is too old to start?"

"Nice try. But we both know you're smarter than that." Off the bridge, he led her down the hill that led to the sea.

She spun in a circle, arms raised. "How about it's difficult because of *all* the other new information I'm simultaneously trying to learn?"

"More believable. Enough that I won't hassle you about it tonight, anyway."

"Wherever you're taking me, thank you in advance for the people watching." Kelsey lifted the brim of her hat with both hands. "You really listen to me, don't you?"

Those violet eyes bored straight into his heart and soul. Kelsey saw through to the real Elias. Not the son reclaiming his father's honor. Not the cloak of duty he wore like armor. Of course he listened to her. Soaked her up like a sponge, was more like it.

"It is my *sincere* pleasure to do so, Your Highness."

. . .

Energy pulsed through Kelsey's body.

All her senses were heightened. The sea breeze coming into the cave grotto whispered over her skin like a caress. Laughter and chatter and clinking china created a busy music for her ears. Garlic, tomatoes, and meat mingled in a rich scent that set her stomach rumbling.

It could be the eye-poppingly romantic location of a restaurant in a cave halfway down a cliff over the ocean. It could be the freedom of finally being outside palace walls for the first time since leaving the airport. It could be the residual adrenaline of feeling the passion of *her* people.

But Kelsey knew those were all merely adjacent to the real reason.

Elias.

His thoughtfulness. His strength. His tenderness. The dry humor that was all the more enjoyable because it was so unexpected, with the serious mask he so often wore. His unwavering commitment to his king, country, and to her.

That was just about the sexiest thing *ever*.

It was impossible to decide about assuming her role in the royal family, staying in Moncriano, without now factoring in Elias. Because the thought of not seeing him again after next week...well, she couldn't picture it. Which was crazy. But with him on bodyguard duty, they'd spent practically all day, every day together, and now several nights. They'd probably spent more time together than most couples who'd been dating for a month.

She wanted him. It was that basic. Like breathing.

And she simply couldn't wait.

Kelsey pulled down the wine menu he'd been studying. "You said they store all their wine in another cave?"

"Yes. It keeps it naturally chilled."

"I've never seen a wine cave. Do you think we could look at it—select our wine amongst the bottles?"

His dark eyebrows shot up his forehead. "Are you finally calling in a princess perk? Asking for special treatment?"

"Perhaps." This was risky, stupid. But damn it, she might not have many moments left with Elias. So she was seizing this one. Kelsey leaned across the table, voice low. "Or perhaps it's just that I'd like to give *you* some special treatment."

A vein popped along his neck as his jaw tightened. "You can't mean what I think you do."

Kelsey removed her hat. Then she fluffed out her fun red hair, toying with the end of one very long strand that brushed the top of her breast. "Hmmm. Maybe it's a language barrier thing. The only way to know for sure is to take me to the wine cave."

Elias spoke into the microphone on his watch, presumably giving a heads-up to the team. The whole time his eyes stayed locked on hers. "Stay here," he ordered. Then he almost jumped out of his seat and stalked over to the maître d's podium.

She looked down at the rest of the restaurant. The sound of the surf made background music unnecessary. Small lanterns hung over each table. Their flickering glow illuminated jewelry on almost every female patron that shocked Kelsey with its sparkle. It made her realize that these people were *very* wealthy. This restaurant, undoubtedly, very exclusive.

Kelsey didn't belong here. And yet, this was the world they expected her to inhabit, that she was told was her birthright.

Yes, the people watching was tremendous, but she'd expected to do it while eating a dollar slice of pizza, with the faint skittering of mice in the walls rather than crashing waves against the rocks. How was she supposed to fit in? Feel like anything more than an observer? An outsider?

There was every chance her jewelry drawer in the palace had diamond earrings and emerald necklaces as nice or finer than the ones she saw below. But if she'd been wearing one right now, it wouldn't make a difference. She still wouldn't *deserve* to be here. Deserve to mingle with the glitterati of freaking Europe.

Her mind wouldn't stop circling back to the absurdity of the situation being reversed—of people, once they knew she was royal, coming here to watch *her.*

The people in the square, having picnics while they listened to politicians. Those people she could imagine fitting in with. Ordinary people. Kelsey was just a girl from Michigan whose only claim to fame was admittedly mad graphic-design skills. That was the only way she'd ever pigeonholed herself.

Now that label had been ripped away from her.

So who was she? Really?

The more time she spent in the palace only made her feel more like an imposter. Yes, she was starting to feel ties to her family. As a daughter, sister, niece, yes. A princess, though? One whom an entire realm looked up to?

Not at all.

What would her family say if she let down the country? If, once the citizens got to know her, or even found out she was American, they called her out for not being good enough? Not royal enough?

Damn it, her one-track brain was spoiling this special night. Kelsey refused to spiral out about this any further. Two a.m. was a much better time to freak-out. She reached for the mineral water they'd ordered. But before she took a sip, Elias reappeared.

"Follow me. You can leave your things on the table." He led her down the steps to the main terrace, then down a hallway to an elevator. Once inside, Elias inserted a keycard to access the lowest level. And took her hand as soon as the doors shut.

His touch smoothed away the last of her ill-timed introspection. "How'd you arrange this? Did you tell them I'm the princess?"

"No." He snorted at the mere suggestion. "Definitely not. I've been here many times with Prince Christian. The maître d knows me and agreed to a private tour."

"Impressively smooth." The doors opened, and she goggled at the cragginess of the natural cave walls. Elias had to prompt her to step out.

A small wooden door with a glass window required another pass of the keycard to enter. Then it was floor-to-ceiling racks and racks of bottles, set into the stone. Sensor lights turned on as they walked. And wow, it was significantly cooler down here. Kelsey rubbed her arms as goose bumps broke out.

"This happens to be the most extensive—and best—collection of wines in the kingdom. The royal family has a rack specially curated, just for their use. But you can't select from it tonight."

The last thing Kelsey wanted was to give up her secret identity too soon. "No problem. I don't think I've ever had a bottle of wine that cost more than twenty dollars. The royal-worthy stuff would be wasted on me. You choose."

"As you wish, but I insist that you sample it. There's a tasting room a little farther in. Heated. You'll be more comfortable waiting in there while I select."

"Perfect." The farther they walked, the lights behind them turned off.

Elias turned left down another branch of the cave. He opened another door, but this room didn't look like the rest of the cave. The walls were covered in brown leather, like she'd picture a Victorian smoking room. A long, high table had a few stools around it. Once she spotted it, Kelsey stopped looking.

And unzipped her shorts.

Elias shot out a hand to grip her wrist. "What are you doing?"

"Getting more comfortable, as you suggested." This would be so much fun. A treat she could give him for all the wonderful times he'd given her. Kelsey's confidence surged. She might not know how to be a princess. But she'd become *very* adept at being Elias's lover. "Don't look so surprised. You knew when you left the table that I didn't want a tour."

"I assumed I was calling your bluff. That you were teasing me."

"This has been a really good night so far. Let's make it

even more memorable." Kelsey wriggled out of her shorts. Left the shoes on, because this still carried an element of risk. The less clothing to be replaced quickly, the better.

"Are you sure?"

"Will anyone interrupt us?"

"No. The sommelier has been instructed not to do anything until we return."

Kelsey knelt. "Then we'd better be quick. Don't want to ruin dinner for the other guests." It only took a few quick flicks of her fingers before his big cock was out, the veins already distended and the tip pointing straight at her.

She wrapped her lips around him and sucked hard, as if trying to get the chocolate shell off an ice cream bar. Once, twice, and then the third time she swirled her tongue. Elias drove his fingers into her hair with a groan. Impossibly, he swelled even more inside her mouth.

Lightly, and with great care, Kelsey raked her teeth along his length. When only the very tip was still inside her lips, she licked in a frenzy of tiny flicks. His knees shook against her ribs. And then she scraped her nails in a twisting circle around his balls.

Elias swore. "You're killing me, Princess." He pulled out and dug around in his pants to get his wallet and a condom.

She hoisted herself up onto the table, legs dangling. "What are you going to do about it?" Then she widened her legs, showing off the white satin panties embroidered with butterflies that had appeared in her drawer. It was weird to have a stranger pick out lingerie for her. But it was *fantastic* to have something sexy to make Elias's eyes smolder like that.

He lunged for the dark wood buffet in the corner. Opened a drawer and pulled out a cloth napkin. Ha. No matter how hard she tried, he always stayed one step ahead of her. Elias tipped her forward over his shoulder, then put the napkin down under her butt.

"*This* is what I'm doing about it." He buried his face between her thighs. Technically, it was unnecessary, as Kelsey was already wet from sucking him off. From hearing his throaty growls. But...she certainly wouldn't *stop* him. Not when he already had two long fingers buried inside her, pumping in time to the slow rhythm he'd set with his tongue.

Her legs fell open, and then quickly scissored together around his head. Kelsey rocked against him, shuddering as pleasure built in waves. This was when everything else—the confusion, the ticking clock, the guilt, the worry—all fell away. With Elias she was simply Kelsey. No expectations, no demands. She was most herself in his arms.

Elias pulled her to the very edge of the table, then he thrust into her, hard and fast. His teeth sank into the sensitive skin right where her neck met her shoulder. Kelsey let her head fall back. He let loose a string of words in his native language.

"Translation?" she panted.

"You drive me wild. You are...extraordinary." He anchored his hands on her hips and jackhammered even faster. "Are you close, my treasure?"

"Always, with you." And then he shifted to rub his thumb across her center, and she was gone. Splintered into a thousand shards of pulsing satisfaction. Kelsey started to scream his name, but he swallowed it with a kiss as he snapped his hips one last time before clenching his fingers into her flesh.

It was quiet, then, with only their rasping breaths and the low hum of the heater. Elias kept kissing her. Deep, long kisses that made it seem as though they had all the time in the world. Kisses that made the room spin every bit as much as her orgasm had. Kisses that *almost* made her admit just how deep her feelings ran.

But Kelsey had watched enough episodes of *The Bachelor* to know you didn't share that with a man until you were positive you weren't on the verge of breaking up with him. The four days she had left with Elias in no way promised any future together.

So she squeezed her eyes shut, imprinting a mental picture of everything about this moment: the softness of the near-stubble on his head, the sharp slant of his cheekbones as she caressed his jaw, the near-bruising pressure of his hipbones against her inner thighs.

Elias finished with a soft kiss on her eyelids. When she reluctantly dragged them open, it was to see him licking the fingers that had been inside her. "I want this flavor in my mouth when I choose our wine."

"You're wicked," she gasped.

"Merely savoring the moment." With a final lick, he winked. "I think we'll need champagne. Nothing else could be as sweet and effervescent as you."

Okay...one more thing to remember about tonight.

That he'd been dirty-talking their wine selection when Kelsey stopped fighting it and admitted she was falling in love with Elias.

Chapter Eighteen

Elias was used to people being obsequious around his best friend, while simultaneously ignoring *him*. It went with the territory when you hung out with the heir to the throne, but he wasn't used to the prime minster all but licking Christian's boots.

Prime Minister Skeggit pointed through the rotunda of the parliamentary building to the stone steps that arched across the front. The attempt at still keeping some level of secrecy had them meeting in the entranceway, rather than going out to the steps that abutted a large park. "After a short speech by myself, we'll—"

Christian cut her off with a sharply raised index finger. "And a speech from the *king*. After all, at its heart, the reappearance of Princess Kelsey is a family matter."

"Of course. After the king's speech, we'll come back to the state receiving chamber for a luncheon with the royal family and parliamentary leadership. Would you like to choose a private room for the family to wait in prior to the announcement?"

Right. Every second in Christian's presence bought Skeggit political capital, or so she thought. It was blindingly obvious to Elias that every additional second was just ticking his friend off.

Time to intercept. Elias stepped forward from his customary four steps behind the prince. "Prime Minister, I believe that's something that Sir Kai is already working on with your staff. We appreciate your time, but we don't want to keep you longer than necessary. It's hard enough to explain Prince Christian's continued presence here."

"Oh. Very good. As for our cover story…" She winked. Oddly. It was painful to watch, it was so out of character. "We have the artist unveiling a new portrait of the prince to hang in the Hallway of Royals. Your Highness, he'll be thrilled if you attend."

"I'll let you know how thrilled *I* am once I see it." They all gave obligatory chuckles. Even though Elias knew Christian wasn't joking. At all.

"I noticed you called your sister Princess Kelsey. Wouldn't it have a greater impact if we continue to call her Princess Valentina?"

Not this again. Elias ground his teeth together. Unfortunately, he couldn't come to her defense. That ball was in Christian's court.

But the prince simply laughed off the suggestion. "Ha! It'd have an impact, decidedly so. Because she wouldn't answer to it."

"Surely the princess can be informed of the optics of her using an American name to be declared the missing Villani. It simply isn't appropriate. What if, God forbid, something happens to the rest of the family and she becomes Queen? With that name?"

Tasteless. In the extreme.

"Well, if *you* manage to survive whatever tragedy takes

out my father, me, and my sister, then you can attempt to have that argument with the new queen. I wish you luck. Until then"—Christian pinned her with a glare the way you'd harpoon a goldfish—"you will respect the wishes of the king and address her as Princess Kelsey."

Well done. Christian didn't throw around his authority very often. He didn't need to, but when he did fully assume the royal mantle, it could be intimidating as hell.

To everyone *but* Elias.

An aide scurried forward, bowing repeatedly. After glancing at the note she'd been handed, Skeggit sent him off. "I'm sorry, but I have to oversee a vote. With your request that we keep this meeting a secret, I must stick to my official schedule."

"I understand. I'll wander about aimlessly until it's time for the portrait ceremony."

Her jaw dropped at his suggestion. "Your Highness, we can get you coffee. Some pastries, perhaps? You may use my office, of course."

"Go. I'll be fine. I've got Captain Trebanti here to keep me company."

She bowed and rushed out of the room.

"Wander aimlessly about the building?" Elias snickered. "Were you trying to give the PM a heart attack?"

Christian shrugged. "Just a mild headache. She was annoying me even more than usual."

"Skeggit got my hackles up, too."

"She sees the reappearance of my sister as a boost to nationalism. Thinks that suddenly the vote will swing her way, and Moncriano won't join the European Union. I won't let her use Kelsey. She's not a symbol to be appropriated."

Bravo. And what a relief that Christian voiced everything Elias was thinking. "You deserve a free beer for that speech."

"I won't stop you." They walked down the white marble

hallway, Christian with hands clasped behind his back. With the vote going on upstairs, the corridors were deserted.

"Do you want to wait in the law library?" It was a dull, quiet three-storied room. It did have couches comfortable enough to nap on, though, and clerks who'd bring you individual teapots.

"I'd rather walk. Find a new room to poke my head into."

Uh-oh. That meant the prince was in a mood. Not just from setting the PM straight, either. He roamed the halls incessantly whenever he was deeply, truly troubled. Like an unsettled spirit, but with louder footsteps.

Better to get it over with quickly. "Is something bothering you, Your Highness?"

"Perhaps. Perhaps it's nothing. But until I know for sure, I won't settle."

For Christ's sake, spit it out, already. Then Elias could sympathize, swear with him, and they could move on. "Is there anything I can do?"

"Yes." Christian stopped walking, looked just over his shoulder at Elias, and asked, "Are you dating my sister?"

Holy *fuck*.

The moment he'd been dreading had come. The one he'd worked so hard to avoid. Because Elias had become quite adept at dodging the truth, evading it.

But he would not, could not, lie to Christian.

Not as his friend. And especially not as his prince.

"Your Highness—"

Christian cut him off by pounding his fist against the doorjamb. "Don't try to pretty it up. Don't you dare talk circles around me. Yes or no, Trebanti. It's a simple choice."

It was *anything* but simple. The question—and the entire situation. "Yes."

"What the hell are you thinking?" Christian's voice rose on each word, until he finished at a near roar.

Elias checked the nameplate on the office. No good. Some secretary of something. But across the hall was the members' cloakroom. It wouldn't be in use on this hot, mid-June day. He opened the door and waited for Christian to enter.

Then he made sure to close it firmly, although he wasn't sure if the soundproofing of a recording studio could contain the prince's bellows as this conversation evolved.

"What made you ask?"

Halfway to the other end of the narrow room, Christian whipped around and narrowed his eyes. "Are you kidding? *How* I found out doesn't matter."

"It does." His duties as a bodyguard, his duty to protect the Villani royal family took first priority. After Elias finished his threat assessment, *then* Christian could kick his ass. "However this affects us personally, as friends, the bigger issue is whether or not this is now public knowledge. That would make it an exponentially larger problem."

"It's a damn big problem already."

"Your Highness, I'm not casting blame, or looking for retribution. I'm trying to do the right thing."

"Should've thought of that before," Christian grumbled, because his friend was nothing if not stubborn as hell. But then, it was almost possible see him piece it together in his head. "No, I don't think anyone else knows. Aside from Kai, I mean."

The prince's private secretary. The one person with as much access—officially—to the prince as himself. The one person who would've risked the royal wrath to share this story. Standing on the opposite side of the low counter from the prince, Elias asked, "What did he tell you?"

"Kai saw you last night, coming out of the elevator at the restaurant. You two were holding hands and looking very much...*enamored,* was the word he used. As soon as you were out of the elevator, you went back into official bodyguard mode. He'd been about to come out of the bathroom. But he let the door close, shocked. So I'm guessing you didn't see him."

"No. I did not."

One moment. One unguarded moment was all it took for his undoing, which was probably the same thought his father had upon discovering the baby princess was stolen.

It was entirely his fault. He'd been sloppy. Distracted. Qualities that should never be ascribed to a member of the Royal Protection Service. Qualities Elias wouldn't forgive in anyone else.

"Well?"

"I can assure you no other inappropriate behavior was witnessed by anyone. This secret is contained to you and Kai."

"Damn it, Elias, that's not what I was asking. What do you have to say for yourself?"

He *should* apologize. Elias knew that being with the princess was wrong.

However, he did not regret it. Not any of their time together. Not any of the deep connection they'd forged. So he could not, in good conscience, apologize. It'd be the same as lying to the prince.

With a bowed head, Elias said, "I beg your forgiveness, Your Highness, for overstepping my bounds."

"As a bodyguard?"

"Yes." *Admitting* to doing wrong was easy. He'd been crystal clear on that concept.

A hard *thwap* by the prince sent at least a dozen hangers spinning on the rack, some flying off to hit the wall. "What about as my friend? My closest friend? You think it's acceptable to take advantage of my baby sister?"

"No. I've been quite sure of that from the start."

"When *did* it start?"

Elias swallowed. "The details are immaterial."

"The hell they are. You do not get to decide what I desire to know." Fully regal fury pumped off the prince in nearly visible waves. Christian might've mentioned their friendship, but right now? He was in full "Prince of the Realm" mode.

As was his right.

But Kelsey had rights, too, which he would protect. "Any measure of forwardness on my part with the princess is too much. I acknowledge that. Out of respect for her privacy, however, I won't go over specifics with you."

"Why not? What are you hiding?" Faster than he'd ever seen him move outside of combat exercises, Christian came at him. Both hands braced on the counter, he leaned forward until his face was mere inches from Elias's. "Did you sleep with my baby sister?"

No evading *that*.

Even knowing what was coming, Elias forced his hands to stay loose, arms down at his sides. "Yes."

The punch came fast and hard. As expected.

Elias had braced his weight for it, so it didn't send him to the ground. Rocked him back, though. Left his jawbone feeling like it'd been hammered by a police baton.

Christian shook out his hand, grimacing. "That's a fucking low-down thing to do, my friend."

Agreed. Christian wasn't saying anything that hadn't been eating Elias up for weeks now. "Would you like to take another shot at me? I won't fight back."

"I know that, which means it's only fair to give you the one." The prince licked at a trickle of blood over one knuckle. "No matter how badly I'd like to give you a pounding for touching Kelsey."

"I'm sorry for…"

Shit.

Here he'd pledged his life to protect the prince, and

instead, he'd made the man *bleed*. All his fault. Sure, it wouldn't even need a bandage, but it was the principle. Those few drops of blood were a tangible symbol of how completely he'd let Christian down.

"Sorry for what?" He picked up the basket full of plastic hanger numbers and chucked it at the wall like it was a cricket ball. "Why don't you delineate exactly how many ways you fucked up, Trebanti?"

Elias shifted his jaw gingerly side to side. And then he met the furious violet eyes of the prince. "Only two ways matter. That I put the princess, the royal family, in jeopardy with my lack of focus. And that I let you down."

"Damn right you did." Christian paced the length of the four empty racks. "There's a code, Elias. Among fellow soldiers—which we are. Among friends—which we are. And among brothers—which I count you as. This crosses a damn line."

"Right. Yes. True." He wouldn't make excuses. There weren't any. He'd gone into this with his eyes wide open. Knowing full well the risks and the lack of a good outcome.

Elias had hoped to get away with it, given the forced and irrefutable end date. Once Kelsey was revealed to the world, whether she stayed in Moncriano or went back to America, they were over. He'd thought they could fly under the radar for two damned weeks.

He'd been naïve. A fool. An idiot.

"Did you think because I'd imagined her dead for two decades that I wouldn't have the same devotion once she returned?" Christian twisted his neck left and right, as though trying to wring out the right words. "We may not have the whole conversation thing worked into a rhythm yet, but Kelsey is wholly my sister. I love her, I respect her, and I shall defend her with my last breath."

"I never doubted that for a moment, Your Highness."

With nothing left to throw in the mostly bare room, Christian struck the wall with the side of his fist. "Stop with the title bullshit. I'm your best friend, Elias. How the hell could you do this?"

That was a weighty question, and almost impossible to answer. It was like trying to quantify the wetness of the ocean. How did you sum up an attraction? An indefinable need to be with a person? The pull at every fiber of your being that said she fits you?

Elias locked his hands behind his back. Took a deep breath. "Kelsey's...special."

"Don't use her being a blood princess as an excuse. You've never chased nobility before."

Elias couldn't help it. Despite the tension in the room, the fury emanating from Christian, the surety that this was *not the moment,* he laughed out loud. "That's not it. Her royal standing isn't an asset, believe me. All it does is complicate things."

"Is it the American accent? She comes off as foreign and exotic?"

"No."

Confusion and curiosity seemed to be calming Christian. He stopped pacing and leaned on the wall across from Elias, arms and ankles crossed. "Then what?"

Part of him wished he'd said what was to come to Kelsey herself first, rather than her brother. But Christian *did* deserve to know that Elias wasn't using her, wasn't toying with her. That he cared—far too deeply, far too fast—for Kelsey. That she *mattered* for her spirit, not her royal DNA.

"The princess is different from other women. Fun, lighthearted without being ditzy. Happy without being juvenile. Tenderhearted. Loyal. Stronger than she even realizes." Elias kept "beautiful" to himself. In his current mood, Christian didn't need a reminder of Elias appreciating his sister's body.

Shock erased the last vestiges of anger from Christian's muscles. His whole body went limp. Sort of collapsed in on itself. "You like her."

"I generally don't risk my career and friendships for women I *dislike*."

"You truly care for her?"

More so than was good for him. More so than it was worth admitting to Kelsey.

More than he'd ever imagined possible.

Elias squeezed his eyes shut. "Yes."

"I don't regret hitting you, but I'm glad I didn't take any other extra whacks. This is a shithole of a situation. I'm sorry."

Ah. Christian had put the pieces together without any more prompting. Saw that there was no happy ending. No future. "As you can imagine, if I could have resisted the princess, I would have. I take full responsibility."

"As a friend, I can tell you're...conflicted, but that's not the only angle here." Christian came around the counter to stand toe to toe with Elias. "You have a duty. You've betrayed it."

The accusation jabbed at him sharper than their uniform swords. "I swear to you, on my honor, I didn't think I was putting the princess at risk. I put my duty, her safety, first."

"You've dishonored your office. Your pledge, your loyalty to the crown."

No. That was unthinkable. "I have pledged my life to keep her, to keep all of you, safe. That hasn't changed. It will not ever change."

"The words aren't enough, Elias. Quite simply, you've betrayed that pledge. You chose to follow your heart instead."

His heart raced as he scrambled to convince the prince otherwise. "It was a mistake in judgment, admittedly, but I swear to you, Christian, there was no choice to be made. My feelings for Kelsey simply grew."

"Don't you see that makes it worse? That means you

can't turn them off, that you'll be pining after her. Distracted. Nowhere close to being at the top of your game."

Every word Christian spoke twisted Elias's gut more. "No. I've accepted our time will come to an end. That it *must*. I won't be distracted. I would not dishonor you, the privilege of guarding you, like that."

"What happened to not having a choice?" Sighing, Christian cocked his head to the side and continued. "I hear what you *want* me to believe. I also hear you trying your damndest to convince yourself every bit as much as you're trying to convince me."

What if the prince was right?

Elias shook his head. "All I can do is apologize. Work to regain your trust."

Christian pushed off the wall. "There's no room for love in the Royal Protection Service. It messes with you. Worse than drugs or alcohol, because it sneaks up on you. It doesn't wear off, either."

"I'm not in love," he said swiftly. Fiercely.

That would be pointless.

"In love, on the way to it...don't split hairs. You're an addict, jonesing for a fix. What's going to happen when you can't get it? When you can't have her?"

There was utter silence in the room while they both pondered that.

When he couldn't bear it any longer, Elias asked, "Are you going to remove me from her detail?"

"I shouldn't have to. The Captain Trebanti I trust with my life, with my sister's life, would *know* the right call to make." Then Christian walked out.

Elias followed him.

Because that was his job, his calling. His reason for being.

The Villanis. The crown.

Above everything—and everyone—else.

Chapter Nineteen

Mallory stretched out her legs on the padded rubber floor of the gym and grinned over at Kelsey. "This is the most at ease I've felt since we got here."

Slowly, Genevieve turned just her head—like an animatronic figure—to face them from her spot against the wall. "You're about to be schooled in how to defend yourself against an attacker. Either you've got a strange kink I do *not* want to know about, or you aren't fully cognizant of the serious nature of today's lesson."

Funny how the Moncriano accent sounded sexy in Elias and Marko and yes, even in Christian's voice. But it just made everything Genevieve said come off as snippier. Bitchier. More condescending.

Or maybe it was that it was always going to be one step forward, three steps back with her.

For once, Mallory—who had turned obsequiousness and dignified respect into an art form over the past two weeks—didn't just nod and try to blend into the metaphorical curtains. She crossed her legs into a Lotus pose. Settled her wrists on her knees and breathed deeply. Then she turned to Genevieve.

"Nobody's judging us, for once. We're all wearing workout clothes—a level fashion playing field. And I'll be learning to take control of a dangerous situation. That's empowering, and puts me at ease. Perhaps *you* aren't fully cognizant of how good it feels to revel in your own strength."

It was a long-winded smackdown, but a smackdown nonetheless. One point to the American team. Not to mention the extra point Kelsey awarded herself for resisting the urge to high-five Mallory.

The twisted grimace that Marko aimed at Elias made it look like he was trying to hide a grin as he clapped his hands for their attention. "Your Highness. Your Highness. Miss Wishner. Today we'll cover basic defensive maneuvers."

Genevieve looked at him from beneath slitted lids. "You mean the basic ones I learned years ago?"

"Yes. But remembering how to do something and making your muscles actually do it are very different processes. I requested your presence today precisely for that reason. It *has* been years since you've done this." She opened her mouth, but Marko shook his head. "I checked with your entire rotation of bodyguards. They've asked, but nobody's been allowed to train with you."

Genevieve's cheeks turned the same mottled red that afflicted Kelsey. "I...I don't want people who work for me pawing at my body. Knowing what it feels like."

"Of course not!" Kelsey couldn't help but rush to her defense. Under the fancy clothes and fancier jewelry, they were still both *women*. "You wouldn't ask a CFO to let the people who report to her graze her boob or squeeze her ass. That's insulting. Inappropriate."

Eyes wide, Genevieve said in a near-whisper, "Thank you."

Marko bowed his head. "My apologies, Your Highness. It did not occur to me, since you have two female guards, that it would be a problem. Clearly an oversight on my part."

"I trust my team, but...I can't wholly trust anybody," she murmured. "One unintentional joke after a few beers about the size of my bra cup could spread like wildfire. Make international news. I have to guard my privacy as fiercely as... well, as you all guard the rest of me."

Elias stepped forward. He'd stationed himself at the opposite side of the room from Kelsey. Genevieve was the only one in there who didn't know the two of them were together...and they intended to *keep* it that way. "I'll make sure that for our next training session, we use officers not on rotation for the immediate royal family. Will that be acceptable?"

"Yes. Thank you."

Kelsey tried to catch Elias's eye, to give him a smile of thanks for smoothing it out. But oddly, he wouldn't look at her.

"Would you like to skip today?" Marko offered as he removed his shoes and socks.

"No, I'm all right with you and Elias."

Mallory said, "I'll partner with you, Your Highness."

Again, Kelsey bit back a grin. No doubt Mallory would enjoy having a legit excuse to slam Genevieve into the ground. Or shove an elbow in her belly. Probably both.

"We'll all be switching off with each other. Good practice to try everything on different heights and body types. Now." Marko raised his hands to get them to stand. Elias joined him in the middle of the floor. Kelsey zipped her gaze away. It was far too tempting to ogle the man in the tight tee that showed off every ripple of his abs, pecs, and biceps. "If everything goes right, you'll never use what we go over today."

"Unless we move back to New York," Mallory said under

her breath. "This'll be as useful against muggers as assassins."

Damn it.

How was it that reminders of the decision Kelsey had to make were coming so often now? She wanted an hour, sixty little minutes, to go by where she was *not* confronted by Destiny with a capital *D*. To not think about all the ways her life could change.

It had been all of maybe seven minutes. On the way down here, Elias had informed her, in an oddly formal, factual manner, that Sir Evan would have two draft statements for her to review when they finished. Both acknowledged that she was, indeed, Princess Valentina. One version embraced her journey to get to know her birth country. The other was a goodbye, of sorts, in case she chose to go back to New York. Kelsey had to approve them before they went on to the king for his approval.

The only part of this she approved of was not having to write them herself.

Elias shouldered in front of Marko, eyebrows furrowed into an almost single line. "No. He's oversimplifying, which isn't safe. You can't assume that things *will* go right, no matter how much faith you have in your protection team. That's sloppy, dangerous. Better to always assume that things will go wrong."

Marko plastered on a broad, reassuring smile that was in stark contrast to the rough threat portrayed in Elias's voice. "Well, we don't want the royal family walking around in fear. Prepare, but don't panic."

Elias's frown expanded to include deep lines bracketing his mouth. "Don't candy coat it for them. They're grown women. They deserve to know the facts."

"Facts, not fear-mongering," Marko spat back, on the verge of yelling.

Now the two of them were facing each other, not the

women. Kelsey hadn't seen this aggressive, argumentative side of Elias before.

She didn't care for it.

Was he *trying* to pick a fight? Or send Genevieve, her, and Mallory into full-blown anxiety attacks? His entire attitude and demeanor were sharper. Harder.

What on earth was going on with him?

Elias thwapped the side of his palm into his other hand, repeatedly. "The irrefutable fact is that every member of the royal family is a target. Every day. There's no letting our guard down. Not for us, but not for them, either."

She couldn't touch him, not without betraying the secret of their relationship. But Kelsey inched forward, mindful of his karate-chop motions. "Elias, that's enough. You're starting to freak me out."

"Good." He swung around to face her. There was no warmth in his eyes, no softening of his stance. The man was in attack mode. "Because you need to be aware. You *are* a target."

She'd had enough of this silliness. Kelsey let a small smile play across her lips as she shook her head. When would this get through to any and every one in Alcarsa Palace? "I'm nobody."

Elias loomed over her, hulking and scary. "You are third in line to the throne. A blood princess of the royal house of Villani." His voice rumbled like thunder over mountains against the walls of the room.

But now Kelsey felt bullied by his continued scaremongering.

No way would she cower before such behavior. Especially not to her boyfriend. "Yes, I'm a princess, but in name only. Not even *my* name, technically. All I am is a problem. An awkward reboot of something that went down decades ago."

Marko shook his head. "You can't believe that, Your Highness."

Couldn't she? How was anything in Moncriano improved by her coming back onto the scene?

The citizens at large didn't need another royal figure. The king was fruitlessly trying to recapture the years he lost with a baby. Christian didn't know what to *do* with her. Genevieve didn't *want* her back in their lives. All her reappearance did was complicate everything.

Kelsey plucked at the neck of her yellow tank top. Not one of her own, from home. Those clothes still seemed to be lost in the palace laundry. Switched out for more appropriate princess-wear. But they couldn't so easily switch her out, or her voice, or her opinions.

"Look, I disappeared once before and life went on."

"That's a selfish, ill-considered thing to say," Genevieve snapped.

Oh, wow. Her sister didn't approve of what she'd said? Color her #notsurprised.

But she was damn well going to finish making her point. *Making* them all listen to her. Even Mallory, who was shaking her head and drawing her hand across her throat in the classic *shut it* gesture.

"I'm not saying I want to be kidnapped. I just think the risk, especially for me, is minimal, because the reward would be minimal. I'm your average American computer nerd. Nations would not rise up in outrage. Citizens would not weep. And I'm quite sure the government would not change course to give in to any demands to get me back."

Elias cuffed her biceps with his big hands, his grip tight almost to the point of pain. His eyes blazed with indigo fire. "I would *make* them do so. I would do anything to get you back. I would not stop until you were safe, here, once more."

His fervent declaration made all the hair on her arms stand up. But not entirely in a good way.

Not when he still was so scary in both his tone and touch.

Not when she didn't understand any of his reactions that he'd had in this room. And not when he risked exposing their secret relationship with a declaration that was far too sincere to be anything but *deeply* personal.

She did, however, believe him.

For all that Kelsey had never thought of herself as anyone special, worth saving? Elias, in this moment, made her *believe*.

She believed without a doubt he'd find her—*again*. And moreover, the depth of his sincerity made her believe that, indeed, the world would and should be turned upside down if she disappeared again.

Because if Elias thought she was worth that effort…it disrespected his fierce faith in her if *she* didn't believe it, too.

Marko clapped his hands once more. "To recap, everyone is safe. Today. And if you work hard for the next hour, you'll have a better guarantee of staying safe in the future. No more talking. Time to get to work."

How was Kelsey supposed to concentrate on moves and grips and stances when Elias had just tilted her entire world on its axis? Could it be that *she* was the only one who didn't believe in her ability to be a princess?

And what the *heck* was wrong with her boyfriend? How could he be so borderline mean to her before saying all that?

When they were alone, she'd get to the bottom of it.

If she had to, she'd play the princess card and *order* him to tell her what was up.

• • •

"You're very quiet," Kelsey remarked in a subdued tone as they jogged through the forest behind the palace.

"We're running, Your Highness. Training." At least, he was trying to get her to do so. The princess kept pace with a steady jog well enough. But every time he tried to push her into a sprint—like she'd need if being pursued—she lagged behind. And Elias couldn't protect her if he stayed in front of her. "If you're running as fast as you should be, there's no air left to chat."

"I'm not in the mood to run." The powdery thud of her shoes against the dirt slowed even more. "I'd rather use all that spare air I'm hoarding to chat. I think we *need* to talk."

Nope. He was barely holding it together while *not* talking. "You agreed to continue training for another hour once we left the self-defense course."

"I changed my mind." Kelsey tossed her ponytail in an unconscious mimicry of her older sister. "Isn't that the prerogative of a princess?"

Really? After fighting the title for weeks, *now* was when she decided to embrace her rank? Elias was tempted to bang his head against the nearest pine tree. "Your schedule doesn't have any other openings. If we do this, we do it now."

"Running for another twenty minutes won't ultimately make any difference."

Well, tough. She wasn't in charge of her security. *Elias* called those shots. "Not today, but it could someday. You know the secret to perfecting a skill? Practice it for ten thousand hours."

She stopped completely, braced herself with her hands on her thighs, and shot him the smile that always melted his heart like a ray of sunshine. "That's hilarious."

"It's proven fact." Elias had read the book about outliers years ago and applied its theories to his shooting and fighting techniques. Putting in the time made all the difference. It was why he felt confident protecting the princess by himself right now.

On royal grounds.

Still connected to his team by earbud.

And wearing a revolver as well as three knives.

"No, it's hilarious you think you can goad me into running for ten thousand hours. That's more than four hundred days. More than a year straight. Not. Gonna. Happen."

Elias adored her stubborn streak. The way she stood up for what she wanted and believed, no matter what. Personally, at least. Professionally, her attitude made his job much more difficult. "I'm not suggesting you do it without breaks. Merely that if you must start sometime, you might as well start today."

She extended her hand to him, fingers outstretched. He didn't rise to the bait. After tossing him a questioning glance, she awkwardly laced her fingers through his. "I'd rather rely on *you* to keep me safe. Becoming a better sprinter doesn't seem like the best long-term solution."

"Correct." Holding her felt so right, and it also felt so wrong. He let go, quickly backing up a few steps to separate them. "That's why you'll need to keep at your hand-to-hand. Start learning karate. Something that will help you use your own weight as leverage against a far bigger attacker. We'll get you down to the gun range, as well. Perhaps a short dagger."

"A knife?" Sunlight shafted through the trees to highlight her look of incredulity. "You want me to walk around with a knife sheathed to my thigh like I'm an assassin?"

"Yes."

"No." Her voice was flat. Like she damn well expected him to do what she said, no questions asked.

Like a princess.

Elias hated them being on opposite sides. Hated not letting her live in a bubble of happy naivete. "Your Highness, this isn't a discussion. You can't pull rank. Not when it comes to your safety. For now, I'm in charge of it. You must follow my direction."

She crossed her arms. "One step at a time. One *measured* step at a time."

"That's not good enough."

"God. Why are you being like this?" She backed away from him. As if to make it clear they were on opposite sides. The yawning chasm between them was palpable. "Look, personal weapons have a high statistical rate of being turned around and used against you by an attacker. I don't want to be stabbed by my own knife. On top of being dead, I'd be mortally embarrassed."

"You want to quote statistics? Fine." Because he had them. Reams of information never released to the general public about thwarted attacks against royalty, all over the globe. If Elias had to scare her into submission, he would. "Meet me back here tomorrow and I'll have pages of statistics supporting my very rational request that you take your personal safety into your own hands."

She lifted her chin. "I have people for that. Not because I'm lazy or not listening to you, but because you and Marko and everyone in the Royal Protection Service are far more highly qualified to protect me from an attacker. I have faith in all of you."

Damn it, why did she have to look at him with those wide, trusting violet eyes? Like she believed he could hold off entire armies with his bare hands? It *almost* made him believe, too.

Which was dangerous.

Elias thwacked his palm against the trunk of the elm tree next to him. "You can't, Kelsey. You shouldn't. Your parents did, and look how that ended up. They left you alone, trusting your safety to the head of the RPS. My father, whom I'd entrust my own life to. And he failed them. He failed *you*. I could do the same."

"Elias, where is all this coming from?" There was a catch in her throat, confusion that he hated knowing he'd rooted there. "You can't have received a specific threat against me because the world doesn't know I'm alive. So why are you harping on this?"

"Because I'm not enough. No one man would be." The thoughts that had been churning through his brain since his talk with Christian finally coalesced into a gut-wrenching decision. "I will do everything in my power to keep you safe, but there's no guarantee I'll succeed. We've been lax, Your Highness. Letting other things distract from the basic tenet that you need to be kept safe."

She threw up her arms, surprising a squirrel into skittering away with loud cheeps. "How about happy? Who's in charge of keeping me happy?"

Elias swallowed hard. Gritted out the words he wished were a lie. "Not me."

Her arms dropped, limply, to her sides. "What?"

He'd always known he'd have to be the one strong enough to let go. To push away. To stop the best thing that had ever happened to him.

Elias hadn't known it would be *this* hard. That they'd spend every day and many nights together, and already meld into a tight, cohesive unit, a couple. That their hearts would already be so intertwined.

Elias hadn't known it would hurt so damn much.

He spread his feet wide and locked his hands together behind his back. Hopefully that would be enough to keep him from reaching out to comfort her as he broke her heart.

"My sole job is to keep you safe, Your Highness. I'm afraid I've let you down. Once the announcement about you is made public, we'll adjust your team. I'll go back to guarding Prince Christian."

Kelsey pinched her eyes shut, rubbing at her temple. "Explain something to me." Her eyes flew open, those violet depths sucking him in deep, like a velvet-lined black hole of feelings. Her voice was thick, clogged with emotions he didn't have the courage to name. "How did you let me down? And, on the ridiculous assumption you did, how is your punishment to guard someone *higher* in rank than me? What on earth is going on?"

"I've let myself become distracted. It is entirely my fault. I've let my feelings for you cloud my judgment. Weaken my focus."

It was happening even as they spoke. With it being summer, there weren't twigs or leaves on the ground to crunch and give away if someone approached. Having this conversation out in the open was just another in the countless risks he'd taken since assuming protection of the princess. And Elias was *grateful* that Christian had pointed it out before things got any more out of hand.

Swiftly, he brought his wrist to his mouth and requested an immediate shift change, because he was quite certain the princess wouldn't want to be escorted back to the palace by him once this conversation ended.

Kelsey fisted her hands on her hips. Her entire body was strung taut, cocked for battle. "You mean because we have sex, you can't properly scan a crowd for potential assassins?"

"More or less."

"Elias, you're the most dedicated person I've ever met." The frustration in her tone was overlaid with a thin edge of anger. "If anything, *I'm* the one who breaks protocol. *I* keep engaging you in conversations when I should let you do your job."

He shook his head. "I should be able to do both."

Almost yelling at this point, she hurled the words across the forest floor. "So you're quitting on me? After putting in considerably less than those ten thousand hours you just touted?"

She was still not getting it. So he'd spell it out very simply and clearly.

"I'm ending our professional relationship." Elias clenched every muscle in his body. Knotted them up into a single, tight fist. Strength with no feeling. Especially his heart. "And our personal one."

"What?" A snort of disbelief cut off almost before it started. Then her eyelids fluttered. God, was that to beat back tears? "I thought this was just a fight, that you were in a lousy mood. You're breaking up with me? Already?"

"This can't be a surprise. We both knew it would have to end on Sunday, when you're revealed as the Princess Royal. I'm simply jumping the gun by three days."

"We could pack a lot more into those three days," she said, her tone pleading.

Why did she force him to keep stabbing at her, painfully, with the truth? "Your Highness. A princess can't date a commoner. This must end. Now."

"I'm not your full-blown, standard princess. I'm mostly a quite common American."

"There is nothing common about you." His arm twitched, trying to surge forward and stroke her cheek. The one with a single tear rolling down it. "A princess most assuredly can't date the son of the man who is responsible for her kidnapping."

"Why not? The king and queen forgave him, kept him on duty back when it happened. Now? Twenty-five years later? Who would dare treat him any differently?" Her arms were flailing, gesticulating wildly.

And again, it ached not to catch them, pull her close and soothe her. More to the point, to stop being the one inflicting the pain...even though Elias knew it was for the best, in the long run.

"You don't understand...yet. But you will. The royals are held to a higher standard. Different expectations."

"My expectation in life is pretty simple. To do good and be happy. You've helped me see the good in this country since the moment our plane touched down. And you've helped me be happier than ever before. How can that possibly be bad?"

"Not bad, Princess. I don't want you to think I regret a moment of our time together." Because he'd cherish it for the rest of his life. "Just...not *right*. I'm not the right man for you. For the country. I won't ever be good enough for you."

Kelsey's mouth turned down and her eyes glared violet-tipped daggers at him. "Funny. That's what I keep saying about being a princess—that I'm not good enough, special enough, to pull it off. Which you contradict every time. So tell me, Captain Trebanti, how is this different?"

"It just is." He refused to say *it's not you, it's me*, no matter how true.

Because it wasn't about anything to do with Kelsey. All the reasons they couldn't be together were Elias's fault. Just like them getting together in the first place and thus leading to this fucking painful moment was also his fault.

How could he have been so stupid? So selfish?

"We're good as a couple." Kelsey stabbed her finger into the air between them. "Don't you dare deny it. Don't lie to me."

"My beautiful, stubborn fighter, I can't lie to you, but I can't give you hope, either." Elias stood at attention; the tight line triggered muscle memory of hours on end holding this position on deck, in review, in their barracks. It ought to be enough to hold him in place—*away* from Kelsey—while he finished this. Forever. "It doesn't matter that I want to stay with you, that I care so much for you. How I adore you. What matters is that Moncriano deserves their Princess Valentina fully restored to them. And that includes her being with the right man. One worthy of royalty."

"You're worthy of *me*, Elias." Tears were streaming down her face.

"No, Your Highness." A crackle in his ear let him know that Marko was almost to their location. "But I wish more than life itself that were true."

Chapter Twenty

"Are you hungry yet?" Mallory asked for about the tenth time since they'd arrived at the imposing stone Parliament building. "I have a PB&J. Well, I think it's almond butter, but close enough, right? Some dried fruit and nuts. And a banana."

Kelsey had been on auto-pilot since Elias delivered his bombshell of a breakup. But Mallory's offered buffet roused her curiosity. Especially since they hadn't been allowed to bring their bags. Or their own clothes. Stylists had dressed both of them head to toe for the grand royal reveal.

She pointed at the baby-blue purse that matched the high-necked sheath dress Mallory wore. "You're only carrying a clutch. Where's all this food you're promising?"

"In the purse. I took everything else out, even left my phone back at the palace. Because my sister's health and well-being is more important than access to social media."

Grimacing in fake outrage, Kelsey blustered, "That's blasphemy. Take it back."

In a far quieter, more serious tone, Mallory said, "You've

barely eaten since Thursday."

Oh yeah, since her world had come crashing down and her heart got ripped out of her chest? Nope. Not so much interested in scarfing down—or even nibbling on—anything. She flashed a tight, "don't worry about me because I'm hunky dory" smile. "I'm not hungry."

"Get there," Mallory said. "The best step in recovering from a breakup is the guilt-free binge eating. And I can't do it without you."

Kelsey fussed with her three-quarter length sleeve. In a paler shade of lavender than Genevieve's purple dress, although otherwise identical. Which she'd let slide this once, but...if she ended up staying in Moncriano? It would stop.

She hadn't worn matching clothes with Mallory in twenty-five years. No way did she intend to start being cutesy now with her *other* sister. Not even in haute couture. Especially not in painful heels and a beauty-pageant-type sash that held a pearl encircled cameo of her dead mother.

But that was an issue Kelsey simply didn't have the bandwidth to tackle today. Her hand covered the cameo with Serena's face, suddenly craving contact with the mother she'd never really known. Wishing that she could sit with her and pour out her problems, and get the type of motherly advice that solved everything.

Because she hadn't solved *anything* by herself.

Staying—and not being with Elias—didn't seem possible.

Leaving because of a bad breakup seemed weak and immature, which just pissed her off.

Either way, the king expected her answer tomorrow.

And today she was about to be presented to the entire country as the missing Princess Valentina. It was time to pull herself together. Pouting was never a good look.

She pushed away the banana Mallory waved in front of her. Mustered up a bit of side-eye. "I thought you used to say that the best step was revenge sex?"

"That also has its merits." Straight-ironed hair fell in a red stream across her shoulder as Mallory looked left at the lineup of minor royals and Parliament members milling near the doorway. "I'm not sure how easy that'll be to accomplish with you being outed to the world in a few minutes. Let's focus on eating all the pizza and pastries instead."

"There's this luncheon right after the presentation. Probably no pizza, but I'm betting the desserts will be killer. The palace chefs are in charge of the food."

"Ludovico," Mallory sighed with a far-off smile. They'd hunted down the pastry chef in the bowels of the palace to thank him after eating a sweet fried dough filled with cream and apricot jam that was basically bliss in a bun. The man was a magician. "You almost want to sleep with him just to see what yummy rolls or pancakes he'd make you the next morning."

Kelsey ticked off points on her fingers. "I'm not sleeping with someone who'll plump me up with impossible to resist sweets." Because she was definitely *off* running as exercise now that she'd always associate it with Elias dumping her. "I'm not sleeping with a member of the staff." Not *again,* anyway. Lesson learned. The hard way. "Oh, and I'm not sleeping with *anyone* in the near future because the only man I want is the man I can't have. The one who refuses to be with me."

"Shhh." Mallory jerked down her hand and clapped a hand across her mouth. "Ix-nay on mentioning the odyguard-bay."

"Mal, everyone in this room speaks not just two languages, but some three or four. You really think Pig Latin's going to stump them?"

"I'm just reminding you to keep, *you know*"—she jerked her head toward Elias, standing against the wall—"a secret.

You don't want any blowback for your relationship, especially if you aren't getting the perks of it anymore."

Perks. Yeah. Kelsey assumed Mallory was talking about the toe-curling sex, which had been spectacular. But what she missed more was Elias by her side, solid as a rock. Listening to her. Laughing with her. Bolstering her. Taking lessons from his enviable sense of duty to his country that so helped her come to terms with her own.

As much as she appreciated Mallory dropping everything to come to Moncriano, it was Elias's steady presence that had made the biggest difference. That had given her the strength to not just flounder in this strange land, but start to flourish.

In this room full of people who bowed to her, people who rejoiced at her simply being alive, people who were her family...

Kelsey had never felt more alone.

Mallory vaulted out of her seat like a Jack-in-the-Box. Having seen it happen repeatedly over the past two weeks, Kelsey knew it signaled another royal approaching. Her sister dropped into a deep curtsey.

"Your Majesty."

"Miss Wishner." The king was spiffed up in a lightgray suit, also wearing a sash. His bore a slew of fancy medallions on ribbons. "I hope you don't find your duties as lady-in-waiting too onerous."

"It's a nice change of pace getting official recognition for putting up with her. I've often said I deserve a medal for it. Kelsey can be a pain in the neck."

She squeezed her sister's arm. "Mallory. Dial it back, okay?"

Her head dropped, red hair hiding her undoubtedly flaming face. "I'm so sorry, Your Majesty. I didn't mean to badmouth the princess."

But the king looked amused. "Nonsense. You should

hear Christian and Genevieve peck at each other. I'm glad you feel comfortable enough to be honest."

"Honestly, Kelsey is the other half of me." Mallory thrust her arm through Kelsey's. "She's wonderful. Once you get to know her, you'll see. There's nobody more loyal or caring or trusting."

That might be more embarrassing than her previous character testimonial. Sheesh. But also sweet. Definitely *enough,* though. "Mallory, would you go grab me a bottle of water?"

"Sure." She did a bow/curtsey combo to the king and darted away.

"I do look forward to discovering all those qualities in you," King Julian said quietly, head cocked to the side as he stared intently at her. He did that, quite often. Kelsey wondered if he was seeing her, his dead wife, or still trying to figure out who this stranger was that happened to be related to him.

"I'm also irrationally competitive at board games. And a massive introvert." She might as well tell him, in case her nerves got the better of her and caused her to let him down. "I always wanted to *watch* people, not *be* the one everybody is staring it."

The king took her hand in both of his and squeezed. "So watch them. *See* your people. Focus in on individual faces, not just the swath of the crowd. Watch the joy and excitement it brings them to be here, sharing in this momentous day."

Instead of trying to get rid of the fear—which was impossible—his advice simply did a one-eighty in focus around it. It could work. "That's...really helpful. Thank you, Tata." Kelsey reached up to throw her other arm around his neck for a hug.

After a few pats on her back, the king kissed her forehead. "I'd like you to walk out right behind me."

"Okay." It was nice that he wanted her close. But... oh. Did that placement *mean* something? Weren't they all walking out together?

"Papa, that's not right." Genevieve's sharp rebuke had most of the heads in the room swiveling toward them. And given the pissy pout on her lips, the king's request did *indeed* mean something.

One eyebrow raised, he replied, "It is my choice, Daughter." And yep, there was more than a little parental "do not test me" in his tone.

"It's a slight to Christian." She tapped at some medal on Christian's heavily decked-out sash that must indicate his awesome specialness. Or that he won a spelling bee back in the day. Kelsey would have to ask Sir Evan for a key to understand all those things. "He's your heir, he should be right behind you."

Christian flicked away her finger. "I don't think anyone will forget I'm the heir if Kelsey walks in front of me, Genny. Lighten up. It doesn't matter."

"It does," she said. "Appearances matter now more than ever, with all this unrest over joining the European Union. Kelsey needs to be recognized not as an extra family member, but symbolically as third in line to the throne. Standing in her place, behind me. Proving that she's one more bulwark in the steady constancy of this monarchy."

Kelsey winced. A lot. "Geez, Genevieve. Please don't call me a 'bulwark.' That word alone adds at least twenty pounds to my mental image of myself."

"I appreciate your instinct to highlight the safer-than-ever line of succession. But my decision stands." Aaaand the king walked away after giving his royal command. Pretty slick trick. All parents should have the ability to shut up squabbling kids that easily.

Genevieve, to her credit, did look more worried than

snitty. Or maybe Kelsey hadn't fully learned how to read her yet. Squinting as though she had a toothache, she headed to the ornately swagged table of drinks and snacks.

Christian stayed put, however, and his violet eyes met hers in reassurance. "Genny wasn't trying to put you in your place. Or make you think you're less important. The three of us, we're all equal, all in this together."

Sort of. For now. Kelsey wavered her hand back and forth. "Until the day you put on the crown."

"Yes, well, then I'm going to turn into a holy terror of decrees and orders and making both of you do my bidding. Be warned." He gave a fake-evil chuckle, deep and long.

"Luckily, that's *decades* away from happening." She'd already lost her mother without getting to know her at all. Kelsey did not intend to have the same thing happen with her father.

"God, I hope so. I'm not ready to be king."

"Is there such a thing as 'ready'?"

"Well, if I was king, there'd be an insistence on my getting married and popping out heirs immediately. Tying myself to someone for the rest of our lives just because our titles mesh up well isn't the love story of the century."

"Why not hold out for love?" Kelsey wasn't at all glad about getting her heart broken, but she did recognize that it was better to have experienced the fullness and fun of being with Elias than never having had that depth of feeling.

Christian scratched the back of his neck while rolling his eyes. "There are seven first-tier choices for my bride-to-be. Twelve second-tier, and twenty-one third-tier. All ranked in order of optimal pairing regards to titles, lands, political usefulness, and bloodlines. The chances of my falling in love with someone appropriate? You'd probably have better luck cleaning up at the baccarat tables in Monaco."

"I don't know how to play baccarat."

"Exactly my point."

They laughed again. Christian was easy to talk to. *Much* easier than Genevieve. He did feel like a brother.

"I just wanted to tell you not to be nervous. The announcement about your return—and your lovely new name—was blasted out overnight, so everyone who shows up today already knows. They won't have any expectations for speeches. All you have to do is stand next to Papa and *look* like a princess."

"Fake it 'til you make it?"

"Exactly. And you, Princess Kelsey, look elegant and quite royal today."

"Even without a tiara?" The stylist had tried to pin one on, encrusted with diamonds in fanciful tiers. Insisted that it would convey her status, as a picture was worth a thousand words. Kelsey had stood firm. She refused to officially meet her subjects dressed like a Disney princess.

Christian roared with laughter. "I heard about that. Genny stood up for you, you know. Slapped back at the stylist for suggesting a tiara could be worn before six p.m."

"I didn't realize she agreed with me. That's nice to hear."

He reached out to touch a pearl on her cameo. "I'm very proud of you for accepting all these changes we've thrown at you. And I'm so very pleased to have my sister back."

"I'm liking having a big brother, too."

With a wink, he walked away. Mallory was instantly at her elbow, brandishing the bottle of water. "Here you go."

"Do you have a pep talk for me, too?"

"Do you need another one?"

Kelsey chugged back a few glugs of water to buy time before answering. She didn't want to come off as too needy. Mallory must be sick of walking on eggshells around her for the last three days.

"I know there's no turning back now. There's a stench of

inevitability about this presentation. Like when I was twelve and had my tonsils out. Once I was on that gurney, I knew the operation would happen no matter how much I objected. So…yeah, I'm nervous."

"Forgive me, Your Highness, but what you are is brave." Elias had snuck up on her, but now that he was next to her, Kelsey *felt* every bit of his presence. "And bravery is having the strength to move forward *despite* acknowledging your fear. I'm very proud of you."

His words bolstered her. She soaked up the compliment like a sponge. Actually felt her torso lean his way for a moment.

But then Kelsey *remembered*.

Remembered that they were crazy about each other, and yet he'd still cut her out of his life. Remembered how raw and sore her heart was. The tears she'd cried the past three nights. The empty ache at not having him anymore. Remembered that it had been his *choice* to be of service to the Crown, and not to be her partner.

She sort of wished she *was* wearing a tiara to go full princess-zilla on him. Lacking that, she drew herself up straighter and lowered her lids snootily. "You don't get to be proud of me. Employees…staff…do not get to opine on my emotional status. It isn't appropriate."

Beside her, Mallory gasped, and Elias physically jolted at her harsh words. His brows drew together, mouth downturned, and he swayed backward. Regret and hurt washed over his features before his face shuttered into bodyguard mode.

"My apologies, Your Highness." He bowed and turned on his heel.

"That was harsh," Mallory clipped out.

"Hard to do, too." Kelsey put her hand on her churning belly. "Could we maybe skip the food binge and go straight to a vat of wine?"

"Tonight. Although I'm going to insist on food if you want to drink away your misery. We're smart enough to know that hangovers are not worth it."

"I have a hangover already. An emotional one. A physical one would at least distract me from that."

A staff member by the door said something she of course didn't understand—the staff didn't always remember she only spoke English—and they headed into a line.

Mallory squeezed her shoulder before getting into place. "My pep talk's pretty short. I love you, Your Highness."

Wow. A shiver chased down her spine. It was the first time her sister had used her title. Now it felt official. Well, that and the herald trumpets blaring an anthem as they crossed through the marble entryway.

The king wasn't actually first. A row of a dozen bodyguards led the way. Even louder than the double line of trumpets was the chanting coming through the enormous curved doorway. "What are they saying?" she asked King Julian.

"Welcome home."

Oh. That was lovely. The sound morphed into a solid wave of energy that practically picked her up and carried her outside, down the wide stone steps. Kelsey kept her eyes glued to the ground so the country's first sight of her wouldn't be a face-plant.

When King Julian stopped walking, she slowly looked up.

Right in front of her, at the bottom of the steps, was Elias. Breathtakingly handsome in an almost brutish way. His jacket bunched as he lifted his wrist to his mouth, communicating with the rest of the security team. Even though he wasn't hers anymore, Kelsey let herself, one last time, siphon strength from him.

Then she looked out at the smiling, clapping, cheering throng. It wasn't just the park in front of the parliament building jammed shoulder to shoulder. Hundreds, no, *thousands* of people filled the streets, rooftops, even across the bridge where Elias had taken her on their last date.

Her father had been right. They were happy, thrilled to see her with the rest of her family. Their joy was both contagious and tangible. Kelsey didn't feel like an out-of-place American.

She felt like a Villani.

She looked right, at her father, so tall and commanding—a father to the entire country. Then to her left were Christian and Genevieve. Maybe they hadn't ironed out all their personality kinks yet, but with siblings you took the good with the bad. This was her family. This was her place.

And Kelsey finally accepted, even *embraced* it.

There was no choice to be made. She belonged right here. This country, these people—they were her birthright. Her duty. Her destiny.

She'd never be the Princess Valentina an entire country had mourned and missed. But she'd stay, and figure out how to be the best possible Princess Kelsey for them.

From right behind her—in what the royal publicist had sniffed at as "unprecedented access for a commoner"—Mallory thwapped her elbow. "Wave. Smile."

It was the least she could do. Kelsey was their princess, and her people deserved the respect of a greeting in return, although she should've practiced how to wave. The queen of England did that weird sideways scoop with her hand she and Mallory always made fun of.

Crap. Was that the official royal way to do it? She peered down at Genevieve. A little elbow action. A little wrist. Totally doable.

A man near the crowd control fences along the edge of the lawn lifted the flag of Moncriano overhead. At least she could recognize that now. He shouted something Kelsey wished she understood. She smiled right at him and waved enthusiastically.

In the next moment, it was like having a car land on her. Kelsey flew sideways and hit the steps with Elias clamped tight around her. It drove the air out of her, and her diaphragm seized up. His hand cradling her head was the only thing that kept her from blacking out.

She felt the crack of her wrist on the stone in a lightning burst of pain at the same time she heard three loud pops.

The cheering turned to screams.

The king was surrounded by four men and all but carried inside at a run. Christian and Genevieve were similarly strewn as her on the steps, bodyguards covering them.

And then Kelsey turned her head to the side to see Mallory lying a few feet away, gasping, with blood spreading across the front of her blue dress.

Chapter Twenty-One

Kelsey heard the pops, just like before. Only this time they wouldn't stop.

Her eyes flew open. No, that wasn't right, either. Her eyelids tried to lift but everything was moving in slow motion. Like gallons of maple syrup weighed down her entire body.

She lifted her hand to her eyes to push them open. *That* didn't help. It banged a heavy plaster cast against her forehead as she overshot. A shockwave of pain burst through her wrist, along with a swirl of nausea.

Those sensations surfaced her more through the dregs of whatever pain medication they'd forced on her. Kelsey had refused any, even while they set her wrist, until Mallory came through surgery safely.

Mallory. *There* was the source of the beeps she'd mistaken for gunshots. It was the steady, rhythmic, and thankfully unceasing sensor of her sister's heartbeat. With far greater caution and far less speed, Kelsey pushed herself upright in the visitor chair next to the hospital bed.

No nausea this time with the more careful movement.

But she was extremely aware that one-hundred-eighty pounds of solid muscle had pushed her onto unyielding stone. Everything ached. In addition to the cast, there was gauze taped over the two stiches along her hairline where a bullet had kicked a shard of stone to graze her.

But she was *alive*, saved from the gunshots meant for her by Elias and his watchfulness.

Under other circumstances, she'd be happy. Grateful. Thrilled.

Hard to be any of those things, though, when her dress was stiff with Mallory's blood. When her sister had endured four hours of surgery, and might yet need more. When Mallory could have *died*, and it would have been all her fault.

Kelsey angled forward to look at the monitors. Heart rate and blood pressure were good. She'd insisted the nurse explain to her what to watch for, what were the normal ranges. She'd also insisted that a translator be on duty so that every nurse who came in with IV refills would explain to her exactly what they were. And she'd insisted that they digitally transfer all of Mallory's OR notes to the specialist in the States her dad recommended for a second opinion.

Her sister might've gotten shot because of Kelsey, but there was no way anything else bad would ever happen to her on Kelsey's watch.

The only thing left to do was find out how soon they could *both* get on a plane and go back to America.

To safety.

The door swished open. Kelsey expected it to be the hourly check-in by the nurse on duty, but it was Genevieve.

A wholly different version of Genevieve. Blond hair rumpled, clad in…loungewear. Sure, the tank top had hot-pink sequins in a heart shape, but it was under a half-zipped velour hoodie and matching pants.

Wow. The world truly was upside down. Kelsey squinted

at the large clock on the wall. Well, it was only five in the morning. Maybe the full princess package didn't kick in until six.

"May I come in?" Genevieve whispered.

Kelsey nodded. They'd put Mallory in the VIP room. It was large enough to have a pullout couch/bed and three chairs in addition to the one she'd pulled right next to the bed. With tasseled curtains, wood paneling, and an oriental rug by the couch, it had more the appearance of a hotel room than a hospital. After a gentle pat to Mallory's arm, Kelsey moved to the couch.

Genevieve stood at the foot of the bed for a long moment, staring at Mallory's so very pale face, framed by the braids Kelsey had done before the pain meds dragged her to sleep. Then she hitched in a ragged breath and went over to the couch. She held out a gym bag.

"This has clothes. I…didn't know if you'd be okay with me going through your things, so they're mine. But they should fit you. Comfy things. Slippers. If you give me a list of anything else you'd like, when your maid comes on duty later today, she can pull everything together."

Kelsey had lost her heels off the end of the ER gurney. A kind nurse had given her socks with rubber grips on the bottom. But other than that, she still wore her blood-stiffened dress and diamond and pearl jewelry.

Uncomfortable was putting it *mildly*. This was the kindest thing Genevieve could have done. "Thank you. And, you know, I'd be fine if you went in my room. Although at twelve, my answer might've been different. But I don't hide romance novels or a diary in my closet anymore."

Genevieve held out her other hand, which held an insulated backpack. "This has a thermos of coffee, and another of chamomile tea, in case you want to sleep. Mixed fruit, an apple, and some pastries. I'll have all your meals delivered as long as you're both here. How's Mallory supposed to get better if she's only given hospital food?"

It went so far beyond simple kindness. So far beyond what Kelsey would've expected from her. Her throat tightened, and she blinked quickly to wisp away any threat of tears. "You think of everything."

"I try." Swinging the bags sideways, Genevieve looked back at the bed. "Will Mallory be okay?"

"She'll pull through." That was the short answer. The most important one, of course.

But the team of doctors had repeated several times how it was too early to tell just how bad and permanent the damage might be regarding ever having children. Kelsey assumed the repetition was them covering their asses, should her sister's fertility be compromised, from a possible lawsuit.

Or a possible beheading, if they were old-school like that here in Moncriano.

The bags hit the carpet with a muffled thud. Genevieve closed the gap between them and put her arms around Kelsey. In a choked voice, she said, "I'm so sorry this happened to her. To you. I was so scared."

"Me, too."

It was a relief to finally admit it.

Kelsey hadn't let herself fall apart inside Parliament, as Mallory's blood pooled beneath her knees. Had stayed focused and calm with the dozens of medical professionals, hour after hour. Had stayed strong as she spoke to her parents in the States. But Genevieve admitting her own fear popped the cork out of everything Kelsey had bottled up.

She threw her arms around her sister as they both began to cry.

Sob.

Ugly cry. With shaking and sniffles and them clinging to each other tighter than shrunken sweaters. It lasted a long time. It lasted exactly the right amount of time. When they drew apart, they both reached for the tissue box on the low side table.

Without the perfect coiffure and couture, looking at Genevieve was similar to looking at herself in a funhouse mirror. Recognizable, but...not quite identical. Although now they did have identically red noses, cheeks, and eyes.

Yet another unexpected treat.

"I'm sorry," Genevieve repeated, more calmly.

"Stop saying that. You didn't shoot her." According to the last report delivered by Sir Evan, the shooter had been making a statement about the upcoming European Union vote. Shockingly, he was a nationalist. Someone who believed Moncriano—and the royal family—was better off without any outside influence.

Someone who'd shouted loud enough for hundreds to hear that *the American girl doesn't deserve to be a Villani. She can't be allowed to taint our royal family.*

Once Mallory woke up, they could both have a laugh over Kelsey's newest title "The Taint."

At least, she *hoped* they could. That was assuming her own superhuman effort to set aside her anger and disgust at the assailant would work, and allow them to move on to more healing laughter.

Genevieve tapped her sternum. "One of *my* countrymen shot her. One of *my* subjects. One of *my* people."

"Mine, too." Kelsey shrugged. "For all we know, he's connected somehow to the people who kidnapped me years ago. Or maybe he's mentally ill. Or maybe he's just evil. But the responsibility lies on him."

That's what the police said.

And the king. And Christian. And Sir Evan.

Kelsey didn't believe it. Not yet. Not at all. She knew, however, it was expected of her to parrot the official line.

"Anyway, I really mean it when I say I'm so sorry all of this happened." Genevieve half-heartedly waved an arm toward Mallory. "That if it wasn't for Elias, you'd be the one lying on that bed—or worse. Probably far, far worse."

Elias. He'd literally jumped in front of a bullet to save her life. Was that really all duty and training? Had any of it been rooted in his caring for her? Kelsey assumed she'd never know. But once he'd carried her inside at a dead run and set her down next to Mallory's bleeding body, he'd held her hand.

And it had helped.

How close she'd come herself to death, rather than her sister's narrow escape? That was too selfish to even contemplate until Mallory was fully out of the woods.

Kelsey removed her earrings. "I'm trying not to think about it."

"I can't *stop* thinking about it," her sister said in a rush. And her violet eyes turned frantic. "Because I wasn't sure you'd be any good for our family. Until I was suddenly confronted with the possibility of you being gone forever." With a drooped head, she murmured, "It made me realize that I've been horrible to you."

"Guarded. Cautious, perhaps. Okay, a *little* horrible," Kelsey conceded. She elbowed her in the side with a small smile. "But I gave as good as I got."

"I'm protective of the monarchy. This family. Our people. Christian is too busy *doing* all the things to look at the bigger picture. That's become my role." With her flawlessly French-manicured index fingers, Genevieve tapped at the sides of her eyes. "Watching it all. Watching out for us. Seeing how we're reflected in the eyes of our subjects. The eyes of the world."

It had been naïve of Kelsey to only see her sister as a pampered princess. To not look hard enough to see that all the princess perks she'd dismissed came with a vast responsibility and ingrained duty. Now? She thought Genevieve earned all those perks, and then some.

She'd never shortchange her in estimation again. "That's too much pressure for you. The weight must be crushing."

"We have centuries of history to live up to. We simply do not have the luxury of screwing up."

Kelsey marveled at how accepting Genevieve was. How calmly she spoke of a life that she'd had no choice in determining. Or was it *easier* when you didn't get to choose?

She sat and patted the cushion next to her until Genevieve sank down, too. "No wonder you didn't want some strange foreigner who didn't even speak the language tromping all over your life."

"I didn't want to risk trusting you. I've learned"—she grimaced, and Kelsey *knew* there was a bigger story there to be unearthed over the Moncriano version of margaritas and nachos—"the hard way not to trust anyone outside of the family."

It hurt her heart that her sister lived so closed a life, emotionally. In Kelsey's little Michigan town, she trusted *everyone*. How could Genevieve exist in that huge palace full of people and only fully trust a handful of them?

"That's sad. So limiting. So unfair."

"It's a reality of the title, but I overlooked the basic fact— you *are* family. I need to be protective of you, too. We are so very lucky to have you back with us."

"Don't make me start crying again," Kelsey said, pushing the words past a suddenly thick throat.

"Would some coffee help?"

"Yes. Always." As Genevieve unpacked the thermos and pulled out actual china mugs from a wall cabinet—*VIP room for the win!*—Kelsey realized how much better she felt with company for this vigil until Mallory woke up. So she asked a question that would've been unimaginable even a few days ago. "How long can you stay?"

"As long as you need. I'm in lockdown whether I stay here or at the palace. The opinion is that the shooter was working alone, but until they finish searching his house, questioning his friends and family, and going over his computer byte by byte, our schedules are officially on hold."

Kelsey was desperate to hear the details she'd been unable to glean from the television mounted near the ceiling. She'd turned it off hours ago after seeing the raw footage of the attack.

She never wanted to see it again.

No doubt she'd see it over and over in her nightmares, though.

And the newscast not being in English just amped up her frustration. Beyond the basic curiosity of trying to make sense of a total stranger wanting to kill her, there was an even bigger question that wouldn't stop ratcheting around in her brain.

It was one she couldn't ask Marko or Christian or even the nurses. Kelsey didn't trust any of them to tell her the truth.

Genevieve, though? Even with the massive olive branch they'd just shared, her sister no doubt still had enough snark in her soul with Kelsey's name on it to give it to her straight.

She pulled over the gym bag. Unzipped it and riffled through at least three sets of comfy clothes. "Before I go change, will you tell me something?"

"Like a party game to pass the time? Have I ever petted a kangaroo, or can I knit?"

Kelsey almost giggled at the seeming randomness that probably hid a very funny story about an official royal visit to Australia.

"That could be fun, later." Her thoughts were all over the place. Genevieve being so nice had popped the top of the raw emotions she'd tamped down while by herself. "But what I want, no *need* to know is"—she bit her bottom lip, so chapped from worrying at it the whole time Mallory had been in surgery—"are people mad at me? For putting all of you in danger?"

"Who? Papa? The Prime Minister?"

"Yes." Elias, too. He'd come within a hair of being shot himself, because of her. Was he mad? "And everyone else. The whole country."

"Our people? Our subjects? They love you. This didn't diminish the thrill of your return at all. And Mallory's now a national hero." Genevieve passed her a mug. "I thought we covered how this wasn't your fault?"

"It was, though," she insisted. Not in a *"Go directly to jail, do not pass Go, do not collect $200"* way. Ethically. Morally. "The responsibility of firing the gun lies with that man. But he did it because of who I am."

"Half American?"

"Or half-European royalty? If it were true, it'd be easier to straddle. But no, I'm *fully* both." Kelsey held her hands out, palms up. "How can I expect our people to accept it when I've struggled with it for weeks?"

"You simply accept it, like grass being green or Belgian chocolate being superior to all others. It is who you are." Genevieve shrugged with the nonchalance of all French women in the classic black-and-white movies she and Mallory binged on every summer. An easy insouciance. Something else intrinsically princess-y.

Kelsey knew that. She didn't know how to pull that off.

She flopped her hands into her lap. Well, flopped one, and carefully set down the one in the cast. "I don't *know* who I am anymore. For so long, I saw myself through very specific lenses. The girl who wanted to move to New York. A graphic designer. Someone who hid behind a computer but loved watching everything unfold. Devoted daughter and sister."

"And?"

The simplicity of the question startled her. "None of those things are true anymore."

"Nonsense. You fulfilled your dream of moving to New York. You accomplished that goal. It didn't last, but you still hit the milestone. The same with your career. You made it." Genevieve curled her legs underneath her and settled back with her coffee.

"I made a mess of it all." Had she jumped over the border from venting to whining? Probably. Kelsey blamed it on the residual painkillers in her system. "I don't know what I'm doing here. I've tried so hard for two weeks, I promise. Moncriano is a wonderful country. But I don't know how I'd fill every day, what my new career would entail."

"Think of it more as a calling than a career," Genny suggested dryly.

Restless, and eager to lay it all out and have her sister diagnose how to fix it, Kelsey got up and paced across the thick rug. "I don't know how to leave my life behind. To see it erased as if it never happened, as if it didn't matter. I don't want my parents vilified by strangers who don't know the full story. Idiots on social media whipping up a storm when they don't understand what was sacrificed to save a helpless baby and raise me."

"Is that all of it?"

"Aside from the fact I spent all this time worrying about the wrong thing." She'd worked it out after the third phone conversation with her parents. The one where they said a police car had parked in front of their house. Not to arrest them again, but for their protection until this crisis passed.

"I'm going out on a very short limb to say you worried about lots of wrong things."

Kelsey rolled her eyes. Guess she'd been right about Genevieve not sugarcoating her thoughts. "This one is bigger than any of my petty personal concerns. My being here has led to danger." She pointed at one sister, and then across the room at the other. "For you. For Mallory. For *everyone* related to me. I've stirred up trouble. I'm the problem."

"Do you have a solution?" Genevieve circled her finger through the air as if to fast forward. "Or may we jump to where I tell you just how deeply wrong you are?"

"The solution is to leave. To go home. As soon as Mallory can get on a plane, I'm taking her back to America and safety."

After choking back a laugh—and the coffee she'd almost spit out—Genevieve said, "There is no such thing as safety for royals. Merely the illusion of it."

"Oh, I felt very safe my whole life, until I came here. Until I acquired a title that can rile people to violence. I can't, I *won't*"—she cut her arm down through the air like a sword—"bring that danger to people I care about."

Genevieve pointed out the window that showed the faint pinkening hint of dawn. "And returning to a city full of muggings and murders will solve everything?"

It'd be a start? "I need to fade back into the background, where I'm comfortable. Where I won't be noticed or cause any more problems."

With a crook of her finger, Genny indicated that Kelsey should come back to the couch. Once seated, she ordered in a very imperious and regal tone, "Don't. Go."

She didn't want to. Not after finally deciding, less than a day ago, to stay. Not merely deciding. *Embracing* the idea. Still... "It's for the best."

"Have you really been angsting over this since you arrived?"

How was it a surprise? "Yes. The king said I had to choose by tomorrow. You were there when he said it."

"Papa and his pronouncements." Genevieve started to

put her hand over Kelsey's heart. Then she frowned at the smears of dried blood, plucked a fresh tissue, and used it as a buffer. "You've been overthinking it. There is no choice to be made. Just as you know exactly who you are."

"I don't." That was kind of the thesis sentence to her whole rant.

"You are *Kelsey*. It is that simple. Inside." She patted once more, then leaned back. "Where you live, your job — those are facts that change for people all the time."

That thought hung in the air like an iridescent bubble of possibility. "Well, that's true."

"You love your family, your sister. Now you just have more of us to love." After a lightning-fast flash of an almost-smile, Genevieve said more softly, "Especially if you're willing to make a fresh start with me."

"I can't help but love the Villanis. All of you. You're a part of me, my heritage, my blood." Surprising, how that felt so natural to say. She'd fought against it, worried about being untrue to the parents who raised her.

But family had always been her touchstone. Had her heart skipped ahead, from day one, to accepting the Villanis as her family long before her brain had?

Genevieve patted her leg this time. *Without* a tissue. "You're kind to people. Interested. Curious. No matter where you go, you carry that inside you."

"It's been wonderful meeting everyone. That part I've enjoyed." Because people were interesting. Universally. At least, they interested her. She hadn't seen the wide swath of stories that would've played out in Manhattan, but Kelsey had been confined to the palace.

"You've been worried about logistics and details. Things like a new language and wardrobe and even food."

"Yes." *Not* as interesting because of the way her control had been stripped away by it all. Kelsey pointed up at the television. "There's a national emergency going on, and I don't have the faintest idea of what's happening because I don't speak the language. I feel helpless. A tidal wave of changes that I haven't figured out how to swim through."

"You will. You'll learn." Genevieve firmed her lips into a thin, serious line before giving a sharp nod. "Because you have to. Because there is no other choice."

"There is. I can go home."

"*This* is your home. If you go back to America, the danger won't disappear. You'll forevermore be a Princess of Moncriano. You'll still need security. It will simply be more complicated in a foreign country."

The decision had seemed so obvious at midnight. Now, it seemed almost obviously wrong.

How had she thought people would ignore her, ignore her title, just by switching her address?

Wishful thinking, that was how.

Kelsey scrubbed the heels of her hands over her eyes. "I…it…you raise a good point."

"I *am* your older sister. Being smarter comes with the extra two years of life experience I've racked up."

In some ways, *all* big sisters were the same. She'd been hearing that nonsense from Mallory her entire life.

"Your pep talk was having a real impact until that last sentence," she snarked.

"You simply have to accept that things are different now, and will remain that way. No amount of hiding or wishing will change the fact that you are, indeed, a princess."

If she did that, if she stayed, it would mean confronting her broken heart every day. It meant seeing Elias, interacting with him, but not in the ways she craved.

She'd give up easy access to nachos and holiday TV marathons. Give up the career she'd trained for, albeit to be handed a new one on a doily-lined, *actual* silver platter that came with unbeatable job security. A million little things Kelsey couldn't even name yet that would be different here than in New York. She could stay and adapt and figure out a way to be herself in the process.

But doing all of that without Elias seemed...empty. Insurmountable.

Because he couldn't see past her being a princess as a problem.

And her problem was being a princess *without* him.

Chapter Twenty-Two

Elias wanted a mint, a nap, and to go on a four-day bender. Instead, he straightened his tie—and his spine—as he entered Christian's office.

Was this what other people felt like before an audience with the prince? Jumpy? Nervous? Because the coffee he'd been mainlining for almost three days straight since the attack had his gut in spasms.

Or it was because he and his best friend hadn't cleared the air yet? They'd had their worst fight of all time and not resolved anything. And then he'd gone and let the prince's sister-by-proxy get shot. Not to mention how he'd hurt Kelsey by pushing her away. How much he'd hurt *himself* with that action, no matter how necessary.

Worst. Week. Ever.

"You summoned me, Your Highness?" That was new, too. The prince never sent for Elias. He just texted him to get his ass up here.

Until now.

"Yes." Christian stood and buttoned his suit jacket.

"Thank you for coming so promptly."

Was this what they'd come to? Polite prattle? "Well, your wish is literally my command, Your Highness."

"Do take a seat." Christian gestured to the chair across the desk. The chair used for *other* people who hadn't laughed and drank and trained and sailed and stood by the man through thick and thin.

Damn it, Elias wasn't giving up on their decades of friendship that easily. He knew he'd fucked up. Knew Christian was furious that he'd moved in on Kelsey. But that was over now. And, as a result, he needed his friend more than ever.

So he remained standing. "Since when do you send a minion for me? Can't text anymore? Did your phone self-destruct after that heiress from Luxembourg sent the topless photos?"

Christian looked over his head to the painting of a sea storm above the sofa and said coolly, "I wasn't sure you'd respond."

Elias knew Christian felt he'd failed in his duties on that date with Kelsey. The thought that he doubted his loyalty, though? That was a donkey kick to the stomach. "You are my sworn liege. My sworn brother-in-arms. I would never ignore you."

"Is that what—" Christian broke off and shook his head. "I assumed you were furious with me."

"Why?"

"Because I blatantly and unforgivably insulted you when I accused you of being a lax bodyguard. Of betraying your duty. Dishonoring your office. And then you risked your life to save my sister. You threw your body between her and a bullet." Christian came around the desk swiftly to stand right in front of Elias. "I'm ashamed that I said those things to you. All I can do is offer my most sincere apology."

And *then* he started to drop to one knee.

It was the most surreal moment of Elias's life, aside from the one three days ago, when he'd kept his ex-girlfriend from being assassinated.

He caught his friend beneath the forearm and didn't let him sink any lower. "Stop. I won't let you apologize."

"Too late, but I'd be grateful if you'd accept it."

He dropped his hand, shaking his head. "I can't, because I *did* let you down. You were right. I led with my heart instead of my head, and it was dangerous. The events of Sunday prove it. If I'd been a molecule less focused, I wouldn't have saved the princess. You telling me to break it off with her made all the difference."

"You did?"

What was with the surprise? "Of course. You told me to."

"You've a mind of your own, Elias." A hint of their usual teasing surfaced in the sting in the prince's tone. "The past two weeks have proven that."

"I'm sorry. I meant to tell you that I'd followed through, but then...well, the world turned upside down."

"No kidding. I meant to apologize sooner but couldn't make it happen. Papa's not well."

Guilt flashed through Elias, remembering the very personal request he'd sent to the king just yesterday. "I thought he was uninjured?"

Christian jerked his head to indicate the sofa, and they both sat. "Physically, yes. Emotionally? He's a wreck. He's been in a state of shock since Kelsey reappeared, blowing off appointments. Almost like he can't accept this new reality where he actually gets to be with his daughter. And then to almost lose her *again* on Sunday? It broke him."

"Kelsey's fine. Her wrist will heal. Her sister's being moved as we speak from the hospital to convalesce here at the palace."

"He hasn't left his suite."

That was shocking. King Julian never missed appointments, rarely took sick days. He said he didn't want to disappoint anyone when half of his job was just showing up. "He didn't go to the hospital to visit Kelsey and Mallory?"

"No. He Skyped them. And he's kept a few appointments that way, or via phone. But he won't come out. I've been running myself ragged, not just picking up the slack, but covering for him."

What a clusterfuck on top of all the other life-and-death drama. Christian must be tearing his hair out. "Does he need a doctor?"

"Hell, yes. There have been daily visits. Pills to calm him down, I guess. I'm not getting the whole story. I'll respect his privacy for a few more days. Then I'll throw the doctor onto the rack until he tells me everything."

"If you need a hand with that…"

"Always." They clasped forearms and squeezed. Hard.

Just like that, they were fine.

Thank *God*.

The prince violently jerked at the knot of his blue tie to loosen it. "Shit. I wish you hadn't broken up with her."

That made two of them. "Kind of sending mixed messages, Christian."

"I hate the thought of Kelsey being upset about losing you on top of worrying about Miss Wishner. Can you fix it? You want to, right?"

Yes, desperately. Every cell in his body ached to be close to Kelsey again. "My wanting her is not, and never was, the issue."

"But you *do* care for her? I mean, you did save her life."

Care for her? Sure. That was the watered-down version of it, anyway. Since breaking up with Kelsey and then being confronted with her almost being killed pierced Elias with the surety that he was falling in love with her.

With a small dip of his head, Elias said formally, "That was my duty and my privilege. Just as it is my duty to stand back and let her find happiness with a suitable man. Of which I am *not*."

"Damn it, I was an ass when I said that. Of course your lack of royal blood doesn't make you any less."

"Technically, it does precisely that."

"Hell, you've been my best friend my whole life. Being a"—Christian cleared his throat and put his hand beneath his lapel in a Napoleon pose—"*most worthy and trusted confidante* of the heir to the throne gives you plenty of street cred."

Right. Because that was all it took. "I don't think street cred is on the list of desired qualities in prospective partners for the princess."

"It makes you not just good enough, but more than acceptable in my eyes. So screw what anyone else says. *Including* your own antiquated notions of worthiness. I refuse to let you distance yourself based on some archaic title, or lack thereof."

Didn't Christian see that, while kind and good for clearing the air between them, this attitude only emphasized the painful finality of his break with Kelsey? "I'm relieved my place at your side is secure. But I'm a commoner. No matter how you try and spin it, our country would not accept me by the princess's side."

"True, undeniably so." Christian rose swiftly, walking to the fireplace to rest his elbow on the mantel. "I haven't thanked you properly for saving Kelsey's life."

"No need. All in a day's work." The guilt that had been eating at him needed to be released. Wincing, Elias said, "A better man would've saved Mallory from losing a few pints of blood. I'm already designing a new training regimen to deal with large crowd identification."

"That's excellent news. And don't let me catch you beating yourself up about Miss Wishner again. You had one job, and you executed it flawlessly. We failed Miss Wishner by not providing her solo protection." His brows drew together into a fierce scowl. Especially fierce with the dark circles under his eyes from doing double duty for the king. "It was an oversight that was quite…costly."

The Royal Protection Service had already implemented her new bodyguard rotation. It stretched their ranks, so Elias was headed out to the training facility in a few days to test who was ready to be cycled up to full royal duty. And if his request to the head of the RPS for permanent reassignment was granted, he'd stay out there.

"We've worked out the schedule to give her full coverage. There's going to be some long shifts as we compensate for the extra assignments on the duty roster."

"Then why did you ask to be cycled out of active rotation?"

Damn it. He'd been hoping the prince wouldn't find out until it was a *fait accompli*. Unfortunately, their deep friendship had probably prompted a check-in with the prince about his unusual request.

"I think I can do more good elsewhere, training others, focusing on how to prevent another assassination attempt, rather than just react to one."

"You don't want to lay your life down for me anymore?"

"No, I don't." Elias had worried it'd be impossible to say that to Christian. But now, in the moment, his mind was clear and calm. This was the right choice. Now. *Finally.*

For Kelsey, and himself.

Eyes wide, Christian gave a low whistle. "That's harsh."

"I will—as your best friend—do everything to protect you. But not as a *job*. Because"—Elias paused, wanting to tread carefully—"my life is as valuable, as worthy as yours."

An odd, secretive smile played over Christian's face. "I agree. My thanking you for saving my sister comes with a reward. A promotion."

Not *again*. Elias waved off the suggestion. "Enough with this. I don't want a promotion for doing my job."

"I let you slough me off last time, when you found Kelsey. You're not allowed to reject my largesse a second time." Christian lifted down his ceremonial sword. He held it out, flat, pointing at Elias. "So you're getting that knighthood. No argument. As of today, you're no longer a commoner. You're Sir Elias, Duke of Arcalia. Comes with a nice income, too."

His head was spinning. No longer a commoner? "I...I don't—"

Christian sliced the sword through the air. "Don't you dare finish that sentence with the words 'want' or 'deserve.' You'll take the damned dukedom. And you'll move off of protection duty to head-up the training program for the royal bodyguards."

Even though it was what he'd requested, Christian's description of the job was odd. That would only be a promotion on paper, to the outside world. What was Christian up to? "That's a lateral move, not a vertical one," Elias pointed out.

"That's one interpretation, but it has the added benefit of keeping you out of danger, which is what I believe Kelsey would want." Smiling broadly, the prince tapped a finger against his temple. "I promised to figure out what you truly want. The favor you need but are afraid to request. This is me coming through, repaying you for, well, everything."

It sounded like Christian had stacked the deck so that Elias could date his sister. And gave him the change of career that was exactly what Elias had realized he needed after his brush with death. *Unexpected* didn't begin to describe these moves. Still, he needed confirmation. Yanking loose his own suddenly too-tight tie, he asked slowly, "What are you saying?"

Christian put the tip of the sword on the floor and stood hip-shot. "Look, I know you're brave enough to sacrifice your life for the good of our country. Nobody asked you, however, to sacrifice your heart."

"*You* did, actually."

"I recanted, apologized. Acknowledged I was an ass. Can we move on?"

A wave of hope surged through Elias, knotting his stomach up again, but in a good way. "Please do."

"The only thing standing in your way now is you. And that boulder of honor and duty that your father's weighed you down with all these years. Are you brave enough to follow your heart? Brave enough to, like Kelsey, let go of your old life plan? Take a different path?"

He'd take that leap in an instant. These last few days without Kelsey had been torture. He'd made a mistake giving her up, and he'd do anything to fix that mistake. There was only one problem... "What if she doesn't want to stay?"

"Give her good enough reason to." Christian leaned his sword against the desk and crossed his arms. Then he lowered the boom with that annoying, princely "do my bidding" look that was only ever a joke to Elias. "Didn't I give you that order a week ago?"

Yes. And he would not let his prince down.

"Like I said, your wish is my command."

Chapter Twenty-Three

Kelsey had a hard time keeping up with Lathan as he escorted her through the Royal Treasury beneath the palace.

There was too much to look at. The walls dripped with antique tapestries. Long glass cases held crowns and scepters. The king's full coronation robes were displayed, along with armor and Queen Serena's wedding dress.

"There's so much history down here. Why didn't I get to see it before?"

"The Royal Treasury is open to tourists daily. Your family only comes down here in the evenings." Then he slid her a knowing glance. "I believe your evenings were otherwise occupied, Your Highness."

What...what was that? She thought Marko was the only bodyguard who knew about her romance with Elias. No way would she risk confirming, especially since it was over. "I know the grand duchess requested this to be a private meeting, but you *will* interrupt us if Mallory needs anything, yes?"

He tapped his earbud. "Your sister's asleep for the night,

according to her guard."

"I'll bet. The move and getting settled back at the palace wore her out." She still had drains in, but her pain was managed and she'd wanted out of the hospital.

Kelsey had celebrated this step in Mallory's recovery by taking a bubble bath to rid herself of *eau de hospital*. Due to the summons by her grandmother, she'd even ditched the yoga pants after three days straight and dressed in a sundress sprigged with pink flowers. Girlier than her taste, but a welcome change from the institutional-green scrubs she'd been surrounded by.

"And her nurse has instructions to let us know if she wakes and asks for you. Even the very real fear of annoying the grand duchess won't keep me from updating you."

"Thank you."

Lathan opened a door that looked like all the others they'd passed. But once open, it revealed a three-inch thick steel vault door, propped open. "I'll be out here if you need anything, Your Highness."

No dig at Lathan's politeness, but what she needed was her old bodyguard back.

Might as well wish to find a unicorn horn in one of the displays they'd passed, though. Kelsey plastered on a smile. Couldn't risk having her grandmother ask what was bothering her and—out of the nonstop worry and exhaustion that had filled her week—accidentally admit that she missed her boyfriend.

Because with Mallory officially out of the woods? It left Kelsey waaaay more time to reflect on how miserable she was without Elias.

The sensor lights flicked on in a sequence with every step. And then she rounded a corner to see a room filled floor to ceiling with drawers of differing heights, a small table with a mirror, and a single velvet-cushioned chair.

Oh, and *Elias*.

Her heart did a triple beat. At his handsomeness in his black suit and deep purple tie. At his nearness. At simply sharing a moment with him again.

"What are you doing here? The Grand Duchess is on her way."

"She's not coming. She granted me a favor by requesting you join her. Of all the people in Alcarsa Palace, I was sure she was the one you wouldn't refuse."

"Why bother with the subterfuge?"

He held out a hand to indicate she should sit. "Our last private conversation did not end well. Entirely my fault, but I wasn't sure you'd give me another chance." Elias stepped forward, eyes suddenly intense and gleaming under all the pin lights. "And I want another chance, Your Highness."

That was a painful carrot for him to dangle. "Why? Nothing's changed. You chose the royal house and your duty over me."

"True. That was, however, the wrong choice. And it's important that you hear how soon I came to that realization."

"I'll play along. You dumped me last Thursday. When did you decide you were wrong?"

"Thursday. When you started to cry and I realized I hurt you."

He could say that, but she'd still been alone and brokenhearted for the past six nights. "Funny how it's Wednesday and this is the first I'm hearing of your great change of heart."

"That's the thing with mistakes. Realizing you made one is easier than figuring out how to fix it. I knew I missed you. I knew I'd regret 'til the end of my days breaking it off with you. I knew I'd do anything to get you back."

"You didn't do *anything*." Yes, that was a pure snark attack on her part. But Kelsey was that worst of combinations:

both mad and sad.

"I wanted to." His hands hung at his sides, limp, just taking what she hurled at him. "I wracked my brain to come up with a solution. The only one I'd come to was leaving the Royal Protection Service. It wouldn't solve the problem of my being a commoner, but my duty to the crown would no longer impede us."

Oh no. Thoughtful, but impossible. "Elias, I'd never ask you to quit."

He wouldn't be able to live with himself, and eventually he'd end up resenting her. Kelsey knew that wasn't the path for them.

"That's because you're wonderful. And there was the next problem. I knew you wouldn't *let* me give up my career for you. So I was back to square one. Missing you. Unable to see a future where I could be with you."

Great. They were both miserable, and nothing would change. Kelsey stood. "This is a really fun little recap. May I go now?"

"Please, Princess. Five more minutes." When she gave a tight nod, he proceeded. "When I saw you on Sunday, you looked so sad."

"Yes. That's on you, by the way."

Huh. The snark just kept popping out of her mouth.

Kelsey didn't even blame it on her near-death experience, or almost losing Mallory. She *hurt*. No matter his noble motivation, Elias was the one who caused it. So yes, a small, mean part of her wanted to hurt him back.

"I know, and I'm sorry." Elias crossed his hands over his heart and gave a small bow. "Then I saved your life. And discovered that while I absolutely wanted to save you, I didn't want to die. That bullet that hit your sister? It impacted me, too."

It seemed impossible. Captain Elias Trebanti lived his

life to *give* it. A bullet wouldn't scare him. It wouldn't dent his impenetrable armor of honor and duty. "How?" she challenged, arms crossed, ready to defiantly shoot down whatever he said.

"I don't want to die, not for someone else. My life isn't worth any less than someone with royal blood."

Oh, he'd said exactly the right thing to melt Kelsey's heart. How had it taken him twenty-nine years to come to this conclusion? "Of course not."

"I gave you up, broke up with you, but I was so wrong. If I died? I'd never get to see you again, not even from afar." He swiped his hand over the top of his head, as if trying to wipe away the image in his mind. "That's simply not acceptable. I can't give you up—forever—on every level. And I couldn't cause you pain like that, either."

"If you died, I'd be quite overwhelmingly bereft," she confessed with a teasing curl to her lips. Wherever this revelation of his was leading, it seemed to be *back* to her. And that put a little pep that she'd been missing for almost a week, a little sass, back in Kelsey.

Elias thumped his chest. "*I* matter. To myself, and to you. And if not to a single other person in the world, that's still more than enough. To fight for, to live for. So I asked to be taken off active protection duty."

"What about your father? Won't he be devastated?"

"It's been twenty-five years. Nobody needs my father to atone—except himself. Nobody blames him—except himself. So I asked the king to give him a royal pardon. Ultimately, it's simply a fancy piece of paper with gold lettering. But the officialness of it might appease him. Either way, it isn't up to me any more to keep trying to atone on his behalf."

Unable to resist, Kelsey squeezed his arm through the thick wool of his coat. "Elias, I'm so proud of you. You've spent all these years being brave for everyone else. You're finally doing it for yourself."

He slid his hand up to cover hers, and then lifted it to press a soft kiss onto her knuckles. "Well, not just for myself. I'm doing it for you, to have another chance with you, Princess. To stop living my life for everyone else. To worry about my happiness. You know what makes that possible? *Your* happiness. Duty, honor, scandal, my oath to the crown...none of that comes close to mattering like you do. I don't want to give up my life. I do want to give up every and anything else that it'll take to get you back."

Kelsey was rocked to her core. He'd chosen her after all. "I never demanded that you jump through hoops for me."

"I'm not. I knew that if I quit my job—or at least transitioned it, which is a story for later—you'd be okay as long as I did it for both of us."

She believed him, truly. A brush with death was powerful enough to shift priorities around, make a person see what mattered the most in life. Nevertheless, she had to state the obvious one last time before jumping into his arms.

"It can't be just for me, Elias. That would be a selfish, unforgiveable act on my part to let you make that sacrifice."

"Don't you see? Choosing to leave the RPS, to abandon my duty to the crown isn't selfishness at all. I choose you. I choose my duty to protect your heart, to keep you whole and happy."

"That's...overwhelming." And wonderful, more than she'd dreamed possible.

"But I didn't want to influence your decision to stay in Moncriano. And then there was the attack. I heard you were going back to America, so I stayed away from you. Luckily, your brother had my back."

The surprises kept coming. "What did Christian do?"

"Long story short? He gave me a new, non-dangerous job. Still serving the crown. Before you give him too much credit, it's one I'd already asked for. But then he gave me a dukedom."

"Why would he do that?"

"Because your brother loves you very much and wants to do whatever is necessary to ensure your happiness."

"*Sir* Elias?" That would take some getting used it. And it was also *hot*. "Can we back up to where you choose me?"

"I do. I did. In my mind, at least. Which is a lousy, half-assed way to go about it." Elias dropped to one knee. "So I apologize, Princess. I'm sorry for hurting you. I'm sorry for being stubborn, for only seeing one possibility. I'm sorry for not knowing all along that being happy with you is better than being unhappy in service to the crown. I'm most of all sorry for not being available to comfort you as you struggled the past few days with Mallory."

That was a lot of groveling. Almost too much to take. All she'd really needed was that first line—the *I'm sorry*.

Kelsey stepped forward and pressed his head to her stomach to keep him from continuing. And oh, the feel of the short, soft stubble of his hair weakened her knees. "You're forgiven."

He breathed in a long, deep sigh as he circled his arms around her legs. "Just like that?"

"It turns out I've had a bit of a head-clearing epiphany of my own along the same lines. Because I was mired in sticking to a single path myself, I didn't accept this new life, and agonized about giving up my old one."

"It's not a simple thing to do, starting over."

He was always on her side. Kelsey loved that. "It's not impossible, either. Not half as hard as I made it out to be." She slid down to kneel with him. She couldn't say who moved first—just that together, they interlaced both hands. And it slid the cracked pieces of her heart back into place. "Want to know what I figured out? Because, in a funny twist of synchronicity, it fits both of us now."

His blue eyes twinkled and his entire demeanor relaxed. "Enlighten me."

"Who you think you are isn't always who you are meant to be."

Elias threw back his head and laughed. "That's... brilliant."

"Isn't it? I can't take all the credit. Genevieve helped."

"*Princess* Genevieve? Your sister?"

"Strange, but true. Yes, I panicked about living up to the expectations of an entire country. But I can handle this change, and whatever else life throws at me, with the right support, and as long as I believe in myself."

Solemnly, Elias said, "I believe you can do anything."

"I know. I'm so grateful for your belief in me. It's as if you lent me your strength, your bravery, until I found my own."

"Does that mean you're staying?"

Kelsey nodded. "The only thing holding me back was the thought of being here every day, with you, and not being *with* you. Having to miss you in plain sight. But I decided to be scared, accept it, and keep going anyway. That's my new life plan."

Elias shifted to lift her hands to his mouth. He softly kissed the back of each one. "Will you? Be with me? Give me another chance to stand by you and work to make you smile as much and as often as possible?"

Eyes filling with tears, Kelsey nodded again. "Yes." She leaned in for a kiss. Started to throw her arms around his neck, but Elias leaned back, out of her reach.

"I suppose that means you don't need your present."

She made a time-out sign with her hands. Did they use those in European soccer? Well, she'd teach him what it meant. Because they had their whole future in front of them. "Whoa. I'm going to chalk that up to English being your second language, because this girl never turns down presents."

He swiveled to grab a white bakery box, tied with a red ribbon, from underneath the chair. "Open it."

Kelsey tucked her legs to the side and lifted the cardboard top. Inside was an enormously tall cheesecake. The puffy edges were golden brown. It was…it couldn't be… "Is this a Junior's cheesecake?"

"Yes, overnighted just for you. I thought perhaps I could bribe you into staying in Moncriano by proving that whatever you miss from America can be brought over."

"Omigosh. This is amazing. Thank you." Kelsey lifted it to her face and sniffed. Glorious. "I don't know if I can make it last until Mallory's allowed to eat more than broth, but she'll kill me if she doesn't get a slice."

"Not a problem." Elias tapped a paper sealed in tape on the lid of the box. "That's their recipe, because it's bloody expensive to overnight a cheesecake. I hoped the palace chefs could try their hand at recreating it for you."

"They can try as often as they like. I'll be a willing victim." Carefully, she set it back down. No point risking a single crumb of deliciousness, no matter how giddy with happiness she was right now. "Will you share it with me? Tonight?"

His voice dropped to a sexy growl. "I hope to share many things with you tonight." Elias stroked a hand up her leg, to make sure she got all the innuendos he'd delivered on a silver platter. "But there's one more thing. The reason we're down here. With your grandmother's permission, by the way."

"You asked the grand duchess for help?"

Grimacing, he said, "I told you I'd do anything to get you back." Elias pulled her to her feet. Then he opened a drawer on the back wall. "I'm so sorry that I made the automatic choice before. That I chose duty over you, over my heart. But it wasn't what I truly wanted. What I *truly* want is the woman

I'm falling in love with, and I vow to put you first henceforth."

Who knew *henceforth* could be so romantic? "I feel the same way. Like everything is better and brighter when shared with you. I'm so head over heels for you, Elias."

"That's a relief."

"You've finally offered me a princess perk I actually want—*yourself.*"

"I'm not ignoring that you're a princess anymore. Whether you stayed or left, I thought you might need a reminder of who you truly are." He rummaged in the drawer, his back to her.

"I can't, I *won't* deny the fact that I'm a princess. It isn't a problem to be solved. It is literally in my blood."

"Good." Turning around, he handed her an exquisite, delicate tiara. The pearl-topped loops on each side rose to a fleur-de-lis in the center, the whole thing encrusted with diamonds. "I want to be next to you as you walk down this new path. To encourage you to embrace everything about being a Villani, to make up for how hard we both fought against it."

"This is beautiful."

"I thought you could keep it in your bedroom. According to the grand duchess, it was your mother's favorite."

The man's thoughtfulness knew no bounds. *That's* what made her feel like a princess—the way Elias treated her. "The bedroom can wait. I want to wear it now. For you." Kelsey set it on her head, pushing the combs into her hair. It fit perfectly. Like it belonged there. "Kiss me."

"It would be my great pleasure, Princess."

Elias's mouth took hers. Another perfect fit.

Epilogue

One Week Later

Kelsey held tight to Elias's hand. Half because she wanted to, and half because she was *able* to in front of everyone, finally. It was such a relief to not hide their relationship anymore.

Although she'd very much like to be in hiding right about now…

"I still don't understand," she said to Genevieve, seated next to her in the row of stiff-backed antique chairs.

"Why we tricked you and claimed this was another family portrait session?" Genny held up her hands, palms out. "Don't look at me. That was Gran's idea."

Odd. The grand duchess didn't seem the sort to play games. She was more the type to give orders and expect them to be obeyed no matter what.

"Oh, dear," murmured Duchess Mathilde. She was pacing in front of the purple floor-to-ceiling drapes of the Peacock Gallery, shut tight against the gathering throng outside. "I was concerned you wouldn't react well to our little ruse. Honesty is always the best policy."

"Except for when it isn't," snapped the grand duchess. She was seated at the end of the line of chairs. With more than a bit of exaggerated sighing and shoving, she twisted her chair sideways and forward to be able to look down the row at Kelsey. "Ten days ago, we gathered as a family to wave at our subjects. And we were attacked. Mallory was shot. It was... traumatic. For all of us."

"Agreed," Kelsey said fervently.

Elias brought his other hand up to sandwich hers in comfort. He did that a lot now. Offered comfort and touches and was an absolute rock when she'd collapsed in tears after loading a sedated Mallory on the royal jet to heal back home to Michigan.

He still didn't speak up much in front of the older royals. Relaxing, dropping his guard around Mathilde and Agathe was a work in progress. Hard to kick years of habit in a matter of days. But he made his *presence* as her boyfriend very much known.

"I thought you might still be...a bit...*ruffled* from the experience. That you might spend all week in a state of anxiousness if told early about our balcony appearance today."

Oh. *Oh*.

Her grandmother had lied to be *kind*. To try and protect her until the last possible moment. It was a very, very grandmotherly gesture. It was also very, very surprising. In the best possible way.

Kelsey almost jumped up.

At the last second, she remembered that she was all princess-ed up, with orange and beige spectator pumps to coordinate with the ornate orange floral design of her cream dress. One she'd chosen after finding out that Genevieve planned to wear a green silk blouse with a white pencil skirt.

And wonder of wonders, her stylists hadn't put up a fight at all about them not matching.

Mindful of her stilettos, she clung tightly to Elias until she'd slowly achieved verticality. Then, silently cursing the thick pile of the carpet, Kelsey kept her eyes glued to the floor as she carefully walked down to the grand duchess.

Once there, she crouched and took her hands. "Thank you for trying to protect me."

"Nonsense," the grand duchess blustered. But she didn't pull her hands away. "That's what you've got that strapping young man for. Sir Elias has more than proven he's all the protection you need."

Wow. A compliment for her boyfriend, too? If it wasn't eleven in the morning, Kelsey would wonder if her grandmother had been nipping at the gin.

"Elias *is* pretty great. But so is having a family who cares about me. And you were guarding my heart. Thank you." Kelsey leaned in to drop a kiss on her powdered cheek. "I'm fine, though."

"Are you?" the older woman shot back.

"Elias explained that you all do this every year. Go out on the balcony, wave at the crowd, and unveil the floral wreath in honor of Queen Serena's birthday. I've never gotten the chance before to do *anything* for my mother. I'm really excited to do this today."

Sure, her knees would be shaking the whole time. The still-fresh memory of bullets whizzing past her from a crowd of clapping people didn't make Kelsey super eager to put herself right back in that situation.

But she meant every word. The meaning behind today's event was *exactly* the right button to push to get Kelsey to want to move past her fear.

"You're very brave," Duchess Mathilde said.

"Hey, we *all* are," Christian replied. He was pacing at

the opposite end of the room, down by the door. And he was majorly dashing in his dress blues Naval uniform. "We're having wine with lunch to celebrate getting through this, right?"

"We will have a champagne toast to Serena, as always." Agathe let go of Kelsey. And then—shockingly—she *winked* at her grandson. "But I believe I accidentally requested twice as many bottles as usual."

The door opened. Christian all but leaped over to greet his private secretary. The man merely shook his head, then retreated.

"Papa's not coming?" Genevieve asked.

Christian tapped the hilt of his sword. "Apparently not."

Kelsey walked back to Elias, wondering just how significant it was that King Julian would skip this annual tradition.

Probably *very*.

The king hadn't left his suite of rooms in days. Ten days, to be exact. Not since the shooting.

"There's only one thing to be done." Christian strode the length of the room to join them. "Elias, you'll join us on the balcony."

He shook his head. "You know I'm not Kelsey's guard anymore. That's all Marko."

"Not as her guard. As her boyfriend."

Elias didn't just flinch with his eyes. He flinched with his entire body. It cracked Kelsey up every time he had a visceral reaction to the reality of his new titles—both as her boyfriend and as a peer. He tended to puff out his chest at being called her boyfriend.

As for being *Sir* Elias, a knight of the realm and fully entitled to stand *with* the royal family instead of two steps ahead or behind? It generally made him twitch as if someone had dropped a spider down his shirt.

"That's not done. That's not my place," he insisted.

Geez. If Kelsey could move past her fear of being, oh, *shot*, then Elias could certainly man up and get past his disinclination toward being lauded and applauded. "What—next to me? It most certainly is."

"Oh yes, Elias would be a wonderful addition!" Mathilde beamed from ear to ear. Of course, she was their biggest supporter in the room, aside from Christian. Kelsey had a feeling it had more to do with her aunt's love of love than any specific approval for *Elias*, but she'd take whatever they got.

"You turned down all those television interviews," Christian reminded him. "The people want to see the hero who saved the day. Saved the princess. Giving them this glimpse today should get it done."

The grand duchess stood. She gave two sharp waves of her hand to the footman, indicating it was time to open the drapes. "Sir Elias, you came to me a week ago and professed to be in love with Princess Kelsey. If that is still true, there is nothing more to discuss. You belong with her." Then she motioned to Christian until he belatedly realized he should lend her his arm to lean on to cross the room.

"Are you all right with this?" Elias said softly in Kelsey's ear. His breath stirred the fine hairs along her neck and made her shiver. Of course, just being near him almost gave her that reaction. The man was so freaking handsome and wonderful.

"You think I have the courage to contradict my grandmother? Heck, no."

He kissed the back of her hand. "I would refuse her, if you wanted me to. In a heartbeat."

So sweet. *S*o supportive. No wonder she was head over heels in love with him. "I know you would. You're my own personal hero. Fearless and tireless in protecting me. But I *want* you out there, holding my hand."

"The royal family does not engage in public displays of

affection," Genevieve butted in, literally hip-bumping them apart. She used her snootiest, snittiest tone, too. But then she kept walking to get in line, and said over her shoulder, "Good thing you haven't learned all the rules yet, isn't it?"

Wow. Kelsey gaped at Elias as they all fell into line in front of the French doors. "Did my sister just basically tell us to hold hands? More importantly, did she more or less say 'screw the royal protocol'?"

Elias nodded. "You've turned the House of Villani upside down since you got here." As the footmen opened the doors, he dropped a kiss on her cheek. "Way to go, Your Highness."

At that, Kelsey *did* shiver. Because he didn't need to use her title anymore, so it was incredibly sexy when he did in that dark, low rumble.

A wall of cheers hit them as soon as they stepped onto the balcony. Each and every member of her family paused for a split second, probably flashing back, just as Kelsey was, to the attack. But then, with the perfect unison of a chorus line, they pressed forward to the purple fabric centered over the railing.

"Just think, Genny, your prince could be down there right now, staring up at you," Christian teased as they waved and smiled at the thousands of people packed in across the garden and down the street.

"That's creepy. I don't want a staring pervert. Maybe I don't even want a prince," she replied with a sniff.

Kelsey snorted out a laugh. "I didn't want a bodyguard following me around. Look how well that turned out for me."

"Genevieve, don't be ridiculous," Mathilde scolded. "Kelsey is not starting a trend with her...ah...unconventional choice of the handsome Elias."

Kelsey's giggles turned into a hoot of laughter. "It'd be impossible to start trend. He's an only child." Okay, maybe their teasing was verging on silly now. It gave them all an outlet for their nerves, though. Which was helpful.

"Genevieve, you will marry at least a duke, if not a prince," the grand duchess commanded, turning to stare down her granddaughter under the guise of smoothing out the fabric covering the wreath. "And Christian, you will choose from the highest female nobility in all of Europe."

Christian untied the ropes holding the fabric. "Why limit myself to Europe? Why not get the RPS to chase down an elusive Russian grand duchess, living in hiding and poverty as the great-great-granddaughter of the most reputable Anastasia pretender?"

"I'm not going on that wild goose chase," Elias chimed in.

Kelsey wished she had her phone to take a picture to send Mallory. Although a balcony crowd selfie would probably be considered bad taste. "Also, you shouldn't hold up me and Elias as examples of couples on track to marry." She didn't want to scare him off with this sort of talk. He'd barely gotten over the problem of her being a princess. It was too soon to wave a ring in his face. "We *just* started dating. One step at a time."

"Will those steps lead to an altar?" her grandmother shot back as Christian uncovered the white and purple wreath. He and Elias both saluted it. The crowd grew almost silent for a full minute.

And when that minute had passed, Elias snapped his arm down from the salute. "That, Your Grace, is up to my brave, beautiful princess." He smiled down at her with so much love shining from those bright blue eyes that Kelsey thought she might just go up in flames.

After one last wave, Christian led everyone back inside. But Kelsey paused on the threshold.

Screw it.

Kelsey threw her arms around Elias and jumped. Of

course he caught her, holding her up high against his chest. And they kissed and kissed as the crowd went absolutely bonkers below them.

"Want to be a few minutes late to lunch?" she asked as they finally made it inside, hand in hand.

"Are you suggesting we make your *royal* family wait while we have a quickie?"

Kelsey pressed on the chair rail, ridiculously proud of herself for having scoped out the hidden entrance to a royals-only bathroom. She pulled him through the door and locked it behind them. "You betcha."

Because it turned out that some princess perks were pretty great. Secret palace sex was way up there on the top of the list. Just because their relationship was no longer a secret? Didn't mean they had to give up on the illicit thrill.

As Elias set her on the marble countertop, his mouth plunging down along her neckline, he said in a voice turned gravelly with lust, "I think we should have sex in all the secret rooms in Alcarsa Palace. This month, in fact."

There were only four days left in June. "How many secret rooms are there?" Kelsey asked, unzipping his pants.

Elias ripped open the condom with his teeth. "Twelve."

"Oh yes. Definitely." Kelsey rolled it onto him while he battled to get off her stupid pantyhose.

"And after we knock that off our to-do list? How about we aim for sex in every room of the palace? By year-end?"

Kelsey locked her ankles behind his back. "How many are there, exactly?"

"Six-hundred and thirty-four," Elias said as he plunged into her.

"*Ohhhh* yes."

"I love you, my princess."

Kelsey closed her eyes, gripping the broad shoulders of the man she adored. "I love you, too." And in that moment, she couldn't be happier than to be a princess. *His* princess.

And maybe, just maybe, someday Elias would be her prince...

Want more?! Turn the page to read a sneak peek of *Ruling the Princess*, the next book in the Unexpectedly Royal series.

Chapter One

Princess Genevieve Eleanor Marie, second in line to the throne of Moncriano, had to use all of her twenty-seven years of training *not* to do a spit-take. But she did allow the shock to pop her eyes wide open. "Your date threw up on you?"

"Well, he wasn't my official date," her sister Kelsey corrected. Amazing how she waved that off with the hand holding the last bite of a dill roll. "Brian Masur was just dancing with me. Nobody took real dates to the eighth-grade dance. We all went in clumps with our friends."

It sounded dreadful. Genevieve couldn't come out and *say* that, though. She'd done far too much cutting down of Kelsey's American hometown since her long-lost sister had arrived two months ago.

Borderline snide bitchiness, actually.

Okay, probably quite a bit *over* the line with the bitchiness. But they'd brokered a truce from their rocky beginning, and Genny now endeavored to be at least respectful when hearing these stories.

In a studiously neutral tone, she commented, "The

customs of small-town Michigan schools are indeed... different than those in Europe."

"I'd say *everything*, not just the customs, are different. Except, of course, for you and me." Kelsey grinned. "Physically, at least."

It was true. Although two years apart in age, they looked similar enough to pass for twins. Same blond hair, fine bone structure, and the striking violet eyes of their dead mother, the queen.

So far? That was where the resemblance ended. They were like comparing apples to zucchini. Cats to worms.

But if the whole "opposites attract" thing worked for romance, surely it could bring two sisters together who very, very much wanted to find common ground.

"That's why we started having these lunches." Genevieve fluttered her hand back and forth. "To discover each other. Good and bad. Similarities and differences."

Ugh. Was that too stilted and formal? Chances were, wondering that at all—it meant the answer was in the affirmative. Genevieve's auto setting for strangers was to be polite, warm, but reserved. And Kelsey still felt like a stranger much of the time.

Maybe they needed to let go and get drunk together...

Kelsey lifted her glass of water with lemon in a toast. "To catching up on everything we missed over twenty-four years." Her laughter broke out on top of the last few words. "That sounds ridiculous."

Mmm-hmm. Rather impossible, too. Because her sister had been kidnapped as a baby, and only found by the royal family a few months ago. How did you recap and share an entire *lifetime*?

No matter how large the project, however, it always began with a single step. Genevieve's tutors, whether in languages, politics, or riding, all had impressed that singular notion upon her.

And goodness knew that both she and Kelsey were more than stubborn enough to do *whatever* they put their minds to.

Lifting her own sparkling water, Genny said, "A ridiculously high goal? Perhaps. But a worthy one."

"Yes." Kelsey nodded emphatically. "I'm so grateful that you squeeze me in for these lunches twice a week. Truly." Then she lunged across the table to take Genny's hand, snagging the lace runner in the process. The Waterford vase of pale peach roses toppled over.

A footman clearing their plates managed to right it before any water puddled out. Genevieve shot him a look of thanks.

Her sister had a natural, ah, *exuberance* unlike anyone else in Alcarsa Palace. Or perhaps they'd all started with it until protocol drummed it out. Regardless, Kelsey kept the staff on their toes as she whirlwinded her way through the halls.

On the other hand, Genny appreciated how genuine her responses were to everything. No practiced platitudes, no polite-yet-meaningless nods and plastic smiles.

There were some days she *envied* her sister.

Not that she'd ever admit it.

"You're family." Genny beamed at her, relieved that she meant the grateful smile. It took Kelsey almost being killed by an assassin a few weeks ago for them to get past Genevieve's initial...wariness. Okay, bitchiness. "I'd happily put off the prime minister to have lunch with you."

"That's because none of you like the snooty-ass prime minister."

"No, that'd merely be the added bonus." So true, though.

Sitting back down, Kelsey straightened the runner and gave an apologetic finger wave at the footman. "Sorry, Ivan."

Amazing. She'd barely learned more than how to count to twenty—and how to swear—in the Moncriano language, but Kelsey made a point of learning the names of every servant, driver, and bodyguard in the royal service.

That, *that* was the mark of a true princess of the House of Villani. That bone-deep caring for their subjects.

Genny was so proud of her.

Leaning back to allow Ivan to serve the lime sorbet, Genny asked, "So the story of your first dance does not end well. Did things improve at the next one?"

Kelsey snorted. "No fair. It's your turn. We'll save my disastrous prom episode for another lunch. Who was your first real dance with?"

"Besides my dancing instructor?" It took a long stare out the arched window at the marble peacock fountain in the courtyard before the memory solidified. "I was twelve. It was the Harvest Ball, and I wanted the first dance to be with Papa."

"Aww, there's nothing cuter than a father-daughter dance."

"Cute" wasn't exactly the aim of the presentational dance of the royal family. "Tradition, however, meant that Papa had to lead off the dancing with the duchess of our biggest farming duchy. Christian was stuck with their fully-grown daughter, who'd just had her fiancé break their engagement so he could run after a princess of Luxembourg."

Oh, the memory was flooding back now. Genevieve set down her spoon so she could prop her chin on her hands to properly dish the dirt. "Christian's partner regaled my fourteen-year-old brother with a bitter diatribe about how all men were evil, cheating bastards."

The woman hadn't been invited back to the palace for five years.

Wincing, Kelsey said, "I get that she was bitter, but... what a rotten thing to unload on a teenager. Is it okay to decide right now not to like her? Or does she foster guide dogs now?"

Ah, such bone-deep loyalty to the brother she barely knew. Yet more proof that Kelsey's inner princess had all the right instincts.

Allowing a tiny, barely there smirk to form, Genevieve said, "Lucia's fortune-hunting down a third husband in Monaco."

"Sounds like karma took care of her." Kelsey rolled her hand in a circle. "Get back to your story."

"I had the distinct non-pleasure of waltzing with the Minister of the Treasury."

"Really? No dashing foreign prince? No dreamy school friend?"

She'd asked to send an invite to a boy she'd been crushing on—but received the standard lecture about Duty over Pleasure. "No other children were at the ball. The minister was chosen because he was so unfortunately short. In other words, the perfect height to pair with me."

"Ouch. That must've been a letdown."

Indeed. Genny spooned up sorbet to help palate-cleanse the memory. "He smelled of black licorice. He quizzed me on economics for the entire dance."

Violet eyes wide with sympathy, Kelsey said, "Oh God. I think that might be worse than my puke-covered pumps."

"But I got to wear a yellow Givenchy couture gown and pearls that the grand duchess let me choose from the Crown jewels. A little boring conversation was balanced out by the spectacular outfit. Something you'll come to appreciate as a princess, I guarantee."

A brisk knock on the door barely preceded the rushed entrance by her private secretary, Sir Stefano.

That didn't bode well. He was a stickler for protocol, just like Genevieve. Unflappable, too, just like Genevieve. And yet a strand of salt-and-pepper hair drooped over his forehead.

"Is something wrong?"

"Your Highness." He bobbed his head at each of them while he hustled across the parquet floor. Polished loafers slid to a squeaky stop at the edge of the table. "Pardon the interruption, but this couldn't wait. It's a missive from the royal auditors."

There was a royal just-about-everything, from milliners to saddlers to cartographers. But... Genevieve raised an eyebrow. "That's a new one. Did somebody's great-great-nephew need a job?"

"This isn't a joke, Princess." Stefano brandished the papers he'd clutched to his gray-striped vest. "This is, in fact, a quite serious threat."

"A bean counter?" Kelsey rolled her eyes. "They're a pain in the ass, but hardly serious. Unless you count the serious time-suck of doing your taxes once a year. Oh. You probably don't do your own taxes, do you?"

A few months ago, Genevieve would've snarked back with something, yes, cutting and bitchy about how the royals don't trim their own hedges, either. Now? She had more empathy for the enormity of the life shift Kelsey was trying to wrap her head around.

So she'd help explain, not just snap out a response. "No. The royal family doesn't pay taxes. That is, we didn't. We're going to start next year, so that we follow the same rules as our people."

"Geez. When you put it like that, I know I can't complain about taxes anymore. Pay up and shut up." Kelsey mimed locking her lips shut and tossing the key. "That'll be my motto from now on."

Stefano cleared his throat. Which was akin to anyone else screaming while pounding a fist on the table.

Genevieve gave him her full attention. "Tell us about the

auditor."

"The audit is part of the vetting process to prepare to join the European Union. *If* that's how the country votes. The royal auditor assigned to you has sent over a threat. A down and out, vicious diatribe."

Stefano was riled. *Nothing* riled him—his ever-present composure was what made him such a good private secretary. Worried now, Genevieve thrust out her hand for the papers. "Let me see."

"Perhaps I should just sum up for you, Your Highness."

What on earth was he trying to protect her from in there? "I can read fluently in five languages, Stefano. I think I can muddle my way through a letter about my own finances."

With a half bow to express his reluctance, he handed them over.

After only scanning the first few sentences, Genevieve's head snapped back up. "Get him over here. Now."

"The royal auditor?"

The Royal Pain-in-the-Ass was more like it. "Yes. Summon him to the palace immediately."

"Right away, Your Highness." Stefano bowed twice and hurried out of the room.

Kelsey ran her aquamarine pendant up and down its silver chain. "Uh, you actually pulled rank and just *summoned* someone? That's so…"

"Regal? Imperious?"

"Ballsy."

"I declare it *necessary*. This…" Genevieve flipped to the end to squint at the signature, the harsh, spiky scrawl that was redolent with a smug—and mistaken—sense of power. "…Sir Theo Holst has a lot to answer for."

"Yikes. Is it wrong that I'm excited to watch an old-fashioned, royal dressing-down? I've only seen this happen in movies."

Genevieve appreciated Kelsey trying to lighten the mood. But she wasn't ready to let go of her anger yet.

Ire.

No, fury.

"He thinks he can order me around? Me, a blood princess of four undiluted centuries of the House of Villani? Trust me when I say I'll disabuse him of that notion."

"I'm dying of curiosity over here. What order did he give you?"

Genny folded her napkin. Which was a major victory given that she wanted to throw it across the room. Preferably with an ice-ball inside of it. And preferably *at* Sir Theo's head.

Then she stood and allowed the tiniest portion of her vexation to set her cream-and-fawn spectator pumps clicking across the floor at a fast clip. "He demanded that I slash my budget. That I allow *him* to tell me how and when and what to spend for the next two months. That I make the myriad of cuts he's outlined, without question or discussion."

Kelsey pursed her lips. "Weeeeeell—I've seen your closet. You have an entire shelf of tiaras."

Of *course* she did. This lifelong job she'd never asked for did have its perks. "I'm a princess. They come with the title. I didn't buy them on a reckless shopping spree. I inherited them."

"Did you 'inherit'"—her sister put finger quotes around the word—"the custom-made red Italian pumps I drooled over last week?"

Those had been her reward for surviving a week-long, twenty-five-stop official visit to Sweden and the Netherlands. In January. "I repeat, I'm a princess. I have my own income. As do you," she reminded, ready to drag Kelsey into her self-righteous snit.

"Oh no. I've never owned a pair of shoes that cost more than fifty dollars before moving here. And I didn't buy any of that expensive stuff in my closet. It just keeps appearing."

Kelsey's mindset was still stuck where they'd found her—in the fourth-floor walkup in Manhattan that, in its entirety, was smaller than her bedroom here in the palace. And buying toilet paper in twenty-four packs, for some reason. She hadn't accepted the birthright of her royal fortune yet.

Fine. Her sister didn't have to be mad on her behalf. Genevieve had enough of a head of steam worked up. "My wealth doesn't come from taxing our people. I should be able to spend it however I please."

"Absolutely."

She stabbed the tip of her French manicure against the paper. "He says I should cut out all my stationery. 'Emails are free.'"

Spooning up the last of her sorbet, Kelsey clucked her tongue. "Impersonal, though."

"Right? People don't treasure emails for decades. They don't print them out and tuck them in a drawer or the family Bible. Handwritten letters show you've made an effort, that the recipient is worthy of your time and respect."

"Agreed. I hate writing thank-you notes, but I do it every birthday and Christmas. That's just good manners."

Genevieve's heart fluttered with gratitude that of *anyone* the kidnapper could've left Kelsey with, he'd chosen such upright, principled people as the Wishners. They'd taken in an unknown baby, risked their safety, and raised her to have the caring and strong ethics befitting of a princess.

"Precisely. However, a proper regard for etiquette is something Sir Theo Holst is completely lacking." It split Genny in half between a burning desire to scream, and an equally strong desire to toss back three gin and tonics in a row. Neither of which could be indulged by a true princess. Not without sneaking off to her suite, anyway. "He doesn't ask for a meeting to review, to discuss, to get explanations.

No, he just took a blow torch to my budget."

"That's arbitrary." Kelsey shook her head. "I mean, apparently it's what he was hired to do, but shouldn't there be a give and take? Figuring out what works best for you and your far-from-normal lifestyle?"

Aha. Kelsey *did* get it, despite the sticker shock she'd voiced at the custom pumps, as well as literally all the clothes stocked in her closet by their aunt, Duchess Mathilde.

Genevieve toyed with the interlocking circles of her sapphire bracelet. It used to belong to Wallis Simpson, the woman who came close to toppling the British monarchy. Genny wore it as a reminder that passion had no place in the palace.

A princess did what her people needed. Her own desires were secondary. Giving in to them could so easily bring havoc to her own royal line.

But those were *her* decisions to make. Not Sir Theo's.

And why did his name sound vaguely familiar?

Genny folded the papers in half. Then she sharpened the crease with her thumbnail. "He's ordered me to not wear nylons. 'An arbitrary fashion holdover from the last century that is utterly wasteful.'"

"Don't we have to wear them? As part of the royal dress code?"

"Yes." Just like they had to wear slips so that nobody would see through their skirts. With weights in the hems so a strong gust of wind wouldn't allow the world to see her blue satin panties.

Old-fashioned? Definitely.

Integral to preserving the dignity of House of Villani? Definitely. In this world of cell phone cameras and a relentless internet demanding information every second of every day, it was more important than ever to be careful. Restrained.

With a strong mix of both hope and wistfulness in her

voice, Kelsey asked, "Couldn't you change it? As the senior female member of the royal family?"

"You're kidding yourself if you think I'm the senior female. That would be our grandmother, the Grand Duchess Agathe. And she would be *appalled* if I stopped wearing them."

"You should definitely sic her on Sir Theo. She'd obliterate him with one glare."

It was tempting. The woman was beyond fierce. But Genevieve was an adult. She couldn't ask her grandmother to fight her battles for her.

"Aside from the absurd total amount he wants me to cut, there are at least two-dozen bullet points of specificity." And the worst was burned in her brain. She made another knife-sharp crease, folding the paper over again. "Kelsey, the man wants me to stop using name-brand tampons."

Kelsey's jaw dropped. "That's despicable. Intrusive."

Not to mention *mortifying* that her period would be a topic of discussion in a royal missive. "He's demanding an immediate switch to generic brands of all feminine products and birth control."

Right. Because the fate of their country being accepted as a member of the European Union—if, and only if, their own subjects voted in favor of it—rested on her preferred brand of tampon?

It was so ridiculous as to be laughable. If only it wasn't happening to *her*, of course.

Stefano came back in. No knock at all this time. And his complexion was dead white beneath his general swarthiness. "Your Highness, I'm afraid he won't come."

"Who?"

"Sir Theo." The older man looked ill. Was he shaking? Clenching and unclenching his hands spasmodically, he continued. "He refused your summons."

That certainly explained Stefano's reaction. This was unfathomable.

Unheard of.

Not possible.

And now Genny found herself an even deeper level of pissed that this obnoxious man would upset her secretary so. His world was rooted in order and protocol and above all else, *rules.*

It had to be a misunderstanding. "He can't." As much to hear the words herself as to explain it to Kelsey, Genny said, "That's what makes it a summons, rather than an invitation."

"But he did refuse, Your Highness. He said the letter was self-explanatory and he had no time to waste repeating himself."

"Yowza. That's a dickish thing to say." Kelsey visibly startled when both Genevieve and Stefano snapped their attention to her. "What? Does that not translate? Do you need me to explain?"

Shooting up a hand to stop her, Genevieve said, "Please don't." At least not in front of Stefano. They could laugh about it later, in private. Because she thought it a *perfect* description. "The context was clear from your usage. But no, that colloquialism does not have an exact translation in Moncriano."

"Would you like me to send a member of the Royal Protection Service to fetch him?" Stefano offered. "That would teach the lad some manners."

"And what—have them rough him up along the way?" If the royal family went around delivering black eyes to everyone who offended them, well, it would be a scandal, to say the very least. And not in any way representative of a confident, caring monarchy.

Kelsey's hand flew to her chest, splaying across the bright orange-and-green print of the Lily Pulitzer dress. "They can *do* that? Elias never mentioned beating up disrespectful punks when he was on duty."

Her knowledge of the Royal Protection Service came from the fact that Kelsey was dating her bodyguard. Well, her very recently made *ex*-bodyguard.

It shocked Genevieve how much she was rooting for them. True, Elias was no longer a commoner and thus not entirely out of the question as a match for a princess. He'd been knighted for saving Kelsey's life in the attempted shooting. Thanks to his heroic action, she'd escaped with merely a broken wrist.

The two of them as a couple was both extraordinary and unconventional—utterly like her sister.

"No, they cannot," Stefano said, an undercurrent of disapproval in his tone that Kelsey had even brought up the idea.

But there was the rulebook to life in the palace...and then there was the reality of what went on outside the lines. Genevieve knew those lines blurred occasionally.

See Kelsey dating the staff as a perfect example.

"It *should* not happen," she amended. "If they ever do, it isn't with my authority."

"Too bad. Because I really dislike this guy." Kelsey took the paper now folded down to the size of a compact and opened it, grimacing as she took in demand after demand. "Even if they didn't land any punches, giving him a good scare might teach Holst some respect."

That was it. He only *thought* he was in control. Genevieve, however, could correct that mis-assumption. "You know what?" She put an arm around Kelsey's shoulders and squeezed. "You are exactly right. Brilliant, in fact."

"Agreed—in general." Grinning, Kelsey reached across her chest to pat Genevieve's hand. Which resulted in her hard cast banging painfully against Genny's knuckles. "Want to let me in on how specifically brilliant I am on this particular day?"

Genevieve let go, and caught a glimpse of herself in the crackling glass of the Baroque mirror. Anger had pinked up her cheeks as though they'd been slapped. It blotched across the pale skin of her chest, too.

That would never do. The world only got to see what she *chose* to reveal.

She turned back to Kelsey. Made sure that her tone was even and low and calm. Because Sir Theo Holst didn't deserve anything more than that. His demands would be dealt with and dismissed with all the attention she gave an annoying fly buzzing around a fruit tray.

"There's one thing more frightening than being threatened by the Royal Protection Service."

Kelsey raised an eyebrow, clearly already there but giving Genevieve the satisfaction of saying it. "What's that?"

"Being threatened by an *actual* royal. Stefano, get me a car. I'll change and leave immediately."

"*You're* going to *him*?" Stefano tugged at the pointed tips of his vest. "Princess, you do not have to—"

"I want to," Genevieve gritted out as she snatched her phone from the table and headed to the door.

In fact, she was suddenly quite looking forward to putting this…what had Kelsey called him?…*bean counter* in his place.

• • •

Be sure to pre-order your copy wherever digital books are sold!

Acknowledgments

I have to start by thanking Christy Altomare and the Broadway cast of *Anastasia*. The idea for this series came to me in the middle of Act I, and I spent all of intermission scribbling it down. Their show was extraordinary, and I'll forever be grateful for the spark it provided!

Thanks to Jessica Alvarez for her unflinching persistence. Thanks to everyone at Entangled for their support of this story that I was desperate to share with the world.

Mary Vaughan single-handedly saved the day by helping me sort out the final twist, so I clearly owe her a night at the Bluebird Cocktail Room. Eliza Knight read the opening chapters and assured me they were more than "okay" and has begged repeatedly for the rest of the book, so I owe her bigtime for the shot of confidence I so desperately needed. And thank you to my Fearsome Foursome, for patiently listening to me vent and worry over all things miniscule to elephantine both writing-related and decidedly *not*...well...I shall do the same for them. As often as needed!

About the Author

Christi Barth earned a Masters degree in vocal performance and embarked upon a career on the stage. A love of romance then drew her to wedding planning. Ultimately she succumbed to her lifelong love of books and now writes award-winning contemporary romance, including the Naked Men and Aisle Bound series. Christi can always be found whipping up gourmet meals (for fun, honest!) or with her nose in a book. She lives in Maryland with the best husband in the world.

Also by Christi Barth

RULING THE PRINCESS

Discover more Amara titles...

SOME LIKE IT PLAID
by Angela Quarles

One minute Ashley Miller is sipping a latte in San Francisco and the next she's zapped to the 2nd century, informed she's wed to a handsome Highlander without even an "I do." Oh, hell no. Nothing prepared Connall, or his tribe, for his sassy new wife from the future. But the more he gets to know her, the more he starts to think she's just what they needed. If only he survives her next demand...

THE AUSSIE NEXT DOOR
a *Patterson's Bluff* novel by Stefanie London

It only took American Angie Donovan two days to fall in love with Australia. With her visa clock ticking, surely she can fall in love with an Australian—and get hitched—in two months. Especially if he's as hot and funny as her next-door neighbor... Jace Walters has never wanted much—except solitude, and now he's finally living alone. Sure, his American neighbor is distractingly sexy and annoyingly nosy, but she'll be gone in a few months... Except now she's determined to find her perfect match by checking out every eligible male in the town, and her choices are even more distracting. So why does it suddenly feel like he—and his obnoxious tight-knit family, and even these two wayward dogs—could be exactly what she needs?

BUTTERFACE
a novel by Avery Flynn

I'm not what most people would call "pretty" and, well, high school was rough. Fast forward ten years and life is good… Until a bunch of jerks put the "butterface" (AKA me) on a wedding Kiss Cam with the hottest cop in Waterbury. But then he kisses me. Then he tells everyone we've been dating for months. Soon everything starts to feel too real. But there's something he's not telling me about why he's really hanging around, and I'm pretty sure it has to do with my mob-connected brothers. Because this is not a make-over story, and Cinderella is only a fairy tale…

ONE WEDDING, TWO BRIDES
a *Fairy Tale Brides* novel by Heidi Betts

Jilted bride Monica Blair can't believe it when she wakes up next to a smooth-talking cowboy with a ring on her finger. Ryder Nash would have bet that he'd never walk down the aisle. But when the city girl with pink-streaked hair hatches a plan to expose the conman who married his sister, no idea is too crazy. And even though Monica might be the worst rancher's wife he's ever seen, he can't stop thinking about the wedding night they never had. What was supposed to be a temporary marriage for revenge is starting to feel a little too real…